PENGUIN BOOKS

MISS GOMEZ AND THE BRETHREN

William Trevor was born in Mitchelstown, Co. Cork, in 1928, and spent his childhood in provincial Ireland. He attended a number of Irish schools and later Trinity College, Dublin. He is a member of the Irish Academy of Letters, and recipient of a 1996 Lannan Literary Award for Fiction. Among his books are *The Old Boys* (1964), winner of the Hawthornden Prize; *The Children of Dynmouth* (1976) and *Fools of Fortune* (1983), both winners of the Whitbread Award; *The Silence in the Garden* (1989), winner of the *Yorkshire Post* Book of the Year Award; and *Two Lives* (1991; comprising the novellas *Reading Turgenev*, shortlisted for the Booker Prize, and *My House in Umbria*), which was named by *The New York Times* as one of the ten best books of the year. His eight volumes of stories were brought together in *The Collected Stories* (1992), chosen by *The New York Times* as one of the best books of the year. Many of his stories have appeared in *The New Yorker* and other magazines. He has also written plays for the stage and for radio and television. In 1977 William Trevor was named honorary Commander of the British Empire in recognition of his services to literature. His most recent novel, *Felicia's Journey* (1994), was a national bestseller which won the Whitbread Book of the Year Award and the *Sunday Express* Prize. His latest short story collection is the bestselling *After Rain* (1996). William Trevor lives in Devon, England.

MISS GOMEZ
AND THE BRETHREN

* * *

William Trevor

PENGUIN BOOKS

PENGUIN BOOKS
Published by the Penguin Group
Penguin Books USA Inc., 375 Hudson Street, New York, New York 10014, U.S.A.
Penguin Books Ltd, 27 Wrights Lane, London W8 5TZ, England
Penguin Books Australia Ltd, Ringwood, Victoria, Australia
Penguin Books Canada Ltd, 10 Alcorn Avenue, Toronto, Ontario, Canada M4V 3B2
Penguin Books (N.Z.) Ltd, 182–190 Wairau Road, Auckland 10, New Zealand

Penguin Books Ltd, Registered Offices: Harmondsworth, Middlesex, England

First published in Great Britain by The Bodley Head Ltd 1971
Published in Penguin Books 1997

1   3   5   7   9   10   8   6   4   2

PUBLISHER'S NOTE
This is a work of fiction. Names, characters, places, and incidents either are the
product of the author's imagination or are used fictitiously, and any resemblance to
actual persons, living or dead, events, or locales is entirely coincidental.

LIBRARY OF CONGRESS CATALOGING IN PUBLICATION DATA
Trevor, William, 1928–
Miss Gomez and the Brethren/William Trevor.
p.   cm.
ISBN 0 14 02.5264 9
I. Title.
PR6070.R4M5   1997
823′.914—dc20   96–9798

Printed in the United States of America
Set in New Baskerville

FOR JANE

'In my opinion,' said Miss Arbuthnot, 'the child is not in her right mind.'

The matron of the Lily Arbuthnot Orphanage inclined her head, not wishing to contradict the orphanage's founder and owner.

'Gomez,' said Miss Arbuthnot. 'Why did we call her Gomez?'

'The father, actually, was a Gomez. She was a child of the Adeline Street disaster. Both parents—'

'Perished,' interrupted Miss Arbuthnot sharply, for this was the word she preferred in her orphanage when death was meant.

Miss Arbuthnot was a white lady of fifty-one who dressed herself always in black, a black suit and a blouse with little pearl buttons, and black polished shoes with fine, neatly tied laces. Her hair was full of hairpins. It was coiled on her head, the hairpins holding it perfectly in place, thick grey hair that once had been black also. Miss Arbuthnot was beautiful; even at fifty-one there was beauty in Miss Arbuthnot's thin face and in the way she moved her tall body; and in her hands and her neck. There were laughter lines about her soft grey eyes, her nose was delicate, her mouth slightly crooked.

Miss Arbuthnot's orphanage was in Port Antonio, Jamaica, founded with money left to her by her father, whose family had been successful in the sugar business. The house that was now the Lily Arbuthnot Orphanage was a gracious mansion with an abundance of pillars. Inside, the pillars were of carved wood, dominating a staircase that majestically rose from a large square hall and after a dozen steps divided into two. Higher up it divided again, into galleries and more modest flights of stairs. These stairs and galleries were the veins of the house, so Miss Arbuthnot's mother, a thoughtful woman, had more than once remarked to friends from England who came to stay. As a child, she'd run about them and her own children had, too: she'd have been surprised to see the children who ran now, a different-coloured blood for the house's veins. Miss Arbuthnot was the last of her family's line, a righteous woman who believed that in the past her family had exploited the natives. As best she could, she sought to make amends but did not always find it easy.

'The child has a vivid imagination,' she said now. 'She has written a distressing composition. About naked persons in hell.'

'I've heard, Miss Arbuthnot. Oh yes, indeed.'

'Yet during my Sunday School lessons she's a constant fidget and always has been. So sombre. Why does she never smile?'

'I've heard, Miss Arbuthnot—'

'She said she disliked you, Matron. She described you, for one thing, as cruel. She doesn't like your eyes. Your hands, she says, are always dank with moisture. I explained, of course, that you couldn't help your personal characteristics. She seemed inclined to disagree.'

'I caught her smoking cigarettes,' the matron cried, her face flaming with anger and embarrassment. 'She's remote from the other children. Dr Harper says there's a definite defect. God knows I've done my best, Miss Arbuthnot.'

'No doubt you have, Matron,' replied Miss Arbuthnot drily, 'but your best has not prevented this child from causing malicious damage in my bedroom. No child should enter my bedroom,' said Miss Arbuthnot in a voice that quite sternly attributed blame to the other woman. 'My bedroom at least is a private place.'

They stood in silence then, awaiting the child's arrival in Miss Arbuthnot's pleasant study. The windows were open. Outside the day was sunny. 'Yes,' said Miss Arbuthnot when the knock was heard on the panels of the door.

The child came in, a tall Jamaican child with spectacles, eleven years of age.

'Iniquity unto iniquity,' murmured Miss Arbuthnot, not asking her visitor to sit down, not sitting down herself. 'You've done bad things, my dear. You delight in causing trouble to those who are kindest to you.'

'You see, Miss Arbuthnot—' began the child.

'It isn't right, my dear. No more is it right to go into my bedroom and break my silver-backed brushes. It isn't easy to break a brush, but you, it seems, have managed to do so. Other things are missing, a comb and pair of scissors. My very favourite looking-glass has had its glass smashed. An ivory shoe-horn—a family heirloom, my dear—has been discovered at the bottom of Matron's lavatory.'

The child was silent. The matron, starched and white, threw out her bosom and rubbed the palms of her hands on her overall. Miss Arbuthnot said:

'I cannot ever use that shoe-horn again, my dear. You understand that?'

Again the child did not speak. Miss Arbuthnot said:

'I could not use a shoe-horn that had been fished out of a lavatory. Matron's lavatory or anybody else's.'

The matron drew a short breath through her nose, snappishly enough to turn the intake into a sniff. Her eyes were on the child's face. Miss Arbuthnot said:

'I would think of your action, my dear, every time I put my shoes on. I'd think of you, dear, dropping the shoe-horn down and attempting to flush away your unkindness.'

There was another silence in the room. The matron appeared about to break it, but Miss Arbuthnot gestured at her delicately.

'I feel alone,' the child said suddenly.

The matron heard this irrelevant statement and thought to herself that it was poppycock, since the orphanage contained thirty-seven girls. Miss Arbuthnot said:

'My dear little one, we are all alone. And yet, as we know, we are not.'

'My parents were burnt alive, Miss Arbuthnot.'

'Your parents perished, my dear. The parents of every girl in this home have perished. In that sense you're not alone because you have companions who are no better off than you. And in

3

another sense because you have Our Lord Jesus Christ. And in a third sense also, my dear, because you have me.'

'I broke your brushes, I put your shoe-horn down that woman's lavatory.'

'That is Matron standing there, my dear.'

'I know it is—'

'Then you must not call her that woman. You must try and like her, even though you find it difficult. She loves you, dear, as I do.'

'My parents, Miss Arbuthnot—'

'My dear, why do you never smile?'

'I feel I am nothing,' the child said.

'Nothing?'

'I feel peculiar sometimes.'

'And act it too,' the matron snapped. 'It's certainly peculiar to take a shoe-horn—'

'Thank you, Matron,' said Miss Arbuthnot, and added that everyone felt peculiar from time to time. When people were ill or worried they felt peculiar, or sometimes for no reason, although it wasn't sensible to feel peculiar for no reason. 'You understand?' she said.

'My parents—'

'Yes, my dear. But you were no more than—what age was she, Matron?'

'Two and a half. To be exact, two years seven months and—'

'Two and a half, my dear. You can't even remember your parents. Children come and go here: hardly any have known their parents.'

'I think about the fire.'

'The fire's past and gone, child. We have the present to think about now. My dear, I have to warn you that you're on the way to becoming a delinquent. You've written a most distressing composition. And pictures, my dear. I've heard you've drawn pictures.'

'Oh, most unpleasant,' cried the matron. 'Morbid, gruesome pictures. Destroyed at once, Miss Arbuthnot. Naturally.'

The child, seeming not to have heard these remarks, stared hard at Miss Arbuthnot through her spectacles. She said:

4

'The fire in Adeline Street went on for a day and a night: Mr Kandi told me. Ninety-one people were burnt alive and I was saved. Only I was saved, Miss Arbuthnot, that's why I feel alone.'

'That's nonsense, my dear.'

'Poppycock,' cried the matron, and again Miss Arbuthnot gestured at her.

'Mr Kandi said the smell of burning flesh carried on the wind. You could hear it sizzling like fat.'

'Mr Kandi has no right to talk to you like that.'

'Another thing,' the matron said, 'he's not whiting the plimsolls properly.'

'Mr Kandi said the fire was started by a person.'

'A person who was demented, my dear.'

'There was nothing wrong with his mind, Mr Kandi said. He was all misshapen: he had an incurable disease of the bones.'

'I'd say demented, dear.'

'The court said sane. According to Mr Kandi—'

'Please, dear. Please now.'

'I'm sorry, Miss Arbuthnot.'

'Ridiculous, all this,' the matron murmured, keeping the words well to herself. Troublesome this girl was and always had been.

Miss Arbuthnot smiled. She said: 'A wretched man, my dear, who truly didn't know what he was doing. Now please tell me you understand that.'

'Yes, Miss Arbuthnot.'

'We love you here, my dear: I cannot repeat that too often. Try always to remember it.'

'Yes, Miss Arbuthnot.'

'Can you feel affection, dear? For me, for the other girls?'

The child shook her head. She found it hard to feel affection, she said.

The matron made a noise. Miss Arbuthnot said:

'Hard, my dear? Is it not that for some reason you do not try?'

The matron mentioned laziness. Miss Arbuthnot smiled. She said:

'No one must be above affection, my dear. It's not a weakness, you know.'

5

'The fire—'

'Forget about the fire.' Miss Arbuthnot's tone was sharper, although her smile was still in place. 'Look into the future that's waiting for you. Try and do better, dear.'

'And return immediately,' the matron peremptorily interposed, 'Miss Arbuthnot's comb and scissors.'

'If you please, my dear.'

The child was dismissed, and the matron followed her from the room.

Miss Arbuthnot stood by the window. She had failed with that child, she thought: for years she'd been aware of it. The sombre child was a bad influence on the other girls, with her morbidities and the unpleasant pictures she drew. Dr Harper was right when he described her as remote, the word seemed somehow to suit her perfectly. Once she'd asked her what she'd like to be when she left the orphanage and she'd said that she'd be called Miss Gomez when she left and that in her whole life she wouldn't permit herself to be called anything else. She loved the sound of Gomez, she said, because it had been her parents' name. Miss Arbuthnot hadn't said anything, believing at the time that Gomez had probably been a name they'd given her at the orphanage, knowing no other, as often was the case. But as Matron had just reminded her, this wasn't so: the child was right about her name.

Miss Arbuthnot parted the unpatterned lace curtains and looked out, across flowering trees in sunshine, to a blue-green dappled sea. The child was atheistic. Was that so because of the circumstances of her parents' death, because she thought that a sane man had deliberately caused a conflagration so that people might die? Yet there was, as well, the fact of her own escape: you'd think she could derive joy from that. If only she could see it, she had more to smile at than most.

She had failed with the child, Miss Arbuthnot thought again. She left the window and angrily pressed a bell, a summons that in a moment would bring to her drawing-room the elderly porter of her orphanage, Mr Kandi.

* * *

That evening in the great square hall of the orphanage the black girls, standing in rows, sang from their hymn books:

> 'So longs my soul, O God, for Thee,
> And Thy refreshing grace.'

They sang the hymn to the end, their voices joined by those of their teachers and the matron and by the voice of Miss Arbuthnot herself. But the child who was atheistic just opened and closed her lips, not releasing any sound. The God thing was a confidence trick, she claimed, which was something she often repeated in her dormitory and to new girls, causing the new girls to weep, for being orphans they now and again felt the need of a God thing.

'O God, our refuge and strength,' said Miss Arbuthnot while her girls knelt, 'who art the author of all godliness, be ready, we beseech Thee, to hear the devout prayers of Thy Church; and grant that those things which we ask faithfully we may obtain effectually; through Jesus Christ our Lord.'

The child, knowing herself that she was remote, was troubled by the fact. Through her tortoiseshell spectacles she surveyed a world in which she did not seem to belong, and she occupied her part of it lifelessly, not caring what she said or did. Sometimes, feeling bitter, she acted with deliberate intent, damaging property or taking what did not belong to her; more often she didn't even bother to do that. She felt as a shadow among real people, which was what she'd meant when she'd described herself as nothing: it was a feeling only, but Miss Arbuthnot hadn't quite understood that. Miss Arbuthnot hadn't understood that peculiar feelings had as much potency at the heart of them as any other feelings. Miss Arbuthnot betrayed no sign that she admitted the existence of feelings at all. What use was talk about love?

Often, privately, she sought a reason for her state. She had been told she was not clever: was it due to simple stupidity, she wondered, that she felt being alive was pointless? 'Would you mind dying if there wasn't pain?' she'd ask at night in her dormitory. 'Pleasant enough to be knocked down, you know, to have everything go blank for ever.' It made the new girls cry again to hear her talk so, although she meant no harm and always tried to comfort the new girls afterwards. But she was punished if this misdemeanour was discovered and in the Lily Arbuthnot Orphanage the legend grew that she was a mad girl, rendered so by the strange circumstance of being the only one spared in the Adeline Street disaster. Occasionally she accepted the legend herself and saw in it the explanation of all that was worrying in her life and her mind. She certainly preferred being mad to being stupid.

With such thoughts the child grew up. As the years went by, her legs became excessively long; thin and dark, like autumn twigs. She was troublesome, the staff continued to repeat, because of some streak in her: she took no interest, she didn't ask normal questions like other children. She overheard them talking about her and didn't much mind when they were unpleasant about her. She continued her friendship with Mr Kandi and didn't much mind when he took small, elderly liberties with her.

She disappeared one night from the Lily Arbuthnot Orphanage and was not recovered by the authorities. She was picked up by a lorry carrying bauxite, eight miles from Port Antonio, near Fairy Hill. The driver said he was going to Port Morant and then on to Kingston by the coast road. He stopped twice on the way, in Port Morant and just outside Yallahs. They smoked cigarettes together and he took liberties with her. He said he'd like to see her again, suggesting a trip to the Hellshire Hills in his lorry. She didn't resist the liberties, considering it wiser not to and anyway quite enjoying them, but she didn't keep the appointment she made with him for seven o'clock the following Saturday, in a café in Gold Street.

In Kingston she worked as a cleaner, saving the money she earned because she wanted to leave Jamaica. She didn't know why she wanted to go, being aware only that she wanted everything to be different. She became Miss Gomez, she smoked incessantly, she was not knocked down. Instead, at a time when it was still easy for a Jamaican to do so, she went to live in London.

8

II

At first Miss Gomez worked in Euston Station, washing trains, and then in a cereal factory in Dagenham, and then in the Edgware Road branch of Woolworth's. After that she worked in the haberdashery department of Bourne and Hollingsworth, into which a man who said he was a Sicilian came one day, ostensibly for buttons. He ran a dancing business, he next revealed, with his brother: he offered her work there, taking her clothes off in front of an audience. She'd earn a lot more money, he pointed out, than selling haberdashery in Bourne and Hollingsworth. He went away, saying that the buttons she'd offered him were no good.

A few days later Miss Gomez went to see the Sicilian and his brother in their club, which was called the Spot-On Club. The Sicilians explained that they would require her to remove all the covering from her body except her glasses. A black girl naked in glasses, they explained, was an excitement for all-white afternoon clients. She should also retain her sombre look.

On that first day Miss Gomez found the Spot-On Club unusual. The Sicilians told her to watch from the side while another black girl operated on a platform that the Sicilians referred to as a stage. 'And now we have the lovely Tina von Hippel,' one of the Sicilians said into a microphone, at the same time turning up the volume of an old and damaged tape-recorder. 'I'm just an old-fashioned girl,' sang the voice of Eartha Kitt while Tina von Hippel, born Eleanor Bush, opened and closed her lips, approximately mouthing the words.

The small basement room was full. Smoke from cigars and cigarettes curled in the air, lager at nine shillings a glass was on sale at the back. There was accommodation for forty-three, the Sicilians had informed Miss Gomez with pride, in tip-up seats that had

9

once been the property of a cinema in Kilburn. 'We get good-class men only,' the brother in charge of the microphone and the tape-recorder said. 'Very nice chaps.' He told her to watch carefully, to watch the men in order to see what pleased them and to note how the other girl provoked the men's desires. 'Very popular girl,' he said.

Miss Gomez watched. Tina von Hippel, having removed most of her clothing, played with a piece of gold-coloured elastic that held in place, over her groin, a triangle of similarly coloured sparkling material. She moved her body as though seeking to represent a snake. Her brown breasts rose and fell, flesh rippled on a fleshy stomach. She turned around and sinuously shook her buttocks.

Miss Gomez saw a man close his eyes in ecstasy. Other men sighed and murmured. One spoke urgently to himself. 'Take off those knickers,' a loud voice demanded from the back, where the lager was.

Tina von Hippel smiled teasingly, and paused before she stepped out of the length of elastic and the triangle it bore. Her movement was skilful; her left hand threw the garment over her shoulder while her right, splayed to its extent, covered the area that the triangle had covered. 'For Jesus' bloody sake!' protested the voice at the back, more impatient than before. The record came to an end, Tina von Hippel held both hands in the air, near her shoulders. For a moment she moved her tongue about in her open mouth, but Miss Gomez saw that none of the men in the Spot-On Club was looking at her mouth. A red curtain swished across, the Sicilian spoke into the microphone: 'That was the lovely Tina von Hippel. Soon we have the lovely Elvira-Anne.'

For a year after that Miss Gomez lived in the world of the Spot-On Club, which was in every possible way different from the world of the Lily Arbuthnot Orphanage and, indeed, from the other worlds she had more briefly known, in particular the Dagenham cereal factory and the haberdashery department of Bourne and Hollingsworth. She became familiar with the faces of men who regularly attended the club, a few of them foreign faces, Chinese, or negroid like her own. The man who talked to himself seemed to spend most of every afternoon on the premises, a middle-sized man immaculately dressed, said by the Sicilians to be a Royal employee. Often there were strangers, men who came in twos or threes in mid-afternoon after they'd presumably lunched together or who came late at night and stood at the back drinking lager. These were always the ones who called out, asking for a garment to be more immediately removed or suggesting to a performer that she might like to go for a drive with them. Unlike the Royal employee, most men usually stayed for an hour, taking up a rear seat when they first arrived and moving forward as others left. The red curtain would swish across, two or three figures at the front would rise to go, and those sitting behind would vie for the vacant seats, elbowing one another and arguing. If more serious trouble threatened, one of the Sicilians mentioned the police over the microphone.

The Spot-On Club employed four black-skinned girls, all of them from the West Indies. Miss Gomez was the only one with glasses, and on the premises she was known only as Miss Gomez. Names were as important as such idiosyncrasies as wearing glasses, the Sicilians told her, and although for the purposes of business and in fairness to her employers she would have adopted any name they cared to offer her, they said that in her case they preferred not to make a change. 'And now we have the lovely Miss Gomez,' the brother who worked the microphone would murmur, the formality of the title pleasing him because it helped to promote a feeling of variation. The lovely Tina von Hippel, the lovely Elvira-Anne, the lovely Carla, and the lovely Miss Gomez: each name had a different ring to it, and a different kind of promise. The brother who worked the microphone employed a different voice for each, suggesting by his tone that Tina von Hippel had a degree of fieriness in her appeal, that Elvira-Anne was more the homely kind, that Carla was generous, and Miss Gomez a law unto herself.

Between their acts the girls sat in a small room smoking, reading magazines and drinking Pepsi-Cola. When the Sicilians weren't about they talked about how shameful it was that one of the brothers, hanging about the doorway of the club, would in-

11

terest some passing inebriate in what was taking place downstairs and then extort exorbitant sums of money from him, charging him first of all at the entrance and then halfway down the stairs and then at the door to the basement room itself. They talked about the behaviour of certain men in the club and dealings they'd had with other men, and about proposals they'd received, in general, in London. Tina von Hippel appeared to have had the richest experience in this respect. When her night's work was over she usually permitted herself to be approached as she walked through the Soho streets and as often as not ended up spending the remainder of the night with a companion in a hotel. Carla and Elvira-Anne did not go in for these adventures, although Elvira-Anne had done so in the past. Both were faithfully married now, and quite often they invited Miss Gomez and Tina von Hippel to their homes, two flats in a house in Shepherd's Bush, where Carla and Elvira-Anne cooked *paella* and they all drank Spanish wine. The fare was always the same in both households, and the girls' husbands, both from the Windward Islands, seemed to Miss Gomez similar also. Carla and Elvira-Anne had been friends since their childhood in Barbados. They'd come to England together, had joined the staff of the Spot-On Club at the same time and had married their similar husbands in a joint ceremony. Soon they would cease their work for the Sicilians and have babies. They were happy girls, married to happy men. Tina von Hippel wanted to become a film star.

One night, when Miss Gomez was moving her lips to the voice of Ella Fitzgerald and occasionally kissing her fingers into the air, she was aware of a man in the front row leaning forward. 'I took to you,' he said when she stepped from the club half an hour later, and she saw that he was a stout man with a brief-case and a canvas bag marked *Canadian Pacific Airlines*. He suggested a large sum of money to her, and then hailed a taxi-cab and ordered it to Thrift's Hotel, not far from King's Cross Station.

In a cold room the man knelt down and put money in a gas-meter so that they could light the fire. He took his overcoat off and by way of conversation said he was in the advertising business. He showed her an advertisement in a newspaper that he took

12

from his brief-case and said that it had been composed by the firm of which he was the managing director. A large picture showed a man and a woman putting paint on a wall of a room. It was, the man said, an advertisement for a brand of tea.

When the room warmed up they took their clothes off and lay together in the bed. They smoked cigarettes after the man had satisfied himself, and she told him about the Lily Arbuthnot Orphanage and Mr Kandi and the matron who had dank hands and the lorry-driver with the load of bauxite, and how she had left Jamaica by saving up her money. She told him that she'd been the only person who'd been saved out of ninety-two in a conflagration, but he didn't make any comment on that, as he had when she'd told him all the rest: she felt he didn't believe her.

At half-past three he put on his clothes again, saying he'd have to be getting on. He'd already paid her the agreed price, but as a parting gift he gave her the Canadian Pacific bag which contained, he said, some cheese. She thanked him and fell asleep.

The next day Miss Gomez told Tina von Hippel about the advertising man. The cheese he'd given her was quite pleasant, three-quarters of a pound of Gouda. They ate it while they waited to perform, cutting it into cubes with a small knife that Tina von Hippel carried in her handbag in case of trouble. She'd spent the night with a man who'd asked her to tie him up on a pulley which he said he'd suspend for her from a lavatory cistern. Fearing to cause the man an injury, Tina von Hippel had refused this request and it was then, while she was explaining the subsequent disappointment of the man, that she broke off in what she was saying and suggested that they should both leave the Spot-On Club and go and work for Mrs Idle in Frith Street. 'Angel, there's ten times this money to be made,' she said in her drawling, film-star voice. 'We're truly mad to stop here, angel.'

They went in a taxi. On the way Tina von Hippel explained that the advertising man had given Miss Gomez the cheese because he would have been unable to eat it in the company of his wife, since it had been present at the occasion in Thrift's Hotel. And probably every time he looked at the Canadian Pacific bag he'd have been reminded of the occasion also, which was why he'd given her the bag. Still, it would be quite useful, a good strong container like that. Nice to get a present no matter what the reason. 'That poor guy with his pulley!' Tina von Hippel suddenly exclaimed, looking out of the taxi window and laughing quietly. Miss Gomez laughed also.

Mrs Idle ran what she called a pleasure house. She, too, was a West Indian, a squat woman who accumulated money but was reluctant to spend it. Her house was tall and very narrow, with small rooms that became smaller with each floor. In one, at the extreme top, she was pleased to place Miss Gomez, turning out an older woman, who was a nuisance, she said, because she wouldn't do anything about the gonorrhoea she'd contracted. The woman was angry, and Mrs Idle threatened her with violence from some source that both of them knew about. Miss Gomez felt sorry for the woman, especially since she was herself the cause of the trouble and it hadn't been really necessary for her to come to Mrs Idle's house at all, whereas the older woman looked as though she desperately depended on what work Mrs Idle could offer her, being the mother, for all Miss Gomez knew, of a large family in a suburb somewhere. She mentioned this afterwards to Tina von Hippel when both of them were having a drink in a nearby public house, but Tina von Hippel only laughed her film-star laugh. Miss Gomez would soon get used to the pleasure house, she said: you couldn't always be thinking of diseased women when money could so easily be made.

Every day, from midday until four o'clock and again from seven until midnight, Miss Gomez occupied her top-storey room, placing herself at the disposal of whatever guests Mrs Idle brought to her. Occasionally she missed the days of the Spot-On Club, the loudly singing voices on the tape-recorder, the cigarette smoke and the faint lights, the crates of lager at the back, men scrambling for seats at the front. There'd been a cosiness about the world of the Spot-On Club that was absent in the top-storey room: no music played, no one gaily drank lager, and as often as not there was only the sound of breathing. Some men asked her to take her glasses off, others preferred her to leave them on; some talked to her, telling her who they were, others were silent. A man cried one time, asking her to forgive him. He went away without requesting anything else of her. 'Your smell on me excites the wife,' another man said to her, 'although she doesn't know what it is.' He smiled at her when he said that, replacing his braces over his shoulders. He was the manager of a Lloyd's Bank, he maintained, out Guildford way: often, uninvited, they proffered such information. 'Would you get into a grave with me?' a different man quietly murmured, and another asked her to kick him in the face. 'Give a good loud shout,' Mrs Idle warned her, 'if they ever put a finger near your throat.'

In time Miss Gomez told Tina von Hippel all about the Lily Arbuthnot Orphanage and the fact that she'd been the only person rescued from the Adeline Street disaster. She wouldn't mind being knocked down, she confessed, provided it was painless, for nothing that had happened in her life since she'd left the orphanage had caused her to change her mind about that. Tina von Hippel said it was all a nonsense. You had to take things as they came, she said, like the man with the pulley: you couldn't go on worrying all the time. Miss Gomez, still feeling remote and shadowy yet not wishing forever to be a bore about it, tried to agree. Everyone had problems, Tina von Hippel assured her. When they'd saved enough money they'd both get into films.

Then one day, quite by chance it seemed, Miss Gomez picked up a publication called *Make Friends in London* that had been left behind in her room by a man. In this she noticed a small advertisement that seemed directed at Jamaicans like herself who were exiles in London. *There is a Meaning in the Life of Each and Every One of Us,* she read.

In light and sunshine, with joy, without fear, let the emptiness within you be filled with understanding. There is a reason and an explanation for every moment of your life, through Our Lord Jesus Christ, who miraculously came to answer his people's questions.

Miss Gomez, who as a child had been introduced to her Lord Jesus Christ repeatedly and every day, had never actually been told that he had come to earth to answer people's questions. Nor had she known it to be admitted by the godly that there was an emptiness within people. 'Thou art the King of Israel,' the girls of the orphanage had sung on Palm Sunday, 'Thou Royal David's Son.' But Miss Gomez had never been able to remember who this royal David was, nor could she see what a king of Israel had to do with her personally. 'At the Lamb's high feast we sing,' the girls had melodiously pronounced at Easter, putting Miss Gomez in mind of sheep.

She read the advertisement again. *The Church of the Brethren of the Way*, it said, *Tacas, Jamaica*. The Brethren were happy, the advertisement stated, because of their prayers for other people. The Brethren smiled in Tacas, led by the Reverend Lloyd Patterson and the Reverend Greated, the Reverend Pearson Simmonds, and the Reverend Palmer. They walked together through Tacas, to a hill outside the town, where they prayed for the world's criminals and picnicked in the sunshine. The Brethren were happy because they understood, each and every one of them, the meaning in their lives.

Reading these words cramped into a small space, Miss Gomez experienced a slight sense of wonder. She read again about the emptiness within people. 'I feel it too,' she said aloud, while Mrs Idle tapped on her door with another visitor.

Eventually Miss Gomez wrote, as requested, to the Church's founder, the Reverend Lloyd Patterson. It amazed her that she should do such a thing, that she, employed by the squat Mrs Idle, should write for details of a Church when during all her time at the Lily Arbuthnot Orphanage she'd avoided contact with the God that Miss Arbuthnot so persistently pressed upon her charges. She'd gone deliberately the other way, being friends with old Mr Kandi in the cellar where he was meant to clean the girls' shoes, drawing pictures and writing stories that upset people, referring to the blankness of death. And ever since she'd gone the other way, continuing a journey in an existence she found to be pointless. On blue air-mail paper she wrote at length to the Reverend Lloyd Patterson, telling him everything she could think of.

Over a drink she told Tina von Hippel what had happened, and Tina von Hippel said she couldn't believe her ears. She read the advertisement and after brief thought pronounced the Brethren of the Way a most peculiar outfit. She urged on Miss Gomez

16

her opinion that the religious could not be trusted: what exactly did it mean, this remark about emptiness being filled? And how could Jesus Christ answer anyone's questions since Jesus Christ was no longer alive? Miss Gomez did not say anything. She gazed through her spectacles into space, causing Tina von Hippel to reflect that her friend was probably as nutty as the crowd she was going in with. She couldn't see it herself, she said, but then she'd never been one for any form of holiness. 'My, you're funny,' she said in her film-star voice, finishing her drink because a man across the bar was making her an offer with his face. She embraced Miss Gomez and told her to take care. An hour later, with some of her belongings packed into the Canadian Pacific canvas bag and the others in the suitcases she'd brought with her from Jamaica, Miss Gomez left Mrs Idle's pleasure house.

Forgive the incurable man, the Reverend Lloyd Patterson wrote to her new address. The patterns of God were mysterious, he stated, and there were patterns laid down from which the evil must be removed by prayer. *Had the man on his way to the crime,* he wrote, *been faced with a procession of the Brethren of our Church and had the Brethren turned and knelt before him, the incurable man would have received salvation and no one would have died in Adeline Street that day.* When eventually he and Miss Gomez met, he promised, they would speak together for as long as she wished about all such matters, for such matters must be spoken of. It was different from the silence that had been pressed upon her in the orphanage, where she'd been punished for speaking of the fire, where Mr Kandi had been reprimanded for telling her the truth. *We do not fear the truth in Tacas,* the Reverend Lloyd Patterson had written in a postscript. *When the truth is clear before us, then only may we truly pray.* Reading his letters, Miss Gomez felt neither mad nor stupid, even though people were now increasingly to say that she was both.

17

III

After her conversion Miss Gomez opened a bank account and placed in it the money she had made during her time in Mrs Idle's pleasure house, money that was already ear-marked for the Church that had found her. She became an office cleaner and received instructions from Tacas to peruse the daily newspaper for reports of criminals who were in need of prayer: convicted murderers and felons, those convicted of indecency and assault, drug-takers, drunkards, would-be suicides. For such people she was asked to pray and requested to return to Tacas the details of their crimes so that the Brethren of the Way might pray also. From Tacas, the Reverend Lloyd Patterson informed her, prayers for such people went out to Melbourne, Vizcaya, New York, Naples, Mombasa, Sèvres, Sofia, Matruh, Sluys, Cardiff, Omara. *Prayer spreads as a mist from Tacas,* he had written. *Prayer intercedes.*

In the London newspapers Miss Gomez read of crime and unbridled passion, of appearances in court and sentences passed. She conveyed, with names and details, the information as requested. *We prayed,* the Reverend Lloyd Patterson wrote, and went on sometimes to describe the occasion, how the Brethren had travelled to the hill outside Tacas, where thanks were given for the work of Miss Gomez and others, and pleas made for the world's criminals.

Without being much shocked because of her experiences in the Spot-On Club and in Mrs Idle's pleasure house, Miss Gomez read of occurrences that left her with a feeling of bewilderment. *Do not condemn,* he had written from Tacas, and she endeavoured to remember the command when she read of a hospital nurse who had stolen a ring from the finger of a road-death victim and of a husband accused of secreting his dead wife in a reservoir. A

18

stockbroker's clerk had dropped from a window to his death during a bout of madness that he had artificially induced. Youths had battered to death a perverted man on Wimbledon Common. Children were hourly enticed to motor-cars. Women were set upon. Even animals weren't safe.

All over London, it was the same; all over the world, as far as she could see. Every newspaper she perused contained details of violence and uninhibited sensuality, or sensuality that was in some way strange. A man had been arrested for walking the streets of Tooting Bec with no apparel on his body other than a pair of green suede shoes, another man had escaped from police dogs after he'd attempted to take advantage of a girl in public, in a bread shop. A woman had discovered one morning that the person who'd entered her bed during the night was not her husband but a stranger who'd been given the keys of the house by her husband while he himself went off elsewhere.

A man had been arrested for interfering with the brakes of a model girl's M.G.B. sports car in an effort to cause her death. 'He must,' the prosecuting counsel said, 'have conceived some sort of desire for her.' Other men had been found at night in the trees of London's commons, wearing masks and eccentric clothes, all for some sensual purpose. Once, in the *Evening Standard*, Miss Gomez read of a wife who'd trailed her husband and another woman from a dance-hall where the husband had been playing the drums. The husband and the woman drove in a 1960 Ford Anglia to a secluded spot on the R.A.F. playing fields at Halton, Bucks; the pursuing wife picked up relatives and a friend, Mr J. C. Meagher, on the way. A paragraph in the report described the wife's opening of the front passenger door of the Ford Anglia and the surprise and confusion that had at once obtained within the vehicle. But the judge, in Miss Gomez's opinion, had been less concerned with the immorality than with praising the wife's friend, Mr Meagher, as a witness. 'I cannot imagine a better witness,' the Judge had stated. 'Mr Meagher is the deputy subregistrar of births, deaths and marriages for the Wycombe district. He was one of the most impressive witnesses I have ever encountered. He was adamant on fundamentals.'

Miss Gomez read this remark several times, wondering what the Judge had meant by saying that Mr J. C. Meagher was adamant on fundamentals. It seemed to her extraordinary that a deputy sub-registrar of births, deaths and marriages should have left his house in order to be present at such an occasion on the R.A.F. playing fields at Halton, Bucks. She imagined the deceived wife opening the passenger door with a flourish, and the relatives and Mr Meagher standing eagerly by, determined to witness impressively. 'Here's a deputy sub-registrar,' the wife cried out in Miss Gomez's imagination. 'Take a look at that, Mr Meagher.'

Miss Gomez cut the report from the newspaper and sent it to Tacas just as it was. Prayers would be offered for the drummer who had deceived his legal wife and for the woman who'd been in the vehicle with him, whose skirt had been above her knees at the moment of discovery on the playing fields. In Tacas they would read about Mr Meagher and might wonder, too, what the Judge had meant when he said that this deputy subregistrar was adamant on fundamentals.

Another judge, trying another case, said that in his opinion there was sickness everywhere. A woman couldn't go out to post a letter without running the risk of God alone knew what. There were people walking the country's streets and byeways who shouldn't be walking anywhere. There were lunatics abroad and people obsessed with murder, violence, and sexual cruelty. His own niece had been insulted on a tube train. He'd heard of a woman who'd received a telephone call from a man who put intimate proposals to her. In public places advertisements were obscenely defaced, radio and television brought filth into decent folks' sitting-rooms. In a hotel in Scotland he'd had to walk from a television lounge because of the one-track nature of a late-night show. Women with drinks in their hands, he said, had been sitting in the television lounge laughing.

No comment ever came from Tacas on the details Miss Gomez forwarded. Instead she was informed that nothing happened by chance. It wasn't chance that had caused her to survive a conflagration, nor chance that had caused her to pick up the publication called *Make Friends in London*. Nor was it chance that she had now changed her mind about being knocked down by a motor-car. *You will find more precisely your mission-ground,* were words she read, *and with it great joy and greater comfort. As the white man brought the word to Tacas so you must return it now to where it is most needed. You are a chosen person, Miss Gomez.*

In London that summer the heatwave was a talking point. In offices and shops people spoke of it repeatedly, strangers on trains and buses exchanged a point of view. 'Keeps you sleepless,' a woman remarked in Golders Green, and one in Wapping said it made her dozy all day long. Some thought it had to do with moon-probes, others disagreed.

In one way or another, all London's people, and its animals, were affected. Long days of sunshine browned the grass of parks and heaths, and the grass of suburban gardens, where local cats, less vigorously now, stalked local birds. Each day for hours, and mile by mile, the city baked: dogs panted, children caught sunstroke, old men died. Buildings and pavements were hot to touch; on scorching windowsills milk rotted in the midday sun. They'd had enough of it, a lot of people said.

But Miss Gomez, used to the climate of her childhood, wasn't worried by the heatwave. She walked about in it, wandering here and there, searching and yet not knowing what she wanted. She thought of Tacas and longed to be called, but she knew that that moment would not come until she had in some way proved herself worthy of her conversion. The Brethren in Tacas had all been proved worthy of their conversions: more than once she had read that, a neatly typed sentence that did not parade its significance.

Miss Gomez mentioned her Church to her colleagues in the office-cleaning world but did not achieve much of a response. None of them had time for religions, they quite pleasantly informed her: were they necessary anyway, with the improved communications you got nowadays, the television and the better class of Bingo halls? She talked to people in streets that weren't crowded, choosing people who were alone. She walked about parks, smiling and looking for people on seats. Through leafy avenues, by neat front gardens, she walked in Brentford, Isleworth, Wembley, Putney, Twickenham and other suburbs of London. She knocked on the doors of houses and was told to go away. She returned to the cereal factory in Dagenham and tried to talk to the girls beside whom she'd once worked. She smiled at them constantly to show how different she was from the sombre black girl they once had known. In the canteen of the cereal factory they chewed while she spoke. When she finished they shook their heads.

She spoke to a man who'd just come out of a cinema. He listened; she smiled encouragingly. There was often a pointlessness about people's life, she explained, and an emptiness within them; people were bewildered, living out each day to no real purpose. The Brethren lived differently, she was saying when the man's wife came out of the cinema and asked him what on earth he was doing, consorting with a coloured.

A woman in a park told her that all the horrors of the world were due to religion. Look at the Middle East, she said, and India and Ireland, think of the Crusades. A man said the whole conception of a Creator was primitive and outmoded. If she wished to do good, he advised Miss Gomez to join the Meals on Wheels service.

She walked about Paddington, St Pancras and Blackfriars. In Hounslow, New Malden and Worcester Park she hung around playgrounds and got into conversation with housewives by admiring their children. In Mitcham a policeman told her that residents had complained about her. She smiled and apologized, but she continued in her activities. 'I'm sorry to trouble you,' she went on saying, having rung a doorbell. 'Excuse me,' she said, to other strangers on other streets.

One evening, after her seven o'clock session of cleaning, Miss Gomez entered a small, late-night supermarket in order to buy a tin of mock-turtle soup. She was not at the time thinking of the Church of the Brethren in any particular way, although her Church was always present, somewhere, in her mind. She wasn't thinking about what had been written to her about nothing happening by chance: she was thinking that she felt tired after cleaning out twenty-two offices, in one of which a tray of food had been upset and walked into the carpet.

As she entered the supermarket the cashier reminded her that it was Jelly Week: jelly, he said, was obtainable at a reduction of forty per cent. He was a West Indian also, a man of approximately the same age as she was, but several stones heavier. He smiled at Miss Gomez in a friendly way.

'Jelly,' she said. 'Yes thank you, I will take some.' She went to the shelves where the jelly was and selected a packet of blackcurrant flavour and one of lemon, while the cashier watched. He'd noticed her on the street before she'd come in. She walked elegantly, he'd noticed, and was elegantly attired in a black, expensive-looking leather dress. You could do much worse, he was thinking now.

'I'm finished soon,' he said, taking a sum of money for the goods she'd purchased. 'You doing much tonight?'

Miss Gomez paused, about to leave the shop. She regarded the cashier seriously. He wanted to take her to some public house, where he would endeavour to make her drunk on rum and orangeade, a drink with which he had made other girls drunk. After that, in some secluded place, he would attempt to commit a rape on her. She saw it in his eyes as he looked at her, all of it happening in his mind. She wanted to go away, simply to shake her head and leave the supermarket, but instead she heard herself speaking, using words that were now more familiar to her than any other words she ever used.

'Will you listen to me,' she asked, 'if I tell you a little about my Church?'

The cashier still smiled. He would listen with considerable pleasure, he said, and added that she was a pretty girl. They would get on well if they went out together, he could tell her that already. Would she fancy going to a dance?

'The Brethren of the Way,' she said. 'We act through prayer and through forgiveness. It is the Church of Tacas, in Jamaica. We sometimes call it that.'

'I ain't never heard of Tacas, child.'

'Tacas is a town.'

He nodded. He would be finished in a quarter hour, he said. She could wait in the shop and then they could have a drink. 'Maybe,' he suggested, 'we should enjoy ourselves at the Rhumba Rendezvous?'

Miss Gomez shook her head. She suggested to the man that they should pray together instead. 'Look,' she said.

She took from her handbag the advertisement that had brought about her conversion and which she had kept since as a special memento. She watched the man's lips moving as he read it.

'The Brethren do not condemn,' Miss Gomez said, smiling. 'Through forgiveness lies peace for each and every one of us. Comfort, which we need. And understanding.'

She touched the man's hand with hers, and as their flesh met he looked at her differently: she felt him saying to himself that she was a religious maniac.

'Only through prayer,' she said. 'One for another. Do you understand?'

Casually, the man spat on the floor. He wiped his lips with the back of his hand. He nodded at her and said he hadn't been inside a church for seventeen years. He whistled a popular tune, moving away from his cash register in order to tidy a shelf. 'Ever eat this stuff?' he inquired, holding out a packet of Cresta Curried Chicken with Rice.

'I would like to tell you,' she said, and added that she had run away from an orphanage in Jamaica and that when she'd first come to London she'd washed trains and worked in a cereal factory and then in a branch of Woolworth's and in the haberdashery department of Bourne and Hollingsworth. After that had come the final descent of her downfall and then, out of her downfall, her conversion.

'You see?' Miss Gomez said, smiling again even though the man shook his head. He still held the packet of Cresta Curried Chicken. She could hear him whistling the same tune, quietly, beneath his breath. He returned her smile, and she realized that

24

all thoughts of sexual pleasure with her had not yet left his mind. While the thoughts remained she would continue to have part at least of his attention.

'I wrote to the Brethren,' she said, 'at the address in this advertisement. Hibiscus Villa, King George VI Road, Tacas, Jamaica. I can leave you that address.'

'Sure, you leave me the address. First we relax in the old Rhumba and then you leave me the address. Then maybe we dance awhile and you tell me what you like to tell.'

The Brethren, she said, required brothers and sisters in London, so that the Church of the Way might expand its work. It was not now possible to send envoys: laws had been passed, Jamaicans were no longer welcome. 'We travel sightless,' said Miss Gomez. 'The Lord rains snares upon the wicked, yet we take no heed. The Lord points, asking us to pray, one for another. Why do we take no heed?'

'Man, we takes no heed of nothing,' the cashier cried, entering for the first time into the spirit of Miss Gomez's conversation. 'We takes no heed of old Jew women that comes into this store and say, 'How much the tapioca, Sambo?'' If that black man'd take heed he'd slit the faces of them Jew-fat ladies.'

'Please don't speak like that. Please listen—'

'That black man's better travelling sightless when the trashcans walks in them glass doors. That black man's better travelling deaf and dumb because that black man's hated in this town. That black man's nothing but a gollydoll. You ask me, girl, I'll tell you: that black man's handsome in a nice black coffin.'

'Listen to me. Please listen now—'

'The Lord ain't got no answer to that, girl. You tell this black man an answer to that and this black man'll open his ear for the good Lord's word. Down in the old Rhumba or anywhere else, man.'

The cashier laughed. He whistled again. Miss Gomez said:

'We're exiles in this city together, even though we're strangers. I discovered nothing until I went into exile. I travelled half across the world—'

'Yeah.'

'You can forgive the women who insult you. You can learn to forgive and not to condemn.'

He went to the back of the shop, whistling more loudly now. Miss Gomez watched him. The sound he was making jarred on her. If she spoke again he would insult her.

She remained a moment longer, standing by the cash register, wondering if he'd come back. He tore open a bag of potato crisps and devoured them greedily, standing with his back to her. He turned round and she smiled at him, drawing her lips far back so that the smile was a celebration on her face, so that he might be a witness to her happiness. He shouted at her, swearing at her and blaspheming.

One afternoon she walked through a great desolation. Unlike the pleasant London parks and the tidy suburbs where she had knocked on doors, it was an area of demolition, a wilderness of wastelands in which hundreds of houses had already been destroyed. There were acres of hard, flat earth on which nothing moved, and streets that were not yet quite demolished. Rubble covered what pavements remained, paper and old cigarette packets lay thickly in the gutters, bottles rolled about. The houses that remained were shells, doors were gone, and windows; glass lay everywhere, crunched beneath the wheels of lorries. In the houses workmen shouted, and brown dust rose in clouds as walls fell thunderously down. Elsewhere, corrugated iron surrounded and separated building sites already allocated, and painted signs were rich in promises of all that was to come. Multi-storey blocks would rise from all the nothingness, and blocks of modern flats, maisonettes for families, with central heating and garage facilities. Miss Gomez walked slowly, looking at everything, smiling at the workmen who called out to her. And then, abruptly, she came to Crow Street.

She had known, she afterwards thought, that on this afternoon something was going to happen. The feeling had increased in her as she walked through the desolation and thought about the people who once had lived there, in terraced houses and shops. She had sensed something, some small excitement had flickered within her, impossible to diagnose. And then Crow Street itself stirred a thread in her memory, for she had read of it in a newspaper: she would find a pet shop if she walked on and a public house called the Thistle Arms.

She looked through the window of the pet shop and saw a youth standing there, in the company of a girl. She stared and then drew back a little and saw, instead of the two within, a reflection of herself in the glass of the window, the sun glinting on her spectacles. A name came back to her: the name of the youth was Alban Roche. The girl she had no idea about.

She looked again, leaning closer so as to avoid her own reflection. The girl was wearing Indian sandals, gold stitching on green. The youth, with long thin hands, had a hint of gauntness about his face. His eyes were deep-set, blackly gazing beneath black hair that reached his shoulders, which was the fashion that summer. The girl's hair was pale, falling straight and tending to lengthen the image of her narrow face, which was pale also. It was the image of an icon, insubstantial, still, and silent.

He was holding a guinea-pig in his arm. Quite near him the girl was doing something with a bird-cage. He was wearing a ginger-coloured suit made of what seemed to Miss Gomez to be velvet. He was neat in it, with a tie of the same material and a blue shirt. The girl wore a dress like an evening dress except that it was made of cotton, a faded green that you could see through. All around them there were small animals in hutches and cages, and fish in tanks. The animals moved; even through the glass she could hear the twittering of birds. A parrot noticed her, but neither the youth nor the girl did.

She remembered as she stood there the evening she'd lifted a newspaper out of the waste-paper basket in one of the offices she was employed to clean, and how she'd read in it about the sentencing of Alban Roche. It had been a purely routine occasion; in a purely routine way she'd afterwards written to Tacas, requesting prayers for the distressed youth. And yet the lifting of the newspaper had been, so now it increasingly seemed, the beginning of everything.

Alban Roche had been sentenced to two months' detention under psychiatric observation because of his repeated illicit presence both outside and within the women's changing-rooms of the Swansdale Badminton Club, S.W.15. He had received previous warnings, having been several times observed in the grounds of the Badminton Club. The glass of the changing-rooms' windows was painted white on the inside, but scratched initials and other markings afforded a degree of visual access from without. 'I warned the fellow on two occasions,' a Mr Robin Gilverthorpe said in evidence. 'I asked him what he was doing in the Club's grounds and he replied incomprehensibly. I observed him in a bending position at one of the windows. He was later observed by the Treasurer of the Club.'

Mr Gilverthorpe was the Secretary of the Swansdale Badminton Club. He told the court of complaints he'd received from the women who were members of the Club, from a Mrs Klonaris in particular, who'd been terrified one wet night by the presence in the car park of a bedraggled youth whom she identified as Alban Roche. It was disgraceful, Mr Gilverthorpe said, that decent women going out in the evening to play a game of badminton couldn't change into their sports clothes without some filthy eye upon them. On three separate occasions the accused had been observed leaving the changing-rooms and had once entered them to find himself face to face with Mr Gilverthorpe's own wife, in a state of undress. For all Mr Gilverthorpe knew, members' clothes had been rifled for a salacious purpose while members were engaged on the badminton courts.

It was told in court how a trap had been laid for the persistent intruder and how as a result he'd been apprehended by the police, with the aid of Mr Gilverthorpe and the Treasurer of the Club, both of whom had formed the opinion that Alban Roche was sick, dangerous and vicious. 'I formed the opinion,' the Treasurer stated in court, 'that all he needed was courage in order to commit a fouler crime: I saw that in his eyes.'

Looking through the pet shop window, Miss Gomez recalled those words, and she knew with certainty then that she had not come to this street by chance. She was aware only of feelings as she gazed through the glass: it was instinct, not thought, which told her that the girl who looked like an icon was a victim already in the youth's conscious or unconscious mind, because of the girl's nature, which was in her face, and because of his. Even through glass she felt herself in the presence of a terrible conjunction, as though God or her Church told her so.

Scenes and images flashed in her own mind, occurrences in her room in Mrs Idle's house, and the face of Miss Arbuthnot who wouldn't answer questions, and the face of Mr Kandi, his mouth opening and closing, telling her the truth. She saw the face of Alban Roche; she saw the incurable man on the way to his crime. The Brethren in procession might have descended to the ground with their hands clasped but she, she knew, could not do that.

'I'm looking for work,' she said, going into the pet shop and smiling at both of them. 'I'm a cleaner.'

They stared at her, astonished at what she said, and she, feeling more strongly now all she had felt outside, could think of nothing else to do so she offered them each a cigarette. They shook their heads simultaneously.

'Work?' the girl said. 'A cleaner?' Her voice sounded as though she didn't often use it. The youth, who didn't speak, looked as though he'd never used his at all. But Miss Gomez remembered that he had spoken in court and in fact had been asked to speak up. She smiled again, covering up the silence.

In such a manner Miss Gomez found her mission-ground. She knew it was her mission-ground, she felt it beyond all shadow of doubt. In this unprepossessing place she knew that she would in some way become worthy of her conversion, that from here, from Crow Street, she would be called to Tacas.

With the owner of the pet shop, a Mrs Bassett, who was small and lean and grey-haired, Miss Gomez made an arrangement whereby she would clean her house. Mrs Bassett was glad to see her, because it had been impossible to get cleaners for some time, there being no one about: Bassett's Petstore and the public house called the Thistle Arms were the only two occupied buildings in Crow Street, and indeed for some miles around. 'Could I lodge with you, Mrs Bassett?' Miss Gomez asked, smiling at the old woman, knowing that she was meant to lodge in Crow Street.

Mrs Bassett was surprised by this request. She lived alone above her pet shop and had done so for a long time: no one had shared the house with her since her husband had died in 1956. Occasionally at night, ever since Crow Street had become deserted, she was aware of a feeling of what she supposed was loneliness, even though she had the television. 'I'd clean in lieu of rent,' Miss Gomez said. 'I like old streets like this.'

Mrs Bassett asked her if she was aware of what was happening, if she knew that this street was to be pulled down. Miss Gomez, knowing she was meant to say this in order to advance her cause, said she thought it terrible. While the other two listened, she and Mrs Bassett went on talking about the street, jointly deploring its destruction. In the end Mrs Bassett agreed that Miss Gomez should lodge with her and clean her house in lieu of rent.

Miss Gomez left the pet shop and walked the length of Crow Street to the Thistle Arms, where for a modest recompense she undertook to clean out daily the bars and a few of the private rooms. Mrs Tuke, a large, scented woman who apologized for being in her dressing-gown in the afternoon, was also glad to see her, and she repeated what Miss Gomez already knew, about how difficult it was to get cleaners and how the pet shop and the public house were the last two occupied buildings in Crow Street. Mrs Bassett had twice returned her compensation cheque to those who were developing the area, and the Thistle Arms, by order of the brewery which owned it, remained open in order to supply the demolition workers with lunchtime refreshment. Miss Gomez asked about the girl she'd seen with Alban Roche and was told that she was Mrs Tuke's daughter Prudence, who helped occasionally in the pet shop and served the lunchtime labourers in the public house. A beautiful girl, Miss Gomez said, and Mrs Tuke, given to flamboyance, said she was her pride and joy.

Miss Gomez came to live in Crow Street and discovered that once in the street there'd been a cinema called the Palace Cinema, and that the Snow White Laundry had in its day employed forty women. Now both were gutted of all valuable fittings and stood in Crow Street as useless caves. Next to the cinema the windows of a fishmonger's had been smashed six months ago by a gang of boys. Among the rubbish on the floor mackerel was advertised, the message chalked on a pitted blackboard. In the Crow Street Dining-Rooms a sign still offered mutton with cabbage and potatoes for three and sixpence and shepherd's pie at one and nine. Grey lace curtains horizontally divided the windows of the Crow Street Dining-Rooms; behind them the last meal had been served three months ago. Tables and chairs and all the kitchen equipment had been bought one cold March day, carted away by the owner of a similar establishment in Wandsworth. Mr Zacherelli, whose father had established the Dining-Rooms in 1889, had then conveniently retired. His terrier, Gipsy, was never again seen in Crow Street; and Mr Zacherelli wept, disturbed to leave a lifetime's home.

There'd been a vegetable shop in Crow Street and a drapery that also traded in small pieces of furniture. There'd been a butcher, Mr Knowlman, and a general grocery, a sweet shop and hardware merchant's. Twice in its history murders had been committed in the street; many robberies had taken place. Men had gambled and drunk too much, and often been faithless. Women had repeatedly given birth. Children had played on the pavements.

Yet when she walked in Crow Street now Miss Gomez met only a cat with the fur gone from one side of its body, an animal that snarled and frightened her, for she went in dread of cats. Occasionally she noticed others or heard their mewing in the night, in the depths of empty houses.

Only the windows of Bassett's Petstore gleamed, and within the shop itself the pets lived softly in their hutches and cages. Every morning, on Mrs Bassett's instruction, she cleaned with Brasso the letter-box and knocker of Mrs Bassett's private hall-door. The door was painted green, and it shone also, a dull glow due to years of polishing and care. Its paint was in no way chipped, nor was the paint, a matching colour, that spelt out the title of the shop above the windows. Nothing about the pet shop admitted the distress of Crow Street: it stood its ground with the flourish that Mrs Bassett intended.

At the far end of the street the Thistle Arms was different, reflecting generously the surrounding decay. Permitted for several years to continue in a run-down condition by the brewery, it had heralded the end of the world around it, and in different ways its people had been affected. By order of officials in a brewery the people of the Thistle Arms had lived in a limbo before anyone else in Crow Street, and they continued to do so long after almost everyone else had gone.

Through her thick spectacles Miss Gomez saw the street as a fearsome region, its evening silence eerie with what might have been ghosts. By day there was the swearing and blaspheming of the Irish labourers who every noontime walked to the Thistle Arms in order to become drunk. They continued to address and wave at Miss Gomez when they saw her. She always waved back.

Mrs Bassett states that neither she nor the pets will ever leave this street, she wrote. *Alban Roche has given her an assurance that he'll stay as long as the pets remain. After his imprisonment he was received back into her employ, and received back also by the parents of the girl. He occupies a first-floor room in the Thistle Arms, and shares with the girl the same stairs and toilet facilities; the parents do not care. Mr Batt lodges also in the Thistle Arms. These are the last people of Crow Street.*

The girl took pills three times a day because there wasn't enough blood in her body. The youth was an exile like Miss Gomez herself, a person impossible to know. They stood among pets that no one came to buy, among hamsters and salamanders, tortoises and slowworms, guinea-pigs, gerbils, jerboas, squirrels, coloured mice, cooters, fish and birds. He murmured to the pets, saying little to anyone else. Mrs Bassett carried cups of tea about. The girl talked of breeding butterflies.

You were granted a divine revelation, he wrote. *Do not condemn, Miss Gomez, but only pray, and remember that every second of your life has led you towards your sojourn in this empty street, where a crime is festering in a sex offender's mind. Do not speak of it. Watch him only, and pray. And tell us here all details of Crow Street that we may constantly pray also.*

Your exile, Miss Gomez, is now as pure as my freshwashed surplice hanging in the sun of Tacas. Your exile is part of the greater pattern laid down. And you are not alone, Miss Gomez, which is the message that the Reverend Greated, the Reverend Pearson Simmonds, the Reverend Palmer and I myself now give you. You have been led to your destiny that you may be worthy of your conversion. For this purpose were you chosen, one out of ninety-two.

IV

Mrs Beryl Tuke liked to express herself. Her husband, she once suggested when she was not entirely sober, belonged in grey shadows that matched his own greyness, while she herself occupied a limelight that her personal decor generated. Her hair was a shade of red, her fingernails matched her lips, eye-shadow was generously deployed. Bright colours had always been her thing, crimson and magenta, royal blue and turquoise. In shops the assistants occasionally advised her against purchasing a flowery or swirling pattern of such shades, suggesting that when the material was made up she might be disappointed. Mrs Tuke questioned these assistants and discovered that all they meant was that, in their opinion, such richness emphasized the outsize figure. 'There's nothing can be done with sixteen stone,' she'd said in reply many a time, laughing and buying at once the material she coveted. Never once had she regretted it.

Among the four other people who lived in the Thistle Arms and against a background of varying brownness, Mrs Tuke stood out. She often looked at the four other people, her husband and her daughter, Alban Roche and Mr Batt, and thought that if you left them in a room together for a given length of time they would somehow not manage to have a conversation. Her husband talked mainly about Alsatian dogs, Mr Batt was deaf, the other two rarely bothered to utter. Extraordinary really, she often thought.

Wallpaper the colour of old milk chocolate covered the walls and ceilings of the Thistle Arms, and the colour, slightly deeper in tone, was ubiquitous on linoleum. Other colours, greens and blues, had once been present in the tiled pattern of flowers on the linoleum, but this liveliness had for the most part now faded. Here and there, near the wainscoting and in corners, the coloured blossoms still bloomed within their neat squares, a varia-tion that was similar in the public bar and the private lounge, on the stairs and the first-floor landing, in Mr Batt's room and Alban Roche's, and above those rooms, in Prudence Tuke's and her parents'. Curtains, once a shade of purple and bearing still a faint pattern of *fleur-de-lys,* hung by selected windows and were now nondescript in colour, reduced by the sun to bluish brown. In the hall and the first-floor landing heavy articles of furniture, match-ing the vast proportions of these spaces, had gained a permanency that made them seem almost part of the architecture. There was a dining-table in the hall, with eight chairs around it, all in deeply-carved mahogany. There was a hallstand, a chesterfield, a grand-father clock, and a number of stuffed birds on pedestals fixed to the walls. Four large pictures were contained within mahogany frames, prints of sheep in different positions on the incline of a mountain.

A staircase with a mahogany banister rose steeply from the hall and twisted back on itself as it ascended. At the turn there was a stained-glass window that depicted a man and a woman in ancient dress walking through a wood, and on the first-floor landing the accumulation of mahogany furniture began again. There were two sofas on this landing, a sideboard, a central table, and a mas-sive mahogany linen cupboard that eighty years ago had been constructed for use in the Majestic Hotel, Brighton, and had since found its way to the Thistle Arms. The bedrooms that led off the first-floor landing and off the one above were similarly furnished, heavily and in mahogany.

Downstairs, in the two bars, tall gilt-framed mirrors reflected the brown walls and floors and ornamental ceilings made browner still with years of smoke. They reflected, also, brown upright chairs of bent cane, and square brown tables, and padded seating in brown velour that stretched beneath the windows, and brown whisky in bottles, and beer in glasses.

The bars lay off the front of the hall, the kitchen off the back, and of all the rooms of the Thistle Arms only in the kitchen did greater gaiety prevail. There was a wide mahogany dresser which Mrs Tuke, in a momentary spasm of expressing herself, had painted red. And a man who'd been a local man once in Crow Street had applied to the kitchen table sections of red Formica that Mrs Tuke had purchased economically. Cupboards on either side of the draining-boards she'd painted red also, and had draped the windows with curtains that bore a simple pattern of tomatoes. The kitchen was jolly, Mrs Tuke considered, even if occasionally a bit untidy. She cooked for four there, for herself, her daughter, her husband and Mr Batt, Alban Roche being supplied with a gas-ring in his room. The large sink was generally full of pans and dishes, a fresh loaf and a pot of jam were generally on the table, with butter and knives in case anyone wanted a slice. This, Mrs Tuke believed, was how a kitchen was meant to look, with the frying-pan ready on the stove and the kettle forever boiling, and a hint of steam and smoke in the air, and the television noisy in its corner.

Endlessly Mrs Tuke had asked the brewery to do something about the rest of the Thistle Arms, suggesting striped paper in two shades of red and wall-to-wall carpeting throughout. Two brass chairs she'd seen in a window of Selfridge's would have done marvels for the hall against the striped red paper once the cumbersome furniture was removed, and she had very definite ideas for the first-floor landing: a cactus world she'd read about in a magazine, with the plants growing on actual rocks and in large brass tubs, the kind of thing young Armstrong-Jones went in for, apparently. She'd mentioned her notions to the brewery man who came every third Thursday, but he never for a second seemed to grasp what she was getting at. Which didn't surprise her in the very least, the brewery man being in her opinion a man of extreme coarseness. His fingers were for ever raised to his nose, feeling it, both inside and out. She'd seen him at it, reflected in the mirrors when he thought himself safe because her back was turned. On two occasions he'd actually blown his nose without the aid of either a handkerchief or a tissue, a performance that had put her off a sandwich she was eating. For more than twenty years she'd had to sustain behaviour like that in the Thistle Arms and still keep up her normal cheerfulness. What with one thing and another, and most especially the intractable position that the brewery had taken up on the subject of decor, she wasn't sorry to be going.

On the evening that was precisely a week after the day of Miss Gomez's arrival in Crow Street, Mrs Tuke at twenty past seven heard her cleaner's footsteps approaching the private lounge, where she was, as always in the evenings now, alone. She knew the footsteps were the footsteps of her cleaner because she always came in about now, not to clean but to drink a bottle of Pepsi-Cola and to bother her. Mrs Tuke herself drank gin and peppermint cordial in the evenings, and it seemed to her ridiculous that anyone should make the journey to an empty public house to drink a bottle of Pepsi-Cola, but then Miss Gomez herself was ridiculous, if not insane.

'Nice to see you, dear,' she remarked as Miss Gomez entered the private lounge. She poured the Pepsi-Cola, chattering about the heatwave in case her cleaner should start on her religious topics, because that sort of stuff, no matter where it came from, gave her the creeps. She always turned it off immediately when one of those earnest Arthurs came on the TV, poking a pipe at you and saying to behave yourself. Ridiculous the way they had them penetrating into the home when you were anxious for five minutes' honest entertainment to relax yourself with.

'Thank you, Mrs Tuke,' Miss Gomez said. She smiled: she didn't mind the heatwave, she said.

There was a pause. Then Mrs Tuke, seeing that her cleaner was going to start, said: 'That Dr Finlay. Did you see him on Sunday, dear? I was saying to Mr Tuke, poor Dr Cameron's beyond it. He's sixty-five if he's a day. Dr Snoddy's no younger. I was saying to Mr Tuke, don't the medical profession have a retirement age? I always thought they did for safety's sake. Don't you love Dr Finlay, Miss Gomez?'

Miss Gomez lit a cigarette. Her employer was referring to a Sunday-night television series to which she was addicted and to which she had regularly referred before: Miss Gomez had never seen it and had said so on each occasion. On a shelf behind Mrs Tuke were a number of paper-backed volumes which also had to do with medical matters and which Mrs Tuke, though familiar

37

with their contents, continued to re-read. She picked one up now and drew her cleaner's attention to it. Miss Gomez saw on the paper cover a girl with green earrings, smiling with her eyes closed, while a man placed the side of his forehead against the side of hers. The volume was entitled *Catch Not at Shadows*, and was number 573 in the Woman's Weekly Library, priced at one and three, Eire one and five.

'Sarah Garlen,' said Mrs Tuke, 'wasting her love on Perivale when she should be going with Dr Tom Airley. Have you read it, dear?' Miss Gomez shook her head. Her left forefinger traced a pattern on the bar in beer that had been spilt by the labourers at lunchtime. She drew on her cigarette and slowly blew out smoke. Mrs Tuke said: 'Another good one's *There Came a Surgeon*, and *Attached to Doctor Marchmont*. I'd lend you any of those, dear. Listen to this. *He had been used to every luxury from his sixth year and had every intention of marrying money. Utterly ruthless, bent on exploiting his good looks and enjoying himself, he had no thought for anyone but himself.* That's Perivale for you.'

Mrs Tuke went on speaking. All the time Dr Tom Airley was there, she explained, paying court to Sarah Garlen and having to stand by while she threw her love away on the wrong bloke. It happened to a lot of girls, Mrs Tuke said, this thing of making an error. It happened to Monica Villiers in *Doctor D'Arcy's Love*, which was the best of them all in her opinion.

'I don't read much really,' Miss Gomez said, smiling again. She looked directly into Mrs Tuke's face, causing Mrs Tuke to shift her eyes uneasily. 'A change came into my life six or so months ago. I think I've told you, Mrs Tuke—'

'Of course you have, dear. I've nothing against religion myself. At Rose St Margaret the services are always well attended and you see some really marvellous TV stuff. Charming men, those TV clergymen—'

'Who's Rose St Margaret, Mrs Tuke?'

Mrs Tuke, wearing tonight a dress with a pattern of trees on it and a necklace that was composed of medals in ersatz gold, laughed shrilly. Six of her fingers carried rings with large bright stones in them, and medals similar to those of the necklace featured on her ears. A jangling noise came from her when she laughed at Miss Gomez's ignorance regarding Rose St Margaret, and there came from her also, more pungently than before, the scent of *Muguet du Bois* by Coty.

'Rose St Margaret's the village, darling. Where Dr D'Arcy meets Monica Villiers in the cottage hospital. *Doctor D'Arcy's Love*, dear.'

'I see.' The emptiness in Mrs Tuke's life seemed to Miss Gomez to be more evident with every word that Mrs Tuke uttered. Whenever she saw her, or even heard her voice in the distance, she was aware of it, like a dry well deep inside her. She had written about Mrs Tuke and had received an answer that confirmed her instinct. *She lives a strange life*, a typewriter in Tacas had written, *although she does not know it*.

'We were saying last night, Mrs Tuke—'

'Listen to this, darling. *Her eyes shone and for a moment she gazed at him without answering, studying his face closely as if to prove to herself that the words he had just spoken were sincerely meant. Then she said: "Can you guess how much I love you, Stephen?"*'

'I would like to have a chat with you, Mrs Tuke.'

'That Stephen's the wrong bloke, see. Stephen Perivale, the bloke we were discussing. Listen, dear. *He embraced her passionately, kissing her white smooth brow, her eyes, her soft and willing lips.* That's Perivale still at it, see.'

'Mrs Tuke, I would like to tell you a little about my Church.'

'You were telling me last night, darling. Very interesting actually—'

'It is possible that my Church can help you, Mrs Tuke.'

'Help, darling?'

'My life was nothing, Mrs Tuke. I drifted in any direction, I let anything happen to me. There was no meaning, Mrs Tuke, no explanation. All that is different now.'

'I'm glad it is, dear. No good being a droopy drawers, I've said to Mr Tuke a hundred times: what good is moping when there's no charge for gaiety? I always think Dr Finlay's like that, you know, holding his head up high no matter what happens, cheerful as a rabbit. Don't you think he has a great sense of humour the way he handles the patients in a practice like that? Mind you, I think someone like Dr D'Arcy is nicer socially. D'you know what I mean, dear? The way Dr D'Arcy can make a girl feel she is the only creature on earth. Mind you, Monica Villiers was never right for him, any more than Perivale was right for Sarah Garlen. Monica and Desmond D'Arcy made just the same type of error except that neither of them was the type for Perivale. It's not hard to make an error in circumstances like that: you can see a girl making an error when she can't for a second see it herself. Funny, really.'

Mrs Tuke, lost for a moment in her thoughts, stared past Miss Gomez at the brown velour of the seating that stretched beneath the windows. The fingers of her right hand played with her glass of gin and peppermint cordial, gently moving the liquid about.

'You've made errors yourself, Mrs Tuke?' Miss Gomez as gently murmured.

The meditative expression in Mrs Tuke's eyes faded. She frowned, wondering if she could have heard correctly, if for a second it could be true that a black cleaner had asked her if she'd made errors. She turned her head slowly and found that the eyes of her cleaner were again seeking the attention of hers. The black head was sympathetically inclined, the thick lips sympathetically parted.

'Errors,' murmured Miss Gomez again, to Mrs Tuke's horror. 'Tell me,' whispered Miss Gomez.

Mrs Tuke lifted her glass to her lips. The black bloody baggage, she thought, coming out with stuff like that, grinning like a piccaninny. There was nothing but impudence in that black face as far as she could see, the glasses flashing and the teeth on show like a row of tombstones. They got teeth like that from eating meal, like chickens ate; abrasive stuff that pushed the gums back. A lot of them couldn't read so much as a three-letter word. Ridiculous having glasses, imitating white people.

Miss Gomez continued to smile at her employer, and it suddenly occurred to Mrs Tuke that the creature was now attempting to imitate her personally, since she was herself given to finding her smile in moments of emotion or stress, and always had been. A smile was a sunbeam, she'd read somewhere as a girl, a ripple of laughter cleared the air. If the black creature was imitating her it was probably some type of compliment, even if it was one which she could easily do without: you couldn't know with foreigners these days. She drank some more, aware that she was still being scrutinized and endeavouring to keep calm. To ease the situation, she hummed an old wartime tune, *Wrap Me up in Cotton-Wool.*

'Tell me anything you like, Mrs Tuke,' Miss Gomez whispered. 'We could talk about anything. We could write a letter together.'

'Letter, dear?'

'To the Brethren of the Way in Tacas. At the time of my second baptism—my conversion, Mrs Tuke—I wrote down everything that had always worried me. I made errors too, Mrs Tuke.'

'You've told me about your second baptism, actually. Most interesting, I thought. Is Mrs Bassett well, darling?'

'Mrs Tuke, are you happy in your daily life?'

Mrs Tuke hummed again, examining the pattern of trees on her dress. The sun affected their brain as well as blackening their skins: she'd heard that said and after all it stood to reason, intense heat like that and most of them not possessing the intelligence to make use of a hat. She smiled at Miss Gomez and laughed a little, not answering the question about her daily life. Extraordinary the way the black baggage came in every night and made a bloody nuisance of herself. And yet in the mornings, when she was cleaning the place out, she never said a word.

'I've told my Church about you, Mrs Tuke. I've said that one day you may pray also.'

To Mrs Tuke's astonishment and distaste her cleaner at this point reached out and briefly touched the back of her hand with the fingers that had been poking about in the spilt beer. Mrs Tuke could feel the dampness of the beer, which at first she assumed to be her cleaner's sweat. Miss Gomez picked up her glass of Pepsi-Cola and took it to one of the square brown tables, saying in a gay manner that she wouldn't bother Mrs Tuke with any more holy chatter tonight. Mrs Tuke shivered. She felt angry and embarrassed, which she knew would pass off when she'd had a chance to relax herself with a drink and a glance at a novel. She said to herself as she watched Miss Gomez settling herself down that she wasn't one to harbour grudges. You had to get on with people no matter what they were like, for your own good as well as everyone else's. If you didn't want to get knocked up doing every pick of the cleaning in a barracks of a public house you had at least to keep up some kind of show, even if it meant being touched by a black and told to say your prayers. Mrs Tuke shivered again, recalling the damp fingertips and the intense eyes behind the spectacles and the white teeth like tombstones. It wasn't just anger and embarrassment, she thought, nor was it disgust: there was something else about the creature, something which made you uneasy, and made you shiver as though you were frightened.

For a moment, alone again, Miss Gomez felt as morose and sombre as she had before her conversion. Every night she came to this lounge to sow seeds, yet never was there a single thing to reap. 'Mention only your Church,' he had commanded her, and he was right of course, even though she longed to mention everything else, to tell the full truth so that everyone in Crow Street might play a part, so that prayers might be said, here, among the people. She had longed also to say urgently to Prudence Tuke that she was every day in danger, to confess to her what she had sensed in the mind of Alban Roche. She longed to remind her of her nature, to make her see herself as she was, a timid girl who would not cry out, who offered him the courage he sought. She took a ballpoint pen and an air-mail form from the pocket of her leather dress and began to write her daily letter, knowing that none of that would commend itself to her Church. The crime felt closer to her tonight than it had been for all her seven nights in Crow Street. If she said it had begun to haunt her, normal people would say she was hysterical. He would say so in Tacas, a gentle reprimand.

Mrs Tuke poured herself further measures of gin and peppermint. She hunted among her paper-backed fiction for *Doctor D'Arcy's Love*, but when she found it and opened it at chapter four, which was her favourite, she read only a few lines. She lifted her eyes from the small print and saw her cleaner attempting to write a letter and heard the voice of Mr Batt in the public bar. Wishing neither to see the one nor to hear the other, her mind filled with the face and person of Dr Desmond D'Arcy of the Rose St Margaret cottage hospital.

He bore the features of a youngish man she'd seen a couple of times on television, a salesman in an advertisement for soap. She'd dreamed of him last night, as she often did, experiencing a fantasy in which he'd knocked on her bedroom door just as she was about to go to bed, her husband being away at the time, having the veins in his legs attended to in a hospital. 'Oh excuse me, Mrs Tuke,' Dr D'Arcy had remarked, dressed up in his white medical coat. 'Excuse me, Mrs Tuke, I was wondering if you could perhaps assist me.' By mischance he'd got himself locked into the Thistle Arms after closing time, owing to the fact that he'd been attending to Mr Batt, who'd developed bronchitis. 'So very sorry,' he murmured, 'to disturb your rest.' She'd led the way downstairs and when they reached the hall asked him if he'd like a cup of tea. He smiled a little at that. There was nothing he'd like better, he replied, being totally exhausted after a long day's work. In the kitchen of the Thistle Arms they had tea together, sitting at the Formica-topped table. He admired the pattern of tomatoes on the drawn curtains, saying the whole kitchen was tasteful and homely. He went on talking, telling her, in a quiet voice, about his work in the cottage hospital.

She'd had another dream in which she and Dr D'Arcy were in a country mansion called Villierscourt, the property of Sir Guy Villiers, father of Monica Villiers, a nurse at the cottage hospital. It was a house that was in part of a castle, with lawns stretching in several directions and elegant silver birches in the distance. In her dream she and Doctor D'Arcy were present at a house-party. Dr D'Arcy, with the features of the man in the soap advertisement, was wearing a paisley scarf and she herself a flowered magnolia dress. The sun shone on close-cut grass decorated with croquet hoops and on the spinney of silver birches. On a terrace when it was almost dark young men and girls ate raspberries with yellow cream on them, and a scent of roses imbued the air, roses with which Sir Guy took prizes at the Rose St Margaret annual horti-

43

cultural show. 'Let's walk in Sir Guy's little rose garden,' Dr D'Arcy suggested to her, and they went together from the terrace, down lichen-covered steps into the dusky evening.

Sometimes the dream turned into a nightmare, everything going wrong: Dr D'Arcy wasn't the man in the soap advertisement any more, but a coarse man she'd once unfortunately known, called Eddie Mercer, a man in a coal business, no better than a coal-heaver really. Sometimes Dr D'Arcy turned into one of the Irish labourers who were at present working on the surrounding demolition. Usually it was a labourer called Atlas Flynn, whom she'd seen looking at her a couple of times when the men came in for their lunchtime refreshment, a big coarse-looking fellow with arms like oak-trunks and curly red hair full of grease that had a smell of a herbaceous border. She felt uneasy when Atlas Flynn looked at her like that, admiring her bulk and comparing it maybe to his, saucy with his eyes when he'd had two or three glasses of beer. Not at all like Dr D'Arcy, or Dr Finlay or Dr Tom Airley of *Catch Not at Shadows*.

Mrs Tuke gave a small shiver, recalling the pleasant dreams that sometimes turned into nightmares. A sewer ran through Eddie Mercer, as she knew to her cost, and she suspected that a sewer was the end-all and be-all of the red-haired Atlas Flynn. She drank some more of her gin and peppermint, trying not to think of any of that.

The private lounge of the Thistle Arms was divided from the public bar by a panelled mahogany partition, ornamentally finished and containing at eye-level a row of gothic-shaped leaded windows in yellow and green glass. This ran to the far side of the bar-counter but left access for those serving to move from one bar to the other. A hinged counter-flap adjoined it in the private lounge and it was from beneath this that Mr Tuke's Alsatian dog Rebel now appeared. He was an animal that gave the impression of dwarfing his master when in his company, a brindled creature of majestic stature with a constantly open mouth. He padded across the floor to where Miss Gomez was sitting and immediately displayed affection. His cold nose touched her legs, his tongue licked her.

44

Noticing this, Mrs Tuke considered it bizarre. Really dippy it was, the girl pretending she could write a letter and a dog coming in and licking her. She wondered if old Rebel knew the difference between black flesh and white or could tell by licking a leg. She noticed that sometimes on the palm of a hand the black had worn away a bit and apparently the soles of the feet were similar. Extraordinary, really.

'Old Rebel's taken a fancy to you,' she chattily exclaimed and Miss Gomez, folding her air-mail form, smiled. 'Rebel's licking Miss Gomez,' Mrs Tuke called through to her husband in the public bar, knowing that he was interested in all the activities of his pet.

Miss Gomez finished her cola and returned her glass to the bar. Then, unable to help herself and even though she had promised not to bother Mrs Tuke with any more holy chatter that night, she spoke of the Brethren. Enthusiastically she described them as the Reverend Lloyd Patterson had described them to her; in procession through the streets of Tacas, carrying no banners and handing out no leaflets, for that was not the Brethren's way. She described the smiling of their happiness and the small hill they arrived at, on which flowers grew, where they sang a hymn before they spread out their picnic in the sunshine. The Reverend Lloyd Patterson, a great smiling man himself, moved among them in his surplice, with the Reverend Greated and the Reverend Pearson Simmonds and the Reverend Palmer. The women among them handed around the cakes they had baked and iced with celebration messages, the men opened bottles of Pepsi-Cola. On the hill there was forgiveness; everyone was happy.

Mrs Tuke, who had drawn well back in case she was touched again, said it sounded lovely, and Miss Gomez longed once more to say what she knew she must not say: that because of prayers said on the hill in Tacas she had been granted a revelation in Crow Street the first minute she arrived there, a revelation concerning Mrs Tuke's daughter and the youth called Alban Roche. She longed to say now, even though she would be considered insane, that the girl should be protected, that she felt it in her bones in no ordinary way and knew what she was talking about.

'Good night, Mrs Tuke,' she said instead. They smiled at one another, and Mrs Tuke reminded Miss Gomez that she'd be expecting her at ten in the morning to hoover everywhere through.

Mr Tuke had gone to work in the public bar of the Thistle Arms at the age of sixteen and had remained there since, succeeding to the landlordship in 1959. He was a small man, with bristly grey hair that was cropped close to his scalp, and a limp. Latish in life, in 1966, he had decided to grow a beard and it had remained with him since, squarely cut, its greyness unrelieved by any hint of what shade it might once have been.

Mr Tuke, in his shirtsleeves but wearing a tie and collar, had heard the voices of his wife and Miss Gomez in the other bar, while reading a newspaper that was spread out on the bar in front of him. He'd endeavoured earlier to have a conversation with Mr Batt because Mr Batt had asked him about Rebel and he'd been anxious to explain another point or two about the breed. But Mr Batt, who declined to wear a deaf-aid on the grounds that deaf-aids were a racket, hadn't been able to understand much of what he said. In the newspaper Mr Tuke read without interest of aggression in the Far East. Rebel, he noticed, having returned from the private lounge, was licking Mr Batt's trousers.

Mr Batt sat at the bar in silence, unaware of the dog's activities. He was a man of eighty-one, a tall, bent man with a shallow face in which the bones stood out, and with only a scattering of hair left now. Dressed this evening, as always, in a suit with a pinstripe in it, he was smoking a pipe and regarding the bottles that were hanging upside down behind the bar, with measures in the form of glass globes attached to them. His mind was involved with the distant past: recalling an advance that had taken place on August 8th, 1918, near Lassigny. He had advanced himself until the advancing, he thought, would never cease, or cease only with death. For more than a minute, on that August morning, he'd thought the whole thing foolhardy. Ludendorff wouldn't stand for this; Ludendorff, they said, played games with the dead. But it had been all right. Afterwards he'd seen Sir Henry Rawlinson, whose triumph it was, seeing him for the first time.

One of the tall gilt-framed mirrors reflected the back of Mr Batt as he sat at the bar and reflected as well the small form of Mr Tuke, with a glass of beer beside his newspaper. Another mirror showed Rebel, who had ceased to lick Mr Batt's trousers and now lay on the seat that stretched beneath the windows, licking his own paws.

Bored by solitude, Mrs Tuke carried her glass into the public bar. She was unsteady on her feet, having consumed since six o'clock three-quarters of a bottle of Gordon's gin. She said good evening to Mr Batt. The heat was too much for her, she confessed, and Mr Batt vaguely nodded.

'The heat, old chap,' shouted Mrs Tuke, smiling at him to show she wasn't being rude. 'The sunny weather.'

'Yes,' said Mr Batt.

Mrs Tuke eased herself on to a chair that was specially there for her nightly visits to the public bar. She narrowed her eyes in order to focus them on Mr Batt, reducing a triple image to a double one. It was a long time since she had seen him in any other way at this time of the evening, one cadaverous face floating from the other, the hairless head in constant momentum. He'd been an assistant in Cave's hardware shop and had lived above it with his wife, number four Crow Street, until his wife died. The Caves, being grander, had moved away to a private residence in 1954. Funny being an assistant all your life, Mrs Tuke reflected as the old man wobbled in her vision, selling screws and handles and all that kind of thing, never having your own business, always beholden. His head was constantly sticking out at you, his hands were calloused from all the handling of metal he'd done. Extraordinary the life he led when you came to think of it, standing about the place in one of the suits he said a tailor had made for him. The world could come to an end and he'd still be standing there, poking at his turnip watch. According to himself, although she often wondered if he hadn't imagined the whole thing, he'd been away from Crow Street during the First World War fighting the Germans in the trenches, and in the Second World War he'd been some kind of air-raid warden. Morbid, really, to keep harking back to times like that, when people were killed like you'd kill a fly. It seemed even more so at eighty-one, which was too old for anyone to be, no matter how you looked at it. Old codgers of eighty-one were definitely better off in a nice home somewhere, with proper facilities. He could be a real old bother-boots sometimes, the way he'd suddenly turn up his nose at a plate of food, not to mention the constant difficulty with his hearing.

'There's a good new aid on the market,' she shouted. 'Two years' guarantee, Mr Batt.'

'Eh?'

Again his face slid about, mutiplying itself. She concentrated, closing one eye. She forgot what she'd been saying. She laughed. 'Gomez was on about her Brethren,' she said.

'Eh?' said Mr Batt, leaning closer to her, across the bar.

Mr Tuke, reading now about India's population problem, heard his wife saying that Miss Gomez had been on about her Brethren again and for a moment he thought about the black girl. Two days ago she had entered the bathroom while he was cutting at his beard and had at once apologized, saying she'd come to clean. She had waited while he'd finished his clipping, standing with the Electrolux by her feet, its flex already plugged into a socket on the landing. 'D'you like it in London?' he'd said to her, unable to think of anything else to say. She'd shaken her head.

'Gomez,' shouted Mrs Tuke into Mr Batt's ear. 'Gomez, the black thing.'

'Yes,' said Mr Batt.

'She's a religious lunatic,' shouted Mrs Tuke.

There had been something about her silence in the bathroom and the way she stood as well, her black hands crossed on her black leather dress. He'd been aware of an odd feeling in his head, a rather pleasant shivery feeling that seemed somehow connected with her presence. He hadn't said anything else to her and she hadn't spoken either.

His wife was talking to him about the Arab's Head, a public house in Kew to which they were all to move in a fortnight's time, leaving the old Thistle to be pulled down. She'd visited it that afternoon and had come back saying that she'd like to do the upstairs out in knicker pink. All during tea she'd talk about the plans she'd formed on the bus. She'd do one bar out in white, like somewhere in the desert, to set an Arabic theme. They could call it the Oasis Bar, with a simple fountain in the centre and dry sand in a bowl that could be used as an ash-tray. The Arab's Head was much smarter than the Thistle, she reported, and according to the outgoing landlord there was a tip-top Sunday morning potential, young chaps and girls after vodka and lime, a drink there'd never been a call for in Crow Street. If they played their cards right, she said, the Arab's Head could be a challenge to the Red Rover at Barnes, which had been done out as a stable in order to attract the Sunday morning potential, or Flanagan's Railway in Putney with its sawdust and bar-girls in Edwardian costume. He'd listened to her going on about all that, thinking only that in the Arab's Head he'd like to have a separate bedroom.

'Prudence doesn't want to leave Crow Street,' he said. He tried to raise his voice in order to explain to Mr Batt the reason for this, but found it difficult owing to a catarrhal complaint.

'It certainly is,' said Mr Batt.

Mrs Tuke remarked that for a long time she'd wanted a place like the Arab's Head, a place with a better class clientele. 'I've always fancied Kew,' she said, 'Nicer really.'

He'd have to speak to Prudence, although it was difficult sometimes to make contact with her. He'd try to point out that it was different for Mrs Bassett to make a protest about leaving Crow Street, because Mrs Bassett was old and had lived there most of her life. Mrs Bassett was sentimental about her property and the animals it contained, it being the lifework of her late husband. He'd put it to her like that, explaining that it wasn't unlike Mr Batt being sentimental, staying on in the Thistle after his retirement and the death of his wife. When you got to that age it was a natural thing; it was different for younger people.

'Prudence doesn't want to go up to Kew,' he explained to Mr Batt as loudly as he could, because Mr Batt had put his hand interrogatively to his ear. 'She's taken up with the pet shop.'

Mr Batt heard part of that. Kew was where the botanical gardens were and the Arab's Head public house to which in a week

49

or so they were all going to move. He was quite looking forward to the botanical gardens, which he knew were enjoyable to walk about in, having once visited them. It was pleasant going into the hot glass-houses and just standing there, looking at the green growth. In winter he could go to a cinema instead, if there was a cinema nearby. It didn't cost much in the afternoon for an elderly person and sometimes the entertainment was excellent. In some of the cinemas they turned up the sound in the afternoons for the elderly and the hard-of-hearing, but that never worried him because he couldn't hear a thing anyway.

'Yes,' said Mr Batt because Mr Tuke was saying something to him. He remembered being in Kew during the Second World War when he'd been an air-raid warden. He remembered an enemy plane that had circled round and round all day, going away and coming back again. There was an end to that memory which at the moment he couldn't recall. Strangely enough, it had something to do with bodies on stretchers in a cinema, but he thought that he'd probably got it wrong and was confusing the bodies there'd been at Lassigny with some afternoon he'd spent since in a cinema. Odd, how some events came back so clearly and others were all in a fog. Only that afternoon he'd been saying that to Mrs Bassett, telling her about Lassigny over a cup of tea. He remembered her as a young girl when she first came to Crow Street to work in the pet shop, no older than Mrs Tuke's daughter she'd been, and then she'd married Henry Bassett, a most surprising marriage, people in the street had said, on account of the age difference. She'd never succeed in holding out against the developers, which was what she was apparently trying to do. No point in it, he'd told her, but she hadn't understood.

'I'll quite enjoy those botanical gardens, you know,' he said and he saw Mrs Tuke's husband nodding and saying something.

'I was there one day in the Second World War,' he went on. 'I took a bus from Kew to Putney. There was an enemy plane that kept flying up into the clouds and then coming down low again. We couldn't make it out.'

'Probably lost,' said Mr Tuke, forgetting to raise his voice.

In Mrs Tuke's vision the heads of Mr Batt and her husband

coalesced. The shallow countenance of the old man bore suddenly the moustache and beard of her husband and the hairless scalp was spiked with her husband's grey bristle.

'Ha, ha, ha,' cried Mrs Tuke, deriving from the grotesque image a degree of pleasure. She narrowed her eyes in the hope that something even stranger might occur, but when she did so her husband's face returned to its own side of the bar. She felt sluggish all of a sudden and found it an effort to keep her eyes open because of the glare. Gomez had made her gloomy with all her talk about a church, and so did old Batt. Funny, really, to remain in the one street all your days, the opposite of Gomez, who came from God knows where. You'd think she'd find it awkward to be among people so different from her that even their skins were a different colour, but Gomez never would, being without sensitivity. Atlas Flynn, of course, was an exile, just like Gomez, and so was Alban Roche, and all the Irish boys who came in at lunchtime. Funny, really, not to be in your own country and have a familiar neighbourhood, always to be a foreigner. Someone had told her once how many foreigners there were in exile in London and she'd been amazed beyond measure at the figure.

Mrs Tuke poured herself a further supply of gin. Mr Batt was saying something: his voice seemed to be whispering and coming to her from a distance, echoing over cliffs. She laughed in order to keep cheerful. 'Rebel was licking Gomez,' she said to her husband. He was looking well that evening, she added. 'Both of you, old chap,' she said. 'Rebel's looking well, too.'

He'd come closer to her and she was aware that he was addressing her, suggesting as far as she could make out that she should go upstairs to bed, which was silly since it couldn't have been more than half-past nine. She tried to tickle him but found it wasn't easy because he was just out of her reach and she didn't want to get up from the comfortable chair she was in. She spoke to Mr Batt, endeavouring to tell him that her husband was an angel, but had difficulty in marshalling the words and laughed instead, feeling that old Batt would understand.

Still laughing, she leaned her head against the partition that separated the public bar from the private lounge, her henna-shaded hair bright on the green and yellow leaded panes. Cheeky black baggage, she thought, grinning like that, terrifying the life out of you. Again the head of Mr Batt slipped about moving from his shoulders and then returning. She closed her eyes.

It was definitely that: Gomez was ridiculous and half-baked and half-witted and probably half human, but Gomez frightened her. In drowsy inebriation that truth arrived with Mrs Tuke and was not rejected by her. Everything else was a show you put on: you did your best to cover things up. You said this and that, finding your smile and asking how Mrs Bassett was. You said it sounded lovely, the prayer-meeting on the hill; you chatted on, calling her darling like you'd call a normal person, remarking when the dog licked her. Yet all the time you felt afraid of her because she was a black savage who'd cook you and eat you as soon as she'd look at you.

V

Mrs Bassett turned on her television set. She watched the grey screen flickering into life and then, instead of something pleasant, there was a dead Arab lying on a pavement. The room she sat in had a potted fern in it and two pictures of Eastern scenes framed in bamboo and a buttoned sofa in purple, with chairs to match, and white china ornaments jostling one another on the mantelpiece.

Mrs Bassett rose from the chair into which she had just comfortably settled herself. She crossed the room to the television set in order to try another channel while a man's voice explained the circumstances of the Arab's death, detailing with precision the violence that had accompanied it. She sharply turned a switch. 'One of today's great tastes,' said another voice.

She watched promotion for chocolate bars taking place and then promotion for peas. An empty pea-pod, made into a child's boat, floated on the surface of what seemed to be a lake. 'Welcome home,' a voice said, 'to Bird's Eye country.'

Mrs Bassett turned the volume low in order to listen for Miss Gomez, wondering if she was making cocoa in the kitchen. But though she strained her ears and reduced the television sound entirely she could hear nothing. She liked it when Miss Gomez made them both a cup of cocoa in the evenings and came to sit for a while for a chat or to look at the television, not that Miss Gomez ever seemed to care for anything that was showing. Sometimes in the middle of a programme or an advertisement she'd suddenly begin to talk, suggesting to Mrs Bassett that she should join her Church, which, as far as Mrs Bassett could make out, consisted entirely of black people in Jamaica.

A woman sang on the television screen, holding a microphone close to her mouth. Mrs Bassett watched. When first she'd come to work in the pet shop she'd had to learn the price of the different cage-birds and how they should be fed and cared for, and the price of dog biscuits and Keating's Powder. In those days she was Dorothy Sweet. 'I have something to suggest to you,' Henry Bassett said to her one evening, quite out of the blue, and after a pause suggested marriage. He was fifty-five at the time, exactly twice her age.

He had himself assisted in a pet shop before accumulating enough money to buy the premises in Crow Street. He had waited all those years without marrying, so that in the end he might own, as he had always put it, a small piece of London, which had been an ambition. She'd watched him building the business up, painting the woodwork of the shop and the house, papering their bedroom with a pattern of lupins. He liked John West tinned salmon and a banana sandwich, with tea, before he went to bed. His back was full of small splinters of metal that had become irretrievably lodged there during enemy action in 1915. He never complained about that, although she knew that often he was in pain. He wished they might have a child, and he never complained about that either. Every Sunday they went together to St Nicholas's Church in Enderby Street, ten minutes away. Both church and street had been destroyed a week ago.

In anger, remembering the destruction of St Nicholas's Church, Mrs Bassett continued to view the television screen from which the woman unmelodiously sang about love. What right had they to come, those grasping men, and talk to her about development of the area as though development of the area interested her? What right had they to spread their unpleasant architectural plans all over the cages, saying they wanted to explain? She cared neither for their arguments nor their drawings, nor for the unsolicited cheques they sent to her through the post. 'We understand,' they said, one of them repeating the words of another. 'Of course, Mrs Bassett.' They could never finish a sentence properly, they were incapable of convincing argument. They appreciated

54

her sentiments, they said. 'And what about our pets?' she asked.

She had watched him rearing the guinea-pigs of a mother who'd died at their birth, soaking a piece of wool in milk and letting them suck it off. He had successfully treated budgerigars for psittacosis, watching over them as a mother over children. He had reared rare squirrels and had continued with the strain. The descendants of his squirrels were still in the shop today: the strain had been locally famous for over thirty years. 'Homes must be found for all the pets,' she had informed the grasping men. They quite agreed, they said, and brought an officer of the R.S.P.C.A. to her who suggested that for their own sakes the pets should be painlessly destroyed.

She would not give in. Homes must be found, she had decreed, but the men in their business suits had done nothing whatever about that. They'd put no advertisements in newspapers, as she suggested. She'd give the pets away to children who were suitable, she promised, but they'd brought no children to her, though she'd explained quite clearly what she'd meant by children who were suitable. The men didn't care; they stood around with their ugly drawings, not wanting the bother of advertising or finding children. Death was all they could come up with.

They could take her screaming; they could drag her along Crow Street and she would still protest. The story would be written in the *News of the World*. Cruelty to animals, and memories, and people: she would scratch the faces of those grasping men: what right had they to kill?

On the television screen a man dressed as a woman winked at her. She couldn't see the point of it, men putting on evening dresses full of sequins and going to such trouble with lipstick, plucking their eyebrows. Mrs Bassett turned the set off. It was past Miss Gomez's hour for cocoa; she would not come tonight. At the door, on the way to bed, she paused, looking about the room, at the fern and the buttoned sofa and the pictures of Eastern scenes. She imagined the wallpaper gone, and the mantelpiece; she paused a moment longer, spreading her affection over the room as though her affection might somehow save it. But her nostrils tonight caught a scent of death: an imaginary thing, as immediately she told herself, but none the less real for that.

At half-past one that night Prudence Tuke dreamed that she was putting on a wedding-dress, and that it kept tearing. She was laughing as it tore. 'I see no point in weddings,' she said, giggling out the words because for some reason she was happy. She was addressing, of all people, her mother's black cleaner, Miss Gomez, who spoke to her about forgiveness in so irrelevant a way that she laughed even more.

In the room beneath hers Alban Roche slept also. He dreamed intermittently that a gerbil had escaped from the pet shop and was lost among the empty houses of Crow Street, that he was a child again, buying sugar for his mother, that he and his mother were walking on a road. 'Can you,' a Dr Krig said, a psychiatrist he'd known in prison, a fat tidy man in a grey suit, 'can you tell me, Alban, how it happens that Mrs Bassett's gerbil escapes? Can you tell me how it happens that you work in a pet shop, Alban?'

Miss Gomez sat in the centre of her room, having just completed the letter she'd begun in the Thistle Arms. On the walls around her there were sacred pictures that she had framed herself in passepartout, and a polished wooden crucifix. On the table beside her there was a bible that she'd been given ten years ago by Miss Arbuthnot, the personal present that every child in the orphanage received on her tenth birthday. In the days of the Spot-On Club and Mrs Idle's pleasure house she'd often meant to throw it away, finding it a slight embarrassment whenever she saw it in a drawer. But she never had, and believed now that she had not been meant to.

Above her bed hung a calendar that bore a picture of a garden, with birds fluttering above a bird-bath, and a summer-house of rustic wood. *You are nearer God's heart in a garden,* ran the legend, *than anywhere else on earth.* A man on the street had sold the calendar to Miss Gomez, assuring her that its construction was the work of the disabled and producing a license to prove that he was authorized to act on the disabled's behalf. She had, in fact, bought a dozen of the calendars, placing the other eleven aside so that she might distribute them as gifts among those whom she converted. She planned to buy other gifts as well and was constantly on the look-out for something suitable.

Miss Gomez had few other possessions. She had thrown away an assortment of dresses when the change came into her life, as well as two frilled lampshades and various figurines. The pictures on the walls and the crucifix, her remaining clothes, a writing-case in light-blue plastic, her two suitcases and the Canadian Pacific canvas bag were all she now owned. She did not feel the need for more.

Miss Gomez licked the edges of the air-mail letter and sealed it. Often she thought of these letters, like birds flying between London and Jamaica, chattering with information. She loved the correspondence: in the past she had written no letters at all and wouldn't have guessed that a correspondence could be a pleasure. *The Church of the Way,* she wrote, *Hibiscus Villa, King George VI Road.* The address had a lilt for her, like poetry she'd once been obliged to learn by heart.

For a moment longer Miss Gomez sat. She thought of all the people she'd tried to interest in the Brethren: the office cleaners and the girls at the cereal factory, and Tina von Hippel, who'd been amazed when she told her, and the people she'd stopped on the streets and the ones who'd been angry because she'd disturbed them in their homes. She remembered the cashier in the late-night supermarket: in the Rhumba Rendezvous he'd probably danced with another girl and told her about a Jamaican with glasses who'd attempted to hold a conversation with him about the snares of the Lord, whispering about it to the girl, with his hands clasped round her buttocks. When she'd first come to London she'd gone to such places too, and to Mecca Dancing in Leicester Square and the Lyceum Ballroom in the Strand. Towards the end of the evening some man would attach himself to her, a white man or a West Indian, whose passion she would later assuage in a motor-car, seeing no reason not to. She imagined the cashier of the supermarket driving about London now in the kind of broken motor-car that West Indians went in for, with a different girl, picked up somewhere else. They couldn't return to the house he lived in because he had a wife and several children.

'Oh Lord, in Thy great mercy,' murmured Miss Gomez and then, quite suddenly, she felt a fresh urgency about the crime that was to be in Crow Street, an urgency that seemed to be a physical sensation within her. She sat still, with the letter she'd written between the thumb and forefinger of her left hand. She closed her eyes and felt immediately that there was another presence in the room with her.

After a moment she slowly rose and went to the window. The room, the whole house, felt intensely silent, and outside it was silent also. The buildings of Crow Street were touched with moonlight. No sound came from the Thistle Arms, no light burned there.

She returned to the centre of the room and stood there, feeling the crime all around her. She felt she carried it with her now, as much as the pet salesman himself did, trailing it through this street and its two occupied houses, leaving a smear on everywhere she'd been. She felt it like some leafless growth, its fleshy tentacles creeping inside her. She sensed it in her mind, and saw it there: pale translucent green, faintly marked with blemishes of pink, curling from putrid fruit that oozed a thick, pale liquid. She'd seen that once, something like it as a child, a plant growing in the garden of the orphanage. And then the image blurred and became the face of Prudence Tuke, the strangled face, the tongue and eyes protruding, the lips drawn madly back, the flesh still twitching.

She sat down because for a moment she'd thought she might fall. Prickles of revulsion needled the skin of her body, making her shiver all over. In a strange, vivid way she saw herself sitting there, crouched blackly in her room, her eyes unblinking in a terror that she didn't understand. The throb of her heart shook her whole body now, and as in the agony of a nightmare she was helpless, while witnessing through the tormented face of Prudence Tuke the violation and death in the pet salesman's crime.

In the corridor she turned the light on, not recalling how she had made that journey, only knowing that she must reach Mrs Bassett's door in order to be in the presence of another human being, even for a second. But the door seemed very small and a long way away and her legs moved so slightly that they appeared hardly to shift her body forward. She tried to pray, as slowly the crime began all over again, but she couldn't because the crime did not permit any other concentration within her. She didn't know if she was sleeping or awake but only that whatever her condition she could not bear to be alone. Her eyes dragged her to the door, forcing her legs to carry her.

Mrs Bassett lay awake. Often recently she had thought she mustn't sleep in case, somehow, she was unable to rouse herself at the correct time: in her bad dreams she'd seen herself descending the stairs and finding that the pets had been taken away, that there was no one in the pet shop except a gang of Irish labourers with pick-axes in their hands. When she wept in distress they laughed: Alban Roche had again been arrested, they told her, for looking in at windows.

He was loved by the pets almost as much as her husband had been, and it had been difficult during those three months when he was away, even though Prudence Tuke had come in to help. She'd felt the strain of it and was glad when he returned. 'I'm sorry,' he'd said and had at once examined every creature in the shop to see if all was well.

Mrs Bassett sighed, thinking of those three months that had taken a toll of her. The developers had put a bit of pressure on, knowing that her employee was absent. They'd stood in the shop for hours, it seemed, their lips pursed over the seriousness of it all. They tried to beat her like that, by not doing what she requested in terms of advertising or finding children, trying to promote the notion that her objections were so ludicrous that they couldn't be replied to, and simulating sympathy at the same time.

One morning, when Alban Roche was in prison and the men had been hanging about for a long time, she'd suddenly felt faint. Not wishing to let them see her condition in case they took it as a sign of the weakness they hoped for, she'd gone into the private part of the house and had sat on the stairs. For a moment she'd experienced an urgency in her chest and had for some reason thought of race-horses landing at the other side of a water-jump, which was something she'd recently seen in a television advertisement. In a few moments she'd felt all right, except for tiredness.

Mrs Bassett closed her eyes. Sleep evaded her, but comfortingly her mind filled with images from her married years, the days when Crow Street was thriving, when women worked in the Snow White Laundry and Mr Zacherelli made a daily profit in his Dining-Rooms. Every Christmas Mr Knowlman kept her a turkey without her ever having to place an order, a small turkey just for the two of them. 'You'll have a glass of port,' Henry said, calling Mr Knowlman John although she herself never permitted herself that liberty. 'Come in on Christmas Eve, John,' Henry said. Sometimes Mr Zacherelli came too, at six o'clock on Christmas Eve, and other traders also. Mr Knowlman had died in 1940; his son six months ago had sold out to the developers.

For a moment the people in her mind played tricks with her, and it seemed that the elder Mr Knowlman was still alive when Alban Roche had become her employee and that Alban Roche was pouring port for him. And Miss Gomez was somewhere there, on Christmas Eve also. And in St Nicholas's Church there were black people in all the pews, all singing loudly and smiling. 'These are the Brethren of the Way,' Miss Gomez said, and the mouths of the black people ferociously opened and closed. 'O Saviour, Lord, to thee we pray,' they sang in powerful voices.

She walked in Crow Street, his hand on her arm. She had put the turkey in the oven before going to Church. She would baste it and then wash the celery. He'd get a good fire going in the sitting-room, piling it with coal, and afterwards they'd sit by it eating Turkish Delight, which they always ate on Christmas Day. Later, after tea, he would bring some of the pets in, to run about. 'There's no one cooks like you, Dottie,' he said. 'You're lovely, really.'

His arms went about her, his voice whispered, she could feel the warmth of him. 'She's funny, that Miss Gomez,' she said to him, and his arms tightened until she found it hard to breathe.

60

She wanted to tell him about the employees she'd taken on since she'd been on her own, a man called Edwards and one called Bright and little Lenny Pash. None of them had really known enough about the pets, not in the same way as he did, not until Alban Roche came. If anything happened to her, Alban Roche would own the pet shop because she'd written that down on a will-form, knowing it was the right thing to do. She wanted to tell him about Alban Roche and how he'd had to go to gaol because he looked in at a window, and about Prudence Tuke who was beautiful in her way, and about Miss Gomez and the Brethren. She wanted to tell him how unusual it all was, that Alban Roche should ever have come to work with the pets in the first place, in a shop that was already condemned and without a future. And that Prudence should also have come, both of them saying they'd stand by her. And that Miss Gomez had wandered in. It was all so different from the past, so irregular and so formless. She wanted to tell him, to explain to him how everything had changed, but he was holding her so tightly that she found it hard to speak. 'Christmas's not the same without a good fire,' he said. 'Can't beat coal, Dottie.' The room was like a bakehouse: he laughed, face red from heat. 'Bakehouse,' he said.

She could feel the pressure of his body like an imprint all around her; his weight pressed down, she didn't want it to go. The faces of people in Crow Street came and went, customers and traders, a man who made bird-cages, children who came for mice. The weight was heavier, warmer and more intense. She told him about the day she'd sat on the stairs so that the developers wouldn't notice her. 'Bakehouse,' he said again, and then she opened her eyes because of a glare of light that had suddenly come.

It went immediately, but a black face lingered from the glare's aftermath, with something on the face, like a bar across the eyes. It was the shadow of a stranger: why was there a stranger in the house when she was having an ordinary conversation? Nice having a conversation on Christmas Day, the next day they'd go to *Jack and the Beanstalk*. There was moonlight in her room, long shafts of it slipping in at either side of the blind, and beneath the blind where she hadn't drawn it quite. She didn't like the moonlight. She didn't like the face. She tried to cry out, to wake herself because she knew if she woke the face would go, but she couldn't make a noise. She tried to tell him, but he went on playing with the animals, unaware of her voice, unaware that it was dark and that the fire had died away, and that the black people they'd seen in church were coming closer all the time. She opened her mouth to breathe, and for an instant opened her eyes and saw them closer still, all around her. She tried to close her eyes and found she could not, and died without experiencing discomfort.

Having reached Mrs Bassett's door and briefly opened it. Miss Gomez almost at once felt normal again. She felt fully awake and fully in control of her movements, and no longer fearful. It was as if she had physically shared the burden of what she carried with a sleeping woman in a bed, as if in that way the horror she experienced had for a time been exorcized. She did not know what had impelled her, or if she had moved at a normal pace in the corridor and had imagined the dragging delay because of her shaken state. She prayed in any case, and gave thanks for the help she'd received, for she knew at least that help had come to her.

In a normal manner she extinguished the corridor light and returned to her room, where she propped up on the mantelpiece the letter she had written, ready for posting in the morning. She set aside a plate from which earlier she had eaten some food and removed her leather dress and her spectacles and her underclothes. She paused for a moment, naked in the room, and then lay naked between the sheets, her slender body stretched out like a stick. In time she slept and her mind became a blank.

Beyond Crow Street, and unaware of the crime that was forecast there, London's natives and exiles continued their lives, some sleeping, some awake. The Maltese stood about the streets of Soho; Chinese girls from the good-time clubs came and went in Lisle Street; Russians, elsewhere, spoke of politics. In Earls Court an Australian dentist made love to a secretary from Ottawa. Two days before he had drilled and repaired three teeth in her lower jaw and had formally noted decay in several others. She twisted her body now in response to his passion, remembering his face close to hers on the other occasion, and instruments in her mouth.

Men who had visited Miss Gomez in Mrs Idle's pleasure house talked to their wives, or slept beside them, or slept alone. The man who'd given her the Canadian Pacific bag with the cheese in it remarked in a bedroom in Hampstead that no break in the heatwave could be seen by the television forecasters. 'Really, dear?' murmured his wife. The man who had asked Miss Gomez to lie in a grave with him made the same request of another girl and was told to leave her room at once. The man who'd asked Tina von Hippel to string him up on a pulley found himself in better luck.

An Indian in Putney Hospital, tired of his bed, rose from it and walked through the corridors of the hospital with a robe made of towelling over his pyjamas. He left the building and slowly strolled away from it, through the warm night along Lower Richmond Road. Nurses, one from the Virgin Islands and one from Borneo, were thrown into a tizzy. The ward sister swore at first that the occurrence couldn't have taken place and then blamed the continuing heat, not remembering that Indians were used to greater heat. A passing motorist, noticing an Indian in pyjamas, telephoned a police station and mentioned the matter.

Of the other people who had read the advertisement of the Brethren of the Way in *Make Friends in London*, only three had written to Tacas and of these only one was now awake, a widowed Englishwoman called Mrs Drate. The other two, a middle-aged cinema usher and a schoolgirl who was unhappy because of her complexion, dreamed of their lives and were stirred, as they slept, to fear and anguish and pleasure. Mrs Drate, whose husband had been a clergyman, had lost her faith after his death. He had fallen from the roof of their rectory in outer London, having climbed through a skylight in order to replace some slates. 'I'll just see to that leak,' he'd said one teatime and had kissed her cheek as he left the room: afterwards she knew that his death had been deliberate. While Miss Gomez and the cinema usher and the schoolgirl slept, Mrs Drate prayed. 'O God, if You are there, help me,' she said, kneeling by her bed. She spoke in desperate tones, born of the same desperation that had caused her to write a letter to a Jamaican sect.

The bells of churches and convents quietly rang, that night in London. In Regent Street two men sang and were asked not to by a policeman. Waiters hurried home from restaurants, night telephonists changed shifts. Disposal lorries collected rubbish and sprinklers sprayed selected streets. In the late-night chemist's in Piccadilly people queued for drugs they had to have. In St James's Park a Zulu walked alone. The House of Commons rose, the Indian returned to his bed in Putney Hospital, a baby was abandoned in Victoria Station. An au pair girl from Sweden accepted a proposal of marriage in Charing Cross Road. In Crow Street Mrs Tuke dreamed of Rose St Margaret. The Queen read.

VI

Awake before dawn, he remembered. 'Promise me, Alban,' his mother said. 'Promise me always, dear.'

She read from a red-backed volume, rocking herself in the cobbled back-yard of the house they lived in. She read about St Alban, the English saint after whom she'd named him. He shelled peas into a chipped enamel bowl, listening to her voice. The bowl was white with a blue rim. The peas at first made a tinkling sound as they dropped into it but soon made no sound at all. His mother smiled at him: he was eight years old.

Ash trees belong to the olive family, he wrote for the Presentation Nuns, imitating as best he could the copperplate headline. *Birds are feathered vertebrates,* he wrote, and *Gnawing animals have chisel teeth.* For the Christian Brothers he later worked more elaborately, conjugating verbs in Irish and other verbs in Latin. His father, employed in Shannon's grocery, had died while slicing rashers: another boy told him because it was known in the town. He'd been too young to remember.

In the darkness of Crow Street the past came back to him, mattering to him. He saw the town, a small town that was the colour of cement, with a razor-blade factory and a church called the Church of the Holy Assumption. From the stillness of a pale blue sky the sun fell fiercely on glass and chromium and the heads of people. Cars filled the small central area of the town, their upholstery hot, their mudguards dusty. A woman sang softly beneath the statue of a local hero, her hand held out for alms. A man stepped from an old Ford car and paused for a moment, attempting to catch the detail of a radio commentary that was drifting across the street. Straining for the sound, he altered the inclination of his head and then walked slowly towards the public house from which it emanated. People passed the singing woman, children with ice-creams, young girls loudly talking. Two men wheeling bicycles drove a bullock towards a butcher's slaughter-house, neither of them speaking. Petrol overflowed somewhere and a tang came in to the air. A mongrel dog moved slowly, sniffing at pieces of dirt and paper.

'Always go to confession,' his mother said. 'Always tell everything.' He'd sat with her in the Coliseum Cinema, where the films were always old, watching the lips of Claudette Colbert beneath the embrace of Don Ameche. Together they'd seen Betty Grable dancing, and Hedy Lamarr smouldering in a temper, and Veronica Lake in a night-dress. She never afterwards mentioned the moments he remembered most, as though they'd passed her by unnoticed. Once in the seats in front of them a man had one arm around the maid from the Munster and Leinster Bank and was moving his free hand about in her lap. 'Well, that was nice,' his mother said afterwards. 'Let's go again next week.'

There was a pack of playing-cards, the property of a boy called Gerald Murphy. The cards moved from hand to hand, shared among boys in the doorway of a shop at night. The back of each card bore a representation of a woman stepping into a bath, a woman tinted pink, with dark hair tied about her head, a well-built woman. They talked about her. They said what they would do. They talked about a girl who was employed in Kelly's Atlantic Hotel. She'd need no encouragement, they said: she was well known for that. She worked in the kitchens of the hotel, cleaning vegetables and peeling potatoes. Some said she was half-witted, which was why she didn't mind. Alone in his bed, he undressed her and undressed as well the maid at the Munster and Leinster Bank. Afterwards he felt sick, and his mother's voice softly murmured to him, speaking of the saint after whom she'd named him, telling him she'd almost died in giving birth to him. Her voice was beautiful. 'If the Holy Virgin spoke,' Sister Tracy said to him in the convent when he was five, 'she'd have your mother's voice, Alban.'

In winter they sat together in the small sitting-room. She helped him with his homework for the Christian Brothers and

66

afterwards, when he became a post office clerk, she asked him to tell her all about the day he'd spent. He told her about the people of the town who'd come in to buy stamps and postal orders, or those who had sent off telegrams. He described certain incidents that had taken place, or what someone had said.

They went together to early mass on Sundays, two familiar figures. She wore black on Sundays usually, and he a dark serge suit that they had chosen together in the Munster Arcade in Cork, and a white shirt and a tie she'd given him one Christmas. His shoes were polished, for no one, she said, should go to mass with unpolished shoes. His dark hair was short and tidy, kept in place with Brylcreem because it tended to stand up on top. He was good to his mother, people said: boys weren't often these days. In the evenings, on the way home from the post office, he bought toffees with nuts and raisins in them, which were the favourite of both of them. 'You're good,' she'd murmur. 'My dear, you're very good to me.' He shook his head. When he looked at her he prayed that he would never be alone again in his bed with girls, nor see Claudette Colbert naked before him, nor the woman stepping into the bath. He wanted her to keep him always close to her as she had when he'd been a child. He loved the smell of soap that was always about her.

The girls from the razor-blade factory, red-faced, with headscarves, rode on bicycles through the town, their skirts pulled up a bit through exertion. He watched for one of them every day, a fat girl who never minded about the position of her skirt. Surreptitious in his glances, he saw her over the pebble-glazed area of the post office window, stockings tight on her broad knees, feet in high-heeled shoes. At lunchtime every day, at half-past twelve, she dismounted from her bicycle and went into Egan's Café. She bought jam doughnuts at the counter and ate them, standing where he could see the calves of her legs. The heels of her shoes were higher than the heels of other girls. She had a way of moving towards her bicycle, she had a way of putting her foot on a pedal. In summer she didn't wear a coat. Once at mass she'd seen him looking at her and had smiled at him, causing him shame because it brought to the surface what was in his mind. He hated watching

67

for her above the pebbled glaze but he could never help himself. She drew him and repelled him. He confessed his thoughts and heard his guilt confirmed. After his penance he felt a little better.

All but that he shared with his mother, and received from her a generous affection. All the love that might have gone to his father and other children went instead to him, and to him alone. He was aware of it, although such words were never spoken. When he walked with his mother on Sunday afternoons he felt that one pair of eyes saw flowers, one mind was shared: she might have said that too, but she never did, knowing that with the love she'd spread around him there was no need.

At night, without her, her face came into his mind: it haunted him with its gentleness, with eyes that had no hardness in them, and soft brown hair a little touched with grey, and her smile of contentment. Sometimes in the morning he could not speak, fearing that any words at all would be a lie. How could he speak casually of the weather or the day ahead when she must have known that in their single mind his hands in the darkness had touched the flesh of local girls and film stars?

She died, and standing at her open grave he fought against his thoughts. 'Release from all bondage of sin,' murmured the voice of Father Dwyer. She'd died in pain, of a growth in her stomach: in the end she'd weighed only five stone four. Rain fell on the varnished wood of the coffin, and holy water too. He watched and heard, but in greater reality, it seemed, he stood in a room with the girl from the razor-blade factory. She showed him flowers she'd pressed between the pages of books and an album of photographs that she'd cut out of a film-star magazine; she liked Cary Grant, she said. Her fingers, red with chilblains, turned the pages of the album and by chance touched his. He put his arm round her waist, under a grey knitted jumper. She laughed. She took his hand and held it to her lips. He felt the tip of her tongue, so slight a touch it was like the petal of a daisy. Laughing again, she put his hand on her knee, where the stocking stretched most tautly. She pressed his fingers, urging him. 'Our Father,' murmured Father Dwyer, 'who art in heaven.'

People came up to him after the funeral, some of them weeping. They touched his arm, a silent gesture of condolence. Afterwards, in the dusk of an autumn evening, he walked from room to room of the empty house, picking things up, unable again to control his thoughts. Once he'd sold a stamp for a Christmas card to the half-witted girl from the hotel and she'd attempted to hold him in conversation. He could go out now, he thought, and hang about the yard of the hotel, waiting for her. He could bring her to the house because it was empty. He could say there were clothes of his mother's that he wanted to give her. He could wait until tomorrow and cross the street to Egan's Café. He could stand beside the girl from the razor-blade factory and return the smile she'd offered him at mass. He could invite her to the pictures and sit with her as he'd seen the man sitting with the maid from the Munster and Leinster Bank. And afterwards he could say that there were things of his mother's that he was giving away, that clothes and jewellery were waiting for her in the empty house.

He made himself tea, knowing that he would never do any of it. He ate bread with butter and meat paste on it, consuming slice after slice because he hadn't eaten much since she'd died. No one came to see him because people thought he'd prefer to be alone. He went to bed and when he opened his eyes in the morning he discovered, while not yet fully awake, that he had disliked his mother.

Lying in another bed, two years afterwards in the Thistle Arms, he remembered that. And yet, when the moment had come, he'd been unable to destroy her personal belongings, the belongings he'd imagined he might give to girls. He'd received twenty-seven pounds for the furniture the house contained, and the house itself was a rented one. He was aware at that time, during those few days of packing and sorting out, only of his desire to go far away. Later, when months had passed, he wrote on the square paper of a science notebook, purchased because it was inexpensive:

I hated the town also. I hated the sight of the post office counter behind which I had worked, and the grey appearance of the post office itself, and its dirty interior. I hated voices I heard, and the faces of people who had done me no harm. I hated the sight of Egan's Café, and the razor-blades wrapped in a green and yellow cover in a chemist's window. The town was proud of them, having been put on the map with razor-blades.

When I walked for the last time by the Presentation Convent I saw behind a window the face of Sister Tracy, who'd spoken of the Holy Virgin's voice. She waved but I did not wave back. People spoke to me, I didn't reply. I passed the Christian Brothers' School, and heard boys learning by rote. Brother Farrell was a terror, boys used to say, if he found himself alone with you. I'd hated talk like that and yet had been unable not to resist listening. Brother Farrell carried sweets in his pockets, hidden away. 'Where's the sweets today?' he'd say and you'd be searching all over him for them.

I stood outside the Church of the Holy Assumption. There was a coloured statue of the Virgin in the wall by the railings. Flowers bloomed in beds all around her, tended with love by the women of the church. Her hands were by her sides, palms presented in the familiar way. 'Good morning, Alban,' a woman said, and I said nothing. I didn't speak again in the town, not to anyone, during those last days.

From the deck of the *Queen of Leinster* he'd gazed into a green-grey sea on which foam bubbled, streaking the surface with vivid white. Sea-spray fell on his sallow features, wind untidied his hair. A yard along the rail a whey-faced priest rid himself of a meal he'd recently consumed, heaving to the depths a conglomerate of chipped potatoes, bacon and tea. Girls, arms linked, strode the deck purposefully, laughing and shrieking, returning unconcerned to an exile they'd known before. 'I was three weeks down in Cahir,' one said. 'Jeez, it'd drive you mad.' Others who knew the town called Cahir exclaimed agreement: Cahir was all right for passing through, one in a blue dress languidly pronounced.

He couldn't talk to any of them. There was his town too, that might have been a town like Cahir for all he knew. Yet how could he say that he was running away from it in so unusual a way that he was bringing with him, in a trunk and two cardboard boxes, his mother's personal possessions? How could he say that he'd been unable to destroy the belongings of his mother, or even to leave them behind? The girls looked at him loitering on his own.

70

They giggled at him. If they had spoken to him, he'd have felt a strangling in his throat when he tried to reply, as in a nightmare: he'd felt all that before. He wanted to be in the darkness, standing with the one in the blue dress, alone with her in some silent part of the *Queen of Leinster*.

The girls giggled and went away, the one in the blue dress lighting a cigarette. *On arrival in London girls are earnestly requested to contact a branch of the Society. There are representatives of the Society at all the main railway stations. For your own safety we earnestly entreat you.* He had read those words on a notice, thinking of the girls who would not heed them, of bad girls who were on for anything, who'd put on his mother's clothes and wear her jewellery.

Awake in the Thistle Arms, his mind drifted through it all and then slid away from that time of his life, filling with other thoughts. In his spacious brown room in the Thistle Arms, with its two windows looking into Crow Street and its heavy curtains and its mahogany, were books he had collected in London, about rare or extinct animals, and animal biology. Neatly in order, they filled the room's bookcase, which was beside the wardrobe. In the town he'd come from he'd had no such interest, nor would he ever have believed while living there that one day he'd work in a pet shop. *In the metazoa,* he'd read in Crow Street, *each cell, while still performing the basic functions, is additionally specialized for a more particular function.*

He recalled those words now and others too. *The ventral wall of the abdomen is soft and distensible . . . The mouth is terminal and the upper lip is divided, thus exposing the front (incisor) teeth . . . The tympanic membrane is no longer superficial as in the frog because in the mammal an outer ear consisting of . . .*

He slept again and dreamed that sunfish and shubunkins swam around the post office he'd known, in and out of pigeon-holes, under wire grilles. People were making a film. He had to stand still while the camera focused on his face: he was as he was now, in his ginger suit, with his long hair. His white shirt and the tie she'd given him were folded over a chair. 'That is Claudette Colbert,' a man said, 'who will play the part of your mother, Alban,

71

dressed in your mother's clothes.' And Prudence Tuke came up to him and said that the jacket of his suit needed a stitch in it. 'This is Claudette Colbert,' the man said again, and the cameras moved. They took a photograph of a woman stepping into a bath. 'Promise me, Alban,' his mother said, coming into the post office. And Prudence Tuke put on his mother's clothes and they fitted her perfectly.

Morning came. Prudence woke up thinking of him. She sat up in bed, in a night-dress of white winceyette that she had made herself from a pattern in a magazine, and she saw her reflection in a mirror on her dressing-table. There was a chilly look about her, she thought, although she was not cold.

Every morning she awoke with his face in her mind. She saw him walking in the distance, moving in his particular way. His head was often bent down, as though examining the ground for small objects. She murmured, watching in the mirror the movements of her lips. She spoke his name. She whispered it, repeating it. She smiled and lay down again, pulling the bed-clothes about her. On the ceiling she traced with her eye a crack that had always been there, from the time when she'd first been aware of her bedroom.

All around her were objects she'd collected since: small china bowls, dolls' cups and saucers, snuff boxes, paper-weights, pieces in the shape of eggs, scarlet and mauve and green, mottled like marble. Framed behind glass, a set of butterflies hung above her mantelpiece. Three monkeys in brass, hearing, seeing and speaking no evil, sat on the mantelpiece directly below it. There was a set of medals, framed also, that had been issued at the time of the Boer War, and quills from peacocks, and cameos and terra-cotta reproductions, in miniature, of Egyptian mummies. Her treasures had little value. She'd begun collecting them from junk shops with the first pocket-money her father had given her, and had continued since. They filled her room now, scattered over all the surfaces and on the walls.

She closed her eyes and was at once alone with him, with all her things around her. They didn't say much because it wasn't their way to speak. He walked about, picking up her treasures, holding them gently like he held the pets.

A bubble of gas that had developed during the night in Mrs Tuke's stomach rose to her mouth and noisily escaped. The sound did not rouse her, but caused her husband's dog, resting in a corner of their bedroom, to prick up his ears. Mr Tuke, in red and black striped pyjamas, gazed into Crow Street from the window.

Outside, a lean cat stretched itself and eyed with eyes like lemon-pips a spider clambering on corrugated iron. Fresh morning air drifted through the partly open window; no sound in Crow Street broke the silence. As Mr Tuke watched, the cat was joined by another, a creature of equal leanness. They moved together, slinking past the broken windows of the fish shop and the Dining-Rooms, past Cave's hardware, where Mr Batt had worked, and Bassett's Petstore. And then, from within the Dining-Rooms, a third cat appeared, jumping on to the glassless window-frame and jumping again, into Crow Street. It was considerably fatter than the other two, puffed up like a fungus. Mr Tuke wondered if it was pregnant. He watched for a moment longer and decided that it was.

These animals had come from somewhere else. Rebel, who once had chased all the cats of Crow Street, kept clear of them. It puzzled Mr Tuke that his pet should do that, that so powerful a hunter should suddenly react with caution in the presence of such wretched creatures. Worried because of it, he'd repeatedly tried to interest the dog in chasing them away, but Rebel continued to display some instinctive wisdom and would pad off in another direction.

'Rebel,' Mr Tuke whispered now and the dog obediently pushed himself to his feet and came to him. Mr Tuke stroked the hair of his pet's neck, murmuring and pointing at the cats below. But Rebel did not growl, nor did he rush to the door, whimpering to be let out, as he would have done in the past. He regarded the cats through the window, not even cocking his head. He recoiled, as though nervous of the sight of them.

Mr Tuke began to dress, not wishing to be in the room when his wife awoke. Another small disturbance came from her, and for a moment his eyes rested on her sleeping face. Twenty years ago, when first she'd served in the private lounge, she'd been a quiet girl with a happy, lazy smile that people found attractive. He'd been the talkative one then: looking back on it, they'd been two completely different people. In the private lounge he'd put his arms around her; he'd kissed her lips and she'd smiled, not saying anything.

He pulled his trousers on and began to button his shirt. In Sir Thomas Wright's book on the Alsatian there was no mention at all of sudden allergy to cats, or indeed sudden allergy to any animal. It was against the nature of the Alsatian to behave irrationally; the Alsatian was the most logical and level-headed of animals, as Sir Thomas repeatedly exemplified and his own experience confirmed. Rebel ate four raw eggs a day and a pound of minced lean meat. He was in tip-top condition, heart and lungs as sound as a bell, not a trace of worms. Mr Tuke had read all the way through Sir Thomas's book again and in desperation he'd even mentioned to old Batt that the dog wouldn't go after cats any more, wondering if old Batt had ever heard of such a thing in a long life. Mr Batt at first replied that it stood to reason, and when the question was repeated said he'd never felt better in his life.

Mrs Tuke murmured in her sleep. Carrying his tie and his waistcoat, her husband left the room.

At the far end of Crow Street the labourers arrived. They were men mainly from the provinces of Ireland, but there were some as well from Africa, Pakistan, Miss Gomez's Jamaica and many other countries; some were natives. The red-haired Atlas Flynn, born twenty-eight years ago in a town in Co. Cork called Bandon, arrived on a racing bicycle.

'I didn't see you last night,' he said to a companion. 'Didn't you say you'd be dancing?'

The other man said he'd taken it easy for himself, and Atlas Flynn informed him that he'd had a sharp old time of it in the Emerald Isle Club. He lowered his voice and said that he was going to get Beryl Tuke down to the Emerald Isle Club before he was a day older. The size of her in the Thistle Arms every lunchtime was driving him mad, especially since she was definitely on for it if you could only get her going: in this hot weather, he explained, he found it difficult to restrain himself. His friend told him to take care, and Atlas Flynn laughed.

Lorries and bulldozers started up. 'Get hold of your picks, lads,' ordered the foreman of the gang. 'We're starting in on Crow Street.'

The body of Mrs Bassett who had been Dorothy Sweet continued to stiffen in the bed she had once contentedly shared with her husband. Her eyes, which had opened as she died, remained so while her bedroom filled with morning sunshine, staring at the ceiling.

Miss Gomez, bearing a tray with early-morning tea, knocked on the door as usual. Receiving no reply, she entered the room and carried the tea to the old woman, whom she addressed and then found to be lifeless.

VII

Miss Gomez received an air-mail letter complimenting her on her continued presence in Crow Street. Prayers went out from Tacas daily, she was informed, with Alban Roche their subject. *Soon it will be the annual Sunday of our Harvest,* the typewritten message continued. *Please forward your tithes now and ensure arrival in good time for that festival occasion.*

Other letters had referred to the Annual Harvest of Tithes, all the Brethren's funds being raised by this voluntary subscription: the Brethren lived from year to year, spending their resources in whatever way seemed most charitable at the time, keeping back only a little for the church itself. No sums were invested, for just as the Brethren did not believe in handing out literature and carrying banners, so they did not believe in the accumulation of profit.

On the back of the air-mail form that she'd sealed the night before Miss Gomez wrote: *Mrs Bassett passed to Our Lord in the night. The pet shop is now the property of Alban Roche.*

She blew on the words, drying the ink. She might have written more: she might have started all over again and said that at a late hour the night before she'd felt herself physically and unpleasantly affected by the crime that was, consciously or unconsciously, in the mind of the pet shop's inheritor. She might have described all that had happened, how she had found herself in the corridor and had experienced the overwhelming desire to be with another person, through some kind of terror.

She did not write any of this, fearing that he would ask her in reply if it couldn't be possible that she'd dreamed the whole episode, and in the sunny light of morning she couldn't be sure that she hadn't. She began to think, also, that it might even have been

Mrs Bassett's dying that had drawn her along the corridor, that the presence of death in the house had in some way heightened her fear of the pet salesman's crime, but she didn't attempt to write any of that either. She had sent to Tacas a simple message of the facts, which was enough, for only facts made sense on air-mail paper.

She prayed for the tranquillity of Mrs Bassett in death and as she rose from her knees she imagined the clergyman, as she often did, reading her words in a quiet room that smelt of sandal-wood. He nodded over them, and spoke sentences in reply that a secretary of the Church took down in shorthand and afterwards reproduced on her office machine. At other times she'd seen him differently; late at night typing out the sentences himself on a small Olympia portable that was his own property, quickly working his thoughts into the keys. She'd liked to have had a photograph of him, and of the Reverend Greated and the Reverend Pearson Simmonds and the Reverend Palmer, and of all the Brethren congregated on the hill outside Tacas. She'd often thought of asking for a photograph but felt too shy to do so.

He saw the people of Crow Street, she supposed, in the same vague way as she saw him. He saw them only as she'd described them, through the clothes they wore and the nature of their behaviour: the long-haired Alban Roche in his ginger suit, a pale girl in Indian sandals, a cheery woman and a man with a limp and a beard, and an Alsatian dog. He saw a retired hardware merchant's assistant who occupied now a world he had cunningly created, in which he did not wish to be disturbed.

Beyond all that they were a mystery to him, the realities they avoided, the obsessions they possessed. Why was the girl silent in the presence of her parents? Why had the youth night after night stared through the window of a changing-room at the women in their underclothes?

She left her room and walked along the narrow corridor of the house. For a moment she stood in Mrs Bassett's bedroom, in the presence of the cadaver that earlier she'd covered by drawing the sheet up. He, too, stood there, looking at the outline on the bed.

77

'I telephoned,' she said. 'A doctor will be coming about the death certificate, and an undertaker later on.'

He nodded. He hadn't guessed that Mrs Bassett would die so suddenly. When she'd mentioned about leaving the shop to him she hadn't said anything about feeling unwell, although often lately she'd complained of tiredness.

'You'll move the pets?' Miss Gomez said. 'You'll take the compensation money?'

'No point in not,' he said, and idly he wondered about her. Everyone thought her a little strange. Mrs Bassett had, even though she'd welcomed her company, and Mrs Tuke had apologized for having to employ her. 'Lock up any valuables,' she'd more than once advised. 'You never know with blacks.' Twice since she'd been in Crow Street she'd spoken to him about her Church, a Church he hadn't heard of before.

'They've started to demolish Crow Street,' she said. 'They'd have forced her out if she hadn't died.'

'Yes.'

She looked at him, knowing that everything was different now because Mrs Bassett had died and because already Crow Street was being demolished. He would have to move the pets at once, as soon as arrangements could be made. Within some brief period of time, a day and a night, maybe less, he would be obliged to vacate his room in the Thistle Arms and to leave Crow Street for a street that was still standing. No longer would the girl be daily beside him. Was that, now, in his mind also?

She felt for him, as he stood in his ginger suit, his long hair tidy on his head. She felt a compassion that she longed to express but knew she must not. She wanted to know him, to hear his voice saying what he wished to say, to offer him solace and understanding. But she knew he would never speak to her, that to know him she would have to search in some other way.

'May I stay here, today at least?' she requested.

He nodded, not caring, and then he left the room. She heard his footsteps on the stairs and then sounds of activity from the animals below.

* * *

Prudence spread butter on to a piece of sliced bread, standing by the kitchen table. Earlier, as she did every morning, she'd watched him from the top of the stairs. She'd seen him crossing the landing with an electric kettle in his hand to fill it from a tap in the bathroom, not whistling or humming as Mr Batt did, his bare feet making no sound at all on the cold linoleum. His pyjamas, unlike her father's and Mr Batt's, were not striped, but were all one colour, green, or blue depending on which fortnight of the month it was. They had been green that morning. She'd smelt his bacon cooking in his room and wished she'd been there, crouched on the floor over the gas-ring that her mother considered was adequate, turning the bacon with a fork for him. Every morning of his life he had a bath. Finicky, her mother had remarked. She never listened when her mother went chattering on about it.

She smeared raspberry jam on to the bread, imagining him now, with the pets in the pet shop.

'Mrs Bassett died,' Miss Gomez said, appearing at the door.

Extraordinary the energy he had, Mrs Tuke considered, the way he bounded out of bed and was away across the waste-grounds with the dog long before it was necessary for anyone to stir. She lay still, worrying about her liver, aware of a familiar sourness in her stomach. She closed her eyes and devoted her thoughts to the Arab's Head, moving from room to room as she'd moved yesterday with the out-going landlord. He'd been a dignified-looking man, quite reminding her of Dr Cameron of *Dr Finlay's Casebook*, which she'd laughingly said at the time, more as a joke than anything else. He'd taken it in good part, and later she'd seen him glancing in a mirror and running a comb through his hair. She hadn't much cared for the wife, a coarse little woman with hardly any flesh on her bones and a common, tinny voice.

Cautiously Mrs Tuke rose. She stood for a moment beside her bed before slowly crossing to the window to see what was happening outside. Workmen were at the end of the street and her husband and his dog were standing watching them. Extraordinary the way he always went about in shirtsleeves as though he didn't possess a jacket, with his waistcoat hanging open and not a vestige of a crease in his trousers. One thing was certain: he'd have to brighten himself up considerably in the Arab's Head. He'd need two good new suits, with a linen handkerchief clean every day and the tie of some good school or hockey club. He'd have to clean off that ridiculous-looking beard he'd grown and try not to limp so noticeably; you'd think he had only one leg to see him hobbling about sometimes, looking for sympathy at his age. And with the type of clientele that the out-going landlord had described it would be much better if he kept as quiet as possible when he was serving the drinks. Nobody wanted to hear a person going on for ever about how to give worm-powders to Alsatian dogs or what to do when a dog had a bowel complaint. She'd have a chat with him about it, starting with the clothing angle and going on tactfully to suggest how he might best adapt himself otherwise. Better for him really not to utter at all, let them think from the start that he was dumb maybe.

She moved from the window and settled herself at her dressing-table in order to put curlers in her hair. One thing she wouldn't have to put up with at the Arab's Head and that was lodgers. Not that she'd ever grumbled in all the years at the Thistle. She'd done her best, trying to find her smile when things went wrong, trying to keep cheerful. It had been no joke at all to discover that young Roche was up on a court case, accused of stuff like that. 'About the room,' she'd said when they'd come for him, and without a word he'd handed her a number of five-pound notes. He'd said he'd like to keep the room on because sooner or later he'd be coming back to the pet shop. He hadn't even mentioned the fact that he was about to stand trial for an indecency. It was Mr Zacherelli, still in Crow Street then, who'd afterwards read all about it in an evening paper.

Funny, she thought, winding a strand of hair around a blue plastic curler, funny a young chap going after women in a changing-room. He'd walked in one day when he'd done the two months, as though nothing had happened. 'Enjoy yourself, did you?' she'd heard old Batt asking him, commiserating with him on the bad weather he'd had.

One way or another there'd been quite a few lodgers in the Thistle during her time, chaps spending a year or so and then shifting off, getting married most of them. There'd been one who'd had ambitions as a tap-dancer, a Mr Tanski, who said he came from Poland and went off owing nearly a month's rental, and an older man, a Mr Shattock, who for no reason at all stood up one day in the kitchen and hit her. There'd been little Lenny Pash, who like Alban Roche had worked for Mrs Bassett, whom she'd had to ask to leave because of the way he left the toilet. And of course there'd been Eddie Mercer.

As always, Mrs Tuke endeavoured to eject the memory of the last-named lodger from her mind. She tried to concentrate on an image of the man in the soap advertisement who was also Dr Desmond D'Arcy of the Rose St Margaret cottage hospital, but in this she was not successful: a lodger who'd stayed in the Thistle Arms in 1961 intervened, a red-faced man called Ovens. Unlike the memory of Eddie Mercer, this one caused her only embarrassment, although at the time she had experienced genuine anguish and hadn't known where to hide her face for weeks. She'd been guilty of a moment of folly and remembering it now she looked quickly away from the reflection in her dressing-table mirror, blushing even after all this time.

What had happened, in fact, was what might have happened to anyone. At a late hour, on her way upstairs after an evening in the private lounge, she'd come across Ovens on the lower landing and had been seized with a friendly impulse. She'd had a few drinks and had been feeling particularly contented, rigged out in a two-piece suit with humming-birds on it, with strings of coloured beads tumbling about on a lilac blouse. She'd smiled at Ovens, swaying slightly and aware that she was swaying. 'You're a fine-looking man,' she'd said to him, simply because she felt like saying it, and then she crossed the landing and took his left hand in hers. In a low voice she told him that without charge he could have any drink he cared to name, gin, whisky, beer, brandy, sherry, port, French liqueurs, whatever he most desired. She pulled at the hand she held, anxious to make him move into his room, where they could more privately continue their conversation, but at that moment her husband ascended the stairs and stood there, staring. 'We was just shaking hands,' she explained. 'Mr Ovens and myself was bidding one another good-night. Good-night, Mr Ovens,' she said.

She'd never forget the sight of the two of them on the landing, standing like statues, both of them looking at her. A week later Ovens said he'd found a different place to lodge, which was just as well really, in the circumstances.

Mrs Tuke completed the winding of her hair on to the blue plastic curlers and covered the lot with a mauve headscarf with horse-shoes on it, which she tied in the form of a turban. She found a packet of Rennie's beneath the stockings she'd thrown down on the dressing-table the night before. She unwrapped one and placed it on her tongue in an effort to combat the sourness in her stomach.

In the kitchen Prudence still ate bread with raspberry jam on it. She ate slowly, her eyes fixed on the pile of dishes that her mother had last night stacked in the sink. When she spoke, although she spoke loudly and normally, the words seemed to be addressed to herself.

'Mrs Bassett said he'd inherit everything,' she said, not looking in Miss Gomez's direction. 'She told me that herself.'

Miss Gomez nodded. Alban Roche was the inheritor, she agreed. She opened her lips to say something else, to issue some disguised warning, to indicate danger, however vaguely. And then, about to speak, instinctively she changed her mind.

She rooted in the dresser drawers for a duster instead, poking among Brillo pads and clothes-pegs, string, scissors, furniture cas-tors, novels of the Woman's Weekly Library, wire, screwdrivers and pliers. Underneath everything there were some photographs in black and white, several of Mrs Tuke, two of Prudence as a schoolgirl, two of a man who was a stranger to Miss Gomez, whom she guessed to have been a lodger in the past. She tore a piece from an old flannel night-dress of Mrs Tuke's, which Mrs Tuke had given her permission to do if ever she needed a cloth and couldn't find anything more suitable.

'She was fond of him,' Prudence said.

Miss Gomez closed the drawers of the dresser, pushing at them because they didn't fit well. 'I think Mrs Bassett was fond of everyone except the developers,' she said.

'She often said she was fond of him. No one since her husband understood the pets like he does, no one was as gentle with them. She told me that while he was in gaol.'

Miss Gomez nodded and then, to her astonishment, Prudence said that she had to tell somebody: she loved Alban Roche, she said.

Miss Gomez stood still, holding the piece of Mrs Tuke's nightdress in her right hand, unable to speak. She watched while Prudence smiled, the smile coming gradually in her narrow face, changing everything about it, like lights coming on in the windows of a darkened house. When Prudence turned and left the kitchen Miss Gomez followed her into the hall, still wanting to speak, to say anything at all, but finding that words would not come to her. She watched the girl move dreamily up the stairs and when she'd passed from sight she went on listening to the flap of her Indian sandals. She heard the voice of Mr Batt saying good-morning to the girl, and then Mr Batt appeared on the stairs on his way to the kitchen for his breakfast. He said good-morning to her also and she went upstairs herself.

Alban Roche removed the cover from the crested mynah's cage.

'Thank you very much!' screeched the mynah, which was all it ever said. Mice scuttled about in their cages, hamsters settled down for their day's sleep, white rabbits nibbled.

He fed the canaries and the lovebirds and then a grey parrot that Mrs Bassett had christened Godfrey. 'Mind the step!' cried the parrot, speaking in a voice that was more human than the mynah's. 'Ha, ha, ha,' cried a cockatiel.

The squirrels were sprightly, peering at him earnestly; the guinea-pigs were nervous. He took off his jacket; the shirt beneath it was a shade of fawn, a Swedish shirt, so the assistant selling it had said. He cleaned the budgerigars' trays and gave them water.

He examined the tortoises. 'Thank you very much!' screeched the mynah.

Upstairs in Mrs Bassett's bedroom a doctor prodded at the cold body. She'd died because her heart had failed her, being too weak to carry on a struggle. He'd warned her about that, but of course she hadn't taken any notice. She'd insisted on fighting a useless battle against the development of the area, eating into her reserves of strength. 'Don't do it, Mrs Bassett,' he'd said when he'd come to see her a night or two ago because she'd been complaining of tiredness. 'Keep an eye on her,' he'd said to the black girl then, and the next thing was the black girl was saying the old woman had copped it.

When the phone rang he'd been eating his breakfast and at the same time attempting to talk sense to his schoolgirl daughter, who as far as he could see had become a drug addict. A new narcotic, manufactured, she claimed, under laboratory conditions in America, had become a craze at the school she attended. She assured him that it was non-addictive and harmless, but what he wanted to know was how a new preparation could be so firmly categorized. Brain damage might not occur for several years, he'd been trying to explain to her, but she'd said that it was a known fact that alcohol, tobacco, butter and tuna fish were now the real dangers to the health of both body and mind. It was often part of psychiatric treatment to prescribe drugs of one kind or another, mescalin in particular: surely he knew that? And had he ever heard of psychiatric treatment that prescribed alcoholic refreshment? He'd left the breakfast table at that moment in order to speak to Miss Gomez on the phone, and it had seemed as he listened to her to be irrelevant that an elderly woman had died in the night at the age of sixty-eight: his daughter would be dead in a year or two, before she was twenty. 'I'll be round as soon as I can,' he'd said into the telephone.

In the bedroom he continued his examination. Other people listened to a doctor, he thought: if a doctor said the cells of the body would rot other people believed him. 'You take it in orange juice,' his daughter had said.

He sighed, looking into the eyes of Mrs Bassett. He pulled the sheet over her, jerking his mind away from the problem of his daughter. He gathered up the instruments he had used and replaced them in his bag. The young didn't care about death. The young today didn't want to live on like Mrs Bassett had: the young didn't like the world.

He descended the stairs and in the shop he said that he'd made his examination and would sign a death certificate giving the cause of death as heart failure due to exhaustion. He was sorry, he said, that Mrs Bassett had died. He was sorry she'd gone because he'd known her and liked her for a long time. There was at least the consolation that she had died neither in pain nor penury, nor with violence nor tears. Her death, like her life, had been good.

'That's something, you know,' the doctor said, surprising himself for speaking so. It was not in his nature to be garrulous on such occasions and he put it down to his distress over his daughter. He would have liked to have talked about this distress, because in the presence of the inheritor of the pet shop it seemed to him that this silent, long-haired person might somehow have understood the death-wish of a schoolgirl, even if only because he belonged to her generation. He refrained, however, and more conventionally said, referring to Mrs Bassett:

'Her world is a thing of the past. Everything is different now.'

Alban Roche said nothing, nor did he nod or gesture in acknowledgement of the doctor's words. The tips of his fingers stroked the feathers of the crested mynah. The doctor, feeling awkward, went away.

VIII

It was afterwards an important point that at half-past nine that morning Prudence Tuke, on her way out of the Thistle Arms, entered the kitchen and handed to Mr Batt, who was eating a plate of fried food, the single letter that was delivered that day to the public house. The fact of Mrs Bassett's death, which had earlier been a subject of conversation in the kitchen, had now been exhausted as a talking point. 'I wish that girl would sit down for her breakfast like the rest of us,' Mrs Tuke said, a remark that she was afterwards to recall. Mr Tuke, seated beside Mr Batt at the red Formica-topped table, was reading the *Daily Express* and eating also.

Upstairs, in Alban Roche's room, Miss Gomez opened the drawers of a large mahogany tallboy that stood between the two windows of the room. She found eventually the science notebook in which Alban Roche had written about the town he'd come from, and about himself. *She is here with me now,* she read. *She is more than a ghost to me.*

She learnt about the Church of the Holy Assumption and the Presentation Nuns and the Christian Brother who hid sweets in his clothes. She learnt about the post office in which Alban Roche had worked behind the counter, looking out over pebbled glass at the limbs of a nameless girl from a razor-blade factory. She read of other girls also, all of them at a distance. They were as close to her now, she felt, as they'd ever been to Alban Roche.

In a house in a terrace he lived with his mother. Regularly they went to his father's grave, to weed it and set fresh flowers in a glass container. He went on messages for her, buying groceries in Shannon's, where his father had died while working a bacon machine. He took their shoes to be repaired by a Mr Duffy, who commented on the smallness of Mrs Roche's feet. He bought sweets with nuts in them, which they ate in the Coliseum Cinema.

I see her body still, she read. *I see her dead face. I feel her eyelids on my fingers as I seek to weigh them down in death. Every day she is with me, her heart still beats, her voice has never ceased.*

Miss Gomez, who had carried Mrs Tuke's Electrolux to this room, replaced the notebook in the drawer of the tallboy and plugged in the Electrolux. She turned it on and then pulled a trunk from under the bed and placed it against the door. If anyone tried to get in she'd pretend not to hear. With the Electrolux making its noise, that shouldn't seem unnatural.

She opened the trunk and found that it contained a number of grey coats, dresses in black or brown, two navy-blue suits, cardigans and jumpers in modest variations of the same colour range, hats, shoes, underclothes, three night-dresses, a wedding ring and an assortment of valueless jewellery. Each article had been carefully wrapped in tissue paper, each shoe, each hat-pin. There was a smell of camphor.

She stood on a chair and lifted down two cardboard boxes from the top of the wardrobe. They were large cube-shaped containers securely tied with string. She undid the knots and opened the first one.

Again there was objects wrapped in tissue paper: knitting needles, a pin-cushion, spools of thread and cards of darning wool, an unfinished piece of crochet, nail-scissors, hairpins, a black handbag, a string of beads with a crucifix attached, a sponge, a toothbrush, a hairbrush, a comb and hand-glass that matched it, a set of artificial teeth, a number of insoles in a paper bag. In the second box there were a cup and saucer with a pattern of roses on them, a small glass vase, a pair of gloves, several hair-nets, a knitted tea-cosy, a purse, some dried flowers, and three framed photographs.

In faded sepia a small girl stood smiling beneath a tree, and the same girl, some years later, stood by a photographer's ornate chair, and stood again as a middle-aged woman against a background that was vague. The face had not changed much: it was oval, beneath brown hair that in the third photograph was turning to grey. The lips in each case were smiling slightly.

Miss Gomez stopped the engine of the Electrolux, pressing a white switch on it with her foot. Anger came to her, a fury like an invasion from outside herself. It trickled into her, coming gently at first and then spreading everywhere, tearing at her. Her heart beat faster, blood went to her head. She moved her foot from the Electrolux switch and slowly walked about the room, to the bed and from the bed to the bookcase and then to the tallboy, to a winged armchair in the centre of the room and then to the dressing-table. She felt the passion of anger in her eyes. She felt her eyes erupting like snarls of fire; she felt the anger in her mouth and in her nostrils and her tongue. She wanted to shout out but could think of nothing to shout except indecencies that belonged to her earlier life, indecencies that men had sometimes shouted in Mrs Idle's pleasure house. They came from her now, not in a shout but as a mutter: quietly they filled the room and seemed to Miss Gomez to hover there, obscenely and correctly.

She searched in the cardboard box for the photographs, rooting for them through the hairnets and the dried flowers. She felt the glass vase snapping. She wanted to break and tear at everything then, the artificial teeth that had lain in the woman's mouth for half a lifetime maybe, the unfinished crochet, the hairbrush that still contained her hair.

In frustrated fury, still muttering, she regarded the three oval faces framed in black ebony with ornamentation in brass. This woman's hands had caressed a child, her lips had touched its cheeks. And yet that gentle love in time had turned to venom, infected with jealousy and fear. Miss Gomez's right hand, seizing a photograph to hurl, was seized in a sudden grip by her left: calmness returned to her, causing her to weep.

She wrapped the framed photographs and replaced them, not pausing to examine the damaged vase. She tied the string about the boxes and pushed the trunk under the bed, and wound the flex around the Electrolux. She wept, trying not to condemn the mother because the mother hadn't even known what she was doing. A cruelty had been permitted, that was all that might be said.

She took off her spectacles and wiped the tears from the lenses.

In the small square room behind the shop he was cleaning out a rabbit-hutch. He heard her voice, and knew that she would not call out again. She'd stand there waiting, knowing that for the moment he was busy. He finished the cleaning of the hutch and then went into the shop.

'Mrs Bassett,' she said.

'Yes: Mrs Bassett has died.'

'What will happen to the pets?'

Looking at his hands, he said that he would try and find a small shop somewhere, a shop to buy with the compensation money. He would move the pets and Mrs Bassett's furniture, which he had also inherited.

She didn't look at him, but thought about him. She remembered the night he'd come to Crow Street, she'd seen him in the hall of the Thistle Arms: she'd watched from the first-floor landing and listened while her mother said that yes, there was a vacant room, the previous occupant, a Mr Tanski, from Poland so he said, having disappeared. 'Forgive the drabness, Mr Roche,' her mother had begged, leading the visitor up the stairs.

He took a hamster from its cage and played with it, allowing it to run up and down his arm. It nibbled at his shirt buttons and crawled along his collar, behind his neck. He knew she wasn't watching him, and yet he could feel her eyes all over his face.

Soon after he'd taken the room she'd said to him that if ever he wanted repairs made on his clothes she'd do them for him. They'd met on that occasion outside his room, he about to enter it, she on the way downstairs. He'd known as she spoke that it was to be a private thing between them, that the repairs would be made without the knowledge of her parents. He had found it pleasant at the time to have a secret that could be shared. He'd deliberately torn a shirt so that she could mend it, and afterwards had sat in his room imagining her on the floor above, her thin fingers swiftly moving a needle, her lips licking thread to stiffen it.

The hamster crawled under his clothes. He felt its sharp feet and occasionally the dampness of its nose. She murmured at a squirrel, her back turned to him. She wore a yellow dress. Her bare heels were raised slightly from her sandals.

The hamster crawled on his back, still beneath his shirt. She moved to the door and stood with a hand on its brass handle.

'I would like to be with you,' she said, 'wherever you are.'

Atlas Flynn cut his hand in the small back garden of a house that was about to be demolished, the first house in Crow Street. He caught the ball of his thumb on a piece of barbed wire and inquired of the foreman if he might go to the Thistle Arms and seek first-aid from Mrs Tuke. The foreman agreed. 'Take care with it now,' he advised. 'That wire's all rusted.'

The other workmen, pleased at the diversion, crowded round and it being well known among them that Atlas Flynn admired the bulk of Mrs Tuke, various remarks were made about what the red-haired man would be doing with his left hand while the landlord's wife attended to his right. 'Hurry on now, Atlas,' the foreman urged, he himself being not much given to badinage of this nature. He told Atlas Flynn to hold the hand upright so that he wouldn't suffer from a dangerous loss of blood, and an African worker spoke of a man he'd known who'd caught his death from a rusted barb. With earnestness, he advised Atlas Flynn to forget about his interest in Mrs Tuke and make certain that she dressed the wound correctly.

'If it's a choice,' said Atlas Flynn, 'I would prefer not to die.' He laughed as he left the small back garden with his hand held upright in the air.

'Well, I'll be jiggered,' said Mr Batt, still reading the letter that Prudence had handed him at half-past nine. The surface of the breakfast table was strewn with crumbs of toast and cups and plates. Three pieces of butter, of different sizes and still partially enclosed by butter-paper, were marked with toast crumbs and raspberry jam.

Mr Tuke was eating streaky bacon, which he'd just fried for

himself. Occasionally he dropped a piece into Rebel's mouth, the dog being crouched beside him. Mrs Tuke, wearing fluffy red slippers and a red dressing-gown over her foundation garments, ate also, with *Nurse Rhona and Romance* propped up against an almost empty pot of lemon curd. Beneath her head-scarf her hair was still charged with plastic curlers, her dressing-gown had fat down the front of it.

'I'm in a competition,' said Mr Batt. 'A Giant Jackpot.'

His voice disturbed Mrs Tuke's concentration, causing her eyes to shift from the print in front of her. Dr Alex Denham had just wished Rhona a happy New Year. He had embraced her at a dance and had embraced her a second time in front of a studded oak door. Mrs Tuke drank more milk, believing it to be good for her liver. 'Competition, old chap?' she vaguely said to Mr Batt, smiling at him, thinking of the relief she'd feel in the Arab's Head at not having a pensioner about the place. If it hadn't been for the fact that he paid up regularly and was occasionally obliging with a loan she'd have turned him out months ago.

'There's an offer of gramophone records,' explained Mr Batt. 'The Andrews Sisters and Ted Weems.'

She closed her eyes, not wishing to see the old man in his tailored suit, or her husband dropping pieces of bacon into an animal's mouth, or the dishes that were scattered all over the kitchen. Her vision was blank for a moment and then she saw herself in a sports car, which was being driven by Dr Desmond D'Arcy from the cottage hospital, through Rose St Margaret, to the mansion called Villierscourt, the property of Sir Guy Villiers. He wore a blue silk scarf that perfectly matched his shirt, and blue and white striped trousers, and dark glasses. She was in her turquoise two-piece, with dark glasses also. Sir Guy shook their hands in the great hall, the oldest part of the house, dating back four hundred years. Just a handful of cocktail guests, he said; he thought they'd be amused. Later on she danced with Dr D'Arcy, who held her most politely, and then the telephone called both of them to the hospital, an emergency in Ward Four.

'*Mr A. J. Batt*,' quoted Mr Batt with some excitement, '*is one of the few in S.W.17 to receive this invitation!*' There was a certificate attached to the letter he'd received, and a yellow stamp which stated that his lucky number was 613662. He was requested to attach the stamp to the certificate, which was called a Once-In-A-Decade certificate, and return it to the address from which the letter had come. If the number corresponded with one of a series of numbers that were securely sealed and locked in a vault of Barclay's Bank he would receive a prize from the Giant Jackpot. He'd been sent as well a small gramophone record manufactured of a lank, plastic material. This was stated to be a special 'Living Sound' edition, but the point was also made that it was an inadequate sample only, providing but a hint of the excitement contained in a series of other records, referred to as 'A treasury called Those Memory Years'.

'The Inkspots, the Modernaires,' said Mr Batt, taking the names from the plastic sample. 'Hoagy Carmichael and Ben Bernie.' He picked up the letter again. 'First prize a car,' he said.

Mrs Tuke took the letter from him and read that her lodger was being offered an opportunity to win a motorcar with white wall tyres and de luxe upholstery. He was also being offered an opportunity to examine, and possibly purchase, the treasury called Those Memory Years. If, having examined the treasury, Mr Batt agreed to purchase it, he would receive as well, without extra charge, a record entitled *Theme Songs of the Big Band Era*, a record which was worth up to £2 in fine record stores. The purchase price of the treasury was 10/- deposit and £1 a month for just nine months, or Mr Batt would save more by sending just £8 8s. as full cash payment. On a leaflet that accompanied the letter there was a photograph of the album in which the treasury was contained, with a picture of a rose and a glass of wine on it.

'Funny, really,' said Mrs Tuke. 'What's records got to do with a car?'

Mr Batt, still perusing the leaflet, did not reply. What he was anxious to establish was that he could take part in the Jackpot without purchasing, either outright or by the month, the treasury called Those Memory Years. *It's no accident we've chosen your name, Mr Batt,* the letter stated. *We know for one thing that you appreciate good music.* This wasn't entirely accurate because owing to his affliction Mr Batt had for many years found it difficult to come to terms with music of any kind, and in the circumstances he had no wish to find himself the possessor of a treasury at a cost of £8 8s. full cash payment. He read carefully, curbing his excitement whenever he thought of the car with the white wall tyres.

Mr Tuke, stroking the neck of his pet, was recalling that he'd gone into Bassett's Petstore at half-past three yesterday to buy some Bob Martin's Condition Powders and Mrs Bassett had been perfectly all right then. He remembered the time old Henry Bassett had died, in April 1936, and how after the funeral a lot of his friends in the area had congregated in the Thistle. The fondness that existed between Henry Bassett and his wife had been a famous thing in the neighbourhood and had been much remarked upon after the funeral occasion, in the public bar.

Funny the way he sat there, she thought, not saying anything, just fingering the neck of an animal. You'd think he'd show an interest in old Batt's bit of luck. He was becoming a real droopy-drawers these days, the way he sat about with the dog. What with poor Pru rarely uttering either, the place was like a mausoleum. She smiled at him, inclining her head towards their lodger, urging him to take an interest. 'Old Batt's on a Jackpot,' she said. 'A nice bit of mail he's had.'

He nodded and rose to his feet. 'Did Pru get the mince?' he asked.

She smiled again, shaking her head, not knowing if the girl had bought the mince for his animal, and not caring. She patted his hand, still smiling. He'd definitely have to tidy himself up in the Arab's Head. The out-going landlord had been as spick as a daisy, with a checked waistcoat and a handkerchief folded in the top pocket of his jacket. There was no reason at all why a man who was small in stature shouldn't cut a bit of a dash instead of boring the skin off the customers with talk about Alsatian dogs. She'd definitely mention to him the idea she'd had about him not saying anything at all. What with the latest ideas of doing lounge bars out as a horse's stable, with bags of oats and harnesses, there was no reason whatsoever why a public house shouldn't draw the crowds if it had a dummy. No reason why he shouldn't learn a bit of sign language just to be amusing with it.

There was a knocking on the hall-door and he left the kitchen to attend to it, with Rebel following him. She moved *Nurse Rhona and Romance* from its position against the lemon-curd pot in order to dip a knife into the curd and smear a little on to a corner of toast. Having done so, she propped the book up again and was about to begin reading when her husband led into the kitchen a man with a bleeding hand.

Prudence walked through the streets that had been destroyed, where she had played as a child. Only half an hour had passed since she stood in the pet shop and said she wanted to be with him wherever he was: it felt like days. She'd heard her mother saying once that Alban Roche was crippled. Miss Gomez, when she'd told her that she loved him, had been unable to keep horror out of her face.

She crossed an expanse of open ground, an acre of hard, caked earth. Behind her, in the far distance, she heard the cries of workmen. Far away, also, masonry fell with a crash. The warm air was enriched with the smell of burning wood and paint. As she walked, she suddenly remembered that she'd forgotten, yesterday, to buy mince for her father. He'd asked her in the afternoon, seeing her setting off in the direction of Abyssinia Street. 'Three-quarters of lean,' he'd said, standing on the pavement outside the Thistle Arms, handing her some money. She wouldn't forget, she promised, but on the way down Crow Street she'd gone into the pet shop and the mince had passed completely from her mind. He'd be upset about it.

She went on thinking about her father. When she was small he used to buy her brittle bars of rock called Peggy's Leg, an old-fashioned confection that even then, he said, was hard to get. In the afternoons, when the public house was closed, they went together to the junk shops where she bought the things she liked, and he took her to other places as well: to the Dolls' Hospital in Hammersmith because he knew a man who worked there, to the river at Putney to watch the schoolgirls rowing, and the fair in summertime on Putney Heath, and the Transport Museum in

Clapham. He enjoyed the Transport Museum rather more than she did, but she didn't mind that because she liked being with him. They sat in the old trams and in a train that Queen Victoria had used; they watched the steam engines when on special days they were started up and moved about the yard. Often on a Saturday he took her to see Fulham playing football because in those days he'd been interested in football and a keen Fulham supporter. 'Fancy taking a child to a football match!' her mother would invariably cry when they returned, her mother smelling of powder and *Muguet du Bois* by Coty, dressed up for an evening in the private lounge.

He'd told her about the past, the days in Crow Street when he'd been a child. There were people then who'd never crossed the Thames, whose whole world was the surrounding neighbourhood. There'd been a woman with no hair, called Rita Tansey, whom children called a witch because she kept a mad cat, an animal that often used to walk backwards. There were red sweets called moneyballs that cost a halfpenny and sometimes had a halfpenny inside them. There was the time some youths set fire to the Snow White Laundry.

It was nice listening to him. He would never be happy anywhere except London, he said. He couldn't understand people moving all over the place, leaving their homes and setting up in strange places. London was different now, with foreigners everywhere, Chinese and black people, the Irish and the Italians: London belonged to nobody these days. Mr Zacherelli was Italian of course, or rather his father had been, but Mr Zacherelli, born himself in Crow Street, spoke quite normally, without either accent or difficulty: Mr Zacherelli was different. Her father would go on and on, talking about everything, about the very first day he'd ever come to work in the Thistle Arms, when he was sixteen; about a teacher there'd been at his school in Lacy Street, a Mr Cox who was a Christian Scientist and wouldn't go to a doctor. He told her about his father and his mother, and his brother in Canada of whom he hadn't heard a word for twenty years. He'd talk for ever, she thought; he was never boring.

And then, very suddenly, as though he had run out of words,

he ceased: they walked together in silence, and she thought at first that he was ill and then that it had something to do with her mother. Her mother caused upsets like that to happen, often without meaning to. No one could tell with her mother: she was a law unto herself, full of contrariness and contradictions. She said herself it was because she had a big heart. People with big hearts, she said, often got themselves into a pickle, giving offence where none was meant. Her mother's way was to cuddle and to touch her, to take her face between the palms of her hands and to smile, to stroke her hair and her arms. Then she'd give one of her laughs. She'd always known her mother didn't like her.

In the past she'd have been able to tell her father about her feelings for Alban Roche, like she'd told him about being frightened when she was fourteen, because of changes in her body. In the past he'd have listened quietly and afterwards would have attempted to reassure her. He might have made her happy by saying that if she loved Alban Roche, then she must hope that Alban Roche might come to love her also. But now her father spoke to her of mince. He screwed up his eyes and occasionally suggested that she should train herself for profitable work, and seemed not to know what to say after that. Rebel was his companion now.

To a black cleaner instead of to him she had briefly poured her heart out, to Miss Gomez who people said was insane. And when the day came, when she was alone with Alban Roche and felt his love in return for hers, she would mention Miss Gomez to him, for Miss Gomez was a special person now, being the first to know.

Prudence walked over to the wastelands, suddenly moving more quickly. She could feel the heat rising from the dry earth. She was thinking of Tintagel Street and Tile Street and Mombasa Road and Appian Way, none of which was due to be demolished, and where small shops were often up for sale.

The sight of the blood, on the red-haired man's clothes and dripping all over the linoleum, made Mrs Tuke feel unwell.

'He needs a plaster,' her husband said, standing there, not

doing anything about it. Then he left the room, pursued by his dog.

'If I could maybe wash it,' Atlas Flynn suggested, going to the sink and turning the cold-water tap on.

She hunted in the dresser for a rag, thinking that it was typical that a wounded man should be inflicted on her at the one time of the day when she'd a chance to sit down and relax herself. She found the night-dress that Miss Gomez had earlier found and tore a strip from it.

Mr Batt, for the moment unaware of the presence of the stranger in the kitchen, continued to examine the details of his mail, murmuring to himself.

'Rusty barbed wire,' explained Atlas Flynn, still at the sink. 'A bloke said he seen a man die from it. Have you iodine, Mrs Tuke? Disinfectant, something like that?' Was she wearing damn all underneath the dressing-gown? he wondered. She had no stockings on her legs and when the dressing-gown parted you could see the suggestion of nude thighs above her knees that reminded him of the thighs of a girl he used to go with in Bandon, Teresa Maloney. She was a stone or two heavier than Teresa and about fifteen years older. She was more sophisticated and more lively, always gassing and laughing. He'd give fifteen pounds to get her on to a bed.

She rooted around for a bottle of Dettol, which was the only disinfectant she possessed, and when she found it she gave him a dishcloth to dry his hand with. There were freckles on the skin of his face and a gap between his two front teeth, which she'd read somewhere was a sign of sensuality. He was whistling softly through this gap, the tune she often hummed in the private lounge herself, *Wrap Me up in Cotton-Wool.*

She bound the wound with the strip of flannel. Beneath each fingernail of his hand there was a black deposit, and the hand itself was rough to the touch, like fine sandpaper. She was glad when the cut disappeared beneath the bandage because she never cared for the sight of open flesh. He stood close to her so that she could get at it better, he said. His right knee pressed against her leg.

'What's the trouble?' demanded Mr Batt, looking up and noticing that there was a man in the kitchen having his hand bandaged. The man said something to him, but he couldn't quite hear what it was. 'Were you ever in a jackpot?' Mr Batt inquired, and Atlas Flynn shook his head.

'I got in on this musical thing,' explained Mr Batt. 'Hoagy Carmichael, Ted Weems, all that style of thing. The Jackpot's an Austin car. Brand-new,' said Mr Batt. 'Never on a road before.' He pushed some of the promotional material across the table so that the visitor could glance down and see for himself.

'Oh yes?' murmured Atlas Flynn.

'Old Batt's stone-deaf,' said Mrs Tuke.

The bandaging of the hand was now complete and Mrs Tuke, whose leg felt bruised from the pressure of her patient's knee, crossed the kitchen in order to replace the bottle of Dettol on the dresser. He was totally coarse, she was thinking, like an animal really. She smiled at him politely, hoping that he'd go now. She'd try and have a word with the foreman at lunchtime and make it quite plain that no further men were to be sent to the Thistle for medical attention. Ridiculous it was, first thing in the morning, before your stomach had settled down.

'That should be all right now,' she politely said, still smiling slightly. To her horror the man sat down at the table and took tobacco and cigarette-papers from his working clothes. For an instant she was reminded of Eddie Mercer, because that was just the type of thing he'd done, sitting down without being asked.

'D'you take a smoke at all?' he asked, rolling a cigarette with the aid of a small machine. She shook her head. He lit the cigarette and threw the used match on to the plate from which Mr Batt had eaten his breakfast.

'Flynn the name is,' he said, and she felt obliged to nod, knowing that his name was Flynn. 'Atlas Flynn,' he said.

It surprised Mrs Tuke afterwards that at this point she'd poured him out a cup of tea. She'd done it mechanically, she afterwards thought, the way you would for anyone, being hospitable by nature.

'Interesting,' he said, returning the promotional material to Mr Batt.

'You get membership of the Automobile Association for one year,' said Mr Batt. 'And petrol to carry you for twelve thousand miles.'

Atlas Flynn laughed. He wagged his head at Mrs Tuke in a manner that she considered familiar. He winked, creating the impression that both of them were amused by old Batt and the mail he'd received. 'Hoagy Carmichael's a great fellow,' he said, laughing again.

'Doesn't cost you a penny,' said Mr Batt, and went on to explain that the certificate he'd received was called a Once-In-A-Decade certificate. All you had to do was stick on to the certificate the stamp with your lucky number on it. You were then officially in the Jackpot and you'd receive for examination at your leisure the song treasury.

'Some of the old songs is definitely the best,' Atlas Flynn said, addressing Mrs Tuke. '*The Woodchoppers' Ball*'s a great thing.' He paused. Then he said: 'Isn't this a beautiful kitchen you have!'

She nodded, still smiling politely, not wishing to make a comment. She noticed that a drop of blood from his hand had earlier fallen on to a slice of bread on the table. He was regarding her provocatively, tipping his chair back as though he owned the place. A smell of sweat came off him and was already permeating the kitchen.

'*Theme Songs of the Big Band Era*,' he said, putting his head on one side in order to examine the wording on the Jackpot leaflet. *'The most universally loved music you've ever heard!'* He laughed and winked, causing her to wonder if he was perhaps a bit touched in the head. '*Who'll ever forget,*' he said, '*Guy Lombardo's rendition of* Auld Lang Syne?' She continued to smile, not knowing what else to do. He said:

'*The Woodchoppers' Ball*'s a great song to dance to. I'm out dancing every night of my life, Mrs Tuke, up in the Emerald Isle Club. D'you go to the West End at all?'

She heard herself saying, quite gaily really, that she hadn't been out dancing for years. She heard herself giving a little laugh, although she hadn't intended to give it or, indeed, to speak in a manner that was in any way gay. It was like the time she'd met the lodger, Ovens, on the landing outside his room and had been seized with a friendly impulse, only on that occasion she had not been in command of herself, having had the few drinks. It was like the time with Eddie Mercer, if it came to that.

'Any time you'd feel like it,' Atlas Flynn said in a low voice, glancing at the door to make certain that no one was about to enter the kitchen. 'We could have a few jars and go on to the Emerald. Or the Shamrock if you'd like it any better. D'you know the Shamrock at all? In Tottenham Court Road?'

She tried to get the smile to leave her face but somehow it still remained. He'd stopped tipping back his chair and was leaning over the table, his good hand stretched out towards her as if old Batt was blind as well as deaf. The exhalation that came from his arm-pits was more potent now. His lips were well drawn back, revealing heavily repaired teeth in both sides of his jaw.

As well as this, Old Batt was annoying her, looking for attention by pointing at a photograph on the leaflet he'd received. The photograph showed a previous winner of the Giant Jackpot sitting in a motor-car, his hand being shaken by another man, while a third figure, a male figure with blond, shoulder-length hair, was standing by, laughing and smoking a cigar.

'That bloke's Jimmy Saville,' said Mr Batt. 'A jockey.'

Atlas Flynn laughed gustily, throwing himself backwards in his chair again. She gave a little laugh herself, amused by old Batt going on about jockeys.

'T. M. Garnett,' said Mr Batt, identifying the two other men. 'S. A. Beecher-Stevens.'

Atlas Flynn was serious again. His eyes were on Mrs Tuke's eyes. 'I did it on purpose,' he said. 'I tore open my right hand, Beryl, so you'd bandage it up. I seen the books you read. "She's interested in that type of thing," I said to myself. D'you understand me, Beryl?'

Mrs Tuke felt a flush spreading over her stomach and then rising to her neck and face. She gave another little laugh to show that she was well used to this sort of attention and could deal with it nonchalantly. She could feel her heart beating from embarrassment. It was like Nurse Ann Topping in *I Take This Love* when she'd been embarrassed by an objectionable house-surgeon with whom she happened to have committed an error in the past: you had to be nonchalant, you had to pretend a calmness even though your heart in your breast was beating twenty-six to the dozen.

'I fancy you, Beryl,' said Atlas Flynn.

Hearing those words, Mrs Tuke thought that she was definitely going to faint. She closed her eyes, knowing that her face was by now the colour of an open beetroot. She could hear old Batt's voice rambling on about T. M. Garnett, a native of Stockton-on-Tees, and S. A. Beecher-Stevens. She thought she could hear the heavy breathing of Atlas Flynn and wondered if she was going to be attacked in the presence of old Batt and if old Batt would notice or would be capable of getting aid.

'D'you understand me, Beryl?' she heard Atlas Flynn saying, and immediately after he spoke, before she had time to open her eyes or to do anything else, she heard the commotion in the hall.

Mr Tuke was on his way down the stairs with Rebel. He had reached the last turn of the stairs and was, in fact, passing in front of the stained-glass window that depicted the woodland scene with a man and a woman in ancient dress. It was then that he saw Miss Gomez in the hall. She wore, as usual, her black leather dress. She held in one hand a packet of Embassy Gold cigarettes and in the other a cigarette that she'd lighted. She was shouting imperiously, as though she wished to summon everyone in the house to the hall. 'Mrs Tuke! Mrs Tuke!' she called, and then she called his own name.

Her voice echoed in the hall, bouncing from one hulk of furniture to another. There was aggression and defiance in the way she stood, with her legs wide apart. Between moments of calling out she puffed at her cigarette, and her eyes were bright behind her spectacles. Only one arm moved, to place the cigarette between her lips and again to remove it. Her feet seemed rooted to the ground.

101

Watching her, not answering when she called his name, Mr Tuke recalled the moment when she'd waited in the bathroom while he finished clipping his beard into the wash-basin. He was aware of the same sensation he'd experienced then, a shivery feeling that began in his head and then seemed to pass through the nerves of his body. He looked down at her, noticing her thin legs and the intensity in her eyes.

Mrs Tuke entered the hall from the kitchen and Atlas Flynn, behind her, saw the black girl who lodged in Bassett's Petstore and was a cleaner by trade. Mrs Tuke's husband, whom he'd thought to be safely out of the house, was on the stairs with his big Alsatian. The hall, which he'd never seen before, he considered unusual, having in its centre a dining-room table with eight chairs around it. All the furniture was on the bulky side, a big long couch affair, a hallstand, stuffed birds on the walls, and a grandfather clock that registered ten past ten.

'I would like to speak to you, Mrs Tuke,' Miss Gomez said. 'To you and to your husband, Mrs Tuke. There are statements that must now be made. Mrs Tuke, where is your husband?'

Mrs Tuke looked beyond Miss Gomez and was irritated by the sight of her husband on the stairs. She was aware, as well, that the man Flynn had sauntered into the hall behind her and she thought to herself that it was embarrassing enough having Gomez throwing fits about the place without being followed around by a labouring man who claimed to love her. To her dying day she'd never forget it when he'd come out with that remark in the kitchen, with old Batt rambling on through it all about T. M. Garnett and S. A. Beecher-Stevens. You had to smile when you thought of old Batt rambling on, even though it was far from pleasant to have a labouring man addressing you by your first name. He'd looked as livid as a sultan when Gomez had interrupted him by shouting in the hall: God knows what he'd been on the point of coming out with.

'Mrs Tuke, where is your husband?'

'Mr Tuke's on the stairs behind you. But, Miss Gomez dear, you're meant to be cleaning.'

Miss Gomez turned round and confirmed for herself the fact that Mr Tuke was on the stairs. She nodded at him.

'We do not give out literature,' she said, moving her head so that she addressed Mr Tuke and Mrs Tuke in turn. 'The Church of the Brethren kneels down to pray, that's all that ever happens: we pray for criminal people. I would like all of us here,' said Miss Gomez, 'to pray in this hall.'

'Miss Gomez dear!' cried Mrs Tuke, unnerved by the peculiar talk after what had occurred in the kitchen and recognizing that her cleaner was no longer of use to her if she got into this condition first thing in the morning. 'Miss Gomez dear, come and sit yourself down in the kitchen.' She crossed the hall towards her, thinking that if she could get Gomez into the kitchen she'd ask the man Flynn to assist the creature through the back door. Once she was out of the house she'd not get in again in a hurry.

Mrs Tuke gestured towards the kitchen, but Miss Gomez did not move. 'Old Batt had a fascinating mail,' coaxed Mrs Tuke. 'Old Batt's in a Giant Jackpot, dear.'

Mr Batt, in fact, stood by the kitchen door with his mail in his right hand, sensing that trouble of some kind had broken out: the man who'd been wounded was looking cross, Mrs Tuke was clearly on the edgy side.

Mr Tuke leaned against the frame of the stained-glass window. She belonged to a dotty religion, the way a lot of these West Indian women did: she couldn't help what she said, she mustn't be blamed for that. Miss Gomez had religion on the brain, but somehow it didn't matter.

'Listen to me, please,' said Miss Gomez, smiling beseechingly, as though seeking to charm her audience. She offered Atlas Flynn a cigarette, which he accepted. She lit it for him and lit one for herself. While she was doing so Atlas Flynn moved closer to Mrs Tuke. In a low voice he said that in his opinion Miss Gomez was round the screw.

'Please listen to me,' Miss Gomez said, 'while I tell you. Sit down,' she said to Atlas Flynn, pulling out one of the dining-room chairs for him. 'Sit down,' she ordered Mr Batt, taking him by the arm, smiling at him.

Mrs Tuke made sounds of protest. They were busy, she said, they couldn't go sitting down in the middle of the morning. 'What's the trouble?' inquired Mr Batt, accepting the proffered seat.

'Please come and sit down, Mr Tuke,' Miss Gomez said, smiling up at him, but he didn't move. Rebel came down and stretched himself out under the table, settling himself for sleep.

The man Flynn, Mrs Tuke noticed, had taken a seat and was now sniggering like a fool, seemingly recovered from his grumpiness. In a typical manner old Batt was stuffing tobacco into a pipe.

'Miss Gomez, whatever are you up to?' cried Mrs Tuke. 'We can't possibly have a prayer-meeting, dear.'

'I must tell you this in my own way,' Miss Gomez replied. She moved about, gesturing with her cigarette. 'Think of me first,' she said. 'Think of how I came here, how one day a week ago I looked into Bassett's Petstore and then came to you, Mrs Tuke, and asked you for work. I didn't need work, to tell you the truth. I didn't need money, having accumulated a lot. But I wanted to be here.'

'Miss Gomez dear—'

'Go back to the beginning of my journey, Mrs Tuke. I sat alone with Mr Kandi in the cellar where he cleaned the plimsolls and Mr Kandi put his hands on me. In the dormitory I made the new girls cry with my talk of death. God was a three-card trick, I said, the Father, the Son, the Holy Ghost: they cried at that too. I meant no harm. I rode in a bauxite lorry from Port Antonio to Kingston by the coast road; I repaid the lorry-driver the only way I could. I moved to London, Mrs Tuke. I washed the exteriors of your trains, I put breakfast wheat into packets, I sold pretty things in a haberdashery department.'

Miss Gomez now addressed herself exclusively to Mrs Tuke, standing in front of her with her back to the others. She asked Mrs Tuke if she understood and Mrs Tuke said she didn't. Miss Gomez moved about again, but still did not address the other people in the hall. She kept her eyes on Mrs Tuke's face while she moved, cutting in on her interruptions. Occasionally she drew on her cigarette.

'That is my life,' Miss Gomez said. 'In Thrift's Hotel a man gave me cheese in a canvas bag. I undressed sixteen times a day in the Spot-On Club. In Mrs Idle's pleasure house a man wanted me to go into a grave with him. I was a prostitute, Mrs Tuke, and so was Tina von Hippel. A man asked her to tie him to a cistern on a pulley, and she was frightened in case it killed him. A manager of a bank said his wife enjoyed the smell of a prostitute on him, only she didn't know what it was. Mrs Idle threw out a woman with gonorrhoea so that I could have her room. What'll become of that woman? What'll become of any of them, Mrs Tuke?'

'Miss Gomez, we don't like this kind of talk in the Thistle. We'd no idea whatsoever—'

'They are people I met on a journey I made. An incurable man, Mrs Tuke, set fire to a street, murdering ninety-one people. If the Brethren of my Church had met that man on the way to his crime they'd have knelt down in the road to pray for him. I made my journey to Crow Street, Mrs Tuke, and I saw through the pet shop window Alban Roche on the way to his crime. I understood, Mrs Tuke, because my life has been what it was. Miss Arbuthnot, who'd never satisfied a stranger in a brothel, would have passed the window by, neither seeing anything nor understanding. I was meant to be what I was in the orphanage, Mrs Tuke, and afterwards I was meant to travel in the bauxite lorry, and to arrive that day with Tina von Hippel in Mrs Idle's house. I am meant to be standing here now.'

Mrs Tuke estimated that in her entire life she'd never for a second been so embarrassed. The man Flynn had actually winked at her when the black lump said she'd undressed herself sixteen times a day in a club. After that she'd kept her head down, avoiding his eyes, and Gomez's eyes. She'd heard him snigger suggestively when Gomez mentioned some woman called Arbuthnot satisfying a stranger. She even thought she'd heard him whispering her first name as if anxious that she should come and sit beside him, but she wasn't sure about that. She leaned against the wall, her left shoulder touching the frame of one of the pictures that depicted sheep on a mountainside, her eyes still fixed on the brown linoleum. The foul odour coming from old Batt's pipe affected her stomach. She felt weak in her legs, the way she often did when she was upset.

'I am going against my Church,' Miss Gomez said. 'In Tacas they talked about all this and gave me my instructions. The Reverend Greated and the Reverend Pearson Simmonds, the Reverend Palmer and the Reverend Lloyd Patterson. They talked about it, and everyone prayed. They agreed I shouldn't mention to anyone in Crow Street the revelation I had: prayer was enough, they said. But I am here, Mrs Tuke. I am on the spot and I have gone against my Church because there must be prayer in Crow Street also. And understanding and forgiveness. I am meant to be saying that, Mrs Tuke: I can feel it inside me.'

Mr Batt made a remark, drawing Atlas Flynn's attention to a fresh point on the Jackpot leaflet. He'd spread the leaflet out in front of him on the table, with the letter and the Lucky Number coupon and the Once-In-A-Decade certificate.

'At the end of my journey,' Miss Gomez said, 'was Alban Roche and your daughter. Alban Roche, whose mother's teeth are in that room upstairs.'

'Teeth?' said Mrs Tuke, considerably startled, unable to prevent herself from raising her eyes.

'The mother's teeth, wrapped up in tissue paper. The sponge the mother cleaned herself with. Her hairpins and a comb, and a brush with hair on it, and a bag of insoles. Perspiration rolled down her legs and ended up in those insoles. Every day she put those hairpins in her hair. That woman's dead and yet in death that woman concerns us more than ever.'

Atlas Flynn gave a loud laugh, thinking it was the best thing he could do, since they could be stuck here for an hour listening to a black who was round the screw. She was a good bit of gas certainly, but he was anxious to make a definite arrangement with Beryl Tuke before he left the premises. No one seemed capable of controlling the black, who was saying the first thing that came into her head, about brothels and stripping clubs and clergymen, and was now opening up a new subject, to do with a dead woman's perspiration. The elderly party was oblivious to everything apparently, with his pipe and his Jackpot. The bearded Tuke was as grim as a priest on the stairs, looking as though he maybe fancied the black, and Beryl herself had a wonky appearance about her, like a woman he'd seen once who'd been run into by a lorry. He clapped his hands together, giving himself a slight dart of pain from his cut. Miss Gomez looked at him, which was what he wanted her to do. He smiled at her briskly, humouring her.

'This Alban Roche,' he said, 'the fellow you found at the end of your journey—'

'Who are you?'

'Flynn the name is, Atlas Flynn as a matter of fact—'

'I'm in the middle of explaining, Mr Flynn.'

Mrs Tuke began to speak, but Atlas Flynn interrupted her. 'Hold on now, Beryl,' he said, and added that it wasn't any business of his, but was Miss Gomez aware that possessions of the dead were often lovingly retained? Usually it was a piece or two of jewellery, or a fountain pen or a tie-pin. He himself had inherited his father's watch since no one else had seemed to want it. He drew attention to this watch, which was on his wrist. A tip-top performer, he said, no trouble at all. He spoke rapidly, anxious to make his point with the minimum of delay. 'You follow me?' he said to Miss Gomez, but Miss Gomez shook her head.

It was all written down, she said, addressing herself to Mrs Tuke. The story of Alban Roche was written in a notebook; his mother's belongings underlined the simple truth. 'There is a pattern, Mrs Tuke. There is Alban Roche in his grey town with his mother. The town presses in on him, like the woman does, like the outer wall of the woman's womb. When the woman dies he goes into exile in order to commit his crime, but all he has the courage for is to look into a changing-room and maybe touch the women's clothes.'

'Miss Gomez, we really can't stand here listening to this,' Mrs Tuke protested, feeling more angry than embarrassed now but quietly keeping her anger in control. 'You've no right to go reading stuff in a notebook, you know.'

'No right at all,' said Atlas Flynn. 'Slip off now, like a good girl, and don't be annoying these people.' As he spoke, he wondered

107

what Tuke was thinking of him for stepping in like he was doing. Tuke appeared to have entered a form of trance on the stairs, or else was having a stroke. The whole thing was extraordinary from start to finish.

'I'm asking you to go,' Mrs Tuke said.

Miss Gomez shook her head. 'There's a pattern,' she said. 'The exile of Alban Roche and my own exile too. In London there is Crow Street, where everything meets together, where an old woman dies, leaving her property to the boy who has been most like her husband with the pets, where Prudence Tuke is waiting. God creates complicated patterns and then commands us to fight against what seems like destiny. If you are sick with a cancer you will fight and sometimes you will win. You will fight because you do not know the outcome. Cancer is God's pattern too: only God is responsible. Those words were written for me by the Reverend Pearson Simmonds and passed on to me by the Reverend Patterson. I am learning to understand them myself.'

Mr Tuke heard Miss Gomez's voice going on and attempts being made to stop her. She took no notice. She spoke louder and faster. She repeated further words that had been written for her. 'What radiancy of glory,' she said, referring to her proposed return to her native land. ' "For the kingdom of heaven is like unto a man that is an householder which went out early in the morning to hire labourers into his vineyard".' The householder of her Church, she said, was the Reverend Patterson, the labourers were the Brethren.

Words of all kinds came flowing from Miss Gomez, quotations from hymns and prayers, and from the letters of the Reverend Patterson. She jumbled everything up, Alban Roche and people from the Bible and the person called Tina von Hippel and various men. She spoke of processions without banners, and picnics, with flowers, on a hill: much of that Mr Tuke had heard before from her, but he did not mind hearing it again. He remembered, when Prudence had been ten, reading to her from her history book about Joan of Arc and how together they'd shared the wonder of that, the country girl hearing voices and then inspiring an army, and dying because they said she was a witch. He'd never really understood any of it, any more than he understood what was being said now.

'Alban Roche is a cripple,' he heard his wife say snappishly. 'You're talking sheer rubbish—'

'We're all cripples, Mrs Tuke. There's something the matter with each and every one of us. It's in us all to burn down streets while people are sleeping in their beds, or to end as a sex offender. Terrible things are in all of us.'

'Now look here, Miss Gomez, we've had more than enough of all this. No cleaning has been done in this house this morning. I must ask you to go at once, Miss Gomez, and not to return please. I must insist—'

'I do not condemn you, Mrs Tuke, nor does my Church. I pray that we may pray together in this hall, and that forgiveness will come. You know the truth, Mrs Tuke: you have attempted to destroy your daughter as though you took a hatchet to her. But for that, even for that, you will receive forgiveness here on earth.'

'Ah now, wait a minute,' Atlas Flynn loudly began, while in an astonishment that deprived her of words Mrs Tuke stared with her mouth open at the cleaner whom eight days ago she'd casually employed for the first time. Her tongue passed between her parted lips, moistening them as an aid to speech. 'Destroy?' she tried to say, but the word did not properly come. 'Destroy?' she whispered.

'Don't speak,' Miss Gomez commanded Atlas Flynn, and Mr Tuke moved from the window and descended two steps of the stairs. He stood there as still as before, with his right hand on the banister rail.

'Why don't you like your daughter?' Miss Gomez cried in sudden anguish. 'Why do people commit these terrible cruelties, one to another, atrocities that are worse than bodies torn apart in war? That woman wrapped him up in vicious love because she feared to be left alone in a terraced house. Why don't you like your daughter, Mrs Tuke? And you?' she cried, turning to the man on the stairs.

'Prudence?' he whispered.

Miss Gomez threw her cigarette on to the linoleum. She lit

another, aware of the amazement around her. Only Mr Batt's face was different because Mr Batt, looking up from the Jackpot leaflet, was only puzzled. It had something to do with the cigarettes, he was thinking: was she justifying the fact that she had smoked on duty?

'In Tacas they shall tell me,' she said, 'what it is inside us that makes us no more than monsters. Sometimes I think that we are all of us, every day, on the way to our crime. Cripples, Mrs Tuke, as you said. Incurable, like that man. Only together, walking as my Brethren walk, can we accept all that we are. And in that acceptance we cannot condemn, neither the mother of Alban Roche nor anyone else.'

Mrs Tuke went close to Miss Gomez and stood with one hand on the back of a chair. She spoke slowly, her voice hardly above a whisper. 'Get out of here,' she said, and as quietly Miss Gomez replied:

'Last night I felt the crime like a slimy plant growing out of rottenness. I had visions of horror that would not cease. I couldn't feel myself moving. I couldn't bear to be alone. I saw the muti-lated body of your daughter, whom you yourself have made a victim.'

'Get to hell out of here,' shouted Mrs Tuke.

'There's a crime against your daughter in the conscious or un-conscious mind of Alban Roche. And your daughter in her simple innocence imagines that she loves him.'

'Will you stop talking that filth—'

'I'm speaking the truth to you, Mrs Tuke.'

'You're speaking a load of bloody rubbish. There's none of us can understand you because not a word you come out with makes any type of sense. You go raving on with pure filth, telling us you're a prostitute. You should have told us that when you first came after work here. What d'you think Mrs Bassett would feel to know she'd had a black whore in the house? What d'you think it's like for me, might I ask, with a young girl around the place?'

'I'm speaking the truth, Mrs Tuke. The truth is upstairs in Alban Roche's room.'

'What Roche did is over and done with. You've no right whatsoever to go poking about in people's private property and insulting my daughter with filth. One minute you have poor Pru's taking a shine on a cripple of a creature who's capable of nothing except looking in at windows, and the next you have him mutilating her body. You have a fellow up on a pulley in a toilet and a bank manager up to God knows what. It's dirty, disgusting talk coming out of a Negro's mind. We're not used to it, Miss Gomez, in this country.'

'You don't care about your daughter, Mrs Tuke. You let her be with him because he pays you rent. You're drunk every night of your life.'

Mrs Tuke shrieked. Red marks came on to her face and her forehead and her cheeks. A dark flush rose in her neck. 'You cheeky black bitch!' she shouted.

'Wait now, I'll fix her,' whispered Atlas Flynn, approaching Miss Gomez and taking her by the arm. But Miss Gomez struck at him sharply, bringing the edge of her hand down on his bandaged wound. He uttered a cry of pain and backed away at once, accidentally treading on one of Mrs Tuke's slippered feet and causing her, in turn, to cry out. 'Get out to hell,' she shouted at Miss Gomez.

Mr Batt's eyes were screwed up, fixed on the packet of Embassy Gold cigarettes that Miss Gomez still held in her left hand. He wondered if she'd stolen the cigarettes from the bar and decided that she had. She'd gone in there when everyone's back was turned and had been caught on her way out by Mr Tuke, who'd been coming down the stairs with his dog. An argument had broken out, which was still continuing; it was more serious, naturally, than just smoking on duty.

'Best ring the police, Beryl,' Atlas Flynn said softly and Rebel suddenly roused himself from his lethargy beneath the table. He leapt up, barking and wagging his tail. He licked Miss Gomez's legs.

Noticing this, Mrs Tuke was reminded of her husband's presence on the stairs. She harangued him, saying he'd been standing there like a dummy while a Negro insulted her. Her dressing-gown, Atlas Flynn observed, had opened at the front, clearly revealing that beneath it she wore only two pieces of underclothing.

Mr Tuke came down the stairs. Rebel, having finished with Miss Gomez's legs, approached the legs of Mrs Tuke, which were mottled from sitting too close to electric fires in the winter. 'Get off to hell,' she cried as the dog's tongue touched her flesh. She pushed at him with her foot, shrilly protesting that she wouldn't be licked just after a Negro had been licked.

'You're bloody disgraceful,' she shouted at her husband, 'not opening your bloody mouth.'

'The Reverend Patterson has written letters about you, Mrs Tuke. In Tacas they pray for you also.'

'What the hell are you talking about?'

'Miss Gomez please,' said Mr Tuke.

'Who's this bloody Patterson?' shrieked Mrs Tuke. 'How dare some man write letters about me! What the hell d'you think you're up to?'

'The Reverend Lloyd Patterson is the founder of my Church, Mrs Tuke—'

'Your bloody Church can get itself stuffed. You're an ignorant savage, Gomez, with your slimy plants and your rubbishy Church. You're not fit for a civilized country.'

Miss Gomez shook her head. She smiled at Mrs Tuke, a slight smile that was no more than a twitch at one corner of her mouth. She had laid her life down before them in the hall, she said, in order that they might understand why it was that she had come to the street they lived in. She spoke again of the people she'd spoken of before, the people that none of them knew. 'God knows the fate of Tina von Hippel,' she said.

'No one gives a tuppenny damn about the Tina von Hippel—'

'The Brethren do, Mrs Tuke. As they do about your fate: the manner in which you will eventually die and your state of mind at that time.'

Mrs Tuke, about to reply testily, was aware of the feeling she'd experienced the night before when Gomez had been talking ignorantly in the private lounge. The savagery of Gomez frightened her, she said again to herself, and the admission made her angry because it was an absurd admission. Rage rose in her once more,

112

a frustrated rage that even itself seemed part of the nonsensical fear she felt.

'You're completely ridiculous,' she shouted. 'The first time I saw you I said to myself you were completely ridiculous. A negroid in glasses, I said—'

'God is present in this hall, Mrs Tuke.'

'I don't care who's bloody present. You come over here and then you imitate white people. Ridiculous they look on you, those leathers you wear. Everything about you is ridiculous. You have teeth like bloody tombstones. You have softening of the brain—'

'Please listen to me, Mrs Tuke.'

'We've listened enough to you. We're sick and tired of standing here listening to you. You're a smutty-minded creeping Jesus. You've got God on your stupid brain-box—'

'There is an emptiness in you, Mrs Tuke, that God could fill: I have had that written from Tacas. God is important, Mrs Tuke, in all our lives: I'm trying to explain that to you. It's not God's will that any cruelty should take place between His children any more than it's His will that atrocities of war should take place, or violence and murder. It wasn't His will that the crime of that incurable man took place. Nor is it His will that the crime hidden in Alban Roche's mind should take place. It's God's will that we should prevent it. God has spoken to us through the Brethren, in answer to prayers from Tacas. God has given us a revelation. We must kneel in this hall and show that we are still His children, that we do not condemn but instead forgive. And after that we must gently speak, all of us together, with Alban Roche.'

It was at this point that Mrs Tuke screamed. She flung her two hands against her ears, her fingers striking the plastic hair-curlers that gripped, beneath her head-scarf, her henna hair. Her body jerked, her feet seeming to bounce for an instant on the linoleum. Her eyes were wild, her face and neck more violently flushed then they had been before.

Miss Gomez, nearest to the distraught woman, remained calm. She did not move closer to her, nor did she issue words of sympathy. She pulled on her cigarette while fresh screams filled the hall and echoed all over the upstairs area of the Thistle Arms.

113

Mr Tuke paused for a moment before limping across the hall to his wife. She was not given to hysteria, but it certainly seemed that she was now in an hysterical fit, twitching and breathing heavily, shrieking in short bursts. As he moved, his eyes did not leave her: her dressing-gown had fallen further back, revealing hairs on the lower part of her stomach. Her thighs were white, like suet. He had married her nineteen years ago: divorce wasn't for people like them.

'You're a small stupid man,' she shrieked when she saw him coming. She screamed again after she'd said that. Her eyes burst at him with wrath, her reddened lips were quivering. She took her hands from her ears and clenched her fists. She held them in the air for a moment. Then she struck him on the head.

He stepped back from her, allowing her to go on screaming. He looked at Miss Gomez and saw that she was still calm, as though she'd been expecting all this to happen. The man whose hand had been bandaged was examining the nakedness that the open dressing-gown displayed. Mr Batt's mouth was open also, hanging in bewilderment.

Abruptly Mrs Tuke pulled the fat-stained dressing-gown around her and turned her back on her husband. The whole bloody lot of them, she thought. Typical of him to bring a filthy labourer into the kitchen, with blood spurting all over the food they were eating. Typical to stand there like a dummy when any other man would have run down the stairs immediately and given Gomez a boot up the b.t.m., or set the bloody dog at her. Who precisely did any of them think she was that a labourer in his working clothes could come into her kitchen and make suggestive proposals to her, that a black savage could tell her to kneel down in her own hall? She pushed past her husband and the black, pushing her way upstairs away from the whole damn lot of them. She saw old Batt goggling at her from the table, poking his head out the way he did. Bloody ridiculous that man was. Selfish and thoughtless, making life totally impossible for everyone who came anywhere near him. 'What d'you think you're staring at?' she shouted at him, making certain he heard.

He shook his head, the way he always did. It was a gesture that irritated her beyond measure.

'You and your bloody Jackpot,' she shrieked. 'You and your bloody pipe. I'll tell you one thing, Batt, there'll be no lodgers in the Arab's Head.'

'What?'

She went up the stairs and Mr Batt watched her, astonished at the words that had come through to him with such clarity and suddenness. The black cleaner came to him and touched his hand, as though sympathizing. It wasn't his fault the girl had stolen the cigarettes, it had nothing to do with him whatsoever. He looked at the cleaner and noticed that she was weeping. Tears ran from her eyes and under her spectacles. He saw one drop on to her leather dress.

Miss Gomez continued to weep, going past Mr Tuke on her way to the hall-door. He saw the tears glistening on her cheeks, and Atlas Flynn saw them also and heard the sobs that came from her as she moved through the hall. He winked at Mr Tuke, thinking to make an effort with him since he hoped to acquire the freedom of his wife, but Mr Tuke didn't acknowledge the communication. Mr Tuke didn't know why she was crying, and assumed it was because she'd failed to make anyone listen to her. He didn't know why everything about her seemed to catch so sharply in his imagination: the tears on her cheeks, her frizzy hair, her glasses, her leather dress, the way she walked on her thin legs. Nothing she said was sensible: her mind was filled with rubbish about sex crimes and prayers and people you'd never heard of, and yet in spite of everything she'd caused something to happen in the hall. She'd caused his wife, for a start, to have hysteria.

She left by the hall-door, weeping more copiously than before. She paused for a moment before she banged the door behind her. She didn't speak.

IX

At noon that day the temperature was 81° Fahrenheit in London. The light blue sky was empty of clouds, no breeze cooled the air. Men walked the streets in shirtsleeves, girls smiled and their teeth seemed whiter in the sunshine. The Thames murkily gleamed.

In Notting Hill Gate the traffic moved slowly through the heat and often did not move at all, in Blackfriars there was chaos because a set of lights had failed. In Battersea a grey Humber Snipe, purchased earlier that year as a second-hand bargain, proved less of a bargain than its purchaser had imagined: its engine ceased in a notoriously busy area, causing impatience on the part of other car-owners, all of whom observed Mr Uziki of Nigeria lifting the bonnet of his bargain Humber Snipe and appearing to be distressed. They passed him by as best they could, sounding their horns as an indication of their disapproval. 'Typical,' a man in a Vauxhall Victor remarked to another man and the other man agreed. The police eventually came to the aid of Mr Uziki, and the Humber Snipe, in which he had been planning to drive his wife Veronica and their two children to Southend the following Sunday, was towed away. 'You got a load of old cobblers with that, mate,' one of the policemen laughingly informed Mr Uziki. 'Kaput,' said a garage proprietor a little later, snapping down the bonnet with a gesture so final that Mr Uziki thought of death.

The heat brought out the worst in people. 'Bloody foreigners,' a suited business-man suddenly shouted in Oxford Street, noticing on the opposite pavement a slow-moving band of what seemed to him to be Tibetans. Their heads were shaven. They wore Eastern robes in patterned cotton. They chanted, some shook tambourines; they had the appearance of esoteric priests. But the man was wrong to say that they were foreigners: they were local people with local London accents, devotees of an ancient cult they'd read about in a book. 'Disgraceful,' a woman said, eyeing the shorn men also. 'Dirty-looking lot.'

In Crow Street the labourers sweated, some of them without their shirts, as they demolished a house where a family called Tance had lived. Their pick-axes flew at interior walls that still had patterned paper on them, they battered down wooden sheds in which the Tances had stored timber and guttering and bags of cement. *J. and A. T. Tance Bros,* they noticed on a sign: *High-Class Building and Decorating. Prices Competitive.* Pneumatic drills tore at the concrete yard that fifteen years ago J. and A. T. Tance had themselves laid down. A man laughed, finding a doll, covered in soot, in a fire-grate.

Further up the street Alban Roche watched while the coffin containing Mrs Bassett's body was carried through the shop. 'Thank you very much!' screeched the mynah. 'Ha, ha, ha,' cried the cockatiel.

Two men pushed the coffin into a black van and banged the doors on it. Alban Roche agreed with a third that he'd pay all expenses since he was the inheritor and there was, apparently, no one else. At her own wish, she would be cremated. He'd attend the funeral, he said, although the undertaker didn't seem much interested in that.

When they'd gone he stepped out into the heat of the day himself, locking the pet shop behind him. All the cages had been cleaned out, fresh straw and bird paper put down. He'd scattered sawdust and filled the food and water containers. For an hour or so the pets would be all right.

He walked away from Crow Street, over the wastelands. In the distance he saw a cat. The cats were breeding, he thought, in homes they'd made among the rubble and in the cellars of empty houses. They were stray cats that were now living a communal life, seeking food where they could find it. They picked at the lunch-time scraps of the labourers, they hung about Crow Street where there were still dustbins at the public house and the pet shop. He paused, watching the single cat. It darted away towards houses that were still standing, and was followed at once by several others who suddenly had congregated. The cats were returning to nature, half-wild already: soon they would hunt as a tribe, which was their nature also.

The sun was hot on his head as he crossed the unprotected wastelands. He felt it on the backs of his hands and on his face and neck. He'd have a meal in Abyssinia Street, he thought, in the Windrush Café where he often went.

She'd taken off her sandals. In her bare feet she walked through small streets, far now from the demolition area. She bought a bar of Cadbury's chocolate which melted in her fingers and was warm by the time it reached her lips. Two boys spoke to her and followed her for a while, saying she was pretty, inviting her to the pictures that afternoon. She looked in the shop windows at small toys for sale and confectionery and bread. She bought a bottle of limeade and drank it in a shop, through a straw. 'What a pretty yellow!' remarked the woman who sold it to her, referring to the colour of her dress. She'd made it herself, she said, and went on talking. She asked if there were pet shops in the area and the woman said there weren't. She kept a budgerigar herself, she said, called Percival. 'I like a comic name,' the woman said.

Prudence smiled. Since she'd left the wastelands around Crow Street she'd felt waves of happiness passing through her, whenever she thought that Mrs Bassett, in typical kindness, had passed on to him her collected pets and what amounted to a sum of money. For as long as she could remember she'd visited Mrs Bassett in the pet shop and had liked being with her, having tea and playing with the pets. Now it was almost as if Mrs Bassett had died on purpose so that everything might be all right for two other people. It was as though she'd wished that the happiness of her life with her husband might somehow be passed on, that out of an end another beginning might emerge. In the pet shop Mrs Bassett had often talked about her marriage, making it seem a kind of heaven.

'I'd like to breed butterflies,' Prudence said to the woman who'd sold her the limeade. It wasn't difficult to, she explained:

all you had to do was to collect the eggs from the plants on which they had been laid and store them where their metamorphosis might safely take place. She went on talking, saying she'd like to breed Camberwell Beauties, which were rare in England despite their name. She smiled again, and handed back the empty lime-ade bottle.

On the stage of the old Globe Theatre in Wandsworth Mr Tuke had once seen a man hypnotized. 'You're a bar of steel,' the hypnotist, a Frenchman, had said to another man, and then with the aid of scene-shifters he had placed the man's heels on the edge of one chair and his head on the edge of another. He had then walked across the man's body, jumping up and down on it in so violent a manner that in Mr Tuke's opinion it could not have been good for the man's stomach. Afterwards the French hypnotist suggested to the man that he was a hen and the man made clucking noises, which delighted the audience at the Globe Theatre.

The French hypnotist hadn't been at all like Miss Gomez, either in manner or appearance, and yet, in the atmosphere that Miss Gomez was capable of creating, there was a lot that was reminiscent of the stage of the Globe. And Miss Gomez apparently affected different people in rather different ways, inspiring this feeling of hypnosis in himself, irritation in his wife and causing Prudence to divulge confidences.

Mr Tuke still dismissed everything Miss Gomez had prophetically said about a sex crime, but found it difficult to dismiss the claim she'd made concerning Prudence's attachment to Alban Roche. Ever since she'd said it he'd been thinking that it was just like Prudence to work up an affection for an unobtrusive youth who'd been around the place for years, a sort of drop-out type who'd appeared to have no interest in anything except pets, until he was caught for being a nuisance in a women's changing-rooms.

Sitting in the public bar by himself, Mr Tuke remembered the companionship there'd once been between him and the girl. They'd done a lot together; he'd helped her to carry her things from junk shops, he'd listened to her and she to him. And then his wife had explained to him one night that Prudence was not his daughter.

It shouldn't have made any difference: in the five years that had gone by since that revelation he'd told himself repeatedly that it didn't matter, but in the end, after he'd argued with himself, it always did. Prudence had his eyes, he'd thought, and a look of him around the lips. She had his nature, which was more important: they were two of a kind. When she'd been born his mother, who was still alive then in Crow Street, said she was the dead spit of him. His mother had been delighted because she was the first child to be born in the family since he himself had been. 'Eddie Mercer,' his wife explained to him all those years later, and he remembered Eddie Mercer, a lodger they'd had whom he'd never cared for.

She told him because they'd been quarrelling about Prudence. She said he made too much of a fuss of her, taking her around everywhere. She was growing up abnormal, she complained, because of being hawked about to football matches and the like. She said he'd brought her to the billiards place in Fulham Road, but in fact he never had and was indignantly denying the accusation when she suddenly flared up and told him that if he thought the girl was his daughter he was making a big mistake. After that she told him everything, weeping and saying she was sorry and ashamed. She hadn't cared for Eddie Mercer either, apparently, but Eddie Mercer had made the suggestion, when she'd had a drink or two, one night when there was a sing-song and dancing. They'd gone to the gents' toilet, he going first and she following a minute later. She hadn't liked any of it, she said, and afterwards she'd been sick.

He'd argued that it didn't prove anything, a thing like that in a toilet: Prudence could still be his. His wife said of course she could. It could happen to a queen, she pointed out, if a queen had had a drink or two; nevertheless he was an angel to forgive her. Sweet F.A., she said, could ever come of a business in a gents' toilet, but later, in another quarrel, she furiously told him that if he imagined there'd been only one occasion with Eddie Mercer he was making a big mistake: when he'd been in St Mary's Hospital having an operation on the veins in his legs Eddie Mercer had several times occupied his bed. After this, Mrs Tuke had wept again. She had carried her shame with her, she said, all these years, reminded of it and of Eddie Mercer every time she looked at her daughter.

In spite of all that he still hadn't believed that he wasn't the father of Prudence, and in her contrite mood she agreed that, even allowing for those further activities of Eddie Mercer, it was unlikely that he wasn't. But in the same way, quarrelling again on another occasion, she said that he couldn't possibly be the girl's father: in a temper she reminded him of the precise time he'd been in St Mary's Hospital, of the duration of his stay, and other relevant dates.

They hadn't quarrelled since. He'd watched his mother imagining the girl was her only grandchild, and when his mother died he'd been glad in a way, because at least she'd never found out. He watched Prudence herself, and every time he looked at her he couldn't help thinking of Eddie Mercer. He came into his mind like a demon, Eddie Mercer who'd had a position in a coal firm, a big man with black eyes and hair, not at all like Prudence. When he was with Prudence he seemed more tormented than ever by this man. He kept thinking that he himself had nothing whatsoever to do with the girl, that to her he was merely another person and no more than that. He had neither rights nor claims, and in time he came to feel absurd in her presence. He found it hard, after that, to say anything to her at all. A shadow was left and still remained, of the love he'd felt for her, but it wasn't much compared with what there once had been. They'd drifted apart in silence, she not knowing the reason why. Feeling lonely without her, he'd one day bought Rebel.

That morning Miss Gomez had brought it all back. She'd dredged up the past and thrown it about the hall. Was it something to do with the past that had caused Prudence to form an attachment for a person like Alban Roche? Prudence might have been destroyed, as though with a hatchet: what did Miss Gomez mean by that? Had that statement, also, a ring of truth? And was

it he and not his wife who had taken a hatchet to the girl he'd
once loved more than anyone he'd ever known?

In the public bar Mr Tuke drew half a pint of beer. He sipped
some, and found himself thinking again of Miss Gomez in her
glasses and her black leather dress, of Miss Gomez who could calm
you and upset you, like a witch in a pantomime.

'Morning, Mr Tuke,' a man from the brewery's catering firm
said, depositing on the bar a cardboard box full of cellophane-
wrapped sandwiches. Mr Tuke signed the man's receipt book, listening to him saying that there'd never been weather like it.

Mrs Tuke lay on her bed. She didn't feel well. No woman in her
senses could fail to feel upset after stuff like that, the black lump
standing there, blaspheming like a heathen at ten o'clock in the
morning, saying she had visions. Ten years ago a lump like that
would have been beaten to a pulp for opening her mouth to a
white woman in her hallway. Lay a finger on them these days and
some nosey-parker would come round with a constable.

She wondered if she had a serious liver complaint the way she
was always experiencing the sourness in her stomach. She often
thought she hadn't long to live because she took it out of herself,
endlessly cooking meals when she wasn't serving in an ill-designed
lounge. In that respect it would definitely be nicer in the Arab's
Head. The Cocktail Den was perfectly designed, as the out-going
landlord had pointed out, with shelves at the right height and the
most called-upon bottles readily to hand. She closed her eyes,
endeavouring to transport herself to the Cocktail Den or to Scotland, to the town of Tannochbrae, where Dr Finlay and Dr Cameron practised, or to the cottage hospital at Rose St Margaret in
Devonshire. She failed and cried out angrily, opening her eyes
with a jerk. 'Stupid black bitch,' she cried. 'Stupid bloody negroid.'

Having released these ejaculations, Mrs Tuke felt better. The
house would just have to get dirty, and it didn't matter all that
much really because in a fortnight or so they'd be shutting up
shop for the last time ever. Every lunchtime the labourers made
a fearful mess of the bars with the filth on their boots, but that

would just have to be because she certainly wasn't going to start going round with a brush again, not at her time of life, not with a liver complaint.

Mrs Tuke glanced at a watch that was embedded in the flesh of her left wrist and saw that the time was twenty past twelve. Soon, even from where she lay, she'd hear the tramp of the labourers and their voices calling out as they approached the public house. In a quarter of an hour they'd have filled the two bars, demanding beer and stout, some of them asking for sandwiches. She wondered if Flynn would return after his performance that morning. She recalled with distaste the dirt caught behind his fingernails and the odour that had been mounting up in the kitchen before the black lump shouted out. It was all the same these days: give them an inch and quick as a flash they were calling you by your first name.

She eased herself from the bed and sat down in front of her dressing-table. She removed the curlers from her hair and combed it out, promising herself that one of these days she'd give it another wash. She applied eyeshadow, darkened her eyelashes and smeared her lips. Imagine the lump saying that Pru had taken a shine to Roche! She could have smacked her nasty black face when she'd come out with that, she wouldn't have trusted herself if she'd been carrying an implement. Poor Pru didn't know her head from her heels in that respect and was never meant to, not at her age. She dabbed her face with powder that was a shade of orange. Life wasn't easy, which was what the kind like Gomez didn't realize. It wasn't easy to keep smiling every minute of the day, although naturally you did your best: it wasn't easy when your husband had shut his shop up as far as you were concerned, just because there'd been a few misdemeanours in the past. No one could say she hadn't done her best with him, coaxing him and giving herself, at all hours of the day and night. She could never understand how it was that he couldn't see it from her point of view, that he couldn't understand how it disgusted her to her backbone to have permitted that business with Eddie Mercer. Mercer was like an animal, a great brute of a creature with filthy conversation and pitted flesh on his forehead. No one but Mercer could have suggested a rendezvous in the gents' toilet, an un-pleasant enough locale at the best of times. Completely coarse it had been, with men laughing and relieving themselves on the other side of the locked door. It wasn't nice to be reminded of stuff like that every time you looked at your own daughter, and somehow, because of it, she'd never been able to care for poor Pru all that much, which was something that an ignorant lump like Gomez wouldn't be capable of appreciating even if you spelt it out in capitals. When she'd discovered the condition she was in she'd tried to get rid of the thing as fast as she could, toppling herself down half a flight of stairs and jigging up and down for an hour in the kitchen. She'd spoken to Mercer about it, but all he'd suggested was that they should slip upstairs together since her husband was in St Mary's Hospital with his veins. In her weak-ness she had done so, her problem having always been her generosity.

To her dying day she'd never forget the first time she'd seen the baby, and how no matter what she did she couldn't help thinking that it had begun its career in a gents' toilet. Poor Pru had been small and thin, not at all like either of her parents, resembling if anyone the man who assumed she was his daughter. He took a pride in her, cradling her in his arms for hours on end, showing her off in the public bar when she was three weeks old. 'She'll be a beauty, that one,' said Eddie Mercer, laughing like a drain. He had babies all over London, he'd confidentially informed her; he often made the rounds of them. But soon after the birth he gave up his room in the Thistle Arms, which she considered was the only decent behaviour she'd ever experienced in the man. Because of him, she'd always felt sorry for the child, and even more so when someone remarked in the lounge one night that Eddie Mercer had bad blood in him. She could well believe it, and imagined that what was meant was that one of Mercer's parents had struck the other dead. Mercer was like that, full of violence both in his speech and his actions. Poor Pru, it would kill her to know.

She owed Gomez four pounds ten, she supposed, but she'd certainly no intention of paying her. She'd take it in lieu of notice and naturally enough Gomez would never show her flattened face in the Thistle again. When it came to the point, you couldn't really worry about stuff like that. You had to forget about it and try and find your smile, no good going round like a dead duck.

She rose from her dressing-table and crossed to the wardrobe. The dress she'd worn the day before was rumpled and a little soiled. She threw it to one side and picked out a flame-coloured two-piece that she'd had in mind when she'd selected her face-powder. She slipped herself into it, ran a puff over her cheeks again, touched up her lips, and patted her hair. The enamel on her fingernails hadn't chipped, her eye-shadow was perfect.

She sat down on her bed, and picked up from the table beside it Doris Rae's *Serenade to a Nurse*. She opened it at chapter 3, always her favourite, and read briefly about Rick and Christine at Madame St Hubert's dinner-party in the Château de Bretelle. After a moment she exchanged the novel for *Dr D'Arcy's Love*, transporting herself easily from Les Pléïades to the ivy-clad cottage hospital and the struggle between love and dedication on the part of Dr Desmond D'Arcy.

Mr Batt, who usually sat in the public bar, did not do so today. From the private lounge he poked his head round the partition and asked Mr Tuke if he'd mind passing his ham sandwich and pint of beer through. 'Makes a change,' he'd said, finding it difficult to admit that he'd chosen the lounge because the lounge was Mrs Tuke's domain. He'd thought about the incident in the hall and had come to the conclusion that there was a perfectly simple explanation: in her extreme emotion Mrs Tuke, normally the jolliest of people, hadn't known what she was saying. It was often so, that when you were upset you said things that were the very opposite of what you really meant. Anyone would naturally be upset when a cleaner turned round and stole packets of cigarettes, he quite saw that; anyone could be carried away to nastiness in the heat of the moment. The only reservation he'd ever had about Mrs Tuke was that the food she cooked wasn't of a high standard but that, like the way she sometimes fell asleep in the evenings, was only a reflection of her easy-going nature. She'd be embarrassed, naturally enough, about the incident in the hall, but he'd say it didn't matter at all, not to give it a thought.

Mr Batt sat at a table near the bar, nodding to himself over these considerations and then, with abruptness, he remembered what he'd been trying to remember the evening before: a German aircraft was flying tiresomely about, disappearing and coming back again, and he himself was on the upper deck of a bus going from Kew to Putney. Some hours went by, their contents lost to him now. He remembered, next, standing in the Norwich Castle public house just off Putney High Street and a man with a red face was saying that the aircraft was still buzzing about. Two minutes later it dropped its bomb on a corner building that had been turned into a dance-hall for the duration. The dead were carried into the cinema next door, placed there in rows as though the cinema were a mortuary. He'd helped with that himself, in his official capacity as air-raid warden. Eighty bodies had there been? Or two hundred and something? He'd passed the corner building not long ago, a clothes shop now. The cinema was still in business.

Odd, how memories came and went. In 1918 Henry Bassett had been with him at Lassigny, on August 8th, and someone else from the district, a chap they hadn't liked. It wasn't at Lassigny that Henry Bassett had got the shrapnel in his back: he couldn't quite remember where that had been. Lassigny was a victory, of course: in the next war the single bomb on the dance-hall was a signal of defeat, a forewarning, people said, of worse to come. Defeat was in the air then, and so was death: Peter they'd called one son, and the other Sam. Absurd, he'd thought at the time, that he should have survived the other war just in order to father the dead. She'd never recovered, of course, and he knew what people said because he'd felt it coming from them: she was queer in the head, well, anyone would be, two boys gone like that, sense-less really.

The labourers came into the public bar, but Mr Batt didn't hear them. Having finished his ham sandwich, he reflected that it was thinking about the Arab's Head last night, and the botanical gardens at Kew, that had put him in mind of the aeroplane circling round. Trains of thought were interesting; it was something to do to trace them back to a source.

In the public bar the labourers were curious about what Atlas Flynn had reported to them about the public house's black cleaner. 'What d'you think of it, Mr Tuke?' one of them asked.

Mr Tuke said he didn't know. He drew beer and put sandwiches on plates. He had no wish to discuss what had occurred with his customers. What had taken place was unfortunate; it was nobody's business.

'Sex would destroy you,' a grey-haired man who was older than the others said. It was sex on all sides these days, he remarked, adding that the world would be a decenter place without it.

Mrs Tuke came into the private lounge and Mr Batt glanced towards her, smiling at her from the table where he sat. He was about to speak when several labourers entered the private lounge also. On the table in front of him he'd spread out the letter he'd received and the leaflet, and the Once-In-A-Decade certificate. *Who will ever forget,* he read, *Eddie Cantor's 'Makin Woopee'?* It had been pleasant first thing in the morning, to receive such a cheerful letter. It reminded you that you had a name and address, and even if you weren't much interested in music and hadn't a hope of winning a motor-car it gave you something to do. Mr Batt stuck the coupon that bore his lucky number on to the Once-In-A-Decade certificate. Everything had been fine, he reflected: the morning had been lively and full of promise, what with his mail and the man bleeding in the kitchen and the barney in the hall. Everything had been perfectly enjoyable until she'd suddenly got into that state, saying things she didn't mean.

'Wasn't that shocking?' a man ordering five pints of beer said to Mrs Tuke. 'Sex crimes, eh?'

Mrs Tuke smiled. It was over and done with, she said. In error she had employed an unsuitable cleaner; she'd know better next time.

A turbaned youth from the town of Gwadan in West Pakistan returned to Mrs Tuke her copy of *There Came a Surgeon*, which he'd understood quite well, he said. She'd lend him *Attached to Doctor Marchmont*, she promised, a beautiful thing by Juliet Shore. She'd bring it down tomorrow.

'Go away and sit down,' Atlas Flynn ordered the turbaned youth in a voice low enough not to carry to Mrs Tuke, who was now serving others. He remained at the bar himself, rolling a cigarette with the aid of his machine. When Mrs Tuke had received payment for the drinks she'd served, he said, speaking quietly:

'Are you feeling a bit better, Beryl?'

Mrs Tuke pretended not to hear. She poured herself a measure of gin and added peppermint cordial to it, dawdling over the task in the hope that the labourer would go away. None of the others had heard him calling her by her first name, which was something at least.

'I did the best I could with the bloody creature,' he said. 'I could see you were upset, Beryl.'

Mrs Tuke smiled coolly. It was over and done with, she repeated.

He lit his cigarette and offered to roll her one also. She told him for the second time that day that she didn't smoke.

'We were talking about a night out, Beryl—'

'Please don't address me by my first name,' she quietly said, smiling a little more in order to cover the nature of her words. A few of the men were looking at her, she noticed. She'd seen one of them poking an elbow into another's ribs, drawing attention to the man at the bar.

'I know what you mean,' he said, lowering his voice even more, embarrassing her with this suggestion of confidences being exchanged.

'I'm not at all interested,' she said. 'I'm a respectably married woman, Mr Flynn. I must ask you to remember that.'

'Ah, why wouldn't you be respectable, Beryl? I'm respectable myself. I was only thinking that maybe—'

'Will you please go away and leave me alone.' She still smiled. She lifted her glass to her lips. To her relief she saw that old Batt was on his feet, approaching the bar.

'A half pint in there, please,' he said, poking his head at her, smiling ingratiatingly.

'All I was meaning,' Atlas Flynn said, 'was that maybe we could take a drink together one evening. I meant what I said in the kitchen.' He dropped his voice again. He leaned over the bar while she drew the half pint of beer. 'What I said, Beryl, about fancying you. I can't help my feelings.'

Mr Batt handed her a pound and she gave him his change. His head was still poked out at her, inclined so that an ear might endeavour to catch anything she said. His teeth were bared, his lips drawn back to their extent. His face was like the skull of a sheep, she thought.

'Lovely day, Mrs Tuke,' he said. 'Glorious, isn't it?'

She smiled at him, and then Mr Batt felt a sudden sharp pain in his ankle. He looked down and saw the boot of the man standing at the bar still hovering in the air. The man gestured with his head at the table Mr Batt had been sitting at, indicating that he should return to it.

'What's up with you?' Mr Batt asked angrily, leaning down to rub the bone of his ankle. 'What're you kicking me for?'

Atlas Flynn took Mr Batt by the arm and led him back to his chair. He took some money from his pocket and placed it on the table beside the Jackpot certificate. He didn't say anything, knowing that there wasn't much use. He tapped the glass of beer in Mr Batt's hand and touched the money, making the point that the latter was a gift with which he could purchase himself further alcohol.

'How's our Atlas making out?' one of the men inquired, and all the other men in the private lounge guffawed. They glanced at Mrs Tuke, whose face for the third time that day began to flush.

'Look here,' said Mr Batt, 'what the hell's going on?' He began to say something further, but noticing that Mrs Tuke was looking edgy again he decided that it was better not to speak.

'Beryl—'

'Stop calling me that at once. I've bandaged your hand, Mr Flynn: you've no further call on my time.'

Mrs Tuke spoke the last sentence loudly, so that everyone in

129

the private lounge except Mr Batt could hear it. There was no point in trying to hide the fact any longer that Flynn was after her. Everyone had seen him kicking old Batt and giving him money to keep him away from the bar. Not that old Batt hadn't deserved the little tap he'd received, bothering her like that with his head stuck out. She poured herself another drink, turning her back on the private lounge. She undid the cellophane on a cheese-and-tomato sandwich, taking her time over it. A silence had developed in the lounge. She could feel eyes on her back. She knew well the stuff they were thinking: their minds were filling with the type of words Eddie Mercer had used, all their thoughts were totally unpleasant. She turned round suddenly and saw that Flynn was sniggering and winking at his companions.

He made a coarse noise in his mouth, pretending some beer had gone down the wrong way; he tried to turn his sniggering into a smile. She could smell the odour that had come from him earlier in the kitchen; the bandage she'd put on his hand was filthy already. In the background their faces leered, their bodies sprawled on the padded seat that stretched under the windows or slouched on the bent-cane chairs. They smoked foul-smelling tobacco, rolled into cigarettes, like he did. All of them were dirty in their working clothes.

'I'm dead serious,' he said, again in a low voice. 'I'm not fooling about, Beryl.'

She looked at him, at his greased red hair and broken teeth. She felt herself wanting to shudder, as she had when Mercer had suggested going into the toilet with him. She'd had half a bottle of Gordon's in her then, or else she'd never have made the error. Her whole existence, she often thought, was nothing more than a string of errors. She'd married a useless man, who'd got her stuck in Crow Street for the next nineteen years. She'd tried to be friendly with Eddie Mercer in a perfectly normal way and the next thing was she was up the stick with a baby. Even today, in the space of a couple of hours, two further errors had come to the surface: she'd made a mistake with a cleaner and out of decency she'd bandaged a man's hand. As a result, she'd immediately been taken advantage of. Out of the goodness of her heart

she'd taken in old Batt a few years ago and now he was apparently
assuming that he could tag along to the Arab's Head like a member of the family.

Mrs Tuke, rendered morose by these thoughts, finished her
gin and peppermint in one long draught and almost immediately
felt better than she'd felt all day. She replenished her glass, thinking that in circumstances like these it was always best to let your
nature come to your rescue. Cheeriness rippled through her; she
found her smile.

'Now, now, boys,' she cried. 'No more taking the Michael out
of Mrs T.' She laughed loudly, suddenly seeing the wisdom of
turning everything into a good joke. 'You're a rascal, Mr Flynn.
Get along with you now, you old bother boots!'

She laughed again, pouring herself another drink. She bit delicately into her sandwich. Best to treat them as children since they
were, after all, little else. Neither anger nor pleas had the slightest
effect with fellows like this. Sophistication worked wonders because they were total strangers to it.

'Listen to me, Beryl—'

'Now, now, Mr Flynn. Mrs Tuke *if* you please.'

'Listen, dear—'

'This ruffian wants me to go dancing with him,' she jollily
cried. 'You're a terrible fellow, Mr Flynn.'

'We could go down tonight—'

'Mr Tuke'll have your guts for garters, old chap. I'm being
made advances to, Dad,' she called out. 'Mr Flynn wants to take
me to a ballroom. Is it the Ritz, Mr Flynn, where we're going?'
She hummed a snatch from *These Foolish Things*. 'A cigarette-end
with those lipstick traces,' she murmured. 'An airline ticket to
romantic places.'

'Listen, Beryl—'

'Da da da da da, remind me of you.'

She laughed again, and all the men except Atlas Flynn and Mr
Batt applauded, and when Mr Batt saw what the men were up to
he clapped his hands also. The men went to the bar for more
beer. The youth from Gwadan asked her not to forget the book
she'd mentioned, *Attached to Doctor Marchmont*. He would under-

stand that too, he said, and she promised faithfully she wouldn't forget it. She smiled generously at the youth and at all the men she served, ignoring Atlas Flynn, who was standing there in a sulk.

In the public bar a few of the drinkers asked Mr Tuke where his daughter was since she was usually present at lunchtime. Conjecturing at the truth, he said she was resting in her room. It had occurred to him that she had heard about the scene in the hall —perhaps, even, Miss Gomez had told her—and was feeling shy, being by nature shy.

Alban Roche entered the Windrush Café in Abyssinia Street and ordered bacon, sausages, toast and tea. Abyssinia Street was bustling and lively, not unlike Crow Street once had been. In seven years' time it was to go, to make way for an arterial road. 'Damn cheek,' the woman behind the counter was saying to a regular customer, referring to this fact. 'I've lived here all my life.'

Other people in the café took up the complaint, saying that Abyssinia Street mightn't be much compared to the West End but at least it was home to them. 'Me and Sidney was walking over towards Crow Street last night,' a woman said. 'A bloody wilderness.' They talked about Crow Street while Alban Roche listened. Extraordinary to see it, they said, the last street standing, with pets in a shop window and a public house doing business. 'Mrs Bassett runs that pet shop,' one said, a bus conductress. 'She's fighting them for rights.' But the woman behind the counter shook her head: Mrs Bassett wasn't fighting no one, she divulged, having died in her bed the night before. A milkman had told her that.

He sprinkled pepper over his food. Would someone ask who'd inherited the pet shop? Would the woman serving say that she'd heard it was the youth who'd been had up for messing around in a women's changing-rooms? He waited, his head bent over his plate, but they were talking again about their own street, about a petition they planned. They were indignant and upset, as the people of Crow Street once had been; they were busy with all that.

'And did you have other thoughts?' the psychiatrist in the prison had asked him, Dr Krig in his grey suit. 'You stood in the empty changing-rooms, Alban: for a moment before you touched the women's clothes were you aware of particular thoughts?' He was a bald man with a long-stemmed pipe. He played with the pipe, moving it from hand to hand while he asked his questions. He never lit it, or even filled it with tobacco. Most of his questions were impossible to answer, requiring replies that were too private to utter: after three visits Dr Krig hadn't come back again.

On the squared paper of a science notebook he had more privately written: *She knitted; sometimes she'd smile. And even then, in the room with her, other women spoke to me, saying they wanted to feel my palms on their bosoms. She died in agony and all the time I could no longer care. I hated both of us.*

He'd stood at the bus-stop outside the badminton club, pretending to be waiting. He'd seen the women, in twos or threes, carrying badminton rackets in their sports bags. Badminton was a winter game: it was always dark on the short drive that led to the club, or in the car park where he often stood also, among macrocarpa trees at one end. He saw the women's faces, their legs moving under mackintoshes or tweed coats, an umbrella held on occasion against rain. Often when they stepped off the bus they glanced at him, a passing glance, hardly anything at all. That one always caught a bus at this time, they might perhaps have thought, and then forgotten him.

Through scratches on the white-painted glass he saw the women again, descending three concrete steps into a green changing-room. He watched, as in the past he'd watched the girl from the razor-blade factory in Egan's Café eating jam doughnuts. The girl had come out and got on to her bicycle and ridden away; these women stayed chatting to one another, swinging their sports bags, unbuttoning their coats. They were all ages, some as young as the girl, others much older. They opened green lockers and hung their coats inside. They kicked their shoes off or tidily removed them. Low green-painted racks, like tables made of slats, stretched between the lockers, towards the centre of the changing-room. On these lay the sports bags from which the women now lifted, almost ceremoniously, white, ironed clothes.

They undid the buttons of the dresses they wore, zips were unzipped. Standing in petticoats, they released their stockings or the suspenders that held them up, or rolled down tights. They removed their petticoats and stepped into white shorts or pleated skirts, and drew on white blouses. Sometimes they changed their underclothes beneath this modest protection, sometimes not. Over socks that were white also they tied the laces of their canvas shoes, and threw a white cardigan about their shoulders.

Afterwards in the lockers the clothes were occasionally still warm, soft to his fingers, scented and personal. His hands touched nylon blouses in many colours, and the silky velveteen of dresses, and fine tweed skirts, jumpers, stockings and other garments. He grasped materials in his hands, closing his eyes, imagining their previous proximity. Often he raised a garment to his cheek and pressed it there, embracing it. He wanted to take things away but he did not ever dare.

He hated it, the first time he'd heard the talk, when he was at the Christian Brothers. He'd hated the words, the descriptions and the thoughts they caused. When he went home to her he felt different, although he'd said nothing himself and hadn't even wanted to listen. It was being alone with her that made the difference: it was returning to the house and finding her there, with no one else. It was remembering the laughter and the jokes, the story that Gerald Murphy told about how he'd spent a night in the same room as his sister at a seaside hotel and how the barman of the hotel had come into the room in the darkness and had entered his sister's bed. Walking home together, the boys would listen carefully, not interrupting, while Gerald Murphy told of what he'd heard the barman saying and what he'd heard his sister saying, and the noises they'd made. Another boy said he'd had a nightmare one night and had run into his parents' room, embarrassing them by switching on the light. Boys from farms talked about animals. Others told the story about the honeymoon couple who'd imagined the facts of life were something else entirely, and about the nun and the candles, and the travelling salesman who became involved in the darkness with a hornet's nest instead of a boarding-house keeper's daughter. In private places Gerald Murphy passed round his pack of playing-cards, with the same woman stepping into the same bath on the back of each.

'Tell me everything,' she'd murmur, waiting for him with scones she'd baked, or hot sponge-cake. Her arms went round him always when he returned to the house, her lips touched his face. 'We're happy, aren't we?' she'd say, quite often, after he'd left the Christian Brothers for the counter of the post office. Her eyes went blank only when he said that maybe he'd go out that evening. 'Out?' she'd say. It didn't happen often, and then not at all, because he discovered soon his isolation from other people, from everyone except her.

In the Windrush Café he cut the lean out of the bacon he'd been given and pushed the fat to one side. He remembered it all, the shame and the isolation, and the love he'd felt for her, which had hardened into canker without his even knowing. Love had always been part of his life until she died, and now there was love again, coming like a silent conversation from a girl who was as silent as he was. It would make him weep, this love, it was too much for him: what did she know of the truth, and of ugliness, any more than his mother had? It could not be, this love, and yet there was something that must be because of it. There was a chance to take and Crow Street would soon be gone, separating them forever. She would not spurn him, nor cry out as the woman in the car park of the badminton club had so fearfully cried out.

Around him the people still talked about demolition. He stirred sugar into his tea and drank it. 'Hi, courageous,' a girl had said to him the first night he walked the Soho streets. She'd smiled at him, saying that her place was only a yard away. Five pounds it would cost him, she said, taking his arm. Her hair was the colour of inexpensive brass, her peaked face was thin, she didn't seem healthy. He'd wanted to be gentle with that unhealthy girl, to make her lie down and cover her with warm blankets, to make her Ovaltine, which often he'd made for his mother when she said she was feeling tired and mightn't sleep. He'd walked five paces with her: she swore at him when he turned away from her.

In the café he paid for the food he'd eaten. 'Ta muchly, dear,' the woman said. Outside, he felt the sun hot on him again, in Abyssinia Street, so curiously named.

He walked, knowing where she would be. He knew the streets she'd go to because he knew why she had gone there. He recalled the heels of her feet slightly raised from her sandals and the way she hadn't turned to face him, and her yellow dress, which you could see through when she stood in bright sunlight, and her long, smooth hair.

On the palms of his hands sweat broke as he walked and thought about her, her body beneath the yellow dress, her warm feet.

X

In the privacy of a lavatory at her school the schoolgirl who had answered the advertisement in *Make Friends in London* read again the letter she had received in reply that morning. *Tell us please the facts of your life,* the Reverend Lloyd Patterson had written, and *let the emptiness within you be filled with the Spirit of Our Lord Jesus Christ. Share your mind with your Brethren, let the emptiness be filled.*

The girl, who suffered agonies every day because of the acne on her face, wept slightly in the lavatory, not knowing how to write down on paper that she was troubled because of spots. How could she say that people looked at her and quickly looked away, that often she trembled in nervous horror at the memory of her reflected face? It was too small a thing, and yet it coloured all her life. It had become her life affecting the words she spoke and the gestures she made, affecting how she walked, her head bent slightly, away from light. Other girls' complexions were not pure, but none was affected to the extent that hers was. Teachers were sorry for her and some other girls were too: she would have told them she didn't want their pity if she'd dared to say anything at all. A month or so ago she'd taken to praying and had kept the activity private because neither her parents nor the girls in her school prayed. She prayed as a last resort, complaining that she felt an abnormal species, less than other people because of the plague she bore. But her prayers had only made her feel lonelier: she wanted other people, she wanted it not to matter to them, she wanted them to be special enough, and different, not even to notice. When she'd seen the advertisement she'd found herself staring at it, and a moment later told herself that this was some answer to the prayers she'd made.

Yet now even writing to strangers seemed too difficult: what words were there to make them understand that while other people suffered and died she thought only of spots on her face? Somewhere there were words, she murmured to herself, looking at the letter she'd received. She'd probably fail to find them but she knew she'd write anyway, clumsily if she had to. She hid the letter inside her clothes and left the lavatory.

Mrs Drate, whose husband had dropped to his death from the roof of their rectory, wrote to the Reverend Lloyd Patterson, saying she would endeavour to rise above her husband's crime in the knowledge that there was a greater pattern laid down. She would endeavour to accept that she had lost her faith only that she might regain it more joyfully. She would continue to pray, and she would take some comfort from the knowledge that strangers were praying for her in Jamaica.

Having written that, Mrs Drate paused: he'd have died, she thought, to know that she'd got mixed up with an obscure foundation without credentials; he'd have been shocked to the core, believing so strongly that only the blessed compromise of the Church of England made any kind of sense. He'd died anyway, poor man, maybe because it hadn't made sense enough. *It was the strangest thing in my life,* she wrote, *that I noticed your advertisement on paper wrapped round a piece of fish. Even now I don't know why I decided to write to you. Perhaps the best things are the things we don't know about?*

In a post office in Holborn the cinema usher who had also answered the advertisement wrote: *I have never in my life made a public speech, but if it has been given to you through prayer that I must take the word of our Church into the market-place, then I will do so, with Our Lord's help. I am enclosing a sum for the Harvest of the Tithes.*

He attached a money-order to his letter and sealed and addressed the envelope. He posted it and then walked out into the busy street. He at once addressed the passers-by, standing with his back to the window of a tobacconist's shop. He raised his voice above the noise of the traffic and the voices of other people. He said: 'Then said Jesus, Father, forgive them, for they know not what they do.' He paused and then repeated the words. 'My friends, listen to me,' he urged. 'My friends.' He paused again, the passers-by did not. He said: 'The Church of the Brethren of the Way takes these words as its power and its glory. Forgive them, for they know not. The Church of my Brethren does not turn its back: it prays eternally for those diseased of crime, for those who are hopeless and in distress. Through prayer for others we may live again. We condemn no one.'

Jehovah's Witnesses, the people passing thought, R.C.s, Baptists, Methodists, Seventh Day Adventists, the ones who didn't believe in doctors: they were all much of a muchness, with their God-bothering and getting in your way on the street.

'We condemn no one,' said the cinema usher again.

At five to two the last of the labourers left. In the private lounge Mrs Tuke emptied ashtrays, occasionally glancing at herself in one of the mirrors and raising a hand to her hair. Her husband collected empty glasses that some of the men had carried to the pavement outside in order to drink in the sun. Crow Street was silent again.

She climbed the stairs, feeling tired. She felt heavy as well, after her few drinks and the cheese-and-tomato sandwich. There was nothing like a good rest when you were like that, shoes falling to the floor, the pillow soft and cool, the curtains drawn against the glare. No fun for the outsize figure, weather like this; a strain on the organs, she'd heard it said.

'Mrs Tuke.'

He was waiting for her on the first-floor landing, his head poked out at her. The thought of having to shout at him made her weaker. She felt as though there was something in her bones that weighed them down.

'Mrs Tuke, did you mean it when you said that I couldn't come to the Arab's Head with you? I was counting on it, actually, Mrs Tuke. I hadn't made other arrangements.'

He was smiling his skeleton's smile at her. A dribble had come from his mouth and was running down his chin. Last winter, she'd noticed, his nose constantly needed blowing.

'It's quite unsuitable for you,' she shouted. 'Completely unsuitable in every possible way. Excuse me, Mr Batt.'

She went by him and visited the lavatory. When she came out he'd gone.

Mr Tuke locked the doors that led to the street. He smoked while rinsing the glasses. Rebel occupied his usual place on the upholstered bench, beneath a clock that advertised a brand of whisky. There was tobacco smoke in the air and a tang of sweat and dust, and a smell of beer. With a grey dish-cloth he dried the plates from which sandwiches had been eaten, wiping away traces of mustard and piccalilli. He'd go up to Prudence's room and try and think of something to say to her. He'd carry her up a couple of sandwiches and a glass of shandy after he'd fed Rebel in the kitchen.

'Come on then,' he said, and the dog jumped from his resting place and crossed the bar to him. He bent down to stroke the tawny head. Rebel licked his face.

They passed through the hall and for a moment he paused, standing where she'd stood when he'd first noticed her, on his way downstairs that morning. The hall looked different, he thought. The table and the chairs, the pictures, the hallstand, the birds, the clock he wound up on Thursdays: everything seemed to gleam in the hall, as though life had been breathed into inanimate objects. At the turn of the stairs the stained-glass window looked brighter than before. The imagination played funny tricks, he thought.

In the kitchen Rebel ate slowly, pushing at the food with his nose before accepting it for mastication. Mr Tuke sat on the edge of the kitchen table, his cropped grey head bent, his chin thrown in on his chest. He was thinking that when they lived in the Arab's Head he'd maybe begin going to Craven Cottage again on a Saturday afternoon to see Fulham play. It wasn't far, along the Upper Richmond Road, over Putney Bridge. He'd probably miss the beginning of the matches due to the lunchtime opening, but in the past he'd always missed the beginning and it hadn't really mattered much. 'You all right?' he said, addressing the dog, and Rebel looked up at him and wagged his tail. He'd bought him when he was only two months old from a Colonel Masters in Sutton, who went in specially for Alsatians. 'He'll grow as high as your shoulder,' Colonel Masters had said, glancing at the brief stature of the man before him. He'd given a little laugh and Mr Tuke had laughed also.

Together they went upstairs, Mr Tuke carrying the sandwiches and the shandy. As they crossed the first-floor landing the face of Eddie Mercer appeared, as though thrown on to a screen in his mind. Eddie Mercer had climbed these stairs also, making jokes on the way probably. 'Who's that small man when he's at home?' he imagined him jocularly saying, adding that he hoped the small man wasn't at home tonight. He remembered Eddie Mercer drunk one time, leaning across the bar and seizing him by the back of the neck with one hand. The grip had hurt him, the points of the fingers were like steel driving into his neck muscles. Blood had come into his head, his feet had left the ground. 'I could eat you off a plate,' Eddie Mercer had said.

He knocked on her bedroom door, but there was no reply. He opened it and found she wasn't there. She'd made her bed, the room was tidy.

In the cottage hospital at Rose St Margaret Miss Gomez was bound hand and foot while Dr D'Arcy prodded at her head with a slender instrument. Dr Tom Airley was in attendance also, and Dr Chris Willson and Dr Marchmont and Dr Finlay, Dr Cameron and Dr Snoddy. 'A dangerous savage,' said Dr Snoddy. But Dr D'Arcy said that no conclusion must be jumped at until a thorough investigation of Gomez's brain-box was made. 'Definitely dangerous,' said Dr Marchmont.

Mrs Tuke, herself in the uniform of a nurse, starched and spotless with a pleasant smile on her face, stood modestly in the background. She might have spoken about the patient, but it was not her place to do so. She might have said that the patient had sex as well as religion on the brain; a lot of them were like that, insatiable to a degree. 'A black whore,' said Dr Chris Willson, and Dr D'Arcy added that as far as he could see the whore's brain-box was entirely corroded. 'They don't wear hats,' said Dr Snoddy, but Dr D'Arcy said he didn't think it was that. What had happened was that the patient had caught a social disease, which had led to madness. Dr Marchmont agreed. He'd read a case like it, he said, in the *Sunday Express*.

'Speak to the patient,' Dr D'Arcy ordered her. 'Ask her the questions.'

She came forward. She laughed because she couldn't help herself. 'What was it like?' she cried. 'All those men in your brothel? What was it like, Gomez?'

The doctor leaned forward, wishing to know, and she leaned forward herself because she wished to know also. It was important that Gomez should give this information, that she should talk as much as possible, telling them what it was like in every detail. 'Men you never saw before,' Dr Marchmont reminded her, but Gomez did not say anything. Which was typical of her condition.

The doctors disbanded then, all of them except Dr D'Arcy. She helped him off with his smock and rubber gloves; she untied the mask that covered his mouth. 'I'm going for a spin over to Villierscourt,' he said. 'Care to come, Nurse?'

They stood in the summer garden. 'Nurse Villiers,' he said, 'is going to the Summer Ball with Dr Redgrave.' He looked away from her while he spoke. Sir Guy Villiers kept open house for all the hospital staff, which made it seem wrong, somehow, that she and Dr D'Arcy should be together so much in the gardens of Sir Guy's mansion, since it was an understood thing in Rose St Margaret that Desmond D'Arcy and Monica Villiers would one day marry.

'Monica's in love with Bob Redgrave,' he said. 'They're going to marry.'

She couldn't reply. His words were honey, too beautiful to question in case she had cruelly misheard. He took her hand and led her down the lichen-covered steps to the rose garden. It was late in the evening, although still warm. The shadows of Sir Guy's yew trees were long on the soft grass between the rose-beds. 'My darling,' Desmond D'Arcy said.

His lips were damp when they touched hers, and then she was lying on the surface of a rose-bed. She could feel thorns on the flesh of her legs. Her feet were bare, her heels pressed into the warm soil. He embraced her, his hands gripped her shoulders. 'I fancy you, Beryl,' he said, and she could smell the odour of sweat trapped in his clothes and acrid tobacco smoke coming from his mouth and the rich odour of hair-grease.

She tried to call out, to tell him that a rose-bush was squashed beneath her, causing her pain, but no words would come. She felt blood running on her back and heard her own laughter, although she didn't seem to be laughing. 'Miss Gomez darling,' she said, 'we don't like that kind of talk in the Thistle.'

He was merciless, like a machine encompassing her. His teeth were in her flesh, some terrible part of him was wrenching her apart. 'In Tacas they pray for you also,' the black whore said, 'because you have attempted to destroy your daughter. Are you frightened of our prayers, Beryl?' ·

She closed her eyes and no longer resisted the thorns of the rose-bush. Her body sank into the thorns and the soil; she felt no more pain. Her arms tightened the other body to her. She felt the teeth again and tightened the arms more, for the teeth were cool and hard and pleasant, the teeth of Eddie Mercer. 'There's no one like you, Eddie,' her voice cried out. 'Oh God above, Eddie!' He was terrible, not leaving her alone, not ever stopping, snorting like an animal. She hated the coarseness of him, she could have hit him with a length of piping, she hated the odour he had, and his discoloured underclothes, and the filth that was pouring out of his mouth. 'Oh God, I love you!' she shouted. 'Oh God, Eddie! Oh God! Oh God!'

Mr Batt awoke after his afternoon rest at half-past three. His eyes opened in an abrupt way and remained open. He'd wash his hands and face, he thought, and then he'd put his jacket on and go for a stroll. He'd watch the bulldozers and the men at work, standing a safe distance away.

Often in the afternoon he went over to the pet shop and accepted a cup of tea if Mrs Bassett had one going. He talked about old times, about Henry Bassett and himself setting off in 1914, which had been, of course, before her time in Crow Street. She'd have been a young girl then, about the age of Prudence Tuke. Henry Bassett had been working in a shop in Abyssinia Street, or in Harrington Lane, he couldn't remember which: a shop that mainly went in for selling dogs.

Mrs Bassett hadn't been able to get used to the idea of leaving Crow Street because she didn't want Henry Bassett's name trodden into the ground, which was how she saw it. Perhaps he'd been luckier himself in how death had left him, with nothing like that to worry about. Knowing the Thistle so well, he hadn't minded moving in and it was pleasanter, really, than trying to cope on his own in the rooms above the hardware shop. He'd gone on working in the shop for another two years and then, because of age, he'd retired. In all he'd spent sixty years there, standing behind a counter that had become far more familiar to him than his own face. He'd once estimated, just for the fun of it, that he'd sold nine tons of nails and over a million cup-hooks. He hadn't minded; he'd quite enjoyed it, talking to people while he counted things out, passing the time of day. He didn't mind now, when he passed the shop, its windows so dirty that you couldn't see through them. In a way it seemed quite right, and nicer than seeing other people serving there. He yawned, thinking that he'd explain all that to Mrs Bassett and see if it made it easier for her to come to terms with the destruction of her husband's memorial. Poor thing, he thought, to worry so, and then he remembered that the night before she'd died.

He thought about that for a few minutes and then he left his room and went to the bathroom to wash his face. When he returned he noticed the envelope in which he'd placed his Giant Jackpot entry and the sight of it reminded him of other events that had taken place that day. 'I'll tell you one thing, Batt,' she'd said. 'Unsuitable,' she'd said, 'in every way.'

He didn't want to think about it. He whistled, not hearing the sound but knowing that the sound was there. He'd post the letter at once; he wouldn't bother to watch the demolition. He'd walk over to Abyssinia Street and post it there, and then he'd order a wreath for Mrs Bassett. Chrysanthemums, he decided, because he knew they'd been her favourite flower, and then he wondered if you could get chrysanthemums in the middle of summer, you saw them more at Christmastime.

Mr Batt was still thinking about chrysanthemums as he emerged from the Thistle Arms, not wishing to depress himself with the other matter. But as he passed the pet shop the thought was forced upon him that if he couldn't accompany the Tukes to the public house near the botanical gardens he'd as soon be dead like Mrs Bassett was, and Henry Bassett, and his own wife and his two sons. What on earth was the point at his time of life in starting off a completely new existence in some boarding-house? With the Tukes, he'd come to think of himself as one of the family, and in the establishment in Kew there'd at least have been their familiar faces. Even if the food that Mrs Tuke cooked wasn't always pleasant to have to eat, at least he knew what to expect and he could tell by the smell if it was a good idea not to turn up for a particular meal. He might move from boarding-house to boarding-house, trying to find somewhere congenial, wandering like a tramp all over London in search of people who understood an elderly person's ways.

All the way to the post-box in Abyssinia Street Mr Batt carried with him the notion of death. It didn't cast him down. He had feared death at Hazebrouck and in the mud of Passchendaele, and most of all at Lassigny, on August 8th, a few months before the whole thing was over. Afterwards they'd said that August 8th was the German Army's blackest day, yet not only he had feared death at Lassigny: everyone had, thinking that luck couldn't hold out much longer. 'Blimey, I'm tired of it,' a chap beside him had said, a chap called Gribbens who'd afterwards killed himself, by shooting into the roof of his mouth.

You could kill yourself by taking a full bottle of aspirin, or by taking weed-killer. He'd read of a man who'd wired himself to the bathroom light and then immersed himself in warm water before turning on the light-switch with a brush. You could seal a room by placing cushions at the door and windows, and then turn on the gas-jets of a cooker. You could hang yourself with braces or a tie or a length of flex. You could cut your arteries, but that sounded painful. Aspirins were the best: you'd lie down for your afternoon rest one day and take a bottleful with a glass of water. You'd go to sleep in the usual way and you wouldn't wake up.

He posted his entry-form in a pillar-box not far from the Windrush Café in Abyssinia Street.

'A wreath,' he said in a flower and vegetable shop. 'Chrysanthemums?'

The boy in charge said something that Mr Batt couldn't quite catch. He smiled at the boy and put his hand up to his left ear, pushing his head forward to indicate that he hadn't heard. 'Pardon me?' he said.

The boy spoke again but still Mr Batt had difficulty. The boy went away and returned with a woman.

'A friend has died,' said Mr Batt. 'I was wondering about a wreath. Chrysanthemums were her favourite flower.'

The woman shouted at him. He could see that she was shouting. Her words came clearly to him: chrysanthemums were out of season.

'No need to shout,' he said politely, smiling at the woman.

'We could do you roses,' she said.

'Eh?'

'Roses,' shouted the woman, and he agreed on roses. 'You need a deaf-aid, Dad,' she shouted at him when he'd paid. 'You're hard of hearing.'

He shook his head: he could hear her perfectly, he explained. In any case, who wanted to hear everything that was going on these days? There was a lot of unpleasantness about.

'Definitely,' said the woman, but since he was sorting out his change he didn't catch the word. He'd call in again, he promised, and let her know when the funeral was and where the wreath should be sent. Fuchsia was his own favourite flower, he said, if there should ever be a query about that. His name was A. J. Batt, he added.

'Miss Gomez.'

In her room she heard the voice, coming from somewhere in the house. Holding in her hand the letter she'd written the night before and had added to that morning, she left her room and walked past Mrs Bassett's sitting-room to the top of the stairs. 'Yes?' she said, going down the stairs, meeting him on the way up.

146

His eyes were very wide; excited and fearful. He was in his shirtsleeves, as invariably he was, his waistcoat hanging open. She thought she saw a shiver pass through his hands.

'Yes, Mr Tuke?' she said.

'Prudence isn't there. She's not in her room. She didn't come to help at lunchtime.'

She put the air-mail letter in the pocket of her leather dress and took from the pocket cigarettes and matches.

'I haven't seen your daughter, Mr Tuke. Not since this morning.' She held out the packet of cigarettes to him but he didn't take one. His dog approached her, to lick her legs. She lit a cigarette.

'Where is Roche, Miss Gomez?'

'In the shop.'

'No, he's not.'

'He's always there at this time. Perhaps he's in the lavatory—'

'You said this morning—'

'Yes, I did.'

'Did Roche tell you something? Why did you say those things?' She went downstairs, pushing past him.

'Mr Roche!' she called out. 'Mr Roche! Mr Roche!'

She mounted the stairs again, her cigarette between her fingers. She opened the doors and looked into rooms. 'Mr Roche!' she called again, but still no answer came.

'Miss Gomez—'

'Excuse me, Mr Tuke.'

She went away and he heard water running in the bathroom. He thought that maybe she was getting a drink because she felt faint, or cooling her forehead for the same reason.

'I don't know what to say,' she said when she returned. 'This had to happen because your daughter has your daughter's nature and Alban Roche has his. We prayed, Mr Tuke. I spoke this morning. My Church and I did all we could.'

She was like a thin queen standing there, he thought, and then was angry for thinking that. With her dotty talk she could easily have put some terrible idea into Roche's head. God knows what she'd said to Roche.

'I'm sorry, Mr Tuke,' she said.

'You could cause any kind of damage, talking irresponsibly.' His voice was thick with nervousness and anger. He stumbled in his speech. 'If Prudence has been injured you deserve to be locked away.'

'I prayed against injury to your daughter, Mr Tuke.'

'She's not my daughter.'

She nodded, not surprised. She drew on her cigarette. In the bathroom she'd been sick into the wash-basin, and now she felt sickness in her stomach again. The truth she'd seen in Alban Roche's eyes was a reality now: it was all around her and around this small bearded man who was not the girl's father. The truth had happened, pushing prayer aside. She had failed, her Church had failed.

'I spoke,' she said. 'This morning I spoke, and nobody listened.' She could think of nothing else to say.

'I listened—'

'And he said to them all, "If any man will come after me, let him deny himself and take up his cross daily, and follow me".'

He gestured emotionally with his hands. He climbed the stairs and went close to her.

'What has happened?' he said.

'In that hall if we'd have knelt together—'

'Oh for God's sake, how could we kneel! What d'you think we are, Miss Gomez? You upset my wife. You were talking wildly—'

'He said He would send prophets and apostles. Some, He said, would slay and persecute.'

He felt again the feeling that her presence caused in him, but such feelings were no use to him now. He turned and limped down the stairs, with Rebel following him. He thought she might speak again, but no sound came from her. She was a wretched, peculiar girl, who through her involvement with a half-baked religious sect had caused all hell to break out in Crow Street.

He passed through the pet shop, where the birds chirped in their cages and the guinea-pigs squeaked. 'Thank you very much!' shrieked the crested mynah, and the parrot called Godfrey said nothing. A hamster rattled on its wheel, the cockatiel didn't laugh.

Eddie Mercer pushed her, and then other people pushed her: the red-haired labourer, and Dr Marchmont, and her husband.

She could see her husband's beard. He was shaking her roughly, and increasingly. She was feeling unwell. She tried to smile at him, hoping he'd let her return to sleep.

'Prudence has gone,' he said.

Air escaped with a slight noise from her mouth. Her eyelids were like ton weights. 'Pru?' she said. 'Gone for the mince?'

'She didn't come in at lunchtime. She's not in her room.'

'Pru?'

'Roche isn't in the pet shop.'

It was most unlike him to disturb her in this way, with information about the movements of her daughter and one of their lodgers. She had a feeling that it was still quite early, that she should have had at least another hour's sleep before it was time to think of going downstairs to fry the supper. Perhaps he'd gone queer with the heat, she sleepily mused; maybe he'd been walking outside without a hat.

'She's not here,' he repeated. 'She's not here, Beryl.'

'Pru's out for a walk, old chap. She's out seeing a friend. Or maybe chatting to old Batt. Is old Batt in his room, darling?'

'Old Batt has nothing to do with it—'

'Batty old Batt,' said Mrs Tuke, and laughed.

'For God's sake, Beryl!'

Laughing had made her feel unwell again. There was a pain at the bottom of her stomach, over towards the left. The sourness, which was always prevalent at this time of the day, began higher up. She didn't want to talk about Pru or Alban Roche or old Batt. Why ever couldn't the man take his dog for a trot and leave her in peace?

The dream came back to her then. She saw herself in the gardens of Villierscourt with Dr D'Arcy and then he'd become the red-haired labourer and then Eddie Mercer. She closed her eyes, trying to return to sleep, but he wouldn't let her. He was pushing at her again, leaning on top of her and muttering at her hysterically, like Gomez. 'My God!' she said, remembering Gomez, suddenly aware of what he was on about.

'They've both disappeared,' he was saying, addressing her in a more lively manner than she had heard him employ for years. She'd have smiled to see the bounce in him again if it hadn't been for what he was on about.

'Miss Gomez put it into his head,' he said.

She opened her eyes. The first part of the dream came back to her: Gomez in the cottage hospital, lying there on the operating table. 'Completely corroded,' said Dr D'Arcy.

'Miss Gomez put it into his head,' he repeated. He went to the window and Rebel followed him.

It wasn't true, she said; he was talking nonsense. She pushed herself off the bed and poked her feet into her slippers.

'It's not true,' she said again and when he didn't reply she raised her voice, pointing out that she was addressing him.

'She hasn't been here since early morning,' he said.

'Pru often goes out. If you believed it was true you'd have rung up the police station. Have you rung up the police station?'

He shook his head. She said:

'Gomez says stuff like that in order to get attention to herself. There's neither rhyme nor reason in a black lump like that.'

'Roche—'

'Roche has stuff to attend to with Mrs Bassett's death. Most likely he's in a solicitor's office.'

'He never leaves the pets.'

'He leaves them at night.'

'At night?'

'He leaves the animals at night, doesn't he? He doesn't sleep in a cage, does he?'

'It's odd, that's all. It's worrying—'

'It isn't the least bit odd. What's odd about a girl going out for a walk when she spends half her life going out for a walk? What's odd about a fellow in a solicitor's discussing a property he's inherited six hours ago? Roche has compensation money to receive.

He has new premises to find for himself. Roche can't just sit there on his b.t.m., you know. Not when they're on the point of pulling the street down.'

'Miss Gomez—'

'That name is taboo in my bedroom,' cried Mrs Tuke with sudden vehemence. 'Gomez was employed here without anyone knowing she was a common prostitute. Gomez is as nutty as a fried fruitcake.'

'Miss Gomez said Prudence had a fixation on Roche.'

'That's bloody not true. You know perfectly well that's a load of wholesale bloody rubbish. And while I think of it, there's another thing: I'd rather you didn't bring cut men into my kitchen, bleeding all over the bread. If you want to bring cut men into the house, telephone for a qualified doctor, like any normal human being. If the slightest thing goes wrong with that man's hand he'll have us up in the courts. I'd just like to point that out to you,' she said, finding her smile in an effort to clear away the nastiness. 'D'you understand, old chap?'

He sighed. She put an arm about his shoulder and told him to cheer up. 'Gomez caught insanity from syphilis,' she said. 'Her brainbox is totally corroded.'

'I'm frightened,' he said, as though he hadn't been listening to anything she'd said.

He left the room and the dog followed him closely. She heard them descending the stairs, the limping footfall of her husband and the scraping noise that Rebel's paws always made on the linoleum. The sounds made her uneasy although they were familiar to her. She felt suddenly very wide awake and knew that she'd not be able to sleep again. She crossed the room to her bedside table and picked up *Dr D'Arcy's Love*, but for once she was unable to concentrate. Her eyes kept jumping from the print, and her mind filled with the dream she'd had and then, yet again, with all that had happened during the day. She returned to the window and stood there, leaning against the woodwork. Pru was dreamy. She forgot things, like she'd forgotten this mince; sometimes she had the appearance of a girl doing things in her sleep. But she'd always come back, she'd always remembered to do that.

151

Mrs Tuke looked down into Crow Street. She'd been wearing a yellow dress, she remembered, a dress she'd made for herself because she liked making clothes, although in Mrs Tuke's opinion the colours she chose were all wrong. Any moment now the yellow dress would appear and above it Pru's long hair, which was the next thing you noticed about her after her clothes. Poor Pru, she thought.

She remembered the infant in her husband's arms and her own reflections at the time: she could have loved the child if her father had been what she wished of a man, a chap who was handsome and charming, tender with a woman. Such a father might have disappeared out of her life for ever and it wouldn't have mattered: there'd be no memory of the stench in the gents' toilet and the whispered filth. There'd have been a pride to take in the deception and in the child, in the simple beauty of everything.

She remained at the window, and Crow Street remained empty. Neither her daughter in the yellow dress nor the slender form of Alban Roche appeared. No breeze rustled the scattered litter. No animal of any kind moved. Mrs Tuke shivered, for the first time in her life finding Crow Street eerie.

The labourers finished for the day. They went in different directions and in different houses cleaned the dust of the demolition off areas of skin, and changed their clothes. Atlas Flynn, with three others, ate mutton-and-vegetable soup, with barley, and then some of the mutton that had been boiled in this way, with potatoes and parsnips. Their landlady prided herself on wholesome cooking: tapioca and stewed rhubarb she offered afterwards, and then tea and Marietta biscuits. At half-past seven the four men left their lodging-house. They boarded a bus, from the upper deck of which, ten minutes later, they saw Alban Roche. He was walking alone and they drew one another's attention to his solitariness. They were interested for a moment because of the premonition of Miss Gomez. They craned their necks. He didn't mix much, one of the four remarked and another said that it was the sight of him, with the long hair, that had put the notion into Miss Gomez's mind. They forgot about him then. In the Cruiskeen

Bawn lounge of the George public house in Hammersmith they drank a quantity of stout before going on to the Emerald Isle Club.

The sky was red. Drivers of vehicles moving westward found the glare of the setting sun an irritant, others remarked on the prettiness of the effect. Crossing the wasteland on which earlier he'd observed the cats, Alban Roche was struck by the crimson landscape: unreal, he thought, like something invented, or something from a dream. He paused for a moment on the wasteland, looking all around it. Then he hurried on, to settle the pets down for the night.

XI

The police were everywhere. They stood around in the Thistle Arms, in the two bars, in the hall, on the first-floor landing, in the kitchen and in Prudence's room. Mr Tuke made them tea.

They poked about in the house that had been the Crow Street Dining-Rooms, and in Cave's Hardware, where Mr Batt had counted out nine tons of nails, and in the shell of the Snow White Laundry and the shell of the Palace Cinema.

'Patterson,' a Sergeant Gove said in Miss Gomez's room. 'A Dr Patterson would it be, miss?'

She said he was a clergyman, not a doctor, and Sergeant Gove wrote that down in a thick notebook. He apologized to Miss Gomez for taking so long in writing everything down: he didn't wish errors to creep in. Miss Gomez said she didn't see what her Church had to do with the fact that a girl was lost, and the Sergeant replied that while her point of view was understandable there were other facts to be considered also.

'You made statements this morning, miss. You implicated Mr Roche before the event. You talked about this Church of yours then.'

'I've failed and my Church has failed. I can't help you. I can't help myself; I can't help anyone. Nobody listens.'

'Did you at any time, miss, mention what was in your mind to Roche, or hint at it in any way?'

He'd come in, explaining that he was a police sergeant and then he'd given his name, which she'd now forgotten. She'd been writing her daily letter at the time, retailing everything that had taken place in the hall that morning, the insults that Mrs Tuke had shouted at her and the fact that she herself had ended in tears. She'd described how Mr Tuke had remained on the stairs

154

by the stained-glass window and how he'd moved down a few steps and had then stood still, how his dog had licked her and had licked her again that afternoon. She'd described the man who'd said his name was Atlas Flynn, and the way in which Mr Batt had been shouted at by Mrs Tuke also.

'Miss?' Sergeant Gove said.

She looked at him. He was a man with crinkly black hair. She asked him his name and he told her that it was Gove. She'd never spoken to Alban Roche in any kind of personal way at all, she said.

All day, ever since the occasion in the hall of the public house, she'd been unable to prevent herself weeping. After Mr Tuke had visited her she'd sat for what seemed like an hour, weeping until she thought she'd never cease. She'd taken off her spectacles and lain down on her bed, and the tears had rolled from the corners of her eyes down either side of her face, into her ears. Her Church was rubbishy, Mrs Tuke had said. *I have told you that you may know,* she'd written in her daily letter. *It's all no good.*

Miss Gomez in the presence of Sergeant Gove wept again. She sat on the edge of her bed, sobbing without making a noise. The information he'd gained at the Thistle Arms was that she'd been on the game in Soho and was now a religious case, which by the miserable look of her at present he could well believe.

'I'm sorry,' she said, blowing her nose. 'I'm sorry.'

'That's quite all right, miss. You take your time with it now.'

Sergeant Gove sighed, briefly closing his eyes without letting her see. He'd been roused from his bed at half-past four that morning because of a breaking and entering case which they seemed to think he could throw some special light on. He'd been working at it all day and had been on his way home when the call came in about the Tuke girl. 'We'd both better go,' Inspector Ponsonby had said, although in Sergeant Gove's opinion there'd been no necessity for that, nor indeed for the vast number of men that Ponsonby had seen fit to deploy as a search party at this early stage. 'Makes your blood fair boil,' Ponsonby had remarked in the squad car. Typical of him it was, saying they'd both better go.

'So you think, miss, that you didn't actually speak to Roche at any time about what was in your mind? You're sure of this now? Take your time, miss. Go back over any chats you may have had.'

She didn't reply. She was staring ahead of her, but he imagined she couldn't see properly because her glasses were all smeared. He'd like a nice cup of cocoa, he was thinking, followed by eleven hours' uninterrupted sleep. He sat there patiently pretending to read the few notes he'd made. Typical bloody Ponsonby, he thought again.

She hadn't sealed the letter in case something happened, some final development to report in what she already imagined would be her last letter to Tacas. *Your prayers have failed,* she'd written, *and I have mocked your failure with further failure on my part.* What good was a pattern and a meaning if no one wanted to know? What good was a God that no one could be bothered with?

'We could have stopped his crime,' she cried, on her feet again and causing Sergeant Gove to rise to his. 'If we'd prayed this morning in that hall we could have stopped him. If we could have brought him among us and prayed while he stood there, if we'd have shown him that we did not condemn.'

'That's possible of course,' said Sergeant Gove, considering it wise to say that.

'I'm not insane, you know.'

'Of course you're not—'

'I've always been considered insane. I have an obsession that has to do with an event when I was a child. I don't know why I'm alive, Mr Gove.'

'We none of us ask to be born, of course—'

'I think we do. I think we ask all the time. We ask and we promise. We promise to be worthy of our lives. Save me, O Lord, my mind cried out when I was two years old. Save me and I will follow in the path of Your Holy Son.'

'When did you last see Prudence Tuke, miss?'

She looked at him, not answering. She said:

'He called the twelve together, Mr Gove. He gave them authority over all devils, and to cure diseases. He sent them forth and he said unto them, "Take nothing for your journey, neither

156

staff, nor wallet, nor bread, nor money; neither have two coats."
There are devils and diseases everywhere, Mr Gove, and their
seeds are fear. Do you understand that, Mr Gove?'

He shook his head. He mentioned Prudence Tuke again, saying that the situation was an urgent one.

'Mrs Tuke's afraid of the truth,' she said. 'She's afraid of reality:
she cannot bear to see herself as she is. She lives in a mist of
alcohol and fantasy, but tonight reality has caught up with her.'

'Miss—'

'Reality is unpleasant, Mr Gove. Ask Mrs Tuke why she can't
love her daughter, Mr Gove, and ask her husband too.'

'When did you last see Prudence Tuke, miss?'

'Early this morning I saw her last. She was eating bread with
raspberry jam on it. She told me she loved Alban Roche. That was
the beginning of everything.'

'Loved, miss?'

'You're scratching about on a surface, Mr Gove. There was fear
also in the life of Alban Roche's mother. There was a terror of
being alone in a terraced house with no one to love and no love
to receive. Do not condemn that woman, Mr Gove, even though
she must bear the blame for the death of Prudence Tuke.'

Sergeant Gove questioned that. Miss Gomez said:

'Miss Arbuthnot was frightened of dying so she made herself a
heaven to go to. Around Miss Arbuthnot we sang hymns about
the King of Israel and I didn't even know who the King of Israel
was. I didn't even care because it wasn't important, because it had
all to do with Miss Arbuthnot and not with me.'

'I see,' said Sergeant Gove.

'These three women passed cruelty on, down into other people's lives. Only Mrs Tuke may be alive now. Miss Arbuthnot may
have died too, I don't know.'

'Well, thank you very much, miss—'

'Don't you see, there's nothing at all?' she cried, tears coming
again. 'Just awful human weakness, and cruelty passing from one
person to another? There's no pattern and no meaning, only
makeshift things like the King of Israel and a Church four thousand miles away that is ineffective when it comes to the point. We

live for no reason, Mr Gove. I'm alone as I've always been, and now I feel I cannot bear it.'

She wept, standing in the centre of the room, and he thought he'd never seen weeping like it. Her mouth was open, her head thrown back, her eyes half-closed. Tears came like rain from her, dribbling over her cheeks and down her neck and her dress. Some fell to the floor or on to her shoes. She was intensely black, he thought, her shiny leather dress accentuating the impression. She was like some dark animal in pain, a creature that had been torn apart and lived on to suffer. He didn't understand what her trouble was even though she'd talked so much. He didn't go in much for religion himself, although his mother had, being quite a keen Methodist, but all that was a long time ago now.

She talked, stumblingly, though her distress. She mentioned some man who was incurable. 'The Lord made everything for its own end,' she cried. 'That was written down for me, Mr Gove. On blue air-mail paper he wrote that clearly down. There is an order, he wrote: of birth and life and death and glory: nothing happens by chance. All people are part of one another, no one is alone. All that he wrote for me, Mr Gove, to rid me of my fear of emptiness.'

Sergeant Gove thought at first that it was the incurable man who had done all this writing and then for a moment wondered if she referred in some symbolic way to the God she worshipped. In the end he realized that she had in mind the man she'd earlier mentioned, the clergyman in Jamaica.

She tried to speak again, but all he could hear her saying was that she was not insane. It would be easier to be mad, she cried, and then her voice was lost in weeping.

Not knowing what to do with her, he left her, reflecting that in a way she reminded him of old Betty Highchilde who used to preach when he was on the beat about fifteen years ago, except that old Betty Highchilde was a happier kind of person. 'The Father gave His Son,' she used to chant, and ask people where they were going. It was said that she came of an aristocratic background but he'd always found that hard to believe, since she dressed herself in rags and slept in the open when the weather was fine. He'd often passed a bench on which she'd stretched herself out. He'd never moved her on because she was harmless. Odd, that religious preoccupations so often made people unstable.

Inspector Ponsonby, who was a heavily-made man with some strands of grey hair drawn over a wide, bald dome and a moustache that was yellow from nicotine, shouted at Mr Batt.

'I'm telling you,' said Mr Batt. He'd got up at his usual time, he repeated, and had read the morning paper in the kitchen, waiting for Mrs Tuke to come downstairs and cook his breakfast. Mrs Tuke's daughter, who always got up earlier than anyone else, had had her breakfast already.

'Did you see her?' shouted Inspector Ponsonby. 'Did she seem depressed or anything?'

'No need to shout,' protested Mr Batt. He'd passed Mrs Tuke's daughter on the stairs, he on the way down to the kitchen and she on the way up. He'd said good morning to her and she had replied. He had then proceeded on his way, passing only the black cleaner. In the kitchen he had read the paper for one hour, waiting for Mrs Tuke.

'The only thing of interest that occurred,' said Mr Batt, 'was that in the middle of breakfast Mrs Tuke's daughter came into the kitchen and handed me a letter containing an invitation to take part in what they call a Giant Jackpot.'

Mr Batt handed the Inspector the letter, together with the leaflet and the sample gramophone record. He'd been given as well, he said, a lucky number and a certificate called a Once-In-A-Decade certificate. He'd already posted those back, he explained.

Theme Songs of the Big Band Era, Inspector Ponsonby read. *For an evening of fun, bring in your friends and neighbours and have them identify each theme with the bands that made them famous.*

'It was then that everything must have happened,' said Mr Batt. 'While attention was on that she stole the cigarettes.'

'Cigarettes?'

Mr Batt shook his head. 'Miss Gomez,' he said.

'Mr Batt—'

'A West Indian girl in glasses.'

'Excuse me,' said Inspector Ponsonby.

He left the room and went downstairs again. He hadn't spoken to Roche yet and he didn't intend to, not until he'd collected all the facts there were. 'O.K.?' he said to Constable Wigg, who was standing in the hall. He jerked his head up the stairs, and Constable Wigg understood this as a reference to the suspect's room. 'He's still there, sir,' he said.

In the kitchen young Akkers was standing by the door, posted there to make certain that the Tukes wouldn't do anything silly, like rushing up to Roche's room, as sometimes happened in cases like this. When the Inspector entered, Mrs Tuke was sitting at the table, staring ahead of her. Her husband was standing against the sink, with his Alsatian dog sitting on the floor by his feet. The dog's ears were cocked up and his mouth was slightly open. He made a growling noise when he saw the Inspector.

'Oh Inspector!' cried Mrs Tuke.

'No news,' he said quickly. 'Nothing at all. I've been attempting to talk to your Mr Batt. He says the girl handed him a letter while he was still at breakfast. This would appear to be the last time the girl was seen by members of the household. Am I right in that, please?'

Mr Tuke nodded.

'She had her yellow on,' Mrs Tuke said in a whisper.

'And there are no friends to whom she might have gone?'

Mr Tuke said he'd telephoned some girls with whom Prudence had been at school.

'No luck at all, sir?'

'No.'

With a hand that wasn't steady, Mrs Tuke pushed a cup of tea towards Inspector Ponsonby over the red Formica of the table. It was cool and milky and excessively sweet. He didn't usually take sugar in tea and he wondered why she'd added it without asking him first. Had they any reason to suspect that Roche had on a previous occasion made advances to their daughter? Had there been any trouble of that kind, with their daughter or anyone else, on the premises of the Thistle Arms? 'You didn't mind having him back,' he said, 'after he'd been in gaol?'

'He hadn't done much,' said Mr Tuke. He looked at the Inspector and then looked away again. His voice was nervous, seeming physically choked.

'Always paid the rent, did he?'

'Yes.'

'What would you call this Roche, Mrs Tuke? Hippy type, is he? Drop-out?'

'I suppose so.'

'No lady-friends, anything like that?'

Mr Tuke, still leaning against the sink, shook his head. Rebel had moved to where the Inspector was standing and was now licking his trousers. Constable Akkers, silent by the door, was thinking that the big woman had handed his superior a cup of tea which a moment before she had poured for him, of which in fact he'd had several sips. He'd placed it on the table when the Inspector had entered the kitchen, deeming it unwise to be seen with a cup of tea in his hand when on duty.

'Keeps himself to himself, eh?' Inspector Ponsonby said.

Mrs Tuke made a noise. She began to whisper vaguely, reminding her husband of the way she spoke in her sleep. Her daughter had grown away from her, she said. She'd taken her out a few times when she was younger, to buy clothes in the shops, but then everything had gone wrong. Poor Pru had begun collecting the stuff she kept in her room, going round junk places you wouldn't be seen dead in: she hadn't understood any of that at all, but even so she'd tried to do her best for the girl. There'd been a time when she'd hoped she might grow up like Deanna Durbin: she'd had a look of Deanna Durbin when she was fourteen. She'd often remarked it to her, but Pru hadn't been interested. She'd gone her own way, wandering off to the junk places, sitting silent at mealtimes.

'An extensive search is taking place for your daughter. Everything possible is being done.' The Inspector's tone had an edge of irritation to it due to the fact that both his trouser-legs were now unpleasantly damp from the Alsatian's continued licking. He'd moved away several times while trying to listen to Mrs Tuke, but Rebel had persistently followed him. 'Would you mind calling this dog off?' he sharply requested, not seeing why, no matter what the circumstances, he should have to put up with having his clothes made a muck of.

Mr Tuke murmured, and Rebel went to him.

'The girl's dead,' Mrs Tuke cried, with a shrillness that was startling. 'She's out there somewhere in the rubble. Pru's dead and gone—'

'Excuse me,' interrupted Inspector Ponsonby. 'Look after these people,' he commanded Constable Akkers.

He left the kitchen, the dampness of his trousers more uncomfortable when he walked. In the hall he found Sergeant Gove waiting for him.

'Gomez?' he said.

'Like old Betty Highchilde if ever you knew her, sir. Bag of rags who used to hang about the Mile End Road—'

'What the hell are you talking about, Gove?'

'Gomez is a religious lunatic.'

'What's that got to do with it?'

'It's just a fact, sir. The girl told her she was in love with Roche, sir.'

'In love?'

'Yes, sir.'

'Was Roche aware of this?'

'I don't know, sir. It's just what she said.'

'You've been over there half an hour, Gove: what else did she say?'

'She was on about religious matters, sir—'

'She told these people the girl was going to be assaulted. Did she mention any of that to Roche?'

'She says not, sir. She was on about Roche's mother—'

'I've heard about that, thank you very much.'

In the kitchen Mr Tuke asked Constable Akkers' permission to go to one of the bars and fetch his wife a drink. Constable Akkers said that would be all right. 'Thank you,' Mr Tuke said.

On his way through the hall he saw Inspector Ponsonby and Sergeant Gove mounting the stairs, the Inspector a step or two ahead of his subordinate. He watched them passing in front of the stained-glass window and then rounding the bend of the stairs until they were out of sight. He went into the private lounge and carried a bottle of Gordon's gin, a glass, and a bottle of peppermint cordial back to the kitchen.

'Any idea at all, sir, why she came to the pet shop this a.m.?'

'She was fond of the pets.'

'She came to see them?'

'She'd heard Mrs Bassett had died. She wondered what would become of them.'

He was sitting in the winged armchair in the centre of the room. Its back was to the bed, it faced the two windows and the tallboy that was between them. Inspector Ponsonby had asked him to sit there and had indicated that Sergeant Gove should sit also, on a chair near the wardrobe and the bookcase. He himself remained on his feet, moving about the room as he asked his questions, glancing at but not yet referring to the two suitcases that were open on the floor, half packed.

'And what will become of the pets, Mr Roche?'

'Mrs Bassett left the property and the pets to me.'

'And you'll naturally be moving from the district?'

'The district is being demolished.'

They were like different species of animals, Alban Roche thought, with different senses and tastes and lifestyles: in the room a map turtle might have been interrogating a tuatura. And the sergeant who sat near the wardrobe was related in kind to the yellow map turtle: the sergeant, brown and crinkly, was perhaps a terrapin.

'And that is all you want to tell us, Mr Roche?'

'I'll answer your questions.'

'You didn't, for instance, run across the girl when you were out and about during the course of this afternoon?'

'Yes, I did.'

'You mean you saw the girl?'

163

'Yes.'

'I see, sir.'

Inspector Ponsonby looked purposefully into the eyes of his suspect. All they contained, as far as Inspector Ponsonby could deduce, was a kind of sorrow, indicating, maybe, that this drop-out regretted what he had done. Or perhaps that look was always there; he'd no way of knowing. However it was, he didn't at all care for the fellow. He didn't care for any of these long-haired wonders you came across these days, and especially he didn't care for them when he was obliged to converse with them.

'Where was it you saw the girl, Mr Roche?'

'She was going into a public convenience.'

'Where?'

'In Luther Way, off Abyssinia Street.'

'What time was this, sir?'

'I don't know.'

'Nonsense, Mr Roche, you must know.'

'I haven't a watch.'

'What time approximately? Whereabouts was the sun, for instance?'

'The sun?'

'Was the sun setting, Mr Roche?'

'It was about four in the afternoon.'

They were in the room with him and yet they couldn't see him: animals were better at seeing than that, some animals anyway. Sense and sight were closer in animals and in any case the optical properties of a given animal's eye might be wholly different from a person's. But tortoises weren't colour-blind. If you offered a tortoise a piece of lettuce and a dandelion it would move first towards the dandelion.

'What did you do next, Mr Roche, after you'd seen Prudence entering the public convenience in Luther Way?'

'I leaned against the window of a cycle shop. My shoes had got dusty from walking over the wastelands. I remember noticing that.'

'What were you waiting for?'

'I wanted to speak to her.'

Inspector Ponsonby, requiring time to think, took a packet of cigarettes from one of his jacket pockets. He opened it and held it out. Alban Roche shook his head. 'D'you mind if I do, sir?' he asked. 'D'you mind if Sergeant Gove does?'

'No.'

He put a cigarette in his mouth and offered Sergeant Gove one. The Sergeant lit both of them with a Zippo lighter. 'And what happened,' inquired Inspector Ponsonby, 'when Prudence Tuke emerged?'

He spoke nonchalantly, as if it didn't matter. He blew smoke into the air.

'Well, Mr Roche?'

'She didn't come out.'

Inspector Ponsonby smiled. Sergeant Gove raised his right hand to his lips. He removed his cigarette and then replaced it.

'Excuse me, sir,' Inspector Ponsonby said. 'Let me just recap. What we've established is that Prudence Tuke entered a public convenience at the junction of Luther Way and Abyssinia Street. You were leaning against the window of a cycle shop, sir, examining your shoes. The girl failed to emerge.'

'Yes.'

'So the girl is still in the convenience, Mr Roche?'

'No.'

'You say she did not emerge, Mr Roche.'

'The convenience in Luther Way has green railings around it. You go down steps. In Abyssinia Street there are other green railings. You can go down in Luther Way and come up in Abyssinia Street. I didn't know that. The convenience itself is actually under a corner shop, a branch of Dolcis.'

'So you went on leaning against the cycle-shop window while Prudence Tuke left the convenience by the Abyssinia Street steps?'

'Yes.'

'And what did you do then, Mr Roche?'

'It occurred to me what had happened. I crossed the street and went round the corner by the shoe shop and saw the green railings on the other side.'

'And you did not see Prudence Tuke?'

'No.'

'How long were you leaning against the window?'

'About ten minutes.'

'You arrived in the Thistle Arms, sir, after the police had actually been summoned. The police were summoned at nine o'clock. It was round about four when you saw the girl entering the convenience. That's your own estimation, Mr Roche.'

'Yes.'

'It doesn't take five hours to walk from Abyssinia Street to Crow Street. I'd hardly say it does, sir. Abyssinia Street to Crow Street, Sergeant?'

'Eight minutes.'

'Well, Mr Roche?'

He rose. He crossed to his bed and took from it a number of papers, which he handed to Inspector Ponsonby. They gave information of properties for sale, business premises, small shops. The Inspector handed them to Sergeant Gove without looking at them himself. Sergeant Gove made a note in his thick notebook and replaced the papers on the bed.

'Having visited the properties you returned home did you, sir?'

'I returned to the pet shop. I exercised some of the animals, I gave fresh straw to the guinea-pigs, I cleaned out some of the cages. I gave them all fresh water and a supply of food. The hamsters and the gerbils, for instance, eat during the night and sleep by day. The map turtles and the terrapins—'

'Thank you, Mr Roche: and after you'd done all that?'

'I cooked a meal in this room.'

'I see.'

'There,' he said, pointing at a gas-ring on some bricks on the floor, and a frying-pan and dishes in a green plastic basin.

'After which you proceeded to pack, sir?'

'Yes.'

'You'd decided to move at once, as soon as you heard Mrs Bassett had died?'

'Yes.'

'To one of the properties you'd been inquiring about?'

'Yes.'

The Inspector nodded, eyeing the half-packed suitcases.

'This girl has a fondness for you, Mr Roche?'

'Yes.'

'And you, sir?'

'What?'

'Do you return this fondness?'

'I am fond of her, yes.'

'I see.'

Inspector Ponsonby glanced at Sergeant Gove. He pursed his lips and nodded at Sergeant Gove who, being familiar with his superior's methods, recognized this as a piece of play-acting for the benefit of the suspect. He pretended to make a note in his notebook, pursing his own lips also. He ceased when he saw that the Inspector wasn't watching him any more.

'So you cooked and consumed your meal, Mr Roche. And pretty soon after that you knew that something was wrong, eh?'

'Wrong?'

'Because of the policemen all over the place. Not usual, eh?'

'I heard the sirens in the distance. I saw the cars from the window.'

'And what did you think, Mr Roche?'

'I thought that something was up.'

'There was another occasion, not long ago, Mr Roche, when a police car drew up at the Thistle Arms?'

'Yes.'

'You were arrested, sir, if I am not mistaken, for an offence which could be called a sexual offence.'

'Yes.'

The Inspector hummed a tune he was fond of, a piece from *The Mikado*. He crossed to the window, pulled up the bottom sash and leaned out. He extinguished his cigarette on the window-sill and pulled down the sash again. He smiled at Alban Roche, showing tobacco-stained teeth. He lit a fresh cigarette.

'What we can't help noticing, Mr Roche,' he eventually said, 'is that you don't appear to be upset. Sergeant Gove noticed that and so did I. You're very calm, sir. In the circumstances.'

167

'I've told you—'

'You're very calm, is what I mean, sir, when a girl who has a fondness for you and for whom you have a fondness yourself disappears in mysterious circumstances. You yourself, sir, being the last to see her when she entered a public toilet.'

He smiled again at the youth.

'We'd very much like to know,' he said, 'why you're not upset, sir.'

'She'll come back in her own time. You don't understand—'

'There are men out with dogs, Mr Roche,' snapped the Inspector. 'An area of several square miles is already being searched. There are some extremely suspicious circumstances in this case, sir: I must ask you to remember that.'

He did not reply. Other words came to him. 'I would like to be with you wherever you are,' she'd said, and her mother, two years ago, had asked him to forgive the drabness of the public house's decor. 'You're a good-looking boy,' her mother had said to him one night, but she'd probably have forgotten that now because she hadn't been sober at the time. *The tympanic membrane is no longer superficial as in the frog,* he irrelevantly remembered, *because in the mammal an outer ear consisting of* . . . 'You do not co-operate with me, Alban,' Dr Krig had accused. Why should he co-operate?

Sergeant Gove tried to keep himself awake by pulling at the flesh of his face when his superior wasn't looking. He eyed the spines of the books in the bookcase beside him: *Animal Biology* by A. J. Grove and C. E. Newell, *The Senses of Animals, The Bongo Antelope, The Death of the Thylucine, Angwantibo.*

'Let's just begin again,' said Inspector Ponsonby. He returned to the window and looked out without speaking for a moment. He moved away. He said:

'You left the pet shop in the middle of the day, the girl having earlier visited you there, the body of Mrs Bassett having been taken away. A death certificate was issued for Mrs Bassett, was it, sir?'

'Yes.'

'Which doctor is that, sir?'

'I don't know the doctor's name.'

'And Mrs Bassett's body is now with an undertaker. I'm right in that, sir?'

'Yes.'

'Which undertaker is that, sir?'

'Miss Gomez summoned both the doctor and the undertaker.'

'Miss Gomez found Mrs Bassett dead, did she?'

'Yes.'

'And when did you yourself, sir, last see Mrs Bassett alive?'

'Yesterday evening. When we closed the shop. About a quarter past six.'

'Not much point in ever opening that shop, was there, sir? Not of recent weeks?'

'Mrs Bassett liked to.'

'Quite so. Still, it must have been a boring business, working in a pet shop, Mr Roche, that didn't have any customers?'

'Mrs Bassett—'

'You expected to inherit the property on Mrs Bassett's death, I understand? You were aware of the contents of the old lady's will?'

'Yes.'

'What in fact you inherited was a cheque in compensation money? And of course the animals?'

'Yes.'

'In the circumstances that have arisen I must tell you, Mr Roche, that there may well now be a post-mortem on Mrs Bassett.'

'The doctor said her heart gave out.'

'Which is what we hope, sir, hasn't happened to the heart of Prudence Tuke.'

Sergeant Gove was thinking that if Superintendent Binds could hear him now that would be that. Binds was a stickler over matters like that: he'd be shocked to the core to hear insinuations about post-mortems and a suspect being asked when he last saw a woman alive when the woman had died a perfectly natural death and one that had nothing whatsoever to do with the matter in hand. It was a known fact at the station that Binds was gunning for Ponsonby, there being no love lost due to their two different temperaments.

Having circuited the room, the Inspector found himself again at the window. He stood with his back to it. He said:

'So at some moment after noon, an hour or so after the undertakers had taken away Mrs Bassett's body, you left the shop that was now your property and walked, you say, to the Windrush Café in Abyssinia Street? Were you thinking of anything special as you walked, Mr Roche?'

'No.'

'You weren't thinking that Mrs Bassett was dead? You weren't thinking of anything this Miss Gomez might have said to you?'

'Miss Gomez?'

'Miss Gomez is direct in her speech, I'm given to understand. She's been saying a few direct things to Sergeant Gove here.'

'I don't know Miss Gomez well.'

'You say that after you ate a meal in the Windrush Café you walked about. You didn't think to go straight to an estate agent's? You walked about in the very considerable afternoon heat, did you? And eventually you saw Prudence Tuke going into a toilet?'

'I've told you.'

The Inspector's manner changed. He lowered his voice, standing in front of his suspect and looking directly at his eyes. 'There's always a toilet,' he said after a pause. 'Did you know that, son? There's always a toilet in cases like this.' He paused again, and then returned to his previous mode of address. 'Why did you wish to speak to the girl, Mr Roche?'

'It's a matter that's private between us.'

'Her death, d'you mean?'

He did not say anything. He looked away from Inspector Ponsonby and for a moment gazed at the head of Sergeant Gove, bent over his notebook in the weak glow of a bedside lamp, which was all that lit the room. He glanced towards the window: outside there were faint streaks of day left in the dark sky. How different it would be, he thought, if he'd never left, if he still sold postal orders and licences and stamps, pushing them under the brass counter-grill at familiar faces. He might be sitting now in the Coliseum Cinema watching a well-worn film, his black hair short as it had been. He might be sitting with a girl, eating Urney chocolates, not knowing a thing about the life of the bongo antelope or the klipspringer or the dhole, not knowing that black pigment in animals was melanin.

'I'm going to put certain facts to you, Roche. I'm going to say to you that you're a perverted drop-out who's recently undergone a course of psychiatric treatment at Her Majesty's expense. I'm going to put it to you that you're sick and vicious. I'm going to say to you, Roche, that you followed Prudence Tuke from Crow Street this morning, that you caught up with her in a suitable place and assaulted her. You returned here, ate your food, and prepared to do a flit. I want a full confession from you, Roche. I want you to tell me, without further delay, where we can find what remains of that girl.'

Again there was a silence in the room. The Inspector let it thicken and intensify. Silence could be a weapon on occasions like this. You let it hang; you'd nothing to lose yourself. Eventually he said:

'You knew you could assault her because she was fond of you. You knew you could lead her anywhere you liked. You took advantage, didn't you, Roche?'

The Inspector nodded at Sergeant Gove, his look suggesting that in a moment they'd hear what they wished to hear. But Alban Roche didn't say anything.

'Hi, young fellow,' said a man to Constable Wigg in the hall. 'What's the dirt, lad?'

The Inspector would be making a statement shortly, Constable Wigg replied.

Car-doors banged outside the Thistle Arms, other voices were raised. 'The Press,' said Constable Akkers in the kitchen.

Sergeant Gove came downstairs with a message from the Inspector, asking the reporters and photographers to remain in one of the bars. 'Are you up to serving them, sir?' he inquired of Mr Tuke in the kitchen, and Mr Tuke nodded. His wife, who'd been silent ever since Inspector Ponsonby had taken his departure, was drinking glasses of gin and peppermint cordial at the table, methodically inducing oblivion.

In the public bar he poured drinks for the newspapermen. They asked for photographs of Prudence and he returned to the kitchen for some that were in a drawer of the dresser. They'd all been taken a year or so ago when she was still a schoolgirl but that, the newspapermen said, didn't matter in the least. Better in a way, a few of them murmured.

With what seemed a physical effort Mr Tuke drove from him the images that the presence of the police and the reporters inspired. He'd seen Prudence in his mind's eye, as everyone no doubt saw her now: her body cool already, in a corner of an empty house, bricks thrown over it. He'd even heard a whimper, two or three times.

Nothing was credible. He couldn't believe that that morning he'd stood at the window looking out into Crow Street, worrying that Rebel wouldn't chase cats any more. He couldn't believe that later he'd stood on the stairs and received some strange solace from the presence of Miss Gomez, even though she had horribly prophesied. It had been easy then to take what she said with a pinch of salt.

'I'm really sorry,' a man said to him, holding a photograph of Prudence in his hand. He was a sad-faced man who seemed, although not sober, to be genuinely concerned. 'Some black woman involved, was there?' he asked. Mr Tuke vaguely shrugged, not knowing what to say to that.

They sat around waiting, some of them conversing in quiet tones, others silently alert. Three cameramen had already taken photographs of him, serving behind the bar. They said they'd like to snap the girl's mother, but Constable Wigg in the hall said that Mrs Tuke and the whole interior of the Thistle Arms would be available for photography after the Inspector had made his statement. That was what the Inspector preferred. They'd get their story, he promised, in good time for their deadlines: it was in everyone's interest that they should.

They searched with flashlights now, moving slowly with dogs over empty ground, through dismantled streets. Walls of buildings stood starkly at angles to one another, other walls were disposed of altogether. The moon came up and its light picked out torn strips of wallpaper still hanging by a shred or two in what had once been rooms. Bedsteads lay in back gardens, and chairs, old gas stoves, refrigerators, bicycle-frames, mattresses, piles of mildewed carpeting, newspapers and linoleum. Ceilings and floors were gone: fire-grates were absurdly placed, high up in walls, above the searchers' heads. The doors of cupboards, half broken off, cast crooked shadows in the moonlight and seemed to gain an extra stillness from the night. The searchers looked inside the cupboards, flashing their beams of light. Elsewhere, they looked for freshly dug ground. They rooted among weeds and took apart new heaps of rubble.

The cats of the area, angry that their domain should be invaded, crept away from the wastelands, keeping close together. They reached the basement of the Crow Street Dining-Rooms and remained together in a single cellar which already contained the cat that Mr Tuke had that morning seen to be pregnant. It was no longer so: four kittens crouched close to its lean ribs, occasionally mewing.

A donkey-coloured tomcat clambered up to the grating that gave out on to Crow Street. Its eyes followed the legs of people going by, and the groomed pelts of dogs.

'You're a drop-out from society, Roche. You're sick inside yourself, you can't relate to other people. But there is nothing in the law of this land that permits you to inflict your difficulties on other people, to go looking at women while they're changing their clothes or to take advantage of a young girl because she has an adolescent fancy for you.'

The voice continued, rapping at him from beneath the yellow moustache, coming out of the dimness of the room. He answered it, remembering Miss Gomez telling him that Mrs Bassett had died and the feeling he'd experienced when he realized that he was the inheritor of a shop. He'd felt as he couldn't remember ever having felt before, as though he had gained a title, as though being an inheritor had some special meaning.

'You have the belongings of a woman in this room, Roche: are you denying that?'

'They are my mother's things in my trunk—'

'That's what you say, Roche: how do we know they're not the things of some woman that's lying at the bottom of a river somewhere? How do we know what killed Mrs Bassett, Roche? How do we know there isn't a stream of girls like Prudence Tuke? Girls go missing every day, Roche.'

'They are my mother's things. When she died I didn't want to throw them away.'

'That's a most peculiar story, Roche. Everything you say is peculiar. You're diseased where women are concerned. Isn't that true? You're diseased?' Inspector Ponsonby shouted. He placed his two hands on the arms of the winged armchair and stared at the eyes of his suspect, hoping to see tears there, because they often cried, cases like this.

'Tell me the truth,' he shouted, and Sergeant Gove, acquainted with his superior's temper, thought he was maybe going to over-step the mark. He'd seen him once raise a hand to a suspect, the hand containing at the time a large pair of scissors which he'd happened to pick up. Fortunately he'd had the good sense to bring the scissors down on the desk that had been between him and the suspect, rather than on a portion of the suspect's anatomy.

'Open that trunk, Gove.'

'Sir—'

'Open that damn trunk,' roared Inspector Ponsonby, a sound that was heard by Constable Akkers in the kitchen.

Sergeant Gove pulled the trunk from under Alban Roche's bed. He undid the catches and unfastened two buckled straps.

'Hurry up, for God's sake,' Inspector Ponsonby snapped.

Sergeant Gove took from the trunk the articles of clothing that

Miss Gomez had taken from it that morning. He spread them on the bed: coats, blouses, skirts.

'So these belonged to your mother, did they?' said Inspector Ponsonby. He picked up a grey coat and held it by its shoulders. 'That was your mother's, was it? You're sure of that, Roche?'

He nodded. All the time he'd been in Crow Street he'd never opened the trunk or the two cardboard boxes that were on top of the wardrobe. He'd seen advertisements about church-hall jumble sales and had often wondered if somehow he could manage to convey the stuff to a hall somewhere. He'd thought as well that now, since years had passed, he would make a bonfire one night, out on the wastelands. But he'd never done anything about it, fearful in case at the last moment he'd fail in his intention. It still seemed a savage act to burn these things that had been hers, or to watch while they were rooted through at a jumble sale. He should have left them behind, he knew that now; he should have left them in the house they'd always been in, and forgotten about them.

Inspector Ponsonby threw the coat on to the bed. He took his cigarettes from his pocket. He selected one and lit it. He spoke with it in his mouth.

'What killed your mother, Roche?'

Sergeant Gove, still standing by the open trunk, heard the question and thought to himself that Ponsonby was now most definitely going too far.

'I asked you a question, Roche.'

'My mother died of cancer.'

'Not heart failure, like Mrs Bassett?'

'No.'

Inspector Ponsonby took a blue satin blouse from the bed and held it in front of his suspect.

'Is it natural to keep the clothes of a dead person in your bedroom? Would you say it was natural?'

'I've told you—'

'You realize you've inherited Mrs Bassett's clothes also? Are you going to keep them too?'

'No.'

175

'What'll you do with them?'

'I don't know.'

'No?''

'I'll leave them behind in the house. They'll be burnt in a bonfire, like the wood of the houses is burnt.'

'Did you bring Prudence Tuke's clothes back here, Roche?'

There was silence, and then Inspector Ponsonby shouted again. 'You have a thing about the clothes of dead people,' he shouted. 'You have a sexual thing, Roche, whether they're your mother's clothes or anyone else's.' He flung the blouse on to the bed and Sergeant Gove picked it up. He folded it as it had been folded before. He replaced all the clothes in the trunk and fastened it and pushed it under the bed again. If he was asked to do any more of this he'd refuse, and take it up with Ponsonby afterwards. It was he who'd get the blame if Binds walked in and found him going through property without a warrant. Ponsonby could deny that he'd ever asked for the trunk to be interfered with, and knowing Ponsonby he wouldn't put it past him.

'You followed the girl to that area: what did you want with her?'

'I wanted to say I loved her.'

'Love?'

'Yes.'

'You wanted to tell Prudence Tuke you loved her?'

'Yes.'

'Why did you want to do that?'

'Because of what she'd said to me. And because I was the inheritor of the pet shop.'

'What difference did that make?'

'It was a feeling I had—'

'We know what feelings you had, Roche,' Inspector Ponsonby said softly. He leaned close to his suspect again in order to examine his eyes. Ash, falling from his cigarette, dropped on to the ginger-coloured clothes. After a moment he withdrew and walked about the room again. He lit another cigarette. In a quieter voice he said:

'Tell us about this feeling you had, the one that came because you were the inheritor of a pet shop.'

'I had been in gaol for an offence that Mrs Bassett knew about, yet she left me what she most valued.'

'A building on the point of demolition.'

'It was her memory of her husband.'

'It gave you the courage to go after Prudence Tuke?'

He didn't reply. The night before, she'd sewn a button on the ginger jacket he was wearing now. She'd knocked on his door when he'd been reading W. H. Hudson and had said good-night, handing it to him. In the pet shop he'd felt her love, day after day, as though it mounted up and became more potent. He'd been frightened of it, and of her, and of the feelings that developed in him concerning her. When he'd returned from gaol she'd smiled at him, not caring, the same as Mrs Bassett. That morning she'd broken the silence that he'd thought would never be broken because he couldn't have broken it himself.

'You're completely mixed up,' Inspector Ponsonby said. 'You don't know what you're doing, Roche, or why you do it. Why don't you simply tell the truth, son?'

Sergeant Gove, at a sign from his superior, turned on the room's main light and in the glare Inspector Ponsonby regarded the youth in the armchair, saying to himself that he'd give ten pounds to know what was in the young bastard's mind. He ground the butt of his cigarette into the linoleum.

'You're leaving the heart of the matter out, aren't you, son?' he quietly said. 'Where is she, son?'

Again there was silence. The Inspector nodded. He went to the window and saw in the distance pinpricks of light that were the flash-lamps of his search party.

'We'll need you at the station,' he said without turning his head.

When Inspector Ponsonby entered the public bar Mr Tuke slipped away. He found a torch in the drawer of the hallstand and went out into Crow Street with Rebel trotting beside him. The donkey-coloured tomcat, still gazing through the cellar grating, saw them go past.

'So that's the story,' one of the reporters remarked in the public bar. 'The Jamaican foretold the whole thing at ten a.m.'

'No one has been arrested,' Inspector Ponsonby pointed out. 'If you repeat Miss Gomez's predictions you'll be repeating a slander.'

The reporters laughed, knowing that they couldn't yet write what Miss Gomez had said. 'May we say, Inspector,' one of them suggested, 'that a man is assisting?'

'It would be misleading.'

'An early arrest, Inspector?'

'We've yet to find the missing girl.'

The Inspector went on talking, explaining how the reporters could help the police by making certain that photographs of Prudence Tuke were reproduced prominently in their newspapers. He filled in areas of background for them. He refused to say anything about the man upstairs and advised them not to say anything either. He wished them all good-night.

The photographers found Mrs Tuke in the kitchen and photographed her. They knocked on Mr Batt's door, roused him and photographed him also, an incident that Mr Batt assumed to be part of a dream he was having. They knocked on Alban Roche's door but found it to be locked. They photographed in Prudence's room the three monkeys who spoke no evil, nor saw it, nor heard it. They followed their colleagues to the pet shop, where Miss Gomez was answering questions. They photographed her also, asking her to pose against a background of cages.

'Best left till daylight now,' the leader of the search party decided at half-past one. 'Best left, sir,' he said to Mr Tuke, but Mr Tuke replied that he'd go on for a bit. He called for Rebel, who had wandered off on his own. He whistled and the sound echoed, darting back at him from the broken masonry all around. But Rebel didn't come. The police vans started up and drove away. Alone he went on looking, going over ground that had already been covered.

Crow Street was quiet.

In the kitchen of the Thistle Arms Mrs Tuke slept, her head

on her arms, her arms sprawled over the red kitchen table. Beside her the bottle of Gordon's gin was almost empty, and so was the bottle of peppermint cordial.

Mr Batt awoke briefly, thinking that it had been extreme of Mrs Tuke to summon the police just because her cleaner had stolen a packet of cigarettes. He turned and slept again, and dreamed immediately that he was back in the fruit and vegetable shop, ordering a wreath for Mrs Bassett. The boy he tried to order it from wasn't able to hear what he was saying, and kept bringing other people into the shop. He brought in the man whose hand Mrs Tuke had bandaged that morning, and then Mrs Tuke herself. He brought in Miss Gomez, and a man with blond hair like a woman's who was smoking a cigar and said he was a jockey, and the policeman to whom Mrs Tuke had reported the filching of the cigarettes. And then Mrs Bassett came into the shop and said a wreath wasn't necessary because she hadn't died. 'I suspected you hadn't,' said Mr Batt, shaking hands with her.

The pets in their cages and hutches slept or were wide awake, according to their breed. The gerbils played together; hamsters, solitary because of their aggression, ran on their wheels. Fish were quiet, birds dozed on perches. It was night and day in the pet shop, as it always was, and the pets continued as though nothing had happened, unaware that the three people to whom they were most accustomed would not be there to tend them at the usual time in the morning.

Miss Gomez, emptied now of tears and sleepless in her concern for all that had happened, walked about her room. She had watched the police-cars driving away, with Alban Roche in one of them, and later the newspapermen's cars and then the police-vans. She had smoked during the evening more cigarettes than Inspector Ponsonby had, almost twenty more. She looked out of the window again and then hurried from her room.

Not far from Mr Tuke, she searched the wastelands and the empty buildings, following him as he limped about, neither of them speaking.

*   *   *

In the distance, as he entered Crow Street, the cats saw Rebel. Alone, head down, occasionally sniffing the ground, he trotted in the moonlight. Without sound, they moved from the cellar.

As he passed the Crow Street Dining-Rooms they sprang at him, pinning him against a wall before he had a chance to gather himself. He snarled and tried to bite, but his defence was ineffectual. In their numbers and newfound wildness they massacred without much effort.

Quite naturally and with pleasure they tore his throat out, and then voraciously they ate. Even the kittens which had that afternoon been born ate flesh that still trailed blood. Hunched in a circle, the cats consumed their gory meal with the efficiency of the starving, clawing at bones, examining entrails. And one by one, then, they returned to their cellar.

XII

Sex Crime Prophecy, they read. *Girl Disappears on Building Sites.*
 Riddle of Crow Street, they read. *Church Member Startles Police.*

There were photographs of the Thistle Arms and of Crow Street, and of Mrs Tuke with a glass in her hand, and Mr Batt in his pyjamas, and Rebel, and Prudence. Alban Roche was not mentioned. In all the newspapers there were photographs of Miss Gomez.

The people of London read the story with interest. Police had searched exhaustively, assisted by the lost girl's father and his Alsatian dog, called Rebel. *Miss Gomez believed that Prudence Tuke was a likely victim because of her kind and trusting nature and her habit of wandering the streets on her own. The redevelopment area around her home consists of acres of uncleared land, streets of empty houses, rubble and the remains of old bonfires. Only yesterday morning Miss Gomez alerted Prudence's parents, dramatically stating that she had heard voices warning her of the child's danger. 'We must pray,' urged Miss Gomez, smartly attired in a leather dress. Inspector Raymond Ponsonby, in charge of the police inquiries, would make no comment at this stage.*

People remembered Miss Gomez. Tina von Hippel, recalling her friend's strangeness at the time she'd decided to leave Mrs Idle's pleasure house, wasn't surprised that she had come to this. A girl employed in the haberdashery department of Bourne and Hollingsworth saw a photograph of Miss Gomez and remarked to a stranger on a bus that she'd worked with her for a matter of months. It surprised her, she said, to see Miss Gomez slightly smiling, because in Bourne and Hollingsworth she hadn't smiled at all.

In Shepherd's Bush Elvira-Anne rang the bell of her friend Carla's flat and they read together, sitting in their pyjamas, an inaccurate account of all that had taken place the day before in Crow Street. The Sicilian owners of the Spot-On Club read the same account, as did many men who in the Spot-On Club had observed the nakedness of Miss Gomez. Few of these men recognized her, having paid in the past scant attention to her face. The man who'd brought her to Thrift's Hotel and left with her the Canadian Pacific bag frowned over her face but in the end couldn't place it. A man who'd twice been her client in Mrs Idle's top-storey room confused her with a girl who worked in the lamp-shade department of a British Home Stores and whom he'd once asked, about six months ago, to come out for an evening's bowl-ing with him. No wonder she'd refused, he thought, if she was given over to religion.

To a few of the strangers whom she'd addressed about her Church her face was as vaguely familiar, but none recalled it more precisely. Only the West Indian cashier in the late-night super-market, the man who'd offered to bring her to the Rhumba Ren-dezvous, recognized her immediately and, like Tina von Hippel, wasn't surprised when he read the story.

The developers whom Mrs Bassett had disliked were amazed to learn about the happening in Crow Street, and the doctor who'd issued Mrs Bassett's death certificate sorrowfully shook his head. He'd attended Prudence Tuke for whooping cough and 'flu. He'd seen her for an instant yesterday morning, in the yellow dress that his newspaper described. He was unable to prevent him-self from imagining her dead, as his newspaper seemed to imply she was, death being on his mind in any case. 'Good-bye,' his own daughter said, on her way to the school where experiments with narcotics were all the time discussed.

Another schoolgirl read about the prophecy of Miss Gomez and felt excited because Miss Gomez's Church was the Church she was in correspondence with. 'Come straight back home,' her mother ordered at the family breakfast table, having read the same account, and the girl, who had that morning tried to cover her acne with face-powder, bitterly laughed. 'Beautiful,' she said, leaving her parents' dining-room. 'The wastelands girl was beautiful.' Her parents sighed in their different ways. 'She really has a thing about it,' the mother murmured. 'So cruel it all seems.'

For Mrs Drate and the cinema usher, the one in an outer suburb, the other in Poplar, the Church of the Brethren acquired an extra status. Both wrote at once to Tacas, enclosing clippings from their two different newspapers.

Have You Seen This Girl? Atlas Flynn read. 'Great holy God!' he exclaimed, and read out to his companions the story that had been made of Miss Gomez and her revelations, and the disappearance of Prudence Tuke. *An elderly resident at the Thistle Arms, Mr A. J. Batt, was present in the hall of the public house when Miss Gomez warned the parents in tones that were reported to have been noisy and religious. An Irish labourer,* read Atlas Flynn, *was present also.*

'Definitely,' said the woman from whom Prudence the day before had bought a bottle of limeade. 'It's definitely the girl.' At the other end of the telephone a desk sergeant asked her at what time she'd sold the limeade and the woman said half-past two. 'She talked about butterflies,' the woman reported. 'Camberwell Beauties or some such. Beauty herself she was, poor scrap.' It might have been two o'clock, she added then, or even slightly earlier; difficult to tell really, a thing like that. 'Your name and full address please, madam?' the desk sergeant inquired.

Other people had seen her too. A man in a Yorkshire village had noticed her more than a week ago, but the local policeman to whom he reported the matter pointed out that the girl had been missing for only a day. 'I'm not a liar,' insisted the man. 'I saw her, I tell you.'

People in Edinburgh and Somerset had seen her, and people in Hampstead Garden Suburb, and in Rugby, Leeds, Doncaster, and Northern Ireland. 'I done her in,' a voice that might have been either male or female announced over a telephone. 'I've done a lot in, actually.'

A schoolteacher asked that a message be given to Inspector Ponsonby. She'd taught Prudence Tuke one time and therefore had an interest in the case and would like to help through contacts she had in the spiritual world. She'd been retired now for

183

quite some years, she told the desk sergeant, but had always had an interest in the other world. She gave her address and asked that Inspector Ponsonby should call on her at eleven that morning, when there'd be coffee.

'Violence in this country,' pronounced a man who gave his name as Charles Spillman, 'is the direct result of weakness at the top. What we learn from our *Times* this morning underlines, yet once again, the wisdom of the late Herr Hitler.'

'I was physically sick,' a cultured lady whispered, 'to see a picture of this Gomez in a British newspaper. Isn't deportation for incitement surely possible?'

'The nig-nog done it,' another voice peremptorily accused.

Superintendent Binds asked Inspector Ponsonby how the case was going, and inquired particularly about the continued interrogation of Alban Roche. The Inspector was shaving at the time, with an electric razor that he kept at the police station for the occasions when he was obliged to spend the night there. Because of the sound of the razor he couldn't hear what Superintendent Binds said, but he guessed without difficulty the questions he was asking.

'He didn't talk,' he said above the whirring of the razor.

He twisted his mouth, running the blades close to his moustache. Superintendent Binds was an inch taller than he was, a man who neither drank nor smoked.

'You can't hold him,' Superintendent Binds said. 'You haven't a tittle of grounds for holding, Ponsonby.'

Inspector Ponsonby nodded. He pulled the plug of his razor out of the wall-socket and wound the flex carefully. He felt exhausted but was determined not to show it. Superintendent Binds didn't like him and he didn't like Superintendent Binds. Binds was always narrowing his eyes and appearing to be suspicious, a piece of psychological warfare that particularly irritated Inspector Ponsonby because he could see through it, being a hardened expert in such warfare himself.

'I'm taking him back with me now,' he said, endeavouring to speak smoothly.

There was a knock on the door, and Constable Wigg came in with two cups of tea. He placed them on Inspector Ponsonby's desk. When he'd gone the Superintendent said:

'If Roche did it, Ponsonby, what'd he do with her body?'

Inspector Ponsonby drank some tea. He lit a cigarette, smiling a little because he knew that the Superintendent believed that people engaged in serious business should maintain serious countenances. There were all sorts of places, he explained, that there hadn't been time to investigate with any degree of thoroughness yet. There were old wells in back gardens, the hidey-holes in walls that mightn't have been apparent in the dusk the night before. Bulldozers would have to be employed to shift tons of rubble, and there was a rubbish dump not far away, and of course the river. As well as which, he'd just had a call to say that a dog had been massacred in Crow Street by cats that had turned wild through starvation. 'Nothing left but bones,' he said. 'That dog was licking my trousers at ten o'clock last night, Super.'

'You think Roche'll talk when the body's found, do you?'

'He'll crack down the middle, sir.'

'I hope you're right.'

In the car on the way to Crow Street Inspector Ponsonby informed his suspect of the death of Rebel. He described the dog's remains as they'd been described to him. 'Chap thought it was the girl at first,' he said, 'until he noticed the head.' He laughed, revealing briefly his tobacco teeth. 'In the middle of London,' he went on. 'You'd scarce believe it, would you, son?'

Alban Roche didn't say anything. He remembered thinking that the cats of the wastelands were returning gradually to their tribal state. He'd heard before of animals attacked by cats.

'Nature's ugly, son,' Inspector Ponsonby remarked, and Sergeant Gove turned round in the front of the car and said that it certainly was.

On the telephone to the desk sergeant a man said that he was positive, and would swear to the accuracy of his statement in any court the desk sergeant cared to name, that at half-past four the previous afternoon he had sold to the missing girl two galvanized buckets, two scrubbing-brushes, a sweeping-brush, a dust-pan made of blue plastic, sundry cloths, a tin of Vim and a tin of Ajax, a packet of Daz and a packet of Brillo pads. His name was Fennell, he said: was there in fact a reward?

Alone for five minutes, Inspector Ponsonby found peace in the unlit public bar. He rested on the window seat, his legs stretched out along the padded velour, his head propped against the window-frame. He smoked with his eyes closed; vaguely related thoughts occurred and loitered in his mind.

He had an overdraft of fifty-seven pounds exactly. Yesterday morning his wife had announced her desire to go on a package holiday to Majorca and had twice rung him up about it during the day. He believed he'd die without cigarettes and a small daily indulgence in whisky. She didn't understand that, nor did Binds. She'd never for a second understand what it was like working with Binds, who was as cold as an iced fish. 'Majorca,' she'd said, as though money grew on trees.

He heard a sound and swore wearily, getting to his feet. Mr Tuke appeared in the door of the public bar, covered in dust. He'd searched all night, he said. There was nowhere else to look.

Mrs Tuke appeared behind him, saying she hadn't slept a wink. She asked then if there was any news.

The telephone rang. The Inspector answered it himself and was told that a man called Joseph Fennell had made a statement to the effect that he'd sold the missing girl a quantity of cleansing materials the afternoon before, at half-past four.

The Inspector replaced the receiver. 'Your daughter bought cleansing materials yesterday afternoon,' he said.

'Cleansing?' whispered Mrs Tuke, sitting down. 'Cleansing?'

'Buckets, brushes, that kind of thing. Why would she do that?'

Mrs Tuke silently shook her head, as did her husband. 'Buckets?' he said in a voice that was a whisper also. A moment ago he'd stared at the head and bones of Rebel, unable to believe that the evidence before him was a fact: how could it be that such a savagery had taken place, performed by animals that had been, once, domestic pets? He'd moved on slowly, not touching any-

186

thing, without the strength to accept the burden of this added grief.

'You've no idea?' Inspector Ponsonby said and as he spoke Atlas Flynn came into the public bar and said that he and three others had observed Alban Roche from the top of a bus the night before. He was only mentioning it, he explained, because it was Alban Roche that Miss Gomez had pointed her finger at.

'Where was it you saw him?' demanded the Inspector wearily, and Atlas Flynn explained, and the Inspector calculated. The time Roche had been seen was seven o'clock, which was just the time, according to his own story, when he should have been where the men saw him. Inspector Ponsonby pressed his teeth together, forcing out of his mind a picture that was forming there. Unease budded in the staleness that seemed entirely to possess him. Within black leather shoes he curled his toes, a reaction that was common with him when anxiety began.

'I'm sorry about it, Beryl,' the red-haired labourer whispered privately to Mrs Tuke, but Mrs Tuke did not acknowledge this sympathy.

Inspector Ponsonby pressed his teeth together again. His toes were tight on the soles of his shoes, hurting him. Binds would love it. Binds would look at him through his narrowed eyes and speak in that dry voice, a sound like sandpaper smoothing sandpaper. He'd had fifteen men out, and cars and vans, not to mention dogs. He'd exceeded his duty in the matter of his questioning of Roche. He'd run up an overtime bill of sizeable proportions and had already set in motion the machinery for door-to-door questioning over a wide area. At half-past seven that morning he'd drafted appeals for radio and television.

'Some of the boys could help in the search, sir,' the red-haired man offered.

He shook his head, wondering if the gesture looked as bitter as it felt. He'd sent Gove over to talk to the Gomez woman instead of going himself. Gove was as thick as a pot sometimes: if he'd gone himself he'd have seen immediately.

The telephone rang again. 'An estate agent swears,' began the desk sergeant, and Inspector Ponsonby said yes, he knew. He left the public bar and the Thistle Arms itself. 'You all right these days?' he imagined Binds nastily saying to him. 'No trouble at home, Ponsonby? Feeling on top of it, are you?' With pleasure Binds would incorporate it all on a report. In his small round handwriting he'd make mincemeat of him over the door-to-door questioning, nor would he compose a single sentence in mitigation or support.

'Not a sausage, sir,' Sergeant Gove reported in Crow Street. 'I just thought I'd pop back and let you—'

'Send the men back to the station. Go back to the station yourself and cancel all investigation arrangements until further notice.'

'You've never found her, sir?'

'Do as you're bloody told, Gove.'

She could hear a milkman's dray in Tintagel Street moving and stopping, moving and stopping again. Milk bottles clinked, people called out. Earlier she'd seen a paper-boy pushing newspapers into the letter-boxes of shops and houses. She'd heard birds singing in Tintagel Street at dawn and she occasionally heard them now, when other noises faded.

Her yellow dress was torn in two places, and smeared with dirt and pieces of cobweb. Her hands were red from scrubbing, her knees scarred. Muscles, unused for some time, were painful when she moved; her stomach was empty of food. She hadn't meant to work so hard, or so long. She'd gone to buy the cleaning things and he'd gone in a different direction, to see a Mr Winstanley who ran a removals service and to see to the pets and to get ready to leave Crow Street. He'd have guessed what had happened: that she'd gone on working because she wanted to have the whole house clean for him.

Inspector Ponsonby said it was an offence to withhold information from the police. 'You had no right,' he said. 'You knew perfectly well where that girl was. You watched me mounting a hunt for her and you maliciously kept vital information to yourself.'

With a packet of Bunnimix in his hand, Alban Roche replied

that he had answered all the questions put to him. He reminded Inspector Ponsonby that he'd been asked about a crime and that he'd repeatedly denied that a crime had taken place. He spoke softly and without aggression, displaying no resentment that Inspector Ponsonby had searched his property without a warrant. In answer to direct questions now, he said that he had run into Prudence Tuke half an hour after seeing her entering the convenience at the corner of Abyssinia Street and Luther Way. She had brought him to the estate agent's he'd mentioned and then they had gone to the house in Tintagel Street, which was a shop also. It was she who had managed everything.

Inspector Ponsonby, desiring only to strike this youth on the face, endeavoured not to let the desire show. For hours during the night he'd regarded that thin face. He'd looked at its dark eyes and had been unswervingly convinced that they were the eyes of a murderer. Yet the eyes now seemed much the same as any other eyes. It was this black woman who had started the thing about the youth's eyes, repeating to the girl's parents what she'd imagined she'd seen there. As far as he could see, it was the black who had been the cause of everything, because of some dotty religion.

'Is that Gomez woman upstairs?' he asked, and the youth, filling a container with Bunnimix, politely nodded.

She opened the door of her room and saw standing outside a man she'd seen before somewhere. She remembered quite vividly the yellow moustache and something about his hands, she couldn't establish what. Had he been a man in the Spot-On Club? Or some man at whose house she'd called, to speak of the Brethren?

'Yes?' she said, returning to the open window through which she'd been looking.

She was crestfallen, he saw. Someone had said she'd been out with Tuke during the night, looking for the girl. Gove said he was sorry for her, not knowing at the time that she was the cause of everything.

'Have you seen the newspapers, Miss Gomez?'

She shook her head and he took one from a pocket of his limp suit and handed it to her. *Jamaican's Strange Powers*, she read. *Police on Sex Manhunt*. There was a picture of herself and of Prudence Tuke in a school uniform. She began to read the smaller print, but Inspector Ponsonby removed the newspaper from her hand.

'I thought you'd be interested,' he remarked. 'It mentions your Church, Miss Gomez. There isn't a literate man or woman in the country, Miss Gomez, who hasn't by now heard of the Church of the Brethren of the Way.'

'Who are you?'

'My name's Inspector Ponsonby.'

He'd come to Mrs Idle's house. One January afternoon when it was snowing. He'd been wearing a mackintosh coat and a greyish hat with a band on it. He'd argued about the charge and then had given in, saying he had plenty of money anyway. He'd made her unbutton his coat and take it off him and then take off his jacket and his waistcoat and his tie. Quite suddenly he'd said he'd like to be married to a black woman: he'd discovered that desire in him too late, he confessed, standing in his socks, with blue suspenders on his pale calves.

'Fifteen men, Miss Gomez, I called out on this case, not to mention dogs and dog-handlers. Last night in the public bar of the Thistle Arms I addressed the Press. This morning—'

'Look, there's Prudence Tuke.' She pointed through the open window, and the Inspector looked. Prudence Tuke had entered Crow Street. Behind her and at a distance were the searchers and their dogs.

'In her yellow dress,' said Inspector Ponsonby bitterly.

They watched; she entered the pet shop below.

'How very extraordinary!' said Miss Gomez, experiencing the same joyful sensation that she'd felt at the time of her conversion, when she'd received the first letter from Tacas. She'd felt it also with subsequent letters, when she'd been told that of course her worries were important.

'You were incorrect, Miss Gomez.'

'What?'

190

'In what you saw in Roche's eyes.'

'It was the Treasurer of the Swansdale Badminton Club—'

'I don't care who it was. You accused that boy. You started a rumour going, you frightened everyone. Just who, Miss Gomez, d'you think you are?'

Her lips parted. Teeth showed and then showed more, whitely gleaming, an echo of a light that had come into her eyes.

'Where was she?' she asked.

'She was cleaning a house, a shop that Roche is arranging to buy. She was out on a perfectly innocent excursion, with buckets and scrubbing-brushes and Daz. No one would have given it a second's thought if it hadn't been for your rubbish. As a police officer, Miss Gomez, I must ask you for some kind of explanation.'

She sat down on her bed, thinking that she'd sat on a bed in his presence before. In the top-storey room she'd always sat on the edge of the bed in order to take her stockings off: clients liked to watch her doing that as a rule.

'The parents of that girl were beside themselves, Miss Gomez. I've been interrogating Roche the entire night. He refused to tell me what he knew because he's been in trouble with the police before and won't co-operate. He was laughing, Miss Gomez, behind those eyes you talked about. From the moment I entered that boy's room last night he was laughing up his sleeve at me.'

'I'm sorry. I—'

'I had his trunk opened in front of him. I said his mother's clothes were the clothes of some woman he'd maybe done in. I told him he had a thing about the garments of the dead. When it was all completely innocent, Miss Gomez. His mother's belongings are lying there because he can't bring himself round to selling them off.'

'No. No, there's more—'

'There bloody well isn't more to it,' shouted Inspector Ponsonby.

She murmured: the truth, she said, was difficult to find: the truth about why he'd been unable to throw away his mother's belongings, the truth about anything, about why people did this

191

or that, or resisted doing this or that, or were kind or cruel, or loved or hated. He interrupted her, saying he hadn't the foggiest idea what she was talking about.

She smiled, still sitting on the edge of her bed. The smile increased, her eyes were dazzling when she turned them on to him. He could see the movement of breathing in her body. He looked at her lips and the wet gleam of teeth between them. He looked away, and said what he had come to say:

'You've made a monkey out of me and out of the girl's parents, and the entire national Press. If you were after publicity for your ridiculous Church, you've certainly got it.'

'I lost my faith last night, Inspector Ponsonby. I lost sight of my Brethren and my Church. I couldn't understand, I couldn't see—'

'The entire national Press, Miss Gomez,' he shouted at her, the words rasping through clenched teeth. 'Every newspaper in this country. What the hell d'you think it's like for me?'

She rose and crossed to where he was standing, by the window through which they'd both looked a moment ago. She felt sorry for him: people would say he was a fool. In Mrs Idle's room he had called her Rose because she'd told him that was her name. She hadn't been wearing glasses. She hadn't had them on when he came in and she hadn't put them on, guessing that he was the kind who'd prefer her without. If she'd been wearing them he might have recognized her now, which would be embarrassing for him and would make him feel worse than ever.

'I'm sorry, Inspector Ponsonby.' She took her cigarettes from the pocket of her dress and offered him one. He accepted it. She took one herself, and lit both of them. 'I'm sorry,' she repeated.

'He talked about being an inheritor,' he said. 'I couldn't understand him.'

He leaned against the wall by the window. He should have known a fellow like that would never have the nerve. He should have guessed the instant he'd seen him, but he hadn't even begun to. He hadn't even put the first two and two together, or any other two and two. 'Pity about all that,' Binds would say, later that day. He'd mention the national Press and go on about it, and the squad cars and the vans, and the dogs and the dog-handlers. For several months, years maybe, until Binds retired or thankfully died, he'd carry an accusation in his face. 'A couple of bloody-minded teenagers,' he'd say. 'Pity about all that.'

She was speaking to him, asking him a question. He opened his eyes, having somehow allowed them to close. There was a kind of triumph in her face that should have irritated him but didn't because he hadn't the energy to be irritated any more. Would he like some coffee? she asked.

He shook his head. He thanked her. He was looking at her in some way, he didn't know how. He didn't know what his gaze contained or what she saw in it: he didn't care. He was looking at her lips and her teeth, and the blackness of her nose and her cheeks and her neck. His eyes moved in a small circuit over her countenance and down to her neck again. He said to himself that she was very young, in her early twenties, although she looked more. He found her lips attractive, and her thin black hands that were poised in front of her now, as though delicately holding an invisible object.

She spoke again, repeating another question.

'Where d'you live?' she asked, to his surprise.

'A place called Southfields, a suburban neighbourhood out near—'

'I know Southfields. I went to Southfields, evangelizing.' She smiled, and spoke a little more about Southfields, remarking conversationally on features she remembered. He said he didn't like it.

He'd finish the cigarette and then he'd go. He didn't know why he'd bothered to come up here, except maybe to shout and lose his temper. 'It's an amazing bargain,' she'd say when he got home. She'd push the Majorca leaflets at him, the pictures of coloured umbrellas on beaches and people dancing and sunbathing. He often thought he'd not go back to that house, just not ever return.

'You're angry with me, Inspector Ponsonby.'

He wanted to close his eyes again and to go on standing there, his shoulder against the wall, the sun on his face. There was nothing like the taste of a cigarette, and the sun. He'd smoked when he was twelve, the first time, crouched by a tree in a field, in the sun.

'I understand your anger,' she said.

He wanted to say he liked black women, but he couldn't of course say that. He'd have to go in a moment. He'd walk through the shop below and try and say he was sorry to Roche, not because he felt it but in case Roche should make a complaint. You could never be sure about complaints. You could never take it for granted that some bastard wouldn't make a fuss just because of a mistake.

She was talking but he didn't listen. There'd be a message for him when he returned to the station: *Mrs Ponsonby rang.* He'd phone back. She'd ask him what time he expected to be home and would probably report a conversation she'd had in the Express Dairy. She'd mention something that she'd mentioned before, about Majorca.

The black girl was saying in her religious way about how all the world's people must look. There was a glass ashtray in her hands. She held it out to him and he pressed the end of his cigarette into it. She offered him another, from a packet in her other hand. He took it. She lit it for him, and lit one for herself.

'Like a roomful of flies might look,' she said. 'And yet there are patterns.'

He remembered Gove referring to old Betty Highchilde who'd been gone on religion too, whom vaguely he'd heard about, years ago. He'd known a man once who'd memorized the entire Bible in order to take on bets in public houses. He'd seen, at a fun-fair, the Lord's Prayer on the end of a pin.

'The prayers of my Church were answered by Our Lord God,' she said. 'He reached down and turned what might have been a crime into something entirely different. Either you believe that or you don't.'

He nodded, in acknowledgement rather than agreement. Not that it mattered if she imagined that he agreed. Why should it matter what anyone imagined? Fifteen years had to go by before he could retire. Fifteen years of listening to screwy Jamaicans and drug-peddlers and small-time embezzlers and thieves and troublesome adolescents, and being polite at the right times, or intimidating, or rummaging through the lies people told. In the house in Southfields he'd watch her becoming more querulous as the years went by. He imagined she'd get thinner and thinner until she was little more than an arrangement of bones, like her mother had been. She'd say it was funny the way they'd never made him a superintendent.

'It's probably something that's even beautiful,' Miss Gomez said. 'Whatever's there instead of a sex crime.'

He nodded again. It was said that religion kept some people going, making a rosier world for them. Binds belonged to some sect or other, the Quakers or the Mormons, or maybe he was a Plym or a Presbyterian. He couldn't imagine Binds praying, although it was said that he'd once caused a sensation by standing in some kind of silent meditation when two of his men had been shot, in Peckham in 1959.

'You do see that something happened, Inspector? You do understand?'

'Tuke's dog—'

'Yes, that happened. But you must see what else there was. Prayer intervened, Inspector.'

'Yes, well, maybe it did. Good-bye, Miss Gomez.'

'It might have intervened before. Some truth might have been revealed to that woman in a grey Irish town that you and I can only imagine: a cinema, a church, the factory where the girls work, the hotel, the shops, the statue of a hero, the post office windows, with pebbled glass. And in Crow Street some truth might have been revealed to Mr Tuke, who took love away from a child, or to Mrs Tuke, who hadn't ever loved the child at all. "Love's a dangerous commodity," the Reverend Greated said in Tacas, and the Reverend Patterson wrote it down for me in a letter. Even the love of God, for which crimes have been committed.'

He was at the door. She held the ashtray towards him and he stubbed out his second cigarette. He had no qualms at taking two cigarettes from her since she'd caused so much trouble. She offered him another, but he refused. He shook his head, and it was while he was doing so, when he wasn't even looking at her, that he recollected Gove saying that she'd been on the game and he knew then, without feeling anything, that he'd met her before. It had been a cold day and he'd climbed up flight after flight of stairs in a house in Frith Street, led to her room by a fat little West Indian woman. They'd lain together, as close as two people could get, her long black legs wound around his corpulent body, her tongue touching his.

He raised his head and looked at her and he knew that she'd recognized him also. He had a sudden desire to stay with her, a feeling that he wouldn't mind her talk about religion and that in time he'd even grow to love her simplicity. He thought he'd like to marry her, and immediately realized that the thought was laughable and eccentric. He tried to smile, to give some slight sign that he wasn't above remembering her, but he could not. 'Good-bye,' he said, and went away.

She watched at the window and saw him in Crow Street, his bald head with strands of grey hair pulled across it, his yellow moustache when he paused and looked up for a moment, his untidy suit. She watched him walking towards the Thistle Arms, smoking one of his own cigarettes now. A policeman in uniform was standing there, beside a blue and white police-car. He opened a door. Inspector Ponsonby got in and the car was driven away.

XIII

There was a silence in the kitchen of the Thistle Arms. Mr Batt had been waiting for more than an hour and a half for his break-fast. Mrs Tuke, five minutes ago, had slowly risen from a chair and had begun to cook it, frying for her lodger the same breakfast that she fried every day: streaky bacon and an egg whose yolk always burst on the pan. Mr Tuke sat at the table. Prudence, stand-ing, buttered a slice of bread.

'I don't get it at all,' said Mr Batt, a statement he'd made sev-eral times already and which had so far not elicited a reply. In the newspaper in front of him there was a picture of himself in pyjamas, and a picture of Mrs Tuke, one of her husband, a large one of her daughter, and an even larger one of the black cleaner, Miss Gomez. *The last time Prudence was seen by her parents,* he had read in amazement, *was when she entered the kitchen of the public house to hand Mr A. F. Batt his morning mail, which was an invitation to take part in a Jackpot competition.*

The telephone rang in the public bar and Mr Tuke went to answer it. No one spoke in the kitchen while he was absent. When he returned he said that the brewery wished the public house to be closed immediately. The brewery had offered its sympathy and he'd explained that sympathy wasn't necessary now. But the order still stood: the brewery would prefer not to keep the Thistle Arms open any longer, not after the publicity.

She basted the egg with spoonfuls of fat. She could feel pricks in her stomach as though gorse had taken root there, and pins and needles in the tips of her toes and fingers. Nausea kept rising to her throat. The whole thing was like the worst nightmare you'd ever had in your life. One minute the girl is given up for dead and the next she saunters into the kitchen and announces she's sorry. She forgot all about them, she casually says; it never occurred to her. And then as cool as a cucumber she announces she's going to live in a house with Alban Roche.

'They're making arrangements,' Mr Tuke said, 'to shift the landlord out of the Arab's Head.' He didn't sit down; he stood by the dresser, behind Mr Batt, looking at Prudence as he spoke. With an effort he injected pleasantness into his tone, trying to make life in the Arab's Head sound attractive. He wanted her to come there with them, even if she stayed only six months and then went off. Six months would be long enough for him to make her feel that he was sorry.

'Pru,' Mrs Tuke said, leaving the stove. 'Pru, listen to me.' She spoke lightly, trying to be nonchalant. She smiled at her daughter and went closer to her. 'You couldn't do a thing like that, Pru,' she said.

Prudence nodded, repeatedly raising and lowering her head. She began to butter a second slice of bread. Smoke came from the pan that contained Mr Batt's breakfast.

'He's a perverted boy, Pru,' Mrs Tuke said. 'Your dad's been out all night. I didn't sleep a wink.'

'I wanted to finish what I was doing. I thought you'd think I was in my room. I'm sorry—'

'Now listen to me, Pru. What you're talking is a load of rubbish. No young girl could go off with a character like Roche, because he's sick to his backbone. D'you understand what I mean, Pru? Can you follow me, child?'

Prudence nodded. She continued to butter more bread. She was hungry, she said.

'Pru, there was a young policeman by the name of Akkers in the kitchen for upwards of four hours, and another fellow in the hall. There were uniformed men in your room. It's in that paper there.'

'I know. I'm sorry—'

'It's no good being sorry, Pru.' She went to the stove and saw that everything on the pan was burnt. She turned it on to a plate and put it on the table, pushing it over to her lodger. The girl had bad blood in her, which was now beginning to show itself. She'd remained out all night, saying she'd been washing a place out, and all she could do was to stand there eating bread and butter. A decent-minded father would have taken her across his knee and smacked her cheeky little b.t.m. until she saw a bit of sense.

Bubbles exploded in Mrs Tuke's stomach, wind rose to her throat and was ejected. She pressed her jaws together, determined to regain her coolness. In *Tell Me, Doctor Brinley* poor Dr Haggers had been struck from the register because of an error made due to lack of coolness when he'd been working with a scalpel. She smiled. She said:

'Listen, Pru. There'll be lots of nice chaps coming in at the Arab's Head. Chaps in blazers. Decent boys, goodlooking boys. Boys from rowing clubs and that, Pru. What d'you say?'

'Prudence,' murmured Mr Tuke and began to murmur something else.

'Oh! shut your face,' cried Mrs Tuke. She smiled again at her daughter. She mentioned cinemas, saying that there were several near Kew. 'And a nice Wimpy Bar, darling, and fashion shops—'

Prudence shook her head. She explained that she liked looking after pets, and that that was all she wished to do.

'You're going to live with that boy.'

'We'll live in the same house—'

'You're going to have sexual relationships with him,' cried Mrs Tuke.

Prudence didn't reply. She poured herself tea and added milk and sugar to it. Mrs Tuke said:

'I wish you wouldn't, darling.'

'I like the pets.'

'We'll buy you pets. A cat. A goldfish. Anything you like. It's hard on your dad, love, to have you going off like this the same day old Rebel died. Your dad's beside himself as it is. Poor man with his limp, Pru,' she whispered.

'I think the milk's a little off,' said Mr Batt with a smile. 'The heat, I dare say.'

'It's sour,' Prudence said.

Hearing this, Mrs Tuke considered it the last straw. In a strong voice and in no uncertain terms she informed old Batt that if he had objections to make he knew what he could do. It was quite ridiculous that at a time like this, when she was worried three-quarters out of her mind, he should start on about milk. He was dirty in his habits, she reminded him, thinking that this remark would give him something to ponder over, and she was pleased to see that he heard her because the smile immediately vanished from his face. He rose from the table and left the kitchen in a sulk.

Prudence left also, still eating bread. She crossed the hall and mounted the stairs. Mr Batt was half a dozen steps ahead of her. She could hear her mother behind her.

In her room she opened two large work-baskets she'd once bought, made of straw, decorated with straw flowers in red and green. She took dresses and other clothes from drawers. She lined the work-baskets with them, and then she collected her ornaments from the mantelpiece and the dressing-table and the shelves. Her mother stood by the door, smiling and weeping at the same time. She blew her nose and wiped at her face with a tissue. 'Please, Pru,' she kept saying.

Prudence wrapped china pieces in handkerchiefs and under-clothes. She found the certificate she'd won for diving when she was eleven, and a scarf her father had bought for her, with Buckingham Palace on it.

Her mother came to her and tried to kiss her. She could feel the warm tears from her mother's eyes and was aware of revulsion. She held herself stiffly, wishing she'd go away.

'Pru, don't do this to me. I carried you inside my stomach, Pru. I suffered for you, love. I'm not well, Pru: I have terrible pains in the mornings, I have drumming in my ears the entire day long. Listen to me, Pru. Don't shame us, darling; don't go with a gaol-bird. You're only eighteen, Pru; that boy's a bag of nails. He'll mess you entirely up, he'll ruin your body with perversions. That boy went to bed with his mother, Pru. I swear it to you, Pru,' whispered Mrs Tuke, holding her daughter by the shoulders, try-

200

ing to pull her closer to her. 'I swear it on the Bible, he had a sexual relationship with his mother.'

Prudence felt the lips again and the warm tears. Her mother's hair was grey at the roots. One of her eyes was a little bloodshot. There was dandruff at the grey roots.

'Ask Gomez, darling. Gomez read his diary. Is that what you want, love? A boy that went with his mother? Don't you care, Pru?'

Mr Batt tried not to think about it. He rolled up ties and placed them in a suitcase that his wife had acquired in 1956 with a collection of Green Shield stamps. The suitcase had subsequently been used only when Mr Batt had moved to the Thistle Arms twelve years ago. It was a commodious case, large enough to hold all his clothes and any other odds and ends he still possessed. He'd often examined it during the time he'd been in the Thistle Arms, pleased with its handsome lines, silently congratulating the Green Shield organization on its good taste and posthumously complimenting his wife on her far-sightedness. At the time he'd rather wanted an ornament that could be obtained for the same number of stamps, a green glass fish upturned on a glass rock. They'd had a brief argument about it, he maintaining that since they never travelled a suitcase was hardly practical and she insisting that anything which had a use was more to the point than an inanimate fish. She'd been right, of course, as now was being proved.

All of a sudden, while taking a shirt from his chest of drawers, Mr Batt recalled the idea he'd had the afternoon before, about buying aspirins. He thought about it for a moment and then began to laugh. He imagined her coming into his room, all set to launch further insults, coming in without knocking, her mouth prepared for speech. He laughed again, a sound that began in a gurgling way and then became shrill. 'Ha, ha, ha,' he cried, imagining her standing at the door, seeing what she'd caused him to do. He was clean and always had been: there was no reason whatsoever for speaking to him in that extraordinary manner just because he'd made a reference to the milk.

* * *

201

'Then get out to hell,' shouted Mrs Tuke. 'There's filthy blood in you, Pru, and always has been. You're sly and you're furtive. You're a bloody disgrace to us.'

She didn't reply. She went on wrapping things up, knowing that any effort at explanation would only make everything worse.

'You'll die, that's what'll happen to you. You'll die without your mother to remind you to take your bloody pills. You couldn't remember a thing like that on your own. You can't hardly remember to go on the toilet.'

And then, half lying on the bed, her mother said she hadn't meant a word. She worshipped her, her mother said, she couldn't bear to see this terrible thing happening with a gaolbird. She'd buy her clothes, they'd go together to the shops, they'd go to Oxford Street that very afternoon, everything would be different.

The voice continued as Prudence with her two work-baskets went down the stairs. She heard the footsteps following her, and the sound of weeping, and odd words.

In the hall the man she assumed to be her father stood by the open door, looking into the emptiness of Crow Street, too far from the Dining-Rooms to see the bones and head of Rebel, which still lay on the pavement. 'I'm sorry,' he said. 'I'm sorry, Prudence.'

She felt no love for him nor did she feel, in that moment, capable of simulation. As she passed him by, she didn't speak, nor did she make a sign. She saw no reason not to punish him in that small way.

Later that morning Mr Tuke telephoned. He laid before a council clerk the facts about the cats that were wild in Crow Street and were now a hazard. The clerk promised to send men promptly. 'Thank you,' Mr Tuke said, and as he replaced the receiver he heard his wife pouring herself a drink in the private lounge even though the time was only ten past eleven.

She called to him, speaking of Prudence, but he didn't reply. She came into the public bar and stood beside him. She felt like death, she said. He looked at her and went away.

Typical that was. He knew she had nerves, he knew she suffered from a liver condition, yet he couldn't resist being nasty, not answering you when you spoke to him. Her hands were still shaking after all the unpleasantness; and just perceptibly she could feel a shaking sensation in her lips and teeth. The little drink made you feel better. It was the peppermint, really: it freshened your mouth after you'd been upset.

She returned to the private lounge and sat down on the stool she kept for herself behind the bar. She continued to feel better, even though the whole thing was disgusting and degrading, enough to make you physically sick. It had a degrading effect on you, causing you to behave in a manner that was completely alien to you. She hated obscenities above all else; she hated bad language and dirty language, yet in the last two days every room in the house had been full of both. She always turned the television off when the violence began, or the smut about toilets and the sexual act. She'd seen the man from the brewery putting his forefinger into his nose; filthy that was, the same kind of thing. She'd never permitted anything nasty in Prudence, she'd done her level best with the girl, knowing where she'd come from. A fat lot of use it had been, apparently.

The intoxicant moved through Mrs Tuke's body. It smoothed away the unease in her stomach. It stopped the shaking of her hands. The euphoria was pleasant, causing her to reflect that if her husband came in now she'd let bygones be bygones and say not to worry about his rudeness, they'd both been upset. She'd find her smile and maybe link his arm. She'd made a mistake when she married him in the first place, but you couldn't go on for ever being a mopey-mop over that. You only had the one life and no matter what was said in the heat of the moment, you had to kiss and make up if you wanted to keep yourself happy.

She recalled the day she'd been married and how she'd carried a little bouquet of lilies-of-the-valley. They'd gone in a hired car to the station and then on to the Isle of Wight. She'd enjoyed it there, dancing in the Beach Palace, like Sally and Nick Orpen in *Sister Sally's Honeymoon*, which of course she hadn't read at that time. She remembered Sarah Garlen's joy at the end of *Catch Not at Shadows* when she discovered that Dr Tom Airley had not married anyone else in her absence. She remembered how her green eyes had been veiled with happiness as she explained to Tom Airley that what she'd felt for Stephen Perivale was only infatuation, and how Tom Airley had gathered her into his arms. She remembered the end of *Nurse Rhona and Romance*, how everything came all right between Rhona and Alex, how Alex lay sleeping from sheer exhaustion and Nurse Rhona tiptoed away, knowing that when he awoke she'd fly to his arms once more.

'God, you're looking great, Beryl,' a voice said, and she turned her head and saw Atlas Flynn.

On a wheelbarrow he placed a sack over Rebel's remains. A donkey-coloured cat stood by the cellar grating of the Dining-Rooms, watching him. He felt the cat's arrogance, as though in some contest the cat had defeated him. He wheeled the barrow up Crow Street, to the Thistle Arms. Already he'd dug a hole in the small back garden. He filled it in, covering the sack and the bones with soil.

He would never have another dog. From the kitchen and from the bedroom he still shared he gathered the books on Alsatians that he'd bought. He walked with them to the garden and poured paraffin on them and lit them. He watched the pages brown and curl, and then blaze. He watched the glow pass from the embers, and felt rid of all sign of the dog that had replaced her. He felt no sadness now over Rebel's violent death, for it seemed to him that Rebel's death had taken place instead of hers, as part of a judgement that had been passed on him.

In the garden he sat on an old armchair that his wife had thrown out a year ago because its springs were gone. He'd stuffed it with sacking, having nothing to do one afternoon, and often during the heatwave he'd sat there with Rebel beside him, reading the newspaper. He thought of Rebel and Miss Gomez and the blank face of Prudence when she'd passed him on her way out of the Thistle Arms. He slept and strangely dreamed.

The cats were going to attack Miss Gomez. Some were crouching, ready to spring, others stood still, upright on their four legs, like thin statues. A few held back, watching the others. They were all over Crow Street between the Thistle Arms and the pet shop. Some had moved back from their cellar, in the direction of the public house, others had crept forward. None moved now.

They were like an army, arrayed in any old uniform: black, white, black-and-white, tortoiseshell, orange, grey, grey-and-white, brown. One stood with its tail stretched out, straight like a poker. Another appeared to have no tail at all. One, with trailing orange fur, was huge except for its thinness, but yet was not the leader. The leader, positioned like a general, was donkey-coloured.

Miss Gomez faced the cats. She, too, stood still. The sun, low in the sky, caused her glasses to gleam blindly. She was dressed as usual. She held no weapon.

In his dream he experienced the same feeling he'd experienced before: he felt entranced by her presence, unable to move or to speak. As she slowly went forward, her hands were by her side, her head was down, angled towards the donkey-coloured cat. He watched her and saw out of the corner of his eye the hair of another cat rise on its back. She moved so slowly that she was scarcely moving at all. A spitting sound began, coming from the donkey-coloured cat.

He could feel that she had no saliva in her mouth. Her mouth was made of cardboard. He could feel her legs moving, like straight sticks without joints. He could feel a sensation in her stomach.

The cats did not retreat. Their eyes did not leave her face, and did not blink. She didn't blink either; they would spring if she blinked. The furred mouth of the donkey-coloured cat showed teeth, its back was slightly arched. There was a potent smell, sickly like chloroform. She would fall and the smell would stifle her. Her eyelids were on pivots, huge, heavy blocks that soon would bang down. In his dream he felt them like that.

The cats were restive now. Miss Gomez smiled, and then they snarled, arching themselves and jerking their heads. Her shoe touched the donkey-coloured fur and at once the cat turned. The others went also, scampering through the barred grating of their cellar. 'You have to pray,' she said. 'And if you pray enough something happens.'

205

'Those cats should be put down,' another voice said, the voice of someone he couldn't see.

'Look,' Miss Gomez said. She was looking upwards, into the sky. In his dream he followed her gaze, shading his eyes, but he could see only the hazy blue of the sky. She was still smiling. 'Look,' she said again. 'Look. Do you see, Mr Tuke?'

He nodded to please her, still looking up at the ordinary blue sky.

'You're lucky,' she said, 'Our Lord looked after us. And He has passed only that small judgement on you, Mr Tuke. A dove returned to heaven,' she said, 'as you saw.'

But he confessed that he had seen no dove, and added that only she would see it because she had been granted powers.

'God demands prayer, Mr Tuke,' she said in reply. 'If powers are granted it is because of prayer.'

He said then, speaking quite naturally, that in his opinion she was a visionary. 'You came among us like Joan of Arc,' he said. 'You prevented a crime. You held back the cats.'

'No, no. I'm just a girl. The Brethren prayed in Tacas, Mr Tuke. The Brethren,' she said in a singsong voice. 'The Brethren, the Brethren.'

XIV

In the room it was almost dark. Only at the edges of the drawn blinds did sunshine penetrate the gloom: thin beams on pieces of the room, on boards and dark furniture and the spriggy pattern of wallpaper.

In a moment he would tell her: he would explain that she had brought it all about, that everything had come from her. In a moment he would tell her of the first time he'd seen her and how then she'd seemed, and since had always seemed, too fragile even to think about, and too special.

She smiled at him, looking down into his face, her long hair falling on to him. She said she loved him.

They lay on Mrs Bassett's bed. They felt no qualm, but felt instead, increasingly, that they belonged there, on the bed and in the room, which was a simple feeling, coming simply from the fact that the bed and the room were a circumstance in their association and seemed already part of it.

They talked in the room. She recalled her childhood in the Thistle Arms, playing among the mahogany furniture, her first awareness that her mother didn't care for her, the days she'd gone to football matches with her father. He said how Inspector Ponsonby had seemed a map turtle and Sergeant Gove a terrapin. He told her of shelling peas and listening to his mother's voice reading from a red-backed volume, *Butler's Lives of the Saints*, and Sister Tracy saying his mother's voice had a timbre that the Holy Mother's might have had, and Gerald Murphy's pack of cards and Egan's Café. They used to laugh together, she said, she and her father; sometimes they couldn't stop. A man objected to them on the street one day, asking them what they thought they were up to, kicking up a racket in a quiet area. She'd never forgotten that man, a man with a walking stick and pinched-up eyes and a protuberant Adam's apple that was as thin as a blade.

Brother Farrell, the Christian Brother who had sweets all over him, rubbed shoulders now with little Lenny Pash who'd worked in the pet shop and was evicted from the Thistle Arms because of the way he left the lavatory; and the girl from the kitchens of the Atlantic Hotel rubbed shoulders with Mr Ovens, a lodger who'd left in a hurry. People were jumbled in the room, teachers and neighbours, relatives, friends, the people of the town and the people of Crow Street. He held her body to his and told her of the passions that had possessed him for so long. He mentioned the girls who'd strutted the decks of the *Queen of Leinster* at the beginning of his exile, and the girl who had seemed to be unhealthy on a Soho street, and the white-painted windows of the Swansdale Badminton Club. In a temper one day her mother had confessed she hadn't wanted her to be born, and then had said she didn't mean it. He'd loved his mother, he said, and then suddenly had seemed to hate her: but now, in the room in which there were only thin beams of light, he could not hate the dead. His mother was distant now, a faded face, beyond emotion. They laughed again, remembering Inspector Ponsonby as a map turtle. Their hands caressed each other's skin, their lips touched and pressed, their arms gripped tightly, their four feet nestled.

She closed her eyes and seemed to be in hazel woods. She couldn't understand how she knew the trees were hazel, until she remembered that she was with him and he must have told her. It was hot, and insects twittered. The pressure of warmth was like a mist around her, the smell of sap exotic: she walked in a drifting way through heat and smell, her bare feet dancing on a surface that was scarcely there.

He stared at her closed eyes. He could see the hairs of her eyebrows coming out of her flesh and the pigmentation of her skin. He felt the beating of her heart; his cheek was damp from her mouth. Blood, he thought, might run between them, into his veins from hers and back again, artery joined to artery, tubes relating to lungs, nerves entwined. And yet he still felt doubt.

They lay apart then, gazing both of them at the ceiling. It could not be, he'd thought the day before in the Windrush Café, and yet there was something that might be: that, at least, they had achieved in this warm room.

Thought moved between them. They did not speak, but slowly, as they rested, she was disturbed by his suspicion. It pricked the surface of their love and was, in silence, accepted by her and confirmed: there was no permanence in what they had, nor could they, either of them, believe without pretence in the reality of such permanence between two people. Intensely she felt that her parents must once have loved as they did now. Intensely she felt that if they could view this moment from a vantage point in time they'd see each other as each other's stepping-stones from their separate pasts. Yet she knew that they were fortunate in their love, even if it lasted only six weeks more.

The silence continued in the room. 'Miss Gomez,' she said at length, breaking whatever spell there was.

They murmured about Miss Gomez, who had got everything so ludicrously mixed up. Miss Gomez, imagining her crime, had imagined then that some miracle had taken place, that in Tintagel Street there'd be an idyll for ever: Miss Gomez saw things in black and white when there were only complicated shades of grey, or so it seemed to both of them.

They forgot about Miss Gomez then. He heard her say again that she loved him. He loved her too, and he knew he did, in the room, in that moment. He said so, and then he pushed his mind away from her, to see what else would happen in it. *Echinodermata are coelomate,* he thought. *Asteroidea,* he thought. *Crinoidea, mullusca, bradydonti, crocodilia, cephalochordata, uruchordata, protozoa.* He loved these sounds. He loved the look of the words on paper. It would be easier only to love such things and not be bothered with minds and bodies, bodies especially. Was it all just imagination, the love they spoke of when they said it to one another, like the heaven in Miss Gomez's imagination? Was love just bodily, a mother holding on to part of herself, a man or woman ordinarily functioning? Bees were better organized without it, and ants, the only insects left that threatened man's arrogant rule.

She smiled at him, touching his wrist. She said she'd start at once to breed Camberwell Beauties and in the garden in Tintagel Street she'd put down sunflower seeds in the Spring. They'd breed more squirrels and jerboas. They'd sell clawed frogs and geckos and axolotls and toucans and fruit bats and chameleons.

'Marmosets,' he said, slipping into her harmless pretence that the idyll waited for them in Tintagel Street and would for ever continue, that they could count on permanence when all around them permanence failed.

They talked of pets and of the future, lying on the bed of Mrs Bassett, whose happy marriage had not in its time been regarded as a human rarity but had been famous none the less, locally. They lay until it was time to go downstairs, to pack up everything.

XV

She was wearing her wine-coloured trouser-suit. At her throat, on a high-necked matching blouse, sprawled a dragon in gold plate, with little red beads here and there on its body and green chips for eyes.

It was quiet in the Thistle Arms as she walked about, noting what they'd be taking with them and what they'd leave behind. Several months ago the brewery man had said that the brewery wouldn't wish to reclaim anything of the furniture at all, but who'd want to cart stuff like this up to the Arab's Head?

She glanced through the side window of the first-floor landing and saw her husband asleep in the garden, on a filthy armchair that she'd thrown out nearly a year ago. He looked like a tramp, surrounded by other objects that had been thrown out, an old boiler that had been there for as long as she could remember and wooden bottlecrates and an iron bed. Beyond where he was sitting she could see freshly-disturbed soil and guessed it was the burial place of his dog.

She looked into Alban Roche's room and saw that some time in the course of the morning he'd removed his property, but had left behind him a trunk and two cardboard boxes, which were the containers Gomez had been on about, with a woman's clothes in them. He'd no right to leave anything, she thought, but she felt it hard to work up greater indignation. She sighed, saying to herself that it probably didn't matter, since the whole place would be as flat as a pancake in no time.

She returned to her own room and began to pack her clothes. She hummed, keeping her spirits up, determined not to be upset by what had occurred after Atlas Flynn had appeared in the private lounge. There was nothing to get depressed about: it had in no way been her fault, she could in no way be blamed. She'd just been through one of the ghastliest twenty-four hours of her life, having to face total embarrassment, with photographs in the newspapers for no reason whatsoever, and then a display of bad-tempered rudeness by a man she'd married in error. You couldn't be expected to be in a normal state after events such as those had occurred, one after another, without permitting you time to breathe. If you took a drink when you were in a condition like that it went straight to your head. She'd said that to him because when he'd started playing around she hadn't been able to prevent herself from laughing. Never again would she go about a public house, at any time of day whatsoever, in a dressing-gown. 'What's that you're wearing?' he'd said, laughing himself, with both his hands pulling at the cord. She'd caught the odour of his sweat the entire time he was taking advantage of her, and the scent of a flower-garden in his coarse red hair. No matter what she did she couldn't control her laughing, which made him think she was on for something, when all the time she was trying to push him off. It had been the same the second time with Eddie Mercer, when he'd said come upstairs and she'd said definitely not and he'd sniggered just like Flynn, and whispered in his coarse way that he wouldn't take no for an answer, not from a big girl like herself. Flynn still had the same bandage on his hand, the piece of her old nightdress, in a filthy condition now. In the middle of everything he said he'd known she was mad for it the first moment he walked into the Thistle two months ago and saw her serving there. On a couple of occasions he'd hardly been able to control himself, he said.

Mrs Tuke hummed *Wrap Me up in Cotton-Wool*. She cleared a drawer and found that it was lined with a newspaper dated March 12th, 1935, placed there by her predecessor. *Royal Marriage Rumours*, a headline said. She'd die stone dead if Flynn ever showed his face in the Arab's Head; imagine the cut of him walking into surroundings like that with the bandage and the greased hair. He'd said he didn't intend to let her out of his life while he had the energy to walk after her; he'd mentioned marriage, saying he couldn't do without her. 'I learnt my lesson,' he said, referring to the occasion the day before when he'd tried something on at a time when the lounge was full of customers: he apologized, saying he hadn't realized at the time the way she was about matters like that. 'I'll hang around at the back,' he assured her, referring to the back of the Arab's Head, but you could never tell with persons like that, they had no sense of discretion at all. If he walked into a lounge and tried on his tactics in the middle of the morning he'd try them on any time and in any surroundings. It embarrassed her to her backbone whenever she thought of it, which was punishment enough, God knows, for something she had in no way been responsible for.

At the bottom of another drawer Mrs Tuke found a flowered blouse she'd thought a cleaner, a Mrs Mather, had stolen from her. The flowers were delphiniums, assorted colours on a pale green ground, a most striking pattern. She held it against her, murmuring to it as to an old friend, welcoming it into her life again.

People came to Crow Street. Three men arrived to put down the cats. A lorry arrived, with the legend *Winstanley's Removals All Parts of London* painted, unprofessionally, on one of its doors, the white letters unformed and varying in size, some of them trailing narrow rivulets of paint. Mr Winstanley himself drove the vehicle and was assisted in the task of carrying furniture by his son Thomas, a wiry youth of fifteen with soft, adolescent down on his chin and upper lip. Mr Winstanley was bigger and broader, with a round red face and springy grey hair. Dark corduroy trousers were held up by braces, his shirt was of blue denim. Thomas was similarly dressed.

'How d'you do,' Mr Winstanley said, presenting himself in the pet shop. Thomas held out his hand and Alban Roche shook it, having shaken also Mr Winstanley's. There was an old-fashioned quality about the Winstanleys; and their lorry, which Mr Winstanley had drawn across Crow Street and backed into the doorway of the shop so that nothing would have to be carried any farther than was necessary, gave the same impression of belonging to the past.

213

'Thank you, very much!' screeched the crested mynah, its head on one side. 'Ha, ha, ha,' laughed the cockatiel.

'My, my,' Mr Winstanley exclaimed. He poked a finger at the cockatiel and the cockatiel pecked at it. 'Cheeky monkey!' cried Mr Winstanley. Thomas laughed and the cockatiel laughed.

Mr Winstanley looked at all the pets, being in no haste to begin the removal. He murmured at the hamsters and the gerbils. He'd had a guinea-pig once when he'd been a child, in 1925 it must have been, and two tortoises. In those days people reckoned to have a tortoise or so around the place.

'Mum'd like that bushbaby,' Thomas said. 'Her birthday, Dad, the twenty-fifth.'

'How much the bushbaby, son?' Mr Winstanley inquired, not looking up, his large form still bent over the tortoises. When he heard the price he quite casually said that that would be all right. 'Put it in the cab, lad,' he ordered, and Thomas carried the large cage to the lorry. 'Mind the step!' the parrot called Godfrey warned. 'Ha, ha, ha,' cried the cockatiel.

'We'll call it von Runstedt,' Mr Winstanley announced, leaving the tortoises when Thomas returned. But Thomas, laughing loudly, suggested that a name for the bushbaby was best left to his mother.

Mr Tuke saw the Winstanleys' lorry and said to himself that that lorry with the badly painted white letters on the door had been in his dream, and the red-faced man and the boy had been in it also. He was certain of all that as he walked towards the pet shop. The lorry and the man and the boy had been shadows because of the importance of Miss Gomez in the centre of everything, but they had been there none the less.

The furniture was being carried out of the pet shop and already, even before he asked the question, he knew that Miss Gomez was no longer in Crow Street. She'd left twenty minutes ago, the red-cheeked man said, carrying a bag. Mr Tuke looked down Crow Street, a reflex action that carried with it its own disappointment.

'Sorry about that, mister,' Mr Winstanley said, as if he himself were in some way responsible for Miss Gomez's departure. It was the voice that had spoken in his dream, the voice that had said the cats should be put down, of that Mr Tuke would swear. He turned and walked back towards the Thistle Arms.

Mr Batt was the last to see her. He went to a chemist's in Abyssinia Street and on the way back he met her, in a street where all the houses had been pulled down but from which piles of bricks and slates had not yet been cleared away.

She carried a canvas bag with the words *Canadian Pacific Airlines* on it. She wasn't carrying anything else except a leather handbag that was slung over her left shoulder, black like her dress. She'd held her right hand out when she was close to him. She smiled profusely and after a time he heard her saying that she was going away.

He was going too, he said. The brewery people were going to close down the Thistle Arms in a hurry because of the carry-on last night. He hadn't known a thing himself, he added, until he opened his newspaper that morning and saw a snap of himself in his pyjamas. He regarded her closely, interested because the paper had said she possessed special powers, second sight seemingly. What would she think, he wondered, if she knew that he'd bought a bottle of aspirins?

She spoke, but he couldn't follow her. He wanted to tell her about the aspirins; he could feel himself wanting to see her face when she heard. She was someone he didn't know, it wouldn't matter what she thought; different entirely from telling one of the people of Crow Street. The urge increased in him as he watched her talking, and then it seemed vital that he should speak, to see how she felt about it.

'I thought I'd take a few of these,' he said, taking the bottle of aspirins from his pocket. He took with it, unintentionally, the photograph of himself, which he'd cut out of the newspaper.

She continued to smile at him, and he considered that unusual in the circumstances. He had been about to state his age and to add that having survived two major wars and having welcomed to the throne of England four monarchs, he felt that he'd really, one way or another, had enough, adding that the advent of death did not depress him. He'd been on the verge of saying all that in case she became upset in any way, but he saw that it wasn't necessary. Her lips moved, but he couldn't quite catch what she said. She continued to smile her profuse smile, examining with delight the somewhat blurred photograph in the newspaper. She handed it back to him, and her voice came to him clearly. She was telling him he should lie down, which again surprised him, because it was surely unusual for one person to give advice to another person on the posture to adopt before self-inflicted death. She was sorry, she said, and mentioned a headache.

'No, no,' he said, taking the aspirins from his pocket again. 'I'm going to eat them.'

He explained that he'd prefer to eat them in the Thistle Arms, which was going to be pulled down anyway, rather than in some boarding-house. It wouldn't be entirely fair on a hard-working boarding house proprietor to wake up one morning and find a dead man on the premises, especially an elderly man who had arrived only the day before. It was like the brewery people and the fuss there'd been last night apparently; nobody liked scandal involving death.

She was angry with him then, which at least was better than smiling. 'Good idea,' Mrs Tuke would probably have said. She raised her voice: it was an evil thing, he heard her say, thoroughly wicked. He quite enjoyed her anger.

'There's your pipe,' she was shouting at him, her mouth opening very wide and then closing up again.

'Pipe?' he said.

'You enjoy your pipe, Mr Batt.'

She went on talking about things he enjoyed and he listened with pleasure because it was nice, someone being concerned, even if it was only a black cleaner. 'Would you like a drink?' he suggested. 'There's The King of Spain in Abyssinia Street.'

They walked together. He talked about war, about rain and mud at a place she'd never heard of, called Passchendaele, about a German aeroplane that had dropped a bomb on a dance-hall. His two sons had been killed fighting, a fact that in time had caused the death of his wife, so he believed. Funny, he often thought, to be still going strong himself.

In The King of Spain she drank Pepsi-Cola, he had beer. People looked at them, recognizing her from the photographs there'd been in the newspapers, and then recognizing him. 'Those sex crime people,' a man said to the landlord.

He filled his pipe and lit it. 'It cheers you, a chat,' he said, and added that he'd enjoyed receiving the Jackpot mail because it meant that people he wasn't acquainted with knew he was still going strong in Crow Street. Quite nice, that, instead of insults. He'd mentioned that the milk was off and she'd raged at him like a tigress in a zoo. She'd probably been upset by the hullabaloo last night, but still it was no excuse. Tracker-dogs apparently, there'd been, and men out searching; he hadn't known a thing.

She said he must not take the aspirins. She said he must promise her not to, that he must give her the aspirins and keep his promise. She'd help him find a boarding-house, she said, but he replied that that wouldn't be necessary. Mr Tuke had promised to help him. Mr Tuke was going to order a taxi.

He went away to buy further drinks and when he returned he said she could have the aspirins if she liked because he never suffered from a headache himself. Thing was, he said, when it came to the actual point you wouldn't have the courage to eat them: you might think about it, you might imagine her coming into the room, her red mouth open to give out an insult, but you wouldn't have the courage to cause her to see a body stretched out, as dead as mutton. You could think about lots of things that you'd like to do, and even begin to do them, like he'd begun by going to the chemist's, but when it came to the actual point you couldn't see your way to finishing off what you'd begun. It was nice going to the chemist's with it all in your mind, it was nice thinking things and chatting about them. He'd really enjoyed their chat, he said.

XVI

They were alone in Crow Street. She still wore her wine-coloured trouser-suit with the dragon at her throat. She'd been talking about the packing that had to be done, every cup and saucer; Roche had left the trunk upstairs, she said, and the two boxes. No joke packing in a heatwave, she said.

They were in the kitchen, just having eaten their evening meal. A man on a horse rode slowly across the television screen. She spoke to her husband again, watching the horseman. 'First thing in Kew,' she said, 'I'll go and see a doctor.'

On the screen a woman danced, on the bar of a saloon. Men dressed as cow-hands watched, one of them fingering a gun, suggesting with the gesture that death was on the way.

They'd all had an upsetting time, she said quietly, but it was over now and you had to accept what there was. Pru was a hippy type of girl, the same as Roche was; the police inspector had said the same, only she hadn't had the energy at the time to tell him he was right. The full truth of the matter was that Pru was a law unto herself and always had been, as silent as an empty grave, Alban Roche was definitely affected, what with women's clothes and that, but when you came to consider it poor Pru wasn't all that different, not of course that Pru had ever gone in for anything with clothing. She'd hoped, as any conscientious mother would, that poor Pru might take a shine on a different type of chap, a nicely-mannered bloke, maybe a medical bloke or something like that. But the difficulty was that Pru was so unforthcoming that young fellows these days wouldn't be bothered.

He didn't reply to her and he wondered if he'd ever reply to her again. He wanted to tell her that everything Miss Gomez said about her was true, but if he said that she'd say that Miss Gomez was no better than a lump of filth. She'd lose her temper and tell him in the end that she was glad his dog was dead.

In the saloon on the television screen the cow-hands applauded, all except the man who was fingering his gun. It was clear now which of the other men he intended to kill, by the way he was surreptitiously regarding him.

The only way to look at it, she said, was to say to yourself that since Pru had set her heart on that type of life the whole thing was probably a blessing in disguise, although at the time it was naturally enough to knock you down dead. You had to find the bright side in every situation, and if Pru decided in six months or a year that she'd had enough of what she'd chosen for herself she'd always get her welcome in the Arab's Head, just like any other daughter would.

'Which reminds me,' she said, 'I was thinking of the type of clientele up there: we'll have to smarten ourselves up a bit. Fingernails, deodorants, all that type of thing. I was wondering if you'd get a blazer? And another thing I was wondering: it might be quite amusing if you didn't speak much, if right from the very start you created a certain impression, old chap.'

He didn't reply. If he was lying on the floor, she thought, she'd kick him with the point of her shoe. She'd leave him for dead, the way he was behaving. 'Ah, you're lovely,' he said, the first night he'd put his hands on her. He'd gone under her skirt in a crude way, being so enthusiastic that she hadn't the heart to prevent him. 'You have lovely arms,' he'd said.

He'd told her, one time in a quarrel, that he'd grown the beard because he was ashamed of himself, and that the arthritis that made him limp about like a cripple had been caused by her, that it came from his nervous system. Ridiculous he was, toilet-training Pru the way he had, changing her clothes like a woman would; unnatural really.

'What I was thinking, darling,' she said, 'was that maybe it wouldn't be a bad idea for a landlord not to speak at all. A gimmick thing, like they have the sacks of meal in the Red Rover.'

'Drop it, honey,' a man said to the man who was fingering his gun and then struck him on the jaw. The woman who'd been dancing screamed. A bottle was thrown, and then a table.

There was a knock on the door that led to the backyard, and a moment later Mr Winstanley and his son Thomas were in the kitchen, saying they'd heard the public house was to be vacated and wondering if they could have the removal work. Mrs Tuke said the brewery would be seeing to all that. She laughed to herself, thinking of the Winstanleys' decrepit lorry arriving at the Arab's Head. 'Not wanting to get rid of anything, are you?' Mr Winstanley suggested. 'Any old pieces?'

Seeing no reason not to make a penny or two out of a load of rubbish that neither she nor the brewery had any use for, Mrs Tuke said that some of the pieces were extremely valuable. 'Let's see what you fancy,' she said, glad to have an excuse to lead the Winstanleys from the kitchen because her husband hadn't greeted them or even looked at them. Extremely embarrassing that type of thing was, behaving like a baby.

A group of horsemen galloped wildly up a rocky incline. They paused on the top and then slowly rode down the other side. Words fell on top of them as they rode over a plain towards a darkening horizon. There was a burst of light and then an advertisement came on, one that Mrs Bassett had viewed two nights ago. A girl moved in an eccentric manner on a street. 'One of today's great tastes,' a voice said.

In the Arab's Head he'd go into a room with her, into the same bed that they'd occupied all their married life. After all that had happened that was the punishment he must accept. It was too late for anything else: he should have picked up a knife from the kitchen table and driven it into Eddie Mercer's stomach; he should have known without being told what Eddie Mercer was up to. His weakness had made her what she was. He knew it because he felt it, like Miss Gomez had said she'd felt things, and also because once his wife had been different.

He had looked up the Brethren of the Way in the telephone directory but they weren't in. He'd imagined they would have a

London branch, but apparently they hadn't, and he knew no address to write to, now that Miss Gomez was gone. He wanted to write, to say to somebody that he knew he was to blame, that he was small and weak and undignified, that everything could be traced to him.

'Well, I think after that,' said Mrs Tuke, leading the Winstanleys downstairs again, 'what we need is a drop in a glass.'

She led the way into the private lounge. Her husband, she was glad to see, had remained in the kitchen. Extraordinary really, how people went into the sulks these days, for no reason whatsoever. 'What would you like?' she inquired smiling at the Winstanleys. He'd been a good-looking man in his time, she reflected, before he'd acquired the high colour in his face.

She poured their drinks, Mr Winstanley having a small glass of whisky and a pint of beer, and Thomas taking only beer. A price had been agreed on for two pieces of furniture the Winstanleys were to take. The remainder she'd leave behind to be set fire to.

'You heard about the commotion we had?' she inquired and the Winstanleys said they had. No harm done, Mr Winstanley pronounced, a storm in a teacup.

Mrs Tuke disagreed with that view. A considerable quantity of harm had been done, she pointed out. A dog had been destroyed, which would not have happened otherwise: had it not been for the fuss the dog would have been safe by his master's side, lying on the carpet in their bedroom instead of roaming out among dangerous cats.

'Did the black have hallucinations?' Thomas asked because the account he'd read of the events in Crow Street seemed to imply that Miss Gomez had had hallucinations.

Mrs Tuke replied that the black was total rubbish and the cause of everything. 'She had mad hallucinations, certainly she did. She stood in the hall yesterday morning and raved like a third-degree lunatic. We had an old lodger here, a poor old devil that she frightened out of his skin. She upset Mr Tuke to the extent that he was standing on the stairs unable to move himself. There was

221

a young labourer who called in for attention to his hand who said he'd never seen the like. There's no knowing why that girl came to this street.'

'Abnormal, certainly,' said Mr Winstanley.

'She gave us chapter and verse, Mr Winstanley, of immoral earnings accumulated since she arrived in London on her black banana boat. Bold as brass in front of the labourer and Mr Tuke.'

'Good God!' murmured Mr Winstanley.

'She had to do with those cats. I was talking to the fellows that put them down. They were totally perplexed by those animals.'

'We heard about the cats—'

'I said to the men, could they be bred? They were amazed to see them all down in a cellar like that. She was breeding the cats, Mr Winstanley.'

Mr Winstanley and his son were surprised to hear this. You read about stuff like that, Mrs Tuke explained: Negroes didn't understand about domestic pets any more than they understood about normal food. She'd heard of cases where they kept cats and dogs just in order to cut them up and tin them. They didn't mind what they ate; they'd tin you as soon as look at you, most of them.

'She had the cats collected in the cellar,' Mrs Tuke continued, 'for the purpose of having them killed by West Indian butchers. They skin them and sell the fur. The rest goes into a tin.'

Mr Winstanley regarded Mrs Tuke closely, his eyes suspiciously narrowed. From the newspaper report and the fact that the black girl had been completely wrong in everything she forecast, he could believe Mrs Tuke's claim that she was mentally unbalanced, but he found it hard to accept these statements about breeding cats and West Indian butchers.

'They get like that,' said Mrs Tuke. 'They go out in the tropical sun without a hat on their heads.'

Mr Winstanley laughed, feeling that in this Mrs Tuke was definitely exaggerating. She laughed also.

'If Gomez hadn't come here,' she said, 'my daughter and Alban Roche wouldn't be going off like a couple of hippies.'

'It said in the paper,' Thomas said, 'how she was brought to Crow Street. God's will, apparently—'

'God's fiddlesticks! She came on her flat black feet. She saw a few cats and decided to settle in. She saw the labouring men knocking down the buildings. Those men paid her for services rendered.'

'The labourers?' murmured Mr Winstanley with interest.

'Every lunch-break. She's spread disease among those labourers like water through a sieve.'

Mr Winstanley nodded and Thomas, less experienced in these matters, thought that the black girl hadn't looked at all like that to him, what with her glasses and everything. He'd heard about the disease that Mrs Tuke was talking about. It could pass through your hand, his father had warned him, or through the lips. In fact, it was a hazard that dentists had to face: they could pick up the disease on their fingers through working with a person's mouth, even though they themselves lived exemplary lives. It was something always to beware of. When he'd been in the army, his father told him, there'd been a special tap that you washed yourself at after being out in the evenings.

'That's the story,' said Mrs Tuke: 'a black negroid gone round the bend due to unmentionable reasons, coming here after labourers and cats.'

Mr Winstanley nodded. 'I see,' he said.

'They have a different way of life from ours. There's things they can't ever understand.'

Shortly after that Mr Winstanley and Thomas carried downstairs the two pieces of furniture that Mrs Tuke had sold them and Mr Winstanley paid Mrs Tuke in one-pound notes.

On the way home they talked about what they'd heard and Mr Winstanley said he believed very little of it. It wasn't easy to unravel the truth these days, he said, and you couldn't even begin when you had to make sense of religion and sex and a woman like Mrs Tuke, who was, in his opinion, just as strange as the black she went on about. The truth wasn't respected these days, he said. You didn't know where you were. Something was wrong, he often thought, but it was hard to put your finger on it.

They talked about the bushbaby then, which they'd hidden in a shed until Mrs Winstanley's birthday on the twenty-fifth. 'Von

Runstedt,' said Mr Winstanley, laughing, but Thomas repeated what he'd stated that morning: that Mrs Winstanley would not wish to call her bushbaby von Runstedt.

The evening papers that day carried a brief paragraph to the effect that the girl who'd been missing from Crow Street, S.W.17, had now been found. No harm had come to her. It was all a misunderstanding.

Inspector Ponsonby, returning by bus to his wife and house in Southfields, read the item with distaste. He didn't wish to think about it any more. He didn't wish to think about the bleakness of Crow Street, or the limping grey man who ran the public house with his big wife, or the two drop-outs who all the time had apparently been up to something else, or the black girl. He'd thought of her, without wishing to, a few times since, remembering the previous occasion and remembering the way she'd held her hands today. They were so very different sometimes; they had a kind of grace that white women didn't possess at all.

'Excuse me,' Inspector Ponsonby said to the woman who was sitting beside him on the bus. She collected up her parcels and let him pass her by. He thanked her and left the bus three stops too soon, in order to have a drink or two at the Royal Oak before facing his wife and his house, and the garden where just now the rock plants were at their best.

Other people read that the girl had been found. Some were disappointed, for they enjoyed a nationwide hunt with appeals on television and pictures of the missing person posted up outside police stations. Others were pleased.

The doctor who'd signed Mrs Bassett's death certificate had heard during the course of his rounds that Prudence Tuke and the youth who was supposed to have violated her were to set up house together, selling Mrs Bassett's pets in Tintagel Street. He couldn't understand it. He couldn't understand that whole generation, or the way they went about, moving so slowly sometimes, like automatons. He couldn't understand the long hair of the boys and the strange Indian-like clothes the girls often affected, or why they should be attracted by a peculiar way of life, or why they wanted to experiment with their minds, under dangerous drugs, caring about neither life nor death, pure in their cynicism. His daughter would soon be wholly like that, half-baked, half-dead.

The man called Fennell from whom Prudence had bought the buckets and the cleaning materials read in the evening paper that she'd turned up and said to his wife that the police were mean these days the way they never gave a reward. The woman who'd sold Prudence the limeade read the news and was pleased. 'Camberwell Beauties,' she said, murmuring to herself.

XVII

Miss Gomez took a room in the Hotel Bon Accueil in Bayswater Road and from that address sent a telegram to Tacas, requesting that now she might return to Jamaica since she felt she had proved herself worthy of her conversion. To this she received no immediate reply. She had expected a telegram in return some hours later, but when she thought about it she realized she had been emotional and could not expect such swift communications from a Church. She wrote at length the following day, explaining everything and giving her address again as the Hotel Bon Accueil, Bayswater Road. She wrote, as well, several other letters.

Dear Miss Arbuthnot, she wrote, still wondering if Miss Arbuthnot was alive, *you will be pleased to hear from me. I am the Gomez girl who ran away, my mother and father perished in the Adeline Street disaster. I am happy now, Miss Arbuthnot. In London I found my way to God, through my own sins and later through the sins of others, for whom I daily pray. I think, Miss Arbuthnot, that you do not know the true Lord and this is just to say that if you would like to know more about the Church that found me please write to me c/o The Church of the Way, King George VI Road, Tacas, where I shall be in two days' time.*

I hope the orphanage is doing well. I'm sorry for the things I said about that matron, whose name I don't remember.

To Mrs Tuke she wrote:

I met Mr Batt and had a drink with him in The King of Spain in Abyssinia Street. I thought I would tell you this, Mrs Tuke, because Mr Batt had bought aspirins which he intended to take in quantity. I have read that the elderly become depressed, as I'm sure you have too. I took the aspirins from Mr Batt, a large bottle containing five hundred, and he promised me that he would not contemplate buying aspirins again. He became his old self in The King of Spain, talking about the Jackpot and some place he was at during the First World War, with bad weather conditions. I think he is great for his age, as I'm sure you do too, but I'm writing this to say that he requires somebody to keep an eye on him because of the dispirited state he can get into, and perhaps you would reconsider your decision not to take him with you to the Arab's Head.

All the best in your new life, Mrs Tuke. I'm sorry I got carried away and upset you in the hall. I did not mean any harm.

If ever you feel the need of my Church please write to me c/o The Church of the Way, King George VI Road, Tacas, Jamaica.

To Alban Roche she said she was sorry too, and she wrote the same to Prudence, saying good-bye to both of them and leaving with them her address in Jamaica.

She recalled for Mr Tuke a verse from a hymn and went on to say that she was sorry about his dog, Rebel. I did not have a chance to say I was sorry about this before I left Crow Street as I did not see you. I hope you can become reconciled to the loss of your dog, who I know was also your friend.

If ever you feel the need to, you can reach me in Jamaica c/o The Church of the Way, King George VI Road, Tacas.

She had not included Hibiscus Villa in the address she'd given these people, knowing that Hibiscus Villa was the private residence of the Reverend Lloyd Patterson, and it would certainly have been presumptuous to have letters for her arriving there. She hoped it would not be regarded as a presumption by her Church that she'd given an address at all.

Hibiscus Villa, wrote Mrs Drate on a blue envelope. As well, she'd written how much more at peace she felt since she'd begun what still seemed to her to be an eccentric correspondence, although she did not call it such in her letter. She'd written that day at very great length, explaining in fresh detail what it felt like to be the widow of a clergyman who'd lost his faith and who'd caused her, through his violent action, to lose hers temporarily. She felt better, having poured everything out. She couldn't ever have done so otherwise, by talking to someone openly or even going into a confessional.

The schoolgirl who suffered from acne wrote also. She had received comfort from the understanding she'd received, she wrote, and then she made certain confessions, about how a month or so ago when confined to bed with 'flu she'd closed her eyes and imagined she was alone with an unidentified man in front of whom she was taking off her blouse. Like Mrs Drate, she found it easy to write, once she'd begun.

The cinema usher, who had spent two years in a mental institution and had, until he'd seen the advertisement in *Make Friends in London,* been haunted by a longing to return there, reported that in Charing Cross Road, Leicester Square, the Strand and the Victoria Embankment he had harangued passers-by with news of the New Testament and of the Church of the Way. He proffered this information in the mornings and lit people to their seats in the afternoons and evenings. He had discovered contentment, he wrote, in addressing the people of London, even if his words so far had not in any way been heeded.

XVIII

Another day went by. The flawless heat continued.

Mr Batt found a boarding-house in Parson's Green, not far from Putney, which he had known so well during the Second World War. 'There's just the two of you,' a Mrs Taggart said. 'Miss Tibbett's here also.' The house was in Delvino Road, a house in a terrace. 'We take to the retired,' Mrs Taggart said. 'Six o'clock meat tea, Mr Batt, and we prefer to stop in after that.'

Mr Batt had difficulty in understanding what the woman was saying because she seemed hardly to be making a noise at all when she spoke. After a time, though, she raised her voice and everything was all right. 'There's the wireless, of course,' she said. 'We haven't gone in for the other.'

Miss Tibbett listened when he told her about his experiences during the two World Wars. The food was better than Mrs Tuke's food and in a way he found the atmosphere cheerful. He walked in the afternoons about Eel Brook Common. Sometimes, by way of a change, he went over towards Chelsea Dock and wandered about the gasworks and the power station.

He had arranged to attend the funeral of Mrs Bassett with Mr Tuke, and on the appointed morning they met in a public house near Putney Bridge. After a drink they caught a bus. Eel Brook Green was quite interesting, he said: young mothers wheeling their babies out, plenty going on. From the top of the bus Mr Tuke could see the floodlights of Fulham Football Club, their huge reflectors sparkling in the sunlight. 'We're moving off of Crow Street tomorrow,' he shouted at Mr Batt, and Mr Batt, quite understanding, said that maybe one morning he'd make the journey to Kew and have a drink for old times' sake. He might bring a Miss Tibbett, he said, a lady he'd got to know in Parson's Green.

'A buzz-bomb landed there,' he said, pointing at the front garden of a small suburban house. 'Didn't do a pennyworth of damage.' The garden was full of gnomes now, one holding a fishing-rod over a tiny pond around which roses grew in profusion. The few feet of lawn were closely shorn, brown from lack of rain.

In the crematorium people walked among the graves and the trees. It was a tranquil place; everyone was early.

'There's Pru,' Mr Batt said.

Mr Tuke saw her also. They weren't holding hands or anything like that, he noticed. They were walking together like a brother and a sister might. Prudence was carrying her Indian sandals, one in each hand. She put them on as they approached the chapel.

No one else attended the funeral of Mrs Bassett. In the chapel a clergyman stood up and said that she had lived to a fine age. Her shell was left on earth, he said, her spirit had ascended. Consider life below as wine in a bottle: when the wine was gone the container remained; what use was an empty bottle?

'And bottles of course have labels,' said the clergyman, a youngish man with sandy hair. 'Dorothy Rose Bassett, kind to God's creatures, thoughtful of His people, born into our Christian family. Dorothy Rose Bassett, stalwart in her life.' The corpse, confined in elm, slid away to be burnt.

'As *our* wine also,' said the young clergyman, 'must one day ascend from its earthly container.'

They walked out into the sunshine. The clergyman shook their hands and said he was sorry. 'Nice little gardens,' remarked Mr Batt, looking around. 'And very nice that service was.'

Mr Tuke smiled through his beard at Prudence and Alban Roche, and Alban Roche said that the pets were selling already in Tintagel Street. They were buying in new hamsters and budgerigars. They'd sold one of the squirrels that Mr Bassett had originally bred. He spoke in his usual quiet way. Prudence took off her Indian sandals again. She didn't smile much at Mr Tuke.

'We buried Mrs Batt,' Mr Batt said to the young clergyman, 'in the graveyard of St Nicholas's, eight years ago now. They've had her up, of course, with all this development plan. They had them all up, actually. I don't quite know what they did with them.'

'Oh, I'm sure—'

'You know where you are with this burning thing, and anyway I like the gardens here. I'll leave an instruction, sir. Batt the name is. A. J. Batt.'

He would write to her, Mr Tuke thought, now that she had sent him her address. He hadn't listened enough to her, he'd say, when she'd been in Crow Street, but he wanted to listen now. Her Church, he'd explain, interested him.

If Mrs Bassett hadn't died when she did none of it would have happened, Prudence thought. Something beautiful, Miss Gomez had written in her letter, repeating what she'd already implied. The words sounded old-fashioned and made her think of people in Victorian dress, girls passing from a drawing-room into a dark garden, and nightingales singing in the branches of trees.

She hadn't seen Miss Gomez leave Crow Street. They'd gone to her room and found she'd left a lot of things behind: the religious pictures were still on the walls, and the calendar with the picture of a garden on it, and personal belongings were still in some of her drawers. It had been nice of her to write.

Mr Tuke wandered alone through flowers and yew trees, upset because Prudence hadn't spoken to him. He watched her walking with Alban Roche on the avenue that led to the crematorium's entrance gates and wondered if he'd ever see her again. Mr Batt, by the chapel, was still talking to the sandy-haired clergyman.

Among the flowers and the yew trees he took Miss Gomez's letter from the inside pocket of his jacket and examined her upright, clear handwriting. *When I survey the wondrous Cross,* she'd quoted, *On which the Prince of Glory died, My richest gain I count but loss, And pour contempt on all my pride.* Her face came clearly back to him. He remembered her voice, quoting lines from the Bible, and hymns. He recollected the clergy she'd mentioned and how she'd endlessly described the procession of her Church through the Jamaican town. Affected by the contents of her letter and by his surroundings and the service he had just attended, he saw

231

quite easily all she had described, the Brethren of her Church in the neighbourhood of the Church's foundation. He saw them as they walked through sunshine, headed by the four big clergymen, smiling in their surplices. 'O God of Hosts, the mighty Lord,' sang all the Brethren, 'how lovely is the place.' They sat on the warm grass and opened the picnic baskets, and the clergymen passed among the people. 'Happy,' said the Reverend Lloyd Patterson, standing a little above them on the small hill. 'Happy, O Lord Our God.'

In the distance he saw the sandy-haired clergyman shaking Mr Batt's hand again. Mr Batt held on to the hand, still talking.

'I was telling him,' he said when Mr Tuke was near enough to hear, 'about Henry Bassett's back.'

They said good-bye to the clergyman and walked together towards the gates, not in much of a hurry. Mr Batt went on talking, about Miss Gomez and Miss Tibbett and the pain that Henry Bassett had quietly endured from shrapnel in his back. Mr Tuke occasionally nodded.

The clergyman returned to the chapel to prepare himself for another service. Other people took the places of Alban Roche and Prudence and Mr Tuke and Mr Batt, another coffin came into view and then slipped away, through curtains, to the furnace. 'I'd like you to think,' said the clergyman, 'of wine in a bottle.'

The sauce of the black lump, coming out with that about old Batt after all that had taken place. She'd torn the letter into shreds, not wishing to contaminate herself with it. If old Batt wanted to do himself an injury it was his own business and nobody else's. You couldn't possibly go through life taking responsibility for stuff like that, especially where a senile pensioner was concerned.

Mrs Tuke lay on her bed, forgetting about Miss Gomez as best she could, and about Alban Roche and poor Pru, and everything that had so unfortunately occurred. She turned the pages of *Doctor D'Arcy's Love*, looking for a piece she was fond of, towards the end of chapter seven.

For several minutes she contentedly read, and was then aware of footsteps on the stairs. She read another line and then placed the volume, face downwards, on the bed beside her. She'd be severe, she resolved: as soon as the door opened and his greased red head appeared she'd tell him to clear off immediately. It was disgraceful the way a woman couldn't relax herself for five seconds without having a labouring man going after her in an empty house. He'd written her a note in crude handwriting, saying he'd heard the funeral was at twelve and asking what the situation would be. She'd naturally torn it up.

'Are you there, Beryl?' she heard his voice inquiring outside her door, and she didn't trouble herself with making a reply. She could have sworn she caught the odour of his sweat through the panels. He spoke again. She waited a bit and then she said: 'What d'you want?'

He opened the door and came into the room. He was grinning like a hyena. He asked her if she'd any tickles, as if he was talking to a child. There wasn't a woman in London to match her, he said, and she had to laugh, hearing stuff like that when she was trying to push him off. 'Get on away with you,' she cried, but naturally he took no notice.

No letter came from Tacas to the Hotel Bon Accueil. It was not unusual, for often in the past some weeks had gone by without a communication. But still she felt concerned, in case her telegram and her letter had been presumptuous and prideful: she'd written in a certain enthusiastic vein that was perhaps not fitting. She lay awake for two nights, listening to the Bayswater Road traffic and worrying. At half-past five on the second morning she decided that unless she heard on the nine o'clock post she'd go on her own initiative, as she'd gone to Crow Street.

No letter came. At ten o'clock she withdrew her savings from the National Westminster Bank in Piccadilly. In the B.O.A.C offices in Regent Street she inquired about air-flights to Jamaica and was informed that the first one on which there was a vacancy was in two days' time, arriving in Kingston at midday local time. She booked herself on to it.

XIX

Crow Street came down. The labourers whistled as they worked.

Cave's Hardware, where Mr Batt had stood for so much of his adult life, fell easily beneath the blows. So did the disused Palace Cinema and the Snow White Laundry, and in Bassett's Petstore pictures framed in passepartout came down with the walls of an upper room and were not noticed. Counters and shelves and doors were ripped out of the Thistle Arms and some of the men felt nostalgic, having drunk in the bars so often during the last few months. The furniture was hauled outside and with it the trunk and the boxes that Alban Roche had left behind him. Bonfires were prepared and damaged doors and door-frames were added to them, and timber beams and floor-boards, cupboards, window-frames and stacks of laths.

The bulldozers moved over Crow Street. Rubble was moved, the cellars of the houses were filled. Paving stones and the tarred surface of the street itself were drilled away. Drains stuck up out of the ground, and electric cables and gas pipes and water mains. Men in lorries came to buy whatever was considered valuable from the developers, lead and scrap metal mainly.

In the Arab's Head in Kew Mrs Tuke served in the Cocktail Den, differently attired each evening. She liked it all much better even though there was more to do. She liked the better type of person, the bit of flash the chaps put on, the jolliness and the pleasant shade of pink that the brewery had agreed to. She liked the soft crystal light in the Cocktail Den, the racy humour of the young crowd on a Sunday morning, and the feeling of *décolleté* in the evenings. She was troubled less by her liver, she felt she had come into her own.

One night she found herself telling a man in the insurance business that earlier in her life she'd been a nurse, and a little while later she found herself saying the same thing to someone else. 'Black stockings, Mrs T?' someone laughingly inquired. She giggled since the remark was lightly meant and called for lightness in return. She wanted to mention the cottage hospital at Rose St Margaret, a Devonshire market town, but thought it better not to. In the Arab's Head she didn't mention her daughter who'd gone off with a youth perverted on women's clothes, nor did she refer much to the public house she'd lived in before, or to Crow Street. Atlas Flynn appeared in the back-yard at half-past four one afternoon. She told him she'd set the police on him if he ever dared to return, but he insisted on arguing with her and in the end she couldn't help giving a laugh because of the way he put something.

Mr Tuke bought some air-mail paper on which to write a letter to Miss Gomez, but when it came to the point he could think of nothing to say. He stared at the blue paper, fiddling with a ball-point pen, and in the end he put the paper and the pen away in a drawer. Two days later, though, he attended a meeting of the Jehovah's Witnesses. The day was a Sunday and as the meeting was early in the morning there was plenty of time afterwards to do what cellar-work was necessary before the morning trade and to make sure that the bars were sprayed with Freshaire. In the Witnesses' meeting-room Mr Tuke prayed for his wife, believing now that he had been induced to marry her for this purpose alone: that through his constant intervention and the intervention of others she should find salvation. Later that day, in the afternoon, he walked through the botanical gardens of Kew, where Mr Batt had hoped to walk. He meditated upon himself and his cruelty, and the sign that had come to him through the judgement that had been passed on him; he recalled some words that had been spoken in the meeting-room that morning and he found it hard not to condemn himself. He walked through the precious shrubs, meditating upon the words and thinking of Miss Gomez, seeing her face without difficulty, and the sun sparkling on her glasses.

Mr Batt showed Miss Tibbett the photograph of himself that

he'd cut out of the newspaper. Not wishing to say that it had to do with a sex crime, he said instead that it had appeared because of his involvement in a Giant Jackpot. Miss Tibbett scrutinized the photograph carefully, wondering why Mr Batt had had it taken while in his pyjamas. 'Extremely nice,' she said, raising her voice so that he could hear it, nodding and smiling at him.

He'd woken up in the middle of one night with the realization that he could not possibly win the Jackpot because he'd put the Thistle Arms address on the Once-In-A-Decade certificate and the Thistle Arms was of course no longer there. He'd lain awake for a while, thinking after a time that it didn't matter all that much. Funny, he thought, that day in The King of Spain when they'd had a drink together. Funny girl she'd been altogether, taking fags and yet not seeming the type. He went on thinking about her, remembering her with the vacuum cleaner on the stairs of the Thistle. He dropped into a doze and briefly dreamed about her, seeing her at Mrs Bassett's funeral, walking out of the middle of a yew tree. She took his hand and led him to a grave that she said was his wife's grave, newly moved from the demolished grave-yard of St Nicholas's church. She went down on her hands and knees and scraped away the earth and showed him the coffin, which hadn't been affected by burial at all. She opened it and spoke to his wife, telling her to get up. His wife, unaffected also, smiled and said she'd like another five minutes.

In Eel Brook Common he strolled the next morning with Miss Tibbett and related to her his dream. He described Miss Gomez as he recalled her, her very thin legs, her skin as black as boot polish. Miss Tibbett said something in reply. He couldn't quite hear what it was, so he went on talking.

One morning, before the pet shop was open, they walked over the wastelands, just to see. They strolled on the nothingness of Crow Street, where she'd been born, to which by chance he'd come. They read the signs which told of all that would be built, and imagined again the different landscape, experiencing neither sorrow nor pleasure, for neither the destruction nor the prospect concerned them now that Mrs Bassett had died. It would be uglier than before, they said to one another, in keeping with the times. They walked back to Tintagel Street, idly talking about that and then revealing a little more, in turn, about themselves.

Not far away, in Abyssinia Street, a different scene took place: Mr Winstanley and his son Thomas presented Mrs Winstanley with the bushbaby, and Mrs Winstanley said it cheered her up. It was lovely, she said, a truly lovely pet. 'Von Runstedt?' suggested her husband, and all the Winstanleys laughed.

'Like wine in a bottle,' said the sandy-haired clergyman, beginning his day in the crematorium.

Miss Gomez flew by BOAC Earlybird. She watched while London receded, motor-cars and houses, building sites, trees, streets, roads, parks, a general confusion. 'All right?' the hostess smilingly said and Miss Gomez said yes, she was all right.

The plane rose and then travelled at thirty thousand feet, against the paleness of the sky. She ordered a Pepsi-Cola and when she'd drunk it she opened a newspaper that the hostess had given her and read that four schoolgirls had killed themselves while experimenting with their minds under the influence of an unnamed drug. The father of one of them, a medical doctor, was stated to have attempted to make his daughter see the dangers of such experimentation. A woman beside Miss Gomez, happening to read the same news item, said it was appalling.

'Four children,' the woman said. 'Four children dead from playing around, trying to induce dreams apparently.'

It would go on for ever, Miss Gomez thought, crime and senselessness and folly. In London and New York, Moscow, Stockholm, Calcutta, in the places where she'd evangelized, Brentford, Isleworth, Wembley, Putney, Twickenham, and other places everywhere. She thought of the lives that were led in the midst of it all, the lives of people she'd known in London, casually met, and the people of Crow Street. She wondered about the man who'd paused to listen to her outside a cinema before his wife came along and asked him what he thought he was doing, consorting with a coloured; and the girls in the cereal factory in Dagenham, who'd marry and have babies and live on an estate; and the Irish labourers who wandered from one demolition to another, dismantling London.

In the humming aeroplane she prayed for the people she left behind, asking that too much hardship should not be sent to them, and she prayed for the parents of the four dead schoolgirls, asking for comfort. She prayed for the men who stole away to the Spot-On Club, just in case they should ever need her prayers, and for housewives who went dancing in London's afternoon dance-halls, just in case they did so because of a lack in their lives. She prayed against loneliness for all these people, the loneliness that she had once felt herself, years ago, in the Lily Arbuthnot Orphanage, before everything had changed.

XX

It was raining hard. The bus had gathered mud on its journey, and inside there was a smell of exhaust. People had slept on the journey from Kingston, but Miss Gomez had remained awake. She'd smoked, wondering if in Tacas they would object to this habit in her.

On the plane she had written:

I must not presumptuously have fancies. I must not take it upon myself to presume that I have powers or have been chosen in any way over others of our Church. The others prayed for the people of Crow Street while I fumbled in the dark and made errors. It was not through me but through prayer from Tacas that the pattern God wished for emerged.

Miss Gomez learnt those words by heart, knowing that when she arrived in Tacas she would wish to repeat them, in order to display to the people of her Church that she considered herself in no way special. She simply wanted to tell them all that had taken place and to hear them say, she hoped, that in her modest contribution she was worthy of her conversion. She brought with her her offering for the Harvest of the Tithes, all that remained of her immoral earnings. She knew she was doing right in coming to Tacas: she felt it in her bones.

The bus halted. 'Tacas, miss,' the driver shouted back at her. She moved down the aisle with her single piece of baggage, the canvas bag of Canadian Pacific Airlines, which she had chosen to contain her belongings because it was convenient to carry. 'Thank you,' she said to the driver of the bus, a heavy man with light-coloured dark glasses and sweat pouring through his grey shirt. He nodded briefly, chewing gum. 'You're welcome to it, honey,' he said as she stepped from the vehicle into Tacas.

The bus moved on, throwing up brown slush. To the bus-driver all the towns he stopped at were probably much the same. He'd probably never even heard of the Brethren of the Way, who'd chosen to have their headquarters in this small town. Bethlehem, after all, had once been even smaller.

Ever since she'd stepped off the plane at Palisadoes Airport she'd felt she was at home again. The adventure of her exile had this immediate reward, of the Caribbean in the rain, and familiar signs and colours, and people who were somehow familiar too.

'King George VI Road?' she asked a child who was hanging about the store where the bus had stopped. The child's clothes were sodden with rain. He smiled at her delightedly, but didn't know where King George VI Road was.

'King George VI Road?' she said in the store, and she was told at once: Hibiscus Villa was the first house she would come to.

She walked through the small town, past its few shops selling rice and tins of food and brightly-coloured cottons and local vegetables. She passed a factory that processed bananas, extracting the essence, and a smaller factory that manufactured table-mats from pampas grass. The rain trickled on her face and neck, running down beneath her leather dress, damping her stomach. Her strapped shoes, bought while she was still employed by Mrs Idle, in Lilley and Skinner's in Knightsbridge, felt heavy on her feet. She took them off and walked bare-footed, reminded for a second of Prudence Tuke and the Indian sandals that she carried more often than wore.

No one was about. Even the shops she passed seemed empty of all habitation. No radio sounds carried through open windows, no dog barked. Only the rain was noisy, falling on the concrete road and on taut canvas awnings and on the lids of dust-bins. Raindrops blurred her vision: she took her spectacles off and walked without them.

Miss Gomez had the feeling that suddenly this rain would cease and that the sun would gleam through the clouds, as often happened in the different climate of England. She felt this strongly, as she had felt when first she walked in Crow Street that she must stay there, and had felt so long ago that she must ask questions about the fire in Adeline Street. The feeling was a continuation of a thread, a connected instinct: the sun would dry the tattered walls of Hibiscus Villa, for in England she had always seen Hibiscus Villa in sunshine, and had always seen the Reverend Lloyd Patterson and the Reverend Greated, the Reverend Pearson Simmonds and the Reverend Palmer in sunshine too.

But the rain did not cease. It fell more heavily, it seemed, when Miss Gomez turned into King George VI Road. A post-box attached to a wooden stake had a name faintly painted on it. She had to peer because of not wearing her glasses, but she still couldn't read the sun-bleached letters. She looked beyond the stake and could see only the lashing rain and rose-mallows and giant bamboos. When she put her glasses on she saw that there was a house.

It had once been gracious, a colonial reminder like the Lily Arbuthnot Orphanage, though not as large. It seemed unoccupied: glass was broken in the windows, the paint on the front door had flaked away, what once had been gardens now were rank. She pulled at a bellchain, but no bell sounded that she could hear. She tapped on the panels of the door.

There was a brief wooden porch: two pillars on either side of the door, a sloping wooden roof that let in rain. In this Miss Gomez stood. Her feet were cold because she'd stopped walking. The concrete step beneath them was cracked and in places had fallen away altogether. Weeds grew through it, slimy now on the soles of her bare feet. There was another house, she thought, beyond this empty one, beyond the rose-mallows and the bamboos that grew so wildly. It was difficult to see in the teeming rain what was there, difficult with her glasses on and equally difficult without them.

'Yes?' said a man.

She turned, for he had come out of the rain, behind her. He was a white man, dressed in khaki trousers and a string vest. The trousers were held up by a belt made of crocodile skin, with a large brass buckle. His black hair, partially grey, was flat on his head due to the rain. He was a medium-sized man, unremarkable in appearance.

'I'm looking for Hibiscus Villa,' she said.

He pushed past her and opened the door. He held it while she passed through and then went ahead of her. The hall inside was dark. There was no carpet on the boards and she felt a sandy deposit of dust and dirt beneath her feet.

'Can you see?' he asked. 'The rain has made it gloomy.'

'Yes, I can see.'

He entered a room that was darker than the hall. 'Stand for a moment,' he commanded, and she heard him crossing boards that were also bare. He pulled back curtains at the windows and the room, from being as black as night, became grey and shadowy. There were basketwork chairs and a desk and a sofa, and hangings of some kind on the walls.

He went to the desk and sat behind it. 'Sit down,' he said. He paused before he added: 'You've come from Mr Ferdinand?'

'No, no. I'm looking for Hisbiscus Villa.'

'You're in Hibiscus Villa.'

The room smelt as though the windows hadn't been opened for months. There was also a smell of curry, and of fust and of strong tobacco.

'This is Hibiscus Villa,' the man's voice said. It was a low, tired voice that somehow matched the surroundings. She couldn't see him properly.

'Mr Ferdinand said he'd send someone. I thought it must be you: I'm sorry. Can I help you?'

'I'm looking for Mr Patterson.'

She could see his arms and hands moving behind the desk. There was the sound of liquid being poured. She heard him drinking before she saw the glass held up to his lips. He put it down on the desk again. Outside the rain came down in a torrent now.

'Patterson is gone,' the man said.

She smiled at the man, knowing that there was some error. She shook her head.

'Oh yes, indeed,' the man said.

She left her chair and went to the desk. It was covered with letters in different hand-writings, all of them on air-mail paper. She saw there several of hers. Behind the man, on the floor, were other letters, some stuck on long wire spikes, others thrown into wooden sugar-boxes.

'Who are you?' she asked.

'I own this house. I rented it to Patterson. My name's Greated—'

'The Reverend Greated?'

The man laughed. He wasn't the reverend anything, he said. Mr Ferdinand was sending someone, he repeated, to go through Patterson's things and see if there was anything of value. Not that Patterson had left much behind as far as he could see.

'The Reverend Pearson Simmonds,' she slowly said. 'The Reverend Palmer.'

He poured liquid from the bottle into a second glass and handed the glass to her. 'It's damn cold,' he said. She drank, discovering that the contents of her glass were white rum.

'There's a man called Pearson Simmonds,' he said, 'an old chap from Elderslie. He used to do a bit of work here in the garden about a year ago. He died a while back. Palmer's in gaol.'

'But the Church, the Brethren of the Way—'

'People overseas wrote letters to Patterson. They're here, you can see them. Yes, they wrote about a church—'

'I wrote. My name's Miss Gomez. I wrote everything down, my whole life—'

'The Harvest of the Tithes, Miss Gomez: Mr Patterson mentioned that?'

'Yes, of course. I came to give him—'

'I'm sure you did. I'm afraid he wouldn't have been pleased to see you. An immensely lazy man, Patterson was. He didn't even bother to invent names for his characters: he used the local ones. He and Palmer used to grow ganja on a patch tucked away among the rose-mallows. It was Patterson's laziness over something or other that got Palmer caught. Patterson's probably back in England by now. Did you know he was English, Miss Gomez?'

'No, I didn't.'

'He'd been a schoolmaster at one time, or so he told me. Some school in Sevenoaks. There'd been some trouble, I don't know what it was. There'd been something before that too, when he

243

was a child. His mother married a second time, something about the stepfather. Later, in East Africa, he got some girl with child. She left him seven years after he married her, because of his depressions. She took three half-caste children with her. He was fond of them, apparently: it hurt him, that.'

She sat down again and took cigarettes and matches from the pocket of her dress. She could feel them sodden in her hand. 'Have you a cigarette, Mr Greated, please?'

He poured more rum into his glass before he searched in his pockets and came round the desk again. He handed her one in his fingers and gave her matches. 'It's Patterson's rum,' he said. 'At least there's that. I'm sorry I can't help you further, Miss Gomez. I'm just the landlord of Hibiscus Villa.' He laughed in sour amusement and she realized he was a little drunk. 'I'm sorry there's no church,' he said.

Wearily she felt tears that were themselves weary coming from her eyes. She didn't want to cry again.

'He did quite nicely,' said the man. 'No doubt he did quite nicely.' He picked up letters and read from them, peering at them in the gloom. People had sent postal orders and other forms of money. They'd seen a heaven, as she had, in which no one was condemned and no one was looked down upon, in which prayer was made for those who most needed it, generously made and constantly. They'd seen a heaven in which there was no loneliness, in which you took the hand that was next to yours.

'I can't see how he did it,' the man said, throwing down a letter. 'Walking through a dump like Tacas to a hill: who could ever have believed the man? I'm sorry,' he said, remembering.

She heard her voice trying to explain; and she knew the man wasn't listening. She could hear the white rum slurping in his glass and the rustle of the air-mail letters as he poked again among them. He had to stay there, he said, interrupting her and unaware that he was doing so: he had to stay there because Mr Ferdinand was sending someone.

She stood up, saying she must go. He shook her hand and pressed it tightly. He was sorry, he said, that she'd been tricked in an unpleasant way. Patterson was extraordinary, he said, a man given to great depression and occasionally of violent temper. For the rest, he had been famous locally only for laziness, a small fat man who used to sit in the porch of Hibiscus Villa smoking and drinking ganja, dreaming, so people said, of something better. She passed through the dark hall again and out on to the porch. The rain had lessened.

'Mr Greated in residence, miss?' a tall Jamaican asked, smiling at her. He'd been looking at the guttering of the house, he said, and all that rotting wood. 'My, my,' he said.

He wore a gaily-coloured blouse, bangles rattled on his wrists. He laughed for no apparent reason. 'My, my,' he said again. 'How Mr Sanger going to jump about!'

It was all another story: a man drinking rum in his string vest, and Mr Ferdinand and Mr Sanger, and ganja grown on a patch among the rose-mallows, and Patterson who had been lazy and depressed, with a violent temper. *Illtreatment,* he'd written to her. *One person by another person. The world is full of damaged people: you know that, Miss Gomez.* He'd drifted all over the place, from a man his mother had married to a school in Sevenoaks, to a girl in East Africa. There'd always been something wrong. *Do not condemn,* he had so often written.

She wept the same tired tears, longing that a blankness would occur in her mind, like empty sleep. She walked through the rain, the sodden canvas bag occasionally striking the calf of her right leg. She'd catch the bus to Kingston. She'd find work in a store, if necessary she'd take another cleaning job. She'd never return to London. She'd keep herself to herself. The man called Greated was probably laughing now with the tall Jamaican, reading bits out of her letters, reading about Mr Kandi in the Lily Arbuthnot Orphanage, and how she'd come to believe that there was a pattern in her life. He was probably laughing now with the tall Jamaican, reading bits out of her letters, reading about Mr Kandi in the Lily Arbuthnot Orphanage, and how she'd come to believe that there was a pattern in her life. He was probably reading about how people had often considered her insane, as a child because she'd seen no reason not to die and later, after her conversion, because she spoke of God. They were probably themselves saying that she was a little touched to have been so foolish.

A dream, she thought: no more than Mrs Tuke's dreams of a cottage hospital. Or Alban Roche's of naked girls. Or Prudence's of butterflies and sunflowers. Four dead schoolgirls had sought dreams in memories. And Mr Tuke would one day find some dream to live in, like everyone else, like the housewives who danced in the afternoon dance-halls and the men in the Spot-On Club and Inspector Ponsonby who dreamed of marriage with a black girl.

'You didn't find no Mr Patterson,' a fat woman said to her in the store by the bus-stop. 'You been looking for that Patterson, girl? He's two days gone.'

She realized, she said. She'd found Mr Patterson gone.

'Bad, that Mr Patterson,' the woman said.

The bus would be some time, more than an hour. 'Ain't much to do in Tacas, girl,' the fat woman said.

She bought some cigarettes and matches, and put them in the canvas bag, under some other things so that they wouldn't get wet. She could wait in the store, the woman offered, but Miss Gomez said she'd prefer to go for a walk in the rain. 'Wasn't nothing but trouble in that villa,' the woman said, 'ganja-smoking, ganja-brewing. Mr Dispirito going to find that Patterson, no matter where he gone.'

'Mr Dispirito?'

'He's going to find him. He swear he's going to find him.'

She walked through Tacas, looking for the hill, knowing it would be there because he'd been too lazy to invent anything. She found it, a quarter of a mile from the town, a pleasant hill on which ferns and wild flowers grew.

The rain stopped. On this hill they had picnicked, and the Reverend Lloyd Patterson and the Reverend Greated, the Reverend Pearson Simmonds and the Reverend Palmer had passed among them. From Tacas they had marched in procession when the sun was out, carrying no banners because that was not their way. They marched like phantoms, like the ninety-one who had died in Adeline Street. 'O Lord, O Lord,' they sang; she heard it clearly. 'O Lamb of God, Whose love Divine draws virgin-souls to follow Thee.'

On the hill where wild flowers grew she heard them speaking to her, whoever they were. She had been meant to come to Tacas, in the same way that she had been meant to go to Crow Street, to test her faith in adversity. Their Lord, and hers, they quietly told her, had an answer, for the death of a dog in Crow Street, and for four dead schoolgirls, and her own feeling of despair, and for Hibiscus Villa, and the world when it looked like just a room-ful of flies, and for the cruel absence of an earthly Church. There was a heaven in which the incurable man now was, in which he had been given an explanation for the nature of his worldly ex-istence. That was a place in which all explanations would in time be made, to Alban Roche and Mr Tuke, to Prudence and to Mrs Tuke, to Mr Batt, whose sons had died while he lived on, to In-spector Ponsonby and the man who'd wanted Tina von Hippel to tie him up on a pulley, and the men who hid at night in the trees of London's commons wearing masks and eccentric clothes, and the man who had run away from Hibiscus Villa. There would be madness everywhere, they whispered to her, if there was no dream of heaven to come true, where order was drawn out of chaos. All heavens came together in the firmament, the cottage hospital and Miss Arbuthnot's fearsome vision of a King of Israel of whom no questions might be asked, and the heaven that Alban Roche's mother pretended, and the pretty one that he and Prudence and all their generation pretended also, disguised in their pretty clothes, with pretty things around them.

Everything continued. Already in the evening newspapers in London there'd be a report of still another tragedy, or a crime. Tina von Hippel would discover she had syphilis and report it in St George's Hospital, Mr Batt would neglect a cold. In Tacas Mr Ferdinand would find nothing he could buy in Hibiscus Villa, and Mr Sanger would be disappointed in some other way. The house itself would fall to pieces. Mr Dispirito would never find the man

247

who'd disappeared because by now the man had moved from Tacas to London, to sell ganja for profit. The ganja would give people dreams, which was why people wanted it.

She sat for a moment on the wet ferns and thought again that
she would find work of some kind in Kingston. She remembered
suddenly the night of Mrs Bassett's death and the feeling she'd
experienced that the crime she had foretold had taken on a
ghostly form. She remembered her painful walk along the corridor to Mrs Bassett's door, and opening the door and standing for
an instant there.

Seated on the hill outside Tacas, she knew then that Mrs Bassett had died in that moment, and that she herself had been intended to make the journey in the corridor, bringing death with
her, as she'd been intended to make her other journeys also. She
knew it with an intuition that was as firm in her as the organs of
her stomach: she would have burnt her hands off in that moment,
protesting that because of death the crime had never risen to the
surface of his mind, that instead he'd become an inheritor, receiving the respect of an old dead woman in spite of the shame
of his imprisonment, that the death, also, had created impatience
in Prudence Tuke, causing her to act as she had. No matter what
might happen now, the death had brought only good with it; the
death was the centre of a pattern.

God worked in that mysterious way: through this reason and
that, weaving a cobweb among all His people, a complexity that
was not there to be understood while His people were any living
part of it. She knew that also; she had been made to feel it. Her
faith was defiant in adversity: it warmly hugged her as the shock
of a wet afternoon gradually wore away.

She rose and slowly went down the hill and walked through
the scattered town. *Evangel Temple*, she read on a blue board in
front of a church. *Assembly of God, 9 a.m. and 7.15 p.m. Sundays.
Gospel and Song Broadcast, Sundays 2.30 p.m.* Beneath, in smaller
letters, there was the address of the Assembly of God Church in
Kingston: 3 Friendship Park, Vineyard Town. The telephone number was 82728.

FOR THE BEST IN PAPERBACKS, LOOK FOR THE

In every corner of the world, on every subject under the sun, Penguin represents quality and variety—the very best in publishing today.

For complete information about books available from Penguin—including Puffins, Penguin Classics, and Arkana—and how to order them, write to us at the appropriate address below. Please note that for copyright reasons the selection of books varies from country to country.

In the United Kingdom: Please write to *Dept. JC, Penguin Books Ltd, FREEPOST, West Drayton, Middlesex UB7 0BR.*

If you have any difficulty in obtaining a title, please send your order with the correct money, plus ten percent for postage and packaging, to *P.O. Box No. 11, West Drayton, Middlesex UB7 0BR*

In the United States: Please write to *Consumer Sales, Penguin USA, P.O. Box 999, Dept. 17109, Bergenfield, New Jersey 07621-0120.* VISA and MasterCard holders call 1-800-253-6476 to order all Penguin titles

In Canada: Please write to *Penguin Books Canada Ltd, 10 Alcorn Avenue, Suite 300, Toronto, Ontario M4V 3B2*

In Australia: Please write to *Penguin Books Australia Ltd, P.O. Box 257, Ringwood, Victoria 3134*

In New Zealand: Please write to *Penguin Books (NZ) Ltd, Private Bag 102902, North Shore Mail Centre, Auckland 10*

In India: Please write to *Penguin Books India Pvt Ltd, 706 Eros Apartments, 56 Nehru Place, New Delhi 110 019*

In the Netherlands: Please write to *Penguin Books Netherlands bv, Postbus 3507, NL-1001 AH Amsterdam*

In Germany: Please write to *Penguin Books Deutschland GmbH, Metzlerstrasse 26, 60594 Frankfurt am Main*

In Spain: Please write to *Penguin Books S. A., Bravo Murillo 19, 1° B, 28015 Madrid*

In Italy: Please write to *Penguin Italia s.r.l., Via Felice Casati 20, I-20124 Milano*

In France: Please write to *Penguin France S. A., 17 rue Lejeune, F-31000 Toulouse*

In Japan: Please write to *Penguin Books Japan, Ishikiribashi Building, 2–5–4, Suido, Bunkyo-ku, Tokyo 112*

In Greece: Please write to *Penguin Hellas Ltd, Dimocritou 3, GR-106 71 Athens*

In South Africa: Please write to *Longman Penguin Southern Africa (Pty) Ltd, Private Bag X08, Bertsham 2013*